Olav Audunssøn

Olav Audunssøn

OLAV AUDUNSSØN

II. PROVIDENCE

SIGRID UNDSET
Translated by TIINA NUNNALLY

UNIVERSITY OF MINNESOTA PRESS
MINNEAPOLIS ◆ LONDON

This translation has been published with the financial support of NORLA.

This volume of *Olav Audunssøn* was originally published in Norwegian as Part II of *Olav Audunssøn i Hestviken* (Oslo: H. Aschehoug and Company, 1925).

Map on page ix by Rhys Davies

Published by the University of Minnesota Press
111 Third Avenue South, Suite 290
Minneapolis, MN 55401-2520
http://www.upress.umn.edu

ISBN 978-1-5179-1160-7 (pb)

A Cataloging-in-Publication record for this book is available from the Library of Congress.

Printed in the United States of America on acid-free paper

The University of Minnesota is an equal-opportunity educator and employer.

26 25 24   10 9 8 7 6 5 4 3 2

Contents

Translator's Note

The first two volumes of Olav Audunssøn were originally published in Norwegian in 1925 under the title *Olav Audunssøn i Hestviken*, with the third and fourth volumes appearing together in 1927 as *Olav Audunssøn og hans børn.* An English translation by Arthur G. Chater was published in four volumes by Knopf in 1928–30 under the collective title *The Master of Hestviken*, with the individual volumes titled *The Axe, The Snake Pit, In the Wilderness, and The Son Avenger.* This new translation reverts to the original Norwegian series title, with different titles for the separate volumes (*Vows, Providence, Crossroads, and Winter*).

Throughout my translation I have retained the original spelling of Norwegian names, as presented in the first edition of the work from 1925. Readers should note that Norwegian surnames were derived from the father's given name, followed by either "-datter" or "-søn," depending on the gender of the child. For example, Olav's surname comes from his father, Audun Ingolfssøn. In some instances I have kept the Norwegian titles of "Fru" for women and "Herr" for men.

Creating a new translation of a classic work is a challenging endeavor, especially when the author is as respected and beloved as Sigrid Undset. In many ways the task is akin to that of an art restorer who seeks to remove decades of accumulated grime and dust from the surface of a painting to reveal the original vision of the artist. Literary translations depend on the individual translator's linguistic skills and artistry, but they are also subject to general attitudes at the time of their creation—whether that involves specific word preferences, stylized dialogue, or expectations regarding the overall tone. Translations can become outdated, causing the novel or story to lose its audience beyond the author's own language. It is my hope that this new English translation will bring the reader closer to Sigrid Undset's beautifully clear and lyrical voice as she recounts the deeply moving story of Olav Audunssøn and his family.

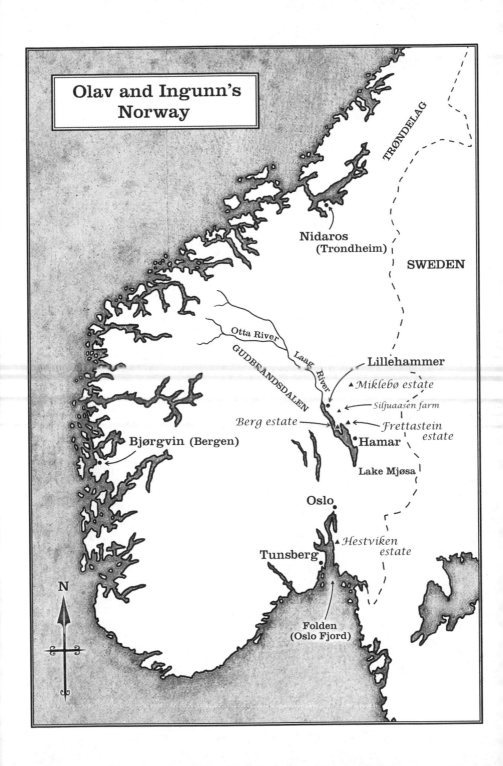

Olav and Ingunn's
Norway

TRØNDELAG

Nidaros
(Trondheim)

SWEDEN

Otta River

GUDBRANDSDALEN

Laag River

Lillehammer

▲ Miklebø estate

← Siljuaasen farm

Berg estate →

▲ Frettastein
estate

Bjørgvin (Bergen)

• Hamar

Lake Mjøsa

Oslo

▲ Hestviken
estate

Tunsberg

N

Folden
(Oslo Fjord)

Genealogy and Kinship

Olav Audunssøn and Ingunn Steinfinnsdatter

Their children:
  Eirik Olavssøn
  Audun Olavssøn
  Cecilia Olavsdatter
Arnvid Finnssøn—Ingunn's cousin
Tora Steinfinnsdatter—Ingunn's sister
Hallvard Steinfinnssøn—Ingunn's brother
Jon Steinfinnssøn—Ingunn's brother
Olav "Half-Priest" Ingolfssøn—Olav's kinsman
Olav Ribbung—Olav's paternal great-grandfather
Torgils "Dirt Beard" Olavssøn—Olav's paternal great-uncle
Ingolf Olavssøn—Olav's paternal grandfather
Signe, Una, and Torunn Arnesdatter—Olav's third cousins
Hallveig and Torgal—Eirik's foster parents
Torhild Bjørgsdatter—housekeeper
Liv Torbjørnsdatter—maidservant
Arnketil "Anki"—hired man
Sira Benedikt—parish priest
Sira Hallbjørn—parish priest

Hestviken Estate—List of Owners

Olav Torgilssøn
Tora Ingolfsdatter
Olav Olavssøn (also known as Olav Ribbung)
Ingolf Olavssøn
Audun Ingolfssøn
Olav "Half-Priest" Ingolfssøn (not the owner, but guardian and
    caretaker for many years while Olav Audunssøn was underage
    and in exile)
Olav Audunssøn

Olav Audunssøn's Happiness

I

Hestviken had been the dwelling place of great chieftains in bygone days. The ruins of many large boathouses could still be seen at the shoreline, and rotting timbers lay on the tidal flats where the Hestviken men had dragged their longboats over slipways in both the springtime and the fall. What looked like the remains of an old log bridge reached from the high-water mark up to the small plateau between stretches of rock.

Then the Christian faith and customs came to Norway. Holy King Olav forbade his countrymen to set out on Viking raids. Men were supposed to believe, whether they liked it or not, that God would not tolerate anyone plundering a fellow Christian, even if he happened to be a foreigner. The Hestviken men then ventured out on trading expeditions. Since ancient times, shipbuilding had always been an important enterprise at Hestviken. Even Olav Audunssøn's great-grandfather, Olav Ribbung, when he was in his prime, had employed a builder of sailing ships on the estate. And when he rebuilt everything after the Birch Legs[1] had burned Hestviken to the ground—the estate houses up on the slope and the buildings at the shoreline—he ordered a boathouse to be erected as well as the two warehouses and the workshop that stood down by the wharf.

Anyone who rowed south for a couple of hours along the fjord from Haugsvik, a site where assemblies or *tings* were held, would come upon a high cliff.[2] The huge reddish-gray rock face that dropped precipitously toward the fjord and was bare of any trees up to the crest was called the Ox. Beyond the promontory the bay of Hestviken sliced inward; it was a small inlet, fairly narrow and constricted. On the north side, the mountain bluff called the Ox plunged abruptly to the water, which at that spot was exceedingly deep and dark. Atop the back ridge of the Ox grew a sparse, windblown pine forest, though it became dense closer to the heights. The base of the mountain resembled a foot thrust out into the sea from the low crest, stretching along the north side of the entire bay and the valley of Hestviken, or Kverndalen as it was also called, and then east toward the main village. Throughout the valley the slope plummeted sharply toward the streambed, where a small river passed through Kverndalen and reached the sea at the head of the bay. Growing at this spot was an abundance of leafy trees and grass and flowers between the cliff and the scree, and atop the ridge stood a spruce forest, though it gave way to deciduous woods up on the flat countryside. And there were still many oak groves belonging to Hestviken.

On the south side of the bay the rocks arching toward the fjord were much lower and less steep. Growing in the mountain crevices were juniper bushes that the wind had combed flat as well as briar rose thickets. And scattered about were small patches of dry grass. But then the mountainside rose vertically toward the north, a looming and almost naked gray-black rock face. And below this cliff, called the Horse, stood the estate, quite high up and facing north. The path from the wharf up to the houses passed along the outermost fields of the estate on the fjord side. Farther inland there was a thick layer of good soil on the slopes, and here the drought did less damage in the meadows and fields than in most other areas on Oslo Fjord, for in many places little streams trickled down from the cliff called the Horse, and there were damp hollows up through Kverndalen. But almost all the arable land at Hestviken lay on the south side of the bay and the valley, facing north.

The Hestviken estate was built in such a way that the houses stood in two rows on either side of a narrow courtyard, with bare outcroppings of rock sticking up everywhere, like a backbone in the middle. Between these rocks and the Horse cliff was a low-lying depression formed by water sluicing off the mountain. For that reason, the buildings standing on that side of the courtyard were sunken and leaky. The lowest timbers had rotted on the side facing the mountain, and it was very drafty inside. The damp seeped in from both above and below, but in the summertime nettles and weeds grew behind in the hollow, reaching almost all the way up to the turf roofs. These buildings served as the stable, the cowsheds, and several storerooms.

Facing the water, on the northern side of the courtyard, stood the main houses, the cookhouse, and the loft rooms. The Ox towered above the fjord and blocked the view. But from the western end of the courtyard it was possible to look across the bay to Hudrheim and toward the south a great distance along Folden, as Oslo Fjord was called. In the old days, when there was strife in the land, the chieftains of Hestviken used to keep watch on the mountain above the Ox. Still standing there was an earthen hut where the sentinels would stay whenever they weren't needed to keep vigil.

At the far end of the courtyard, toward the meadows and Kverndalen and a good distance away from the other buildings was the barn; it was the only structure that remained from the old estate. It was immeasurably large and solid, made from rough timbers. The other buildings were small and not particularly well made, constructed of notched logs that were not very sturdy. Olav Ribbung had found it difficult to rebuild his estate after the fire. He had suffered great losses when his wharf warehouses, filled with goods, were burned down. And at that time it was often hard for landowners to collect what was owed to them by their leaseholders. But it was rumored in the countryside that the old houses at Hestviken had been both spacious and splendid. A large main hall had been of post-and-lintel construction, with a shingled roof, like a stave church. Inside, two rows of carved posts supported the roof, which had supposedly been richly adorned with woodcarvings as well as paintings. And woven draperies had been displayed in the main hall on special occasions—tapestries with blue borders and a wall hanging that was stretched out along all the walls close to the roof. It was made of red woolen cloth and embroidered with beautiful images. Two pieces of this cloth still existed— one had been given to the church and one remained at the estate. The latter was so long that it stretched across both of the long walls and one gable end of the new main hall. Yet a good portion of the cloth had been lost, which gave some notion of how different in size Olav Ribbung's hall was from the old one. Otherwise nothing else remained of the previous splendor except for a carved plank. Folks said that one of Olav's hired men had supposedly pulled off the wall plank to use it for protection when he fled the burning building. In the new hall the plank was now fastened next to the door to the sleeping alcove.

Olav Audunssøn recognized the carved plank the moment he stepped inside his own hall, though he hadn't seen it since he was a seven-year-old boy. Never had he given any thought to this object, nor was he even aware that he remembered it, but the instant he caught sight of the plank, a memory arose like a gust of wind sweeping across the surface of a lake and darkening the water. It was the plank from his childhood. Carved into the wood was the figure of a man surrounded by writhing snakes that filled the whole area and encircled the man's waist and limbs, while one gnawed at his heart. Crushed under the man's foot was a harp. There was no doubt that this depicted Gunnar Gjukessøn in the snake pit.[3]

The carved plank was the only adornment in the hall, which otherwise was no different from the hearth room of any ordinary farmstead. It was a long, rectangular building with a thin board partition at the eastern end that created two small rooms beyond the hall: both a sleeping alcove and an antechamber at the door leading to the courtyard, at the end of the house. For safety's sake the entrance had been placed as far away as possible from the sea. At the opposite end, farthest from the door, were two bedsteads with a bench on a dais in between. Earthen benches stood against both long walls of the room. The only other furnishings were several small three-legged stools; there wasn't so much as a table meant for ale bowls and tankards next to the antechamber door, or a high-backed chair or settle bench. The top of a long table hung on the north wall, but apparently it had been taken down only rarely after Olav Ribbung died.

The bed in the alcove was meant for the master's family. Yet Olav Audunssøn invited his old kinsman Olav Ingolfssøn to make use of this resting place, just as he always had. The younger Olav would sleep in the south bed in the main hall; that's where he'd slept as a child.

Olav Audunssøn had no desire to move into the alcove. When he caught sight of the doorway to that pitch-dark room, something stirred inside him like a phantom of the revulsion he'd felt as a child toward the black opening. This was where his great-grandfather had slept with his lunatic son. Whenever the seizures took hold of Torgils—or Dirt Beard as he was also called—they would tie him up, and then he would lie there on the floor in the dark as he bellowed and wailed and struggled against his bonds. As a child, Olav Audunssøn hadn't been particularly frightened. Or at least what he'd felt was more like a composed and quiet dread, for he'd witnessed Dirt Beard's fits for as long as he could remember, and the crazed man had never caused anyone harm. The only thing they needed to fear was that he might do harm to himself. Yet the boy never willingly went near the alcove. A horrible stench always filled the space; the pestilential stink would waft out of the door opening whenever anyone went past. The father and Aasa, the old servant woman, did their best to keep the space clean around Torgils, but it was difficult, for it was so dark inside. They changed the straw in the bed as often as they could manage, and they spread fresh earth on the floor so frequently that from time to time Old Olav had to get someone to shovel out some of the dirt that had collected into mounds and hillocks inside the alcove. Yet all this did very little good.

Olav Audunssøn now recalled them so vividly: those two old men who would appear in the alcove doorway. Whenever the son had suffered a spell and thrashed about until he'd worn himself out and was calm again, his father would lead him outside to sit in the sun if the weather was good.

First to step out of the alcove would be Olav's great-grandfather. He was a giant of a man with long, thick hair and a full beard that covered his chest; his beard was still as much black as it was white. He would help his son by placing one arm around his neck and bending him forward so that he wouldn't run into the doorframe. Torgils didn't have the wits to avoid anything. He always plunged straight ahead at whatever was right in front of him.

Torgils Dirt Beard seemed small because he was so shriveled and stooped. His entire head was overgrown with hair; his beard reached all the way up to his eyes. These disheveled whiskers of his were covered with dried filth, with gray and yellow bits in the grime. In the center of it all shone his big eyes, the irises a clear gray-green like seawater, the whites bloodshot, his stare eerie. His nose jutted out, small and straight and finely shaped, but red, because it had been frostbitten one time when he'd escaped from his father and slipped outside on a winter night. But whenever Old Olav took his son to the bathhouse, Torgils's shaggy head would gleam a soft, silvery-white like a big tuft of sedge. Torgils looked much older than his father.

Old Olav fed his son as if he were a child. Sometimes he had to shake or strike Torgils in order to make him open his mouth. Other times the son would fail to close his mouth again, and he'd sit there letting the food spill into his beard. Occasionally his father could get Torgils to eat by stuffing meat and other pieces of food into his son's mouth and then pressing his own face close to the younger man's while pretending to chew, moving his jaw up and down with all his might. Then Torgils might imitate his father and begin chewing too.

Aasa would sigh when she saw this. She was meant to serve as Olav Audunssøn's foster mother, and the boy slept in her bed. But Aasa thought most about keeping an eye on Dirt Beard and caring for him, just as Olav's great-grandfather did. The old hired man named Koll was the only one who paid attention to the boy. Olav couldn't remember anyone other than those four ever living on the estate, though people came and went, doing work on the farm and down at the wharf. Presumably it was during these years that Hestviken had begun to decline. And after Olav Ingolfssøn, also called Olav Half-Priest, took charge, the estate had steadily gone downhill.

Farming had never been the primary focus at Hestviken. But neither Olav Ribbung, during the last years of his life, nor Olav Ingolfssøn had made use of the sea as had been the custom among their forebears in the old days. And then Olav Audunssøn, as the next estate owner, had been outlawed, and the big ships that he still owned at the time were confiscated by the king's representative. Olav Ingolfssøn had never managed to acquire new ships, nor had he replenished the estate's stock of cattle and horses.

Olav realized that the inheritance left to him when his father, Audun Ingolfssøn, died had been so large that back then he was a very wealthy heir, though he'd been unaware of this. His foster father, Steinfinn Toressøn, had never tended to anything on his behalf, so even before Olav was outlawed, the estate had been greatly diminished. Now he owned nothing more than the family's main residence and a few farmsteads up in the countryside, as well as some over in Hudrheim, directly across the fjord. He had sold the allodial property[4] he'd owned in Elvesyssel, inherited from his paternal grandmother, when he needed to make arrangements to pay restitution for the murder of Einar Kolbeinssøn and to ensure his own safety in Norway. Yet Olav Audunssøn still possessed sufficient funds from the monks at Dragsmark, who had bought most of the property, that he was able to obtain what was necessary to take up the shipping trade at Hestviken again.

By this time there were few farmers in the villages around Oslo Fjord who lived on allodial estates that had never been divided or dispersed. A great many of the farmsteads had fallen into the hands of the big landowners or now belonged to the king or the church. For that reason Olav Audunssøn had to be considered a prosperous and prominent man in his home district, and he was embraced in accordance with such a high standing when he finally returned to his family estate.

Folks thought that he had shown great generosity when he took over his properties from Olav Ingolfssøn, the old man who had been his guardian yet had carried out his caretaking duties so poorly. Yet no one had heard the younger Olav utter any complaints about this, and he treated his namesake with filial respect. When several men attempted to learn what Olav Audunssøn's opinion was regarding this matter and asked him how he had found the condition of his property, he had replied with great restraint, "Not the best." But things could not have gone any other way, considering the judgment that had been leveled against him. And everything that had taken place here had undoubtedly been more than Olav Ingolfssøn could handle, crippled as he was. One of his legs had been broken, rendering it permanently rigid, with the foot turned out. He limped badly and couldn't move without the aid of a stick. He also found it difficult to ride a horse or travel by boat because of this stiff and dragging leg of his.

Olav Ingolfssøn was a good deal more than sixty winters old, and he looked even older. In fact, he seemed to be ancient. He was tall and thin and stooped; his face was narrow and finely shaped with a handsome beaked nose. It seemed to the younger Olav that his namesake bore some resemblance to his own father, judging by what the son could recall of him. But Olav Ingolfssøn was completely bald, with embittered red eyes. The skin hung in great folds under his eyes, and wrinkles drooped over his sunken cheeks and below his chin. To treat the rheumatism in his ailing leg he applied dog pelts and cat skins and many different kinds of liniments. Because of this, or perhaps for some other reason, a peculiar odor clung to the old man—like the smell of mice. It also smelled of mice in the alcove where he slept.

He was the son of Olav Ribbung's twin brother, the priest Ingolf Olavssøn at Halvard Church in Oslo. When the edict was issued that priests in Norway should no longer marry, the priest Ingolf sent his wife home to the Tveit estate in Soleyar, which had been part of her dowry. All the children accompanied their mother there except for the youngest son, Olav. It had been decided that he too would become a priest, and he was a newly ordained deacon when the accident occurred that made him a cripple. But he had always maintained a celibate life, and folks thought he possessed such great insight into so many things that some considered him both more learned and more pious than their own parish priest. It was especially when folks were haunted by the ghosts of the dead or phantoms on sea and land, or when they were suffering from some ailment they thought had been caused by sorcery or supernatural beings, that they sought the counsel of Olav Half-Priest, for he had a better understanding of such things than any other man.

Olav Audunssøn at once turned for support to his namesake, above all because Olav Half-Priest was his closest kinsman but also because he was the first man of his father's family that he'd met. The younger Olav thought it strange to be at Hestviken and know that it was his allodial estate and that this area was his home district. Here he would spend the rest of his life. He would have grown up here, if his circumstances had not been so remarkably different from that of other young lads. But fate had cast him far from his home when he was still a child, and ever since he had been homeless and as rootless as a timber adrift in the sea.

Now he had returned to where he had started out. To a certain extent he did recognize some places, both indoors and outside, yet much was different from what he'd remembered. When he went to the mill in the valley of Hestviken, it seemed familiar, but he couldn't recall having seen anything that lay on the other side of the bay—the Ox, the forested ridge—nor the soggy valley along the river that was both desolate and filled with leafy trees. It turned out that he had never been aware of how things looked on the north side of the bay—imagining instead a countryside and farmsteads like those surrounding Lake Mjøsa. But from Hestviken not a single human dwelling could be seen.

He had remembered the buildings on the estate to be much larger. And the little stretch of seashore in a gap between the rocks had seemed to him an entire country with many landmarks—including a big bluish stone on which he used to lie and some bushes where he could hide. Now he saw that this small strip of sandy shoreline was hardly longer than fifty paces measured out by a grown man. In the meadow above the estate he couldn't find the hollow where he used to sit in the sun. Perhaps it had been a small depression in the field east of the barn that had now become overgrown with willows and alder trees. In a crevice in the earth of the courtyard he'd once found a peculiar snow-white ring. He now thought it must have been a bird or fish vertebra from which the points had broken off. But back then he had considered it a precious object, and he'd hidden it away. Afterward he would often dig in the cracks of the rock to see if he could find more such treasures. Now he felt as if he were recalling old dreams. Bits and pieces of everything from those days swirled around him. Occasionally he would remember some long-forgotten and eerie feeling, as if from a hideous dream, yet only the sense of disquiet remained.

Olav seized upon anything that might help him conquer this

sensation of uncertainty, this mix of dream and shadow, and enable him to feel that the Hestviken estate was his and that whenever he walked across the fields, he had the ground of his forefathers beneath his feet. The Ox was his, as well as the forests atop the mountains on either side; everything belonged to him. He took pleasure in thinking that he now lived under the same roof as a kinsman, his own grandfather's flesh-and-blood cousin who had known all the men and women of his family all the way back to the generation of his great-grandfather, Olav Ribbung. In the evening, when he would sit and drink with his namesake, and the old man told him about their forebears, Olav felt a connection to his father's family that he'd never experienced when he was living in Denmark with his mother's kinsmen.

And he felt drawn to the old man because he thought that Olav Half-Priest was so pious and learned. During those weeks, as he waited for the day when he could head north to bring Ingunn home, the younger Olav felt as if he were somehow standing to account before God.

He was fully aware that he would not find it easy to display a steadfast composure and a cheerful demeanor when he arrived at Berg to finalize the agreement with Haftor and receive Ingunn as his wife from the Steinfinnssøns. But there was nothing to be done about that. It was his wish to take her as his wife, in spite of everything, and so he would have to be man enough to hide his own feelings. But he couldn't escape from the childhood memories that arose—including the once secure knowledge that he and Ingunn belonged to each other and would always stay together. The very notion that something might come between them had never entered their minds, and for that reason being together had never stirred their hearts either to joy or astonishment. They had simply taken it for granted. That was how it would always be, precisely as it had been decided for them. Until the summer, that is, when, wrapped in each other's arms, they had tumbled out of their childhood and innocent state, frightened yet also giddy with joy at the new sweetness they had discovered in each other—regardless of whether it was right or wrong for them to surrender to it. Even after Olav had roused himself to both defy and fear everything and everyone who tried to intervene in their fate, he had been convinced that in the end they would win their case. Such memories would suddenly come upon Olav, and the pain burned like the stab of a knife. Now the dream was about to come true, although differently than he'd ever imagined. Remembering himself from back then was like recalling someone else he'd once known—a boy who'd possessed such boundless trust that he now felt both pity and scorn for him, as well as a searing envy. He had been a child who knew nothing of betrayal, never thinking that he or anyone else might be duplicitous. But he knew that there was only one thing to do about the treachery inside his own soul: he would have to conceal his suffering so that no one, least of all Ingunn, would notice that he carried a secret wound.

These thoughts might seize hold of him in the midst of a conversation with his namesake, and then he would come to an abrupt halt. The old man hardly noticed as he kept on talking and talking while the younger man sat in silence and stared with a stony and closed expression, until Olav Half-Priest asked him a question. Then the young Olav would realize he hadn't heard a word that had been said to him.

But Olav Audunssøn was preparing himself to bear the burden he would have to carry—and without complaint if God should punish him harshly in the coming years. The memory of the ski expedition and the night spent in the mountain pasture was never far from his mind, though he now seemed unable to fathom that he was the one who had done the killing. Instead, it felt as if he'd been a witness to a confrontation between two strangers. Yet he did know, with an odd sense of indifference, that he was the murderer, and the sin was his sin. The killing itself was no great sin, for he had not ambushed the youth. The Icelander Teit was the one who had initiated what happened, and he had fallen with sword in hand. Olav had heard that in the old days even a thrall had the right to defend the honor of his wife. It was a man's right and obligation, according to the laws of both God and man.

But it was what occurred afterward . . .

And Olav felt as if he were bartering with God when he now straightened his back and made himself ready to take on the burden of Ingunn's disgrace. Never would anyone know how arduous this effort might become for him. From now on he would live a pious and God-fearing life—as much as that was possible for a man who harbored an unconfessed sin. He would do right by his fellow men and treat poor folks with compassion; he would protect those who had been left abandoned and defenseless; he would honor God's house and his parish priest, offering them all that it was his duty to give; he would say his daily prayers with reflection and devotion and often repeat the *Miserere mei, Deus* and contemplate the meaning of the words.[5] He realized that as a child and youth he had been given far too little learning in the Christian faith. Brother Vegard had done his best, but he came to Frettastein only once or twice a year, staying at the estate for a week's time. Otherwise, there was no one who had even made sure that the children said their prayers each day. As for the good teachings that Olav had heard while he was a guest of Bishop Torfinn, those lessons had gone the way of the parable: so much ryegrass and couch grass had been sown among the wheat during the years he had wandered out in the world, that the wheat, which had just begun to sprout, had become overgrown with weeds.

For the first time a certain sense of remorse occurred to Olav Audunssøn when it came to the killing of Einar Kolbeinssøn. He regretted what he'd done because it was a poor way in which to reward Bishop Torfinn for his kindness, and because it was the most unfortunate action he could have taken, given his position at the time. He was also aware that he was supposed to show remorse because the murder was considered a sin, even though he couldn't understand why it was so sinful. Now he began to perceive that there was a deeper meaning and wisdom behind the Lord's commandment not to kill than what he'd known before. God did not wish for the death of any sinner. And behind the commandment there was compassion for the murderer as well—this person who had opened his soul to many kinds of evil forces that then found an unexpected opportunity to attack.

Now it might prove useful for him to live with such a pious old man as Olav Half-Priest. This kinsman of his could undoubtedly offer him all sorts of helpful guidance, in accordance with the precepts of the psalms, a good many of which Olav had learned from Arnvid and

Fat Asbjørn that time in Hamar, though by now he'd forgotten most of them.

Olav Audunssøn invited guests to the homecoming feast he would soon hold at Hestviken, and he told folks in the village that the wife he was about to bring home was the daughter of Steinfinn Toressøn. She was his foster sister, to whom he'd been betrothed when they were both young children. As soon as he'd had a little time to get settled and take stock of matters here at home, he would return to Oppland County to bring back his wife. But he said nothing about whether the wedding had already taken place or would first be celebrated now, and he didn't ask anyone from the area to accompany him, even though it would be impossible for his old kinsman to make the ride with him. Folks soon noticed that the young owner of Hestviken was somewhat taciturn and reticent about how much he was willing to explain. They got little out of him by asking questions.

Olav had given a great deal of thought to whether he ought to mention that there was a child. Perhaps it might be easier if he spoke of this beforehand. But he couldn't bring himself to do it. He also thought the child might have died, even though he'd been born alive. He'd heard it said that infants died easily. Or he and Ingunn might find some other solution, perhaps sending the child to live with foster parents somewhere along the way. He now saw that what he'd said in his initial despair and confusion—that Ingunn should claim he was the child's father—was sheer foolishness. He couldn't understand how he'd come up with such an idea, which would mean thrusting an outsider into the lineage. If only the child had been a daughter. Then she could have been sent to a convent, and no man would have been wronged if he'd claimed her as his own. But Ingunn had given birth to a boy. Oh, he'd been out of his wits back then, overcome by anguish and anger. But he felt compelled to accept the child if the mother wished to keep the boy. He would just have to allow fate to take its course. There was no need to resolve that dilemma in advance.

Yet one day Olav crept up to the small space above the alcove and antechamber. He happened to think that the child and his foster mother might stay up there if Ingunn wished to have her son in the house. Olav Ribbung's daughters had slept in this loft with their maid-servants. But it seemed an eternity since those young women had lived there. At least twenty years of dust and spider webs had been allowed to collect undisturbed, and mice tumbled out of the bedstead when he made an attempt to see what had been stored there. Several old looms stood next to the gable, as well as trestles on which to place a tabletop. There was also a chest carved with crests, which made Olav think it must have belonged to his mother. He opened the chest and found inside several whorls and shafts from drop spindles, wool carders, and a small box. Inside the box was a book and an infant's swaddling clothes made of white linen, most likely a christening gown, thought Olav, probably the very one that he'd worn when he was lifted out of the baptismal font. For a moment he remained there, squatting down, as he let the embroidered border of the fabric slide between his fingers.

He took the book downstairs with him and showed it to Olav Half-Priest. Even though the old man had always claimed he could read and write as well as any priest—and much better than Sira Benedikt, their parish priest[6]—it turned out that he wasn't able to read much from Cecilia Bjørnsdatter's psalter. That evening Olav sat looking at the book. There were little illustrations in the capital letters, and delicate red and green vines wound their way down the pages. When he went to bed, he stuck the book in the bed underneath the headboard, and there he let it stay.

Several days before Olav was due to travel north, a poor woman arrived at Hestviken, asking to speak with the master of the estate. He went out to see her. She carried an empty sack over one shoulder, so he realized what she wanted. But first she greeted Olav with a voice on the verge of tears—from joy, she told him. It was so good to see the rightful master standing in the doorway at last. "And a handsome and noble man have you become, Olav Audunssøn. If only Cecilia could have seen her son. And they speak well of you in the village, Olav. So I thought I had to come to see you for myself. I was among the first to greet you here in this world, for I was a servant at Skildbreid back then, and I came with Margret, my mistress, when she arrived to aid your mother. I helped her swaddle you."

"You knew my mother?" asked Olav when the woman paused to catch her breath.

"We saw her in church once in a while, you know, when Audun first brought her here. But by midwinter her health was so poor that she never went out. It was too cold in the house where she was living, that's what her maidservant said, and finally, she had to move into the main hall with the old men, just to stay warm. Torgils was in a bad state that winter and spring. I remember how dreadful he behaved that night when you were born, and his fit lasted a whole week. Cecilia was so frightened of him that she was shaking as she lay in bed; not even Audun could calm her. I suppose that was what broke her, that and the fact that she had suffered too much from the cold. Audun carried her over to the loft above the storeroom when the weather grew warmer. He saw that she couldn't bear to live in the hall with that crazed man, but she died shortly afterward. You must have been a month old by then."

The woman said her name was Gudrid, and she lived in the hut that Olav might have noticed when he rode east to the church village. It was on the north side of the marshes, right before the road turned up toward Rynjul. During her first marriage she had lived on a small farm in the Saana district. Her husband was a good and respected farmer, but she'd had no children with him. When he died and his brother moved to the farm with his wife, and she could not make peace with them, she had married Bjørn, the husband she now had. That was the worst mistake she could have made. He wasn't poor back then. If they combined everything they both owned, she thought they might have a good life. He was a widower with only one daughter, so they thought things might work out well. She'd set her sights on finding another husband, and she longed so much to have children. That was the only thing that had turned out as she'd expected. Eight children, five who still lived. But already during the first winter of their marriage Bjørn had committed manslaughter and had been forced to pay restitution. That soon put an end to their prosperity. Now Bjørn spent most of his time out at the fjord, hunting harbor porpoises and seals and seabirds or rowing for Tore of Hvitastein when he went fishing, while she sat in their hut with all the little children and her stepdaughter, who was spiteful and mean.

Olav patiently listened to the woman's outpouring of words. Finally he invited her to follow him over to the storehouse. He had acquired everything that would be needed for his homecoming feast, and he now generously filled Gudrid's sack. "If things become difficult for you this winter, you must come back and speak to us here on the estate, foster mother."

"May God bless you, Olav Audunssøn. How like your mother you look when you smile! She had such a gentle smile, Cecilia did, and she was always kind to poor folks!"

Then, at long last, the woman took her leave.

There was no one in the hall when Olav went inside. He paused, lost in thought. With one foot propped up on the edge of the hearth and his hands wrapped around his knee, he stood there, staring down at the small pile of charred logs that were still smoldering. Tiny delicate sounds, a whistling and creaking and quiet inhalations, issued from the dying embers.

Mother, he thought, recalling what little he'd heard about her. She had been so young. And fair, it was said. She had been brought up in the ways of the nobility in the wealthy convent, as the playmate of a king's daughter.[7] Then she had been removed from the women's house of the queen and brought to this lonely estate, far away from everything she'd known. In these modest farmhouses she had carried him under her heart, suffering from the cold and left alone with those two aged men—the madman who had frightened her, and the estate owner who disapproved of his grandson's marriage. How appalling that was.

Olav gave his thigh a hard slap with the palm of his hand. It must be unbearable to be a woman, he thought, with so little power to decide her own fate. He felt a compassion for all women—his mother dressed in silks and linens, the beggar woman Gudrid, as well as Ingunn. It did little good for any of them to counter harshness with harshness. Ingunn . . . A wave of desire and longing rose inside him. He pictured the delicate, white nape of her neck. She had been forced, poor thing, to bow that proud girlish neck of hers. First for his sake. And by now she must be bent very low. But he would draw her head to his chest with gentle tenderness and softly caress the poor, slender nape of her neck. Never would she hear a word from him about this whole misfortune. Never would she notice any sign from him, in either word or deed, that he bore her any ill will. At this moment he sensed no ill will in his heart toward the defenseless young woman who would soon be placed in his care. He wanted nothing more than to protect her and treat her well.

Later in the afternoon Olav saddled his horse and rode east, heading for the village church. He didn't really know why he wanted to go there, but his mind was in great turmoil on this day. When he arrived, he tied his horse to the post and walked up through the cemetery to the church.

He placed his hat and sword on the bench next to the wall, but then he happened to catch the sword on a corner of his cloak, and it fell to the floor. The clang that echoed between the stone walls unsettled him. And the light in the room was eerily pale and strange, for the walls had recently been whitewashed in preparation for the images that would be painted on them in the summer.

Audun and Cecilia had been interred at the very front, to the left of the nave, between the Mary altar and the chancel arch. As Olav knelt on their tomb and prayed as quietly as he could, his attention was caught by a figure that the master painter had finished on the wall near the arch. It was a gracefully tall and slender woman wearing a blindfold over her eyes and holding a broken reed in her hand. Her posture and expression, even the color of her dark clothing, were so inexpressibly sorrowful. Olav had often seen this image in other churches, but he had never remembered to ask what it meant. Yet nowhere else had the woman appeared as despairing or as beautiful as she did here.

Bishop Torfinn's words about the children without kinfolk suddenly came back to him. For the first time he was almost glad he'd never demanded of Ingunn that she give up her child. At this moment he felt he could think of the infant with some measure of compassion. Now that she'd had this child, surely he could bring himself to raise the boy.

When he came out of the church, he saw that the priest, Sira Benedikt Bessessøn, was standing next to his horse. Olav greeted him courteously, and the priest responded with cheerful kindness. Though Olav had seen little of his parish priest, he was most favorably disposed toward the man. The priest had a dignified and imposing appearance. He was short and sturdy of build, with broad shoulders. Reddish-brown hair and beard framed his face, which was wide but well formed, with prominent features and countless freckles. He had big, clear blue eyes, sparkling with life. Olav thought he perceived in this man someone who was pious, intelligent, and good-natured. He also liked the priest because he had such a lovely, strong, and gentle voice, whether he was speaking or singing.

At first they talked about the gelding that Olav had acquired in Skaane. It was seven years old, a big, stocky, and handsome horse, white in color with blue dapples on its flanks. Olav always tended to the horse himself, brushing and grooming its coat until it was sleek and shiny, for he held great affection for this steed. For that reason he was pleased to hear that the priest appreciated the worth of the gelding. Then Sira Benedikt carefully examined the harness, which was made of red-dyed leather. Olav hid a smile. The priest spent a good deal of time tanning and dyeing leather, so he was impressed with such workmanship. This was one of the things that Olav Half-Priest had found fault with when it came to Sira Benedikt. He considered such work most unseemly for a priest, for it meant he had to put his sanctified hands in the worst muck and filth. Sira Benedikt's response was that he didn't think such filth was any worse in God's eyes, since his hands would be just as clean as before when he washed them. Our Lord Himself had displayed His humility and honored manual labor by taking a small axe and chisel in those same blessed hands that had formed and created humankind. And He went out to the courtyard of His holy foster father to cut and shape logs. Surely He would not think

His humble servant was disgracing himself when he carried out such a noble and resourceful task.

The priest invited Olav to accompany him home, and Olav gladly accepted. Olav Ingolfssøn also grumbled that the priest's estate smelled like a shoemaker's workshop in town. But inside, the house was clean and pleasant; it was a much more stately space than the main hall at Hestviken. Three lovely young maidens brought in butter, white bread, and ale, then greeted the guest with gentle courtesy before leaving at once. They were the daughters of the priest's nephew. The oldest was in charge of the estate's household, and her sisters were visiting.

The ale was excellent, and the two men stayed at the table for a good long time, talking about one thing and another. Olav's opinion of Sira Benedikt grew more and more favorable. Then the conversation turned to Olav Ingolfssøn, and the priest praised the young Olav for showing such familial warmth toward someone who had done such a poor job of safeguarding his welfare. Olav Audunssøn replied that for the most part it was his own outlawed state that was to blame for the grievous decline of Hestviken. The old man had done his best, crippled and in such weakened health as he was. But he could tell that Olav Ingolfssøn was a remarkably wise and holy man.

"That fool?" said the priest.

Olav didn't say a word.

The priest went on. "He would have done well to try for a little more holiness. Judging by the company he kept in his youth, his holiness was not much to boast of. And if he were wise, he'd think and speak more about Christ and the Virgin Mary, and less about sorcery and the ghosts of dead children and mermen and sea phantoms. He should be praying instead of spending time on those conjurings and incantations of his. It wouldn't surprise me if much of what he does is sheer idolatry. But he finished his schooling·as a half-educated priest—and the half he did learn was wrongly learned. It can be pleasant enough to listen to his tales on an evening or two, but you seem to be a sensible man, Olav Audunssøn. Surely you don't believe all the foolishness he spouts?"

Ah, thought Olav, so that was it. He'd already begun to suspect that such was the case. Aloud he said with a small smile, "There seems to be little in the way of warm friendship between you and my kinsman."

The priest said, "I've never liked him. But it's not merely because he was the foster brother of the person who treated me and mine so badly. None of us harbored any hatred toward the other Hestviken men. They were brave and honorable—all of them except him. You must have seen that for yourself, Olav. I have looked on you with favor from the first time we met, and it has been my intention that you should know I wish you well. In my view the old enmity between those of us from Eiken and your family from Hestviken should be set aside and forgotten. Not that we have ever considered Olav Ribbung and his other sons to be our enemy, but it shouldn't surprise you that we have avoided each other as much as we could."

Olav began wiping up some ale that he'd spilled on his chest. He did not look up as he said, "I don't know what you mean, Sira Benedikt. I have only recently returned home, and I'm a stranger in this district. I've never heard anything about this enmity between your family and mine."

Sira Benedikt seemed quite surprised, and also a little embarrassed.

"I thought Olav Half-Priest must have spoken of it to you."

Olav shook his head.

"Then I'd better tell you myself." The priest paused to think for a moment, batting at the little hen-shaped ladle floating in the ale bowl, making it sail in circles.

"Did you notice those lovely children of mine, the young maidens who came in, Olav?"

"They certainly were lovely. And if I didn't have a young bride waiting for me in Oppland, I might have taken a closer look when your kinswomen were here, Sira!" said Olav with a brief smile.

"If I understand your meaning correctly," replied the priest as he too smiled, though with some discomfort, "then you must not know that they are your kinswomen as well, and closely related."

Olav looked at the priest, waiting for him to explain.

"You have the same great-grandfather. Torgils Dirt Beard was the father of their father. He disgraced my sister."

Olav's face involuntarily took on a horrified expression. Sira Benedikt saw this and realized what the young man must be thinking.

"No, this was before God stripped Torgils of his wits. Or perhaps it was the Evil One who did that—the one Torgils had obeyed so steadfastly while sin and desire tempted him.

"God knows I'm not unbiased when I speak of Olav Half-Priest. He and Torgils were foster brothers, and Olav stood by him in thick and thin. Olav Ribbung, who was an honorable, courageous, and stalwart man, tried to threaten his son Torgils into marrying my sister Astrid. But Torgils abandoned her, leaving her to the shame of raising his wayside bastard son while he stayed with that whoring woman in Oslo and claimed that she was the one he wanted to marry. Olav Ribbung then ordered his son to return here to this district. Your paternal grandfather Ingolf as well as Olav's daughters and Ivar Staal, his son-in-law, all said they would refuse to sit at the same table or speak with Torgils if he insisted on the course he'd taken. But Torgils was staying with the priest, who was the father of Olav Ingolfssøn, and it was an even greater shame that they were willing to receive him. One was already a priest, and the other was meant to become one.

"In the end my father and brothers accepted payments of restitution and reconciled with the men of Hestviken when we realized that neither Olav Ribbung nor Ingolf would be able to budge Torgils or force him to rectify Astrid's misfortune. It was a better and more Christian resolution. That's true. But if I had been full grown and able to wield a weapon, I know that I would not have given up until I had put Torgils in the ground. I would have done that even if I was a priest at the time and devoted to serving God. I have hated that man so much that . . . God can see into my heart, and He knows this. But surely He also knows that it is the most difficult thing He can demand of a man, that he refrain from avenging his kinswoman's honor with steel. I was ten years old when all of this happened. For me, Astrid had taken my mother's place. She was the oldest of us siblings, and I was the youngest. I slept in her bed that summer. She wept and wept.

It seemed to me she would cry herself to death. Let me tell you, Olav, any man who has it in his heart to forgive such a thing, he is someone I would call holy."

The priest fell silent. Olav waited, as quiet as a stone. But finally he felt the need to say something.

"What happened to your sister?" he asked softly. "Did she die?"

"Eight winters have passed since she died," said the priest. "She lived well into old age. Several years afterward, she married Kaare Jonssøn of Roaldstad, north in the parish of Skeidis. And they were happy together. Father was much too harsh toward her, and he couldn't stand the sight of her child. If the boy had been another man's . . . But Father couldn't bear knowing that his daughter had added to the offspring of Torgils's paramours. Yet Kaare was kind to both of them. He was the one who arranged a good marriage for his stepson, to the daughter who was the heir to Hestbæk. When misfortune struck Olav Ribbung of Hestviken, and the lineage was about to die out after him, he sent word to Astrid. If she would let him have the child, whose name was Arne, he would proclaim the boy to be the lawful heir after his father. Kaare replied that the boy no longer needed the support of his father's kinsmen, and both he and Astrid loved Arne Torgilssøn far too much to send him out to Hestviken to inherit the fortunes of the Hestviken men. That's when Olav Ribbung brought in Aasa, who had once served on the estate, and her son who had been fathered by Torgils. But the boy didn't live long.

"Yet all this is now in the past. In my view we ought to forget the enmity, and you young people should behave with the dignity of kinship and meet each other with affection. I think that you and Arne of Hestbæk would take a liking to one another. Someday you should accompany me up there, Olav, to meet the kinfolk you have in this part of the country."

Olav said that he would be more than glad to do so. Then he asked, "You said something about the fortunes of the Hestviken men. What did you mean by that?"

The priest looked embarrassed.

"Your great-grandfather, you know, was not blessed with a large family who might inherit from him. That was the time when he was living out there on the bay with his demented son. And his other children had died, all except Borgny, who had become a nun. He had no lawfully born heirs to come after him, other than the young lad Audun, your father. Ingolf's widow had taken Audun with her when she went back to where she'd come from, south in Elvesyssel. So Kaare and Astrid must have thought that the lineage would not thrive when Olav Ribbung of Hestviken died."

Pausing for a moment to think, Olav then said, "It's true, after all, Sira Benedikt, that they were not fortunate men. I gather as much from what my kinsman has told me."

"They were men who were both courageous and steadfast, Olav, and that is worth more than good fortune."

"Not Torgils," said Olav. "I didn't know what you've now told me about him. I thought that he'd always been lacking in wits. Old Olav Half-Priest has never spoken of him."

"As bitter as was my hatred toward Torgils," said Sira Benedikt, "I have to tell you the truth about him. He was a brave man, and loyal to other men. And everyone says that no one can remember a more handsome lad ever living here in the villages around Oslo Fjord. It's actually strange that I regarded you with such favor the moment I saw you, for you bear a strong resemblance to Torgils. But Arne also looks much like his father, as do Arne's daughters. I thought perhaps you might notice this when the three maidens came in. They look so much like you that they could be your sisters. All of you have the same small, straight nose and the white complexion, as well as hair the pale color of sedge. And yet none of you is as handsome as Torgils was. Even though I hated him, I have to admit that I've never seen a more fair-looking man. So there must be some truth to the legend that he had no need to chase after women or seduce them with flattery and false words. Women hung on him and became mesmerized if he so much as fixed on them those strange blue-green eyes of his. And you have the same pale-colored eyes, Olav."

Olav couldn't help laughing, and he kept on laughing in an attempt to ignore the oppressive uneasiness he felt.

"No, Sira Benedikt, I can't bear much resemblance to my kinsman Torgils—at least not as far as my eyes are concerned. For I have never noticed that women are drawn to me in that way."

"Yet you do look like him, Olav, though you are not as handsome. And you and the young maidens all have those same eyes. But, praise be to God, none of you has in your eyes the evil power to dupe others. And all the talk about misfortune plaguing certain estates and families . . . I'm willing to accept it may have been true in heathen times. But you are surely wise enough to place your life and fate in the hands of God the Almighty and not believe such things. May God have mercy on you, my Olav. I wish you both happiness and bliss in your marriage. And may your lineage be known as fortunate men from now on!"

The priest raised his glass in a toast. Olav drank with him, though he could find nothing to say. Now Sira Benedikt summoned the three daughters of Arne: Signe, Una, and Torgunn. Olav greeted his kinswomen with a kiss. They were so lovely and seemly that Olav gradually began to thaw, and he sat at the table for a long time, conversing with them merrily. They didn't think they'd be able to attend the homecoming feast at Hestviken, for it was to be held at the same time as a grand wedding in their home district. Yet they would be back in the fall to visit the priest and they would stay with him for a while, so they promised then to come see Olav and meet his wife.

Olav was in a profoundly uneasy mood as he rode home. Why had he felt drawn to visiting the church today? And why had he there met Sira Benedikt and heard the story about his grandfather's brother and the priest's sister? It seemed to Olav so strange that he had trouble believing his visit was mere happenstance.

It was no doubt true that only the bishop himself could grant Olav absolution for the killing of Teit. Yet he might first confess his sin to Sira Benedikt. And with a sense of horror, Olav realized how overwhelming was his yearning to do just that.

He knew that if he knelt down before Sira Benedikt and revealed to the priest that he had on his conscience a secret murder—and if he explained what led him to commit such a sin—then he would find before him a servant of God who was not merely a spiritual father. Sira Benedikt would regard him the way a father does, someone who understands his flesh-and-blood son.

Olav had loved Bishop Torfinn because the monk from Tautra had allowed him to experience firsthand a world of wealth and beauty and wisdom, a world that he had previously known only as something distant and unfamiliar. Christianity had been for him a power like that of the laws of the land and the king. He knew that it was meant to govern his life, and he had bowed before it, without resistance, with both reverence and a sense that it was something to which a man owed loyalty, if he were to live among his peers and look them freely in the eyes without shame. In Bishop Torfinn Olav had seen a man who might take him by the hand and lead him forward to everything that could provide him with happiness and self-knowledge, to serve and to love. He had no idea what sort of person he might have become if he'd been able to follow Lord Torfinn for a longer period of time. For Olav, the bishop was now and would forever remain a spokesman who had come from the eternal heights, while he himself was like a child who had caught only a glimpse of what the bishop had wished him to see with open eyes. And then Olav had taken actions that caused him to flee from the path of his kind, spiritual teacher.

Olav was fond of his friend Arnvid, but they were so unlike in temperament that he had felt Arnvid's piety was something he couldn't understand. Olav perceived Arnvid to be quite reserved, although he was far from being a taciturn man. Arnvid's talkativeness was part of his helpful nature. Occasionally Olav had to remind himself that he was the one who had always received help, and his friend had always been the one to offer it. But such was Arnvid Finnssøn's disposition that Olav never felt humiliated; he could have taken even more from Arnvid and yet they would have remained close friends. Olav thought that Arnvid knew him to his very core yet still was fond of him. He, in turn, did not know Arnvid well, but he was still fond of him.

He'd found it highly entertaining to listen to Olav Half-Priest's talk of spiritual matters. But everything the old man recounted—about angels and devils, about nøkk,[8] troll women, and other supernatural

creatures, about hulder[9] and holy men and women, about uncanny oc-
currences and portents—all those things seemed to be from a different part of life than where he found himself, suffering through his own
troubles. Even the Mother of God seemed more like a king's daughter
in a fairytale, the loveliest rose in Paradise. But Paradise seemed exceedingly far from his own part of the world when Old Olav spoke of it.

Sira Benedikt was the first man Olav Audunssøn had met in whom
he recognized himself—a man who had fought the battle in which he
himself was now engaged. And Sira Benedikt had triumphed to become a God-fearing man, strong and steadfast in his faith. Olav felt a
sense of longing and hope pulse through his veins. All he needed to
do was gather his courage. He needed to ask for strength, as Brother
Vegard had said, without any reservations, unlike the man who asked
the Lord to grant him a pure life, but not at once. "God, hear my
prayer, but not until sometime later."

Olav lay awake most of the night. He realized that he now understood one thing: a battle had been raging in Heaven between God
and His Enemy since the dawn of time, and everything that possessed
life, soul, or spirit had joined in the fight in one phalanx or another,
whether they knew it or not—angels and supernatural creatures, humans here on earth and in the world after death. And it was most often a man's fear that allowed the Devil to tempt him into his fold. This
happened when a man feared that God would demand too much of
him—that he must speak a truth that was difficult to utter, or that
he must renounce a coveted desire that he didn't think he was strong
enough to live without, such as rewards or prosperity, sensual plea-
sures, or the approval of other people. Then the ancient Father of Lies
would appear to capture the man's soul with his old assertion that
he demanded less of those who sided with him and rewarded them
better—for as long as it lasted, that is. Now Olav had to make his own
choice regarding which army he wished to serve.

◆ ◆ ◆

It was a mild but heavily overcast day when he stepped outside the next morning. The fog drizzled over him tiny drops of water that felt blessedly cool on his face and refreshed his lips after the sleepless night.

He walked out to the hill west of the estate, where the mountain slope curved, with its bare rocks and flower-filled crevices, and turned toward the open waters of the fjord. Olav had become accustomed to heading in this direction every morning, and then pausing to observe the weather. He was gradually getting to know the fjord's voice. Today it was largely quiet. Lapping against the base of the smooth face of the Ox were small waves, visible in little white glimpses that broke through the fog where the foaming spray reached highest whenever a slight wind gusted off the sea. Water trickled between the rocks on the shoreline and licked at the wreathed kelp right below him, where the expanse of rock sloped toward the sea. A pleasant smell of saltwater rose up toward him.

Olav stood there motionless as he listened to the faint sounds of the fjord below. Occasionally the fog would grow so thick that he could hardly see the water.

He had realized long ago what a terribly stupid thing he had done by not announcing the death he had caused when he came to the first dwelling place as he descended from the mountain. If only he had done that, it wasn't even certain that he would have been sentenced to pay restitution for the killing. Teit's death might have been judged unworthy of compensation if Ingunn's kinsmen had been willing to testify that he, Olav, had a previous right to her. By now he'd given so much thought to every aspect of the matter that he could hardly remember anymore what he was thinking when he chose to remain silent and erase all trace of the deed, but he'd fooled himself into believing that the shame could be concealed. No one must know that he had gotten rid of Teit Hallssøn; then no one would find out that Ingunn had been disgraced by Teit. It seemed to Olav incomprehensible that he could have imagined anything so utterly foolhardy.

And now he was held captive in a prison of his own making. Never would the bishop grant him absolution for a killing unless he first publicly admitted to his actions so that justice might be fully served. Yet it had become a duplicitous murder, a dishonorable deed, and it would never be anything else.

Behind him was his estate, the fields rising up through Kverndalen, the forested ridges on either side of Hestviken. His property stretched far inland through the fog. Down in the bay he glimpsed the boathouses, the wharf, and the boats that were his. Rising up toward him was the smell of nets and tar and fish guts and saltwater and sea-drenched wood. And far north in Oppland was Ingunn. God only knew how she was faring now. His first obligation was to take her away from her misfortune and bring her to a safe place here.

No. He would have to continue to bear the burden that he'd been reckless enough to take on. He could not relinquish it now. He might have to carry it until he saw death's door standing open to receive him. And he might die a sudden death. But that too was something he had to risk. His disposition was not such that he could turn around and go back to the spot where he'd taken the wrong path. He would simply have to keep moving forward.

It was with such thoughts on his mind that Olav headed north. When he arrived at Berg, he learned from Arnvid that Ingunn had tried to kill herself. Six weeks later he returned home to Hestviken for the second time, bringing his wife with him.

It was noontime, and the sea glinted white with sunlight beneath the blazing hot rock face of the Ox, when Olav brought Ingunn ashore at the Hestviken wharf. It was the day after Saint Lavrans's Feast Day.

The water gurgled under the boat and smacked against the wharf posts. The air was sated with smells: saltwater, sweated tar, rotting bait, and fish viscera. Yet every once in a while the scent of flowers wafted past, so sweet and warm and fleeting. Olav was surprised when he noticed this, for it seemed so familiar and caused memories to rise inside him, though he couldn't recall what the fragrance was from. Suddenly Vikingevaag and Høvdinggaard appeared so vividly in his mind. He'd forgotten all about those places in Denmark when he left them behind to join the earl. At that instant he recognized the source of the scent: linden trees. That delicate and damp breath, as if from honey and seed blossoms and mead. Flowering lindens must be somewhere close by.

The fragrance grew stronger as they walked up the slope. Olav couldn't understand it. He'd never seen any lindens at Hestviken. But when they reached the courtyard, he saw a linden growing out of the steep rock face behind the cowsheds. It had taken root in the crevices. Pressed flat and clinging to the stone wall, the tree allowed its branches to sweep downward. The heart-shaped, dark green leaves lay on top of each other like shingles on a church roof, covering the waxy golden clusters of flowers. Olav caught a glimpse of them underneath. They were brown-tinged and slightly withered. The scent was also a bit cloying and no longer fresh, but a faint, pleasant buzzing and whirring of bumblebees and swarms of flies could be heard from up there.

"Oh, Olav, what is it that smells so sweet?" asked Ingunn in surprise.

"It's a linden tree. You've probably never seen a linden before. They don't grow in Oppland."

"Oh, of course. Now I remember. There was a linden in the monks' garden in Hamar. But I don't see the trees."

Olav pointed toward the mountain.

"The type of linden that grows here isn't like the other trees that are planted on flat ground."

He thought about the enormous, towering linden that stood in the courtyard at Høvdinggaard—the waxy pale, honey-misted flower clusters hanging within the crown, as if under a haystack of leaves. When the linden blossomed at Høvdinggaard, he had always felt a great longing, but not for Frettastein or Heidmark or any of the places where his fate had taken shape. Instead, it was his half-forgotten childhood home that he would recall. It must have been the scent of the linden blossoms that he recognized, even though he had no memory of linden trees at Hestviken.

Toward sunset he headed across Kverndalen. He wanted to have a look at the fields from up there. The scent of linden blossoms was so strong and pervasive. Olav moved his feet sluggishly, as if the sweet fragrance were weighing him down. He felt utterly weak with happiness. Now he saw that linden trees were growing everywhere on the mountain to the north.

The sun had vanished from the valley, and dew fell as he turned back toward the estate. He passed through a lane of alder trees and thought he could recall mowing a pasture that had once been here, though now it was overgrown with alders. A rustling and rushing sound came from the leaves and bushes when the cattle broke their way through the thickets. They were such strange animals, those Hestviken cows, with their long, shaggy coats and swaying bellies, their misshapen legs and oddly twisted horns, their big heads and sorrowful eyes. Most of them had only three teats, or their udder was malformed in some other way. Olav patted them on the cheek and spoke to them gently as he passed through the herd of these melancholy beasts that were his.

Ingunn appeared on the path behind the barn. She was tall and slender as a wand in her blue gown, with the linen wimple fluttering around her. Somewhat hesitantly, she walked calmly forward along the path at the edge of the field. Meadowsweet and common valerian, almost finished blooming, reached as high as her waist and practically closed around her. She was coming to meet him.

When Olav reached her, he took her hand and led her forward as they walked back home together. Their guests were to arrive the following day, but tonight the two of them, and the old man in the alcove, would be alone in the main hall.

II

The good weather lasted through late summer. In the middle of the day the expanse of bare rocks was blazing hot. Heat poured off them, and the sea glittered, with foaming spray dancing white beneath the cliff in those spots where the swells always broke slightly.

Olav rose early every morning, but he no longer went out to the hill. Instead, he was in the habit of leaning on the rail fence surrounding the northernmost field, where the path led up from the wharf. From there he could look down at the bay and across the valley, taking in nearly all the estate's cultivated fields. But the view toward Folden and the south was blocked by a ridge of bare rock that rose up and provided shelter for the outermost stretch of arable land at Hestviken. Of the fjord he caught only a glimpse to the north, looking past the shiny pate and forest-covered nape of the Ox. Opposite was the flank of Hudrheim, swathed in morning sunlight. It was a low and desolate ridge with sparse pine trees. Up on the heights was a village, as well as large estates. He'd once ventured up there, but from here the village couldn't be seen.

In the fields the rocky outcroppings stuck up in so many places that the pale carpet of grain stubble seemed punctured with holes; here and there only a strip of planted ground lay between stretches of reddish rock. Yet the land produced excellent crops, for the fields were fertilized with fish guts from the wharf, and the grain matured early. In the rock crevices grew flowering plants that Olav had never seen before. When he'd gone there in the early summer, he'd found lovely purplish-red stars, but now the slender spiky leaves of the grass itself had turned blood-red and rust-red, bristling lushly with seed-pods that looked like the heads of herons with long beaks.

Running the farm was what Olav understood best. He could see that there were plenty of improvements that needed to be made. The old meadows had to be cleared of weeds, the livestock herd had to be replenished, and the houses needed to be repaired. He had hired Gudrid's husband, Bjørn, to take charge of the fishing and other hunting activities on the fjord for the next half year. Olav had no experience with such things, but he intended to go out with Bjørn during the winter to acquire some knowledge of the pursuits that had been the source of Hestviken's prosperity in the past. Bjørn also recommended that when summer again arrived, they should resume the practice of burning seaweed to obtain salt in the bay south of the Horse.

Yet underlying all these thoughts about the work at hand and the work in the future, a deep calm sated with happiness had settled in Olav's heart. The days now passed over him like a stream of moments that held nothing but good. And because he knew that the dangerous memories lay buried beneath the stream and it was only by sheer strength of will that he was able to make them stay there instead of re-entering his thoughts, he was proud that he now felt so happy and secure.

He was icily aware that the old misfortunes could return to haunt them, but he readily accepted the good days while they lasted.

Morning after morning he would stand at the fence, staring into the distance and thinking about one thing and another while this dreamlike sense of happiness surged beneath all his thoughts. His fair face would look stony and defiant, and the black pupils of his eyes would grow as small as pinpricks. When he knew it was time for Ingunn to be up and about, he would go back to the estate. He would greet his wife with a nod and the shadow of a smile when they happened to meet, noticing the delighted flush rise to her bright face and the quiet and modest joy emanating from both her movements and demeanor.

Ingunn was now exceedingly beautiful, lovelier than she'd ever been. Her figure was fuller, her complexion radiantly pure, and her eyes seemed even bigger and a deeper blue beneath the white wimple of a married woman.

She carried herself with a gentle and placid air. She behaved in a quiet, even-tempered, and kind manner toward everyone, but she was almost deferential toward her husband. Yet everyone could tell that she was happy, and everyone who met Olav's wife looked on her with favor.

Olav was still sleeping very little at night. Hour after hour he would lie awake without moving, except for shifting a bit the arm on which Ingunn lay if it began to feel numb. She rested so securely next to him when she slept, and he would breathe in the sweet hay-scent of her hair. Her entire being exuded warmth, youth, and health. And in the pitch-dark it seemed to Olav that the bad smell of old folks had been banished to the corners, defeated and chased out. He would lie in bed, feeling the hours pass, with no desire for sleep to overtake him. It was so good to lie there, sensing her presence. At last they had ended up together. He ran his hand over her shoulder and arm. Her skin was silky soft and cool to the touch. The coverlet had slipped down. Olav pulled it up over Ingunn, then leaned down to caress her, and from her hazy somnolence she greeted him with tiny, sleepy words of endearment, like a bird chittering from its nighttime perch.

But Olav's heart was always on alert and easily frightened, startling the way a bird abruptly takes flight. He was acutely aware of this and was careful to ensure that no one else noticed.

One morning as he stood at the rail fence and watched his cows that had been released to graze in the stubble field, he saw the big ox among them. It was the only truly handsome animal to be found in the Hestviken livestock sheds. The ox was a large and sturdy beast with a coal-black coat, except for a pale yellow streak along its spine. As Olav looked at the ox advancing down the slope, moving slowly and heavily, it suddenly seemed to him that the pale streak on the black back began wriggling like a snake. And for a moment he panicked. The fear was only fleeting before he pulled himself together. But afterward he was never as pleased with the ox as he'd been before, and this aversion stayed with him during all the years he owned that animal.

◆ ◆ ◆

For as long as the summer weather lasted, Olav enjoyed going down to the foreshore every day during the midday rest. He would swim out far enough that he could see the houses of the estate above the expanse of bare rock. Then he would turn over to float on his back before swimming some more. Bjørn often went with him to bathe.

One day when they came out of the water and sat down on the shore to dry off in the wind, Olav happened to look at Bjørn's feet. They were big, with a high arch and exceedingly narrow sole—the clear sign of a man who was the descendant of free men. He'd heard folks say that it could be immediately determined from a man's feet whether he had even a drop of blood from the old thrall families. Bjørn's face and limbs were as weather-beaten and brown as wood, but his body was milky white, and his hair was very fair, although heavily laced with gray.

Before he could stop himself, Olav blurted out, "Are you related to us, to the Hestviken men, Bjørn?"

"No," said Bjørn curtly. "What the Devil! Don't you even know who your kinsmen are, man?"

Olav felt slightly embarrassed. He said, "I grew up far away from my kinfolk. And sometimes a person may not be fully aware of certain branches of his family."

"And you thought I might be one of those offspring left behind by Dirt Beard?" said Bjørn harshly. "No, I was lawfully born, as were my forefathers, going back seven generations. I've never heard of any wayside bastards in our family!"

Olav bit his lip. He was offended, yet he was the one who had provoked the man, so he didn't say a word.

"But my kinsmen are known for a certain fault," Bjørn went on. "It seems that the axe leaps into our hands of its own accord with even the slightest goading—if you want to call that a fault. But we don't take joy in wielding our weapons for long, unless there's enough gold for us to seize upon afterward."

Olav didn't reply.

Bjørn laughed and said, "I killed my neighbor after we had quar-reled over some ropes made from animal hide. What do you think of that, Master Olav?"

"It seems to me they must have been quite costly ropes. Were they so remarkable?"

"I had borrowed them from Gunnar to use when we brought in the hay. What do you say to that?"

"Knowing what I do of you, I can't believe that you're in the habit of repaying folks for a favor in such a manner," said Olav. "So surely there must have been something special about those ropes after all."

"Gunnar must have thought that was my view," replied Bjørn. "For he accused me of cutting pieces from them."

Olav nodded.

As Bjørn bent down to fasten his shoe, he said, "What would you have done in my place, Olav Audunssøn?"

"That's not easy for me to know," said Olav. He had stood up and was struggling to pin his brooch to the neck opening of his shirt.

"No. For no one would think of accusing a man of your standing of stealing a miserable piece of hide rope," said Bjørn. "But you were also quick to act, Olav, when it came to defending your honor."

Olav was about to put on his cotehardie, but he let his hand drop. "What do you mean?"

"What do I mean? Word spread here in the district that you had punished your future kinsman because he wanted to deny you the maiden who had been promised to you, and he also spoke ill of her. When I heard this, I thought to myself that I might be inclined to offer you the services of a friend when you one day returned home. Other-wise I would not have taken work so close to the place where I once owned a farm myself, even though it was not a big farm."

Olav was now fastening his belt. He took off the dagger that hung from the belt. It was a good weapon made by a foreign bladesmith and with a silver plate and hook for attaching it to a belt. He held it out to Bjørn.

"Will you accept this as a sign of my friendship, Bjørn?"

"No, I will not. Do you not know, Olav, that knives should never be given to friends? They will cut asunder any friendship. But you could do me a favor and stop giving anything to the woman who keeps coming here."

Olav blushed. All of a sudden he looked quite young. To hide his embarrassment, he replied casually as he leaped over a hillock and headed up the slope, "I didn't realize folks hereabouts knew so much about what has gone on between me and the Kolbeinssøns."

Bjørn had startled Olav with his comment that the master of Hestviken was quick to react when his honor was challenged. Olav had forgotten all about the killing of Einar Kolbeinssøn; it weighed so little on his mind except as the cause of the difficulties from which he was now free. It hadn't occurred to him that Bjørn was referring to that particular event.

Olav had taken a liking to Bjørn when the man came to offer his services, and he continued to regard him favorably. But he saw that Bjørn was not well liked in the village. Every once in a while his wife, Gudrid, would come down to Hestviken. Bjørn displayed little joy whenever they met, and he rarely went home. Olav soon noticed that she was the worst sort of gossip. She preferred to wander from one farmstead to another, skulking about with her beggar's sack, instead of tending to her own household. And the family over there at Rundmyr wasn't nearly as impoverished as she claimed. Bjørn took better care of his family than Gudrid said, sending home meat and fish, as well as a little flour, and they owned both a cow and a goat. But Olav had once called the woman "foster mother," and so she never left without receiving some gift from him. By now he was sorry he'd ended up in such a dilemma. He realized that Bjørn found the situation insufferable, for he supposedly enjoyed the highest standing among the hired men at Hestviken, yet his wife would show up to beg for alms.

Olav had developed an inclination to seek the counsel of older men. Though he hadn't been aware of it when he was growing up, he'd missed having someone who would take the time to teach and guide him. He now showed great courtesy and respect toward all older men who were equal in standing to him. He was also willing to help and assist aged folks who were poor, and he patiently listened to the advice of elderly men and accepted their recommendations if he thought them to be beneficial. Olav himself was quite taciturn whenever he found himself among strangers, but old folks were happy to keep a conversation going so he didn't need to offer many comments or pay attention the whole time. For this reason they took a highly favorable view of the young master of Hestviken.

For the most part, his peers also held him in esteem, although they noted that Olav Audunssøn couldn't be said to display much merriment or joy. And some of them mistrusted his quiet and reticent manner, taking it for a sign of arrogance. But others simply thought the man was somewhat gloomy by nature and not overly intelligent. Yet everyone could agree that Olav and his wife were unusually attractive in appearance and knew how to conduct themselves properly toward others.

One Saturday shortly before the late afternoon meal, Olav and Bjørn and both hired men were headed up the slope from the wharf. That's when they saw a group on horseback come riding out of the copse in Kverndalen and set off for the estate. There were two men and three young maidens whose flowing hair, as pale as flax, billowed over their saddles. Their gowns were red and blue. It was a lovely sight against the backdrop of the meadow, which was still fresh and green after the haying. And Olav was filled with joy when he recognized the daughters of Arne.

He greeted them cheerfully, embracing and kissing them as he helped them down from their horses. Then he led them over to his wife, who stood in the doorway. Ingunn received their guests in a quiet and gentle manner.

The maidens had not attended the homecoming feast, and now, over the sabbath, the two youngest were to return home to their father. The priest had sent all of them to Hestviken so they might meet their kinsman's wife and bring her gifts. The priest's hired man had accompanied the maidens, and when they rode past Skikkjustad, the son of the estate decided to join them. The previous week he'd had a brief discussion with Olav about a matter of commerce.

Olav went over to the loft living quarters to take off the clothing he'd worn at the wharf and to wash before donning his sabbath best. He was glad to have these young kinswomen living nearby; perhaps Ingunn would feel less lonely. He'd heard a rumor that Sira Benedikt and Paal of Skikkjustad were contemplating a marriage between Signe and Baard Paalssøn, and the two young people didn't seem to have anything against such an arrangement. If the marriage agreement was made, it might be pleasant for everyone living here at Hestviken as well.

Outside, it was cold with no wind. The pale, clear weather was definitely a portent of frost arriving in the night. It was also cold indoors. They kept putting more wood on the hearth fire, and after everyone had eaten, the young people decided to warm up by going out to dance in the courtyard for a while, until dark fell. But Ingunn didn't want to join in the dancing. She wrapped her cloak tighter around her, looking as if she were freezing. She was so quiet that it seemed she must be disconsolate about something. Olav left the dancing to sit down next to his wife. After a while it grew so dark that everyone had to go back inside. It then turned out that the three sisters knew plenty of games, diversions, and amusements that were suitable for indoors, and they had lovely singing voices. They were in all ways courteous and well-mannered maidens. Yet Ingunn continued to look out of sorts, and that made it difficult for Olav to enjoy himself, for he couldn't understand what was distressing his wife.

Olav put his arm around Torunn and led her over to Ingunn. Torunn, who had not yet turned thirteen, was a beautiful and lively child. But even she was not able to cheer up the mistress of the house.

Later in the evening Olav accompanied their guests part of the way after they took their leave. It was a lovely night, with the full moon shining brightly high overhead, but a frosty haze was starting to rise up from the fjord and erase the shadows across the meadow. Olav walked along, leading Torunn's horse.

"Your wife doesn't like us, Olav," said the young maiden.

"How can you think such a thing?" said Olav smiling. "Why wouldn't she like you? I don't know what came over Ingunn tonight."

Ingunn was in bed when Olav returned home, and when he lay down beside her, he noticed that she was weeping. He patted her arm and begged her to tell him what was making her so sad. At long last he managed to persuade her to speak. She was feeling terribly unwell. No doubt it was from the mussels she had eaten when she was down at the wharf in the morning. Olav told her not to do such a thing again. She should ask him or Bjørn if she had a longing for food of that kind, and they would find her some mussels that were good. Then he asked her whether she found his kinswomen to be lovely and decorously behaved young women.

Ingunn said she did. "Those daughters of Arne were quite lively," she added, sounding displeased. "You became very high-spirited yourself, Olav, and that is not like you. I can tell that you're fond of them."

Yes, Olav told her, he was. And his voice took on a joyful tone as he thought back on the merry evening. Then he repeated what a great pleasure it was for both of them to have these sweet and polite young kinswomen nearby.

Olav could hear Ingunn sighing heavily as she lay next to him. After a moment she whispered, "We were like your sisters, Tora and I, when we were growing up, yet I can't recall that you ever bantered and jested so merrily with the two of us."

"Oh, I'm sure I did occasionally," replied Olav. "But I was living on the estate of a stranger," he added quietly. "If I had grown up among my own kinfolk, where I belonged, I think I would have been less stalwart and withdrawn as a boy."

A little while later he noticed that Ingunn was weeping again. And this time she was so overcome with sobs that he had to get up to bring her some water. When he lit a twig, he saw that her face was so red and swollen that he feared she had eaten something truly poisonous. He threw on some clothes and dashed out to find fresh milk, which he made her drink. With that she finally felt better and fell asleep.

◆ ◆ ◆

One day just before All Saints' Day, Olav had gone to the presbytery along with other landowners to compose several documents. Several times during the meeting Olav exchanged sharp words with another man, whose name was Stein, though they hadn't actually fallen out.

When everyone was about to head back home, some of the men came over to look at Olav Audunssøn's horse, Apalhviten. They praised the steed and also mentioned how well cared for the animal looked. And they teased Stein, for he too had a white horse, but it was scruffy and dirty-yellow in appearance, and it was easy to see that the horse had been badly treated by its rider.

Stein said, "It was Olav's job to groom and ride horses, so it's only reasonable that the steed belonging to a knight's man should be well tended. But just wait until you've been farming for a few years," he told Olav. "By then you'll undoubtedly have forgotten some of those nobleman tricks of yours. Then you'll realize the truth of the old saying that white horses and beautiful women aren't meant for farmers, for there is never any time to safeguard them."

"Things can never be so bad for me that I can't afford to keep two white horses," said Olav arrogantly. "Will you sell me yours, Stein?"

Stein named a price. Olav reached out his hand at once and asked the others to witness the agreement. Then and there it was decided where and when Olav would arrange to make the payment. Stein removed the saddle from his horse and went into Sira Benedikt's house to borrow a halter. The other men shook their heads and said that Olav had made a bad bargain.

"No matter." Olav shrugged and gave a little laugh. "But I don't want to be so cautious that I always have to divide a louse into four parts."

He placed his saddle on the horse he had just purchased and let Apalhviten run behind. The other men remained where they were and watched him ride off. A few grinned maliciously. The first test of wills between the horse and rider occurred at the bend in the road. It looked as if Olav was bound to sweat a great deal before he made it back home to Hestviken.

◆ ◆ ◆

Ingunn was sitting alone in the main hall and sewing when she heard hoof beats on the stone surface of the courtyard. She went over to the door to look out, astonished when she saw her husband. There he was, in the pale, hazy autumn sunlight, sitting astride an agitated horse she'd never seen before. Olav's face was bright red, and both he and the horse were spattered with foam pouring from the bridle bit as the horse, refusing to stand still, chomped and swerved, making its hooves ring against the ground. Olav laughed when he saw Ingunn and the hired man, who came toward him.

"I'll tell you all about it when I come inside," said Olav to his wife. He dismounted and then followed the hired man who led the new horse over to the stable.

"What happened?" asked Ingunn when Olav came back. He paused just inside the doorway, looking as if he were drunk.

"Is the old man here?" asked Olav.

"No, he went down to the sea. Shall I send Tore to get him?"

Olav laughed and closed the door behind him. Then he went over to his wife and picked her up as if she were a child, holding her so tight that she gasped.

"Olav," she said with alarm. "What is it?"

"Nothing except that you're so fair," he murmured, uttering another burst of drunken laughter. He pressed his hot face so hard against hers that she thought he might snap her neck in half.

Later that afternoon Olav climbed the slope to the mill while Ingunn went over to the cookhouse. She had left a wooden tub with cheese next to the back hearthstone.

The lid must not have been fastened tightly, because a great deal of ash had settled inside. And the tub gave off a bad smell. The cheese must have stood there too long, but earlier the whey had refused to drain out. Ingunn was never able to make her cheeses ferment properly. The cheeses that she had made the previous week had begun to drain again, running out all over the shelf where she'd placed them to dry.

Her lips quavered as she stood there, slowly and listlessly kneading the sticky and foul-smelling cheese in the tub. She was not a skillful mistress. She found the work tiring and arduous, and she was constantly plagued by mishaps. With every setback she encountered, she would feel beside herself with despair. When was Olav going to realize that his wife was also incapable of managing a household? At the end of such a day, when everything she tried had gone badly, she would feel as bruised as if she'd suffered a series of falls.

Olav had not been drunk after all. At first she had found solace in the idea that he must have imbibed more than was his habit when offered ale at the presbytery, ale that the priest boasted of so often. But Olav had been completely sober. And her heart began pounding hard as she stood there, lost in thought. What could have possessed Olav to make him behave so differently? He had never been anything but loving and kind and tender in his lovemaking. She had often felt a slight yearning for him to show a little less composure.

A weight seemed to settle over her. He was calm by nature and master of his emotions—for the most part. But she had witnessed times when Olav had lost control over himself. Yet even on that night when he, in a wild state, had come to tell her that he'd killed Einar, she had sensed his love for her and found it comforting. His fury she had witnessed only once, and it was aimed at her. That was when she'd shrunk from him in terror, having come face-to-face with his white-hot rage. She couldn't bear to think of it, and she hadn't until now. But suddenly it all came back to her with suffocating clarity. Surely she could not have done anything this time to provoke such anger in him.

She had thrived during the past four months after they were wed. She instinctively regarded their marriage as beginning from the moment her kinsmen, before witnesses, had given her to Olav Audunssøn. And he had been so kind to her that the memory of all the dreadful past events seemed no more than a horrible dream. And she had to admit that he had been right. Hestviken was far away, and it had been easier than she'd imagined to forget about everything that had happened up north. But she had also tried hard to show him that she was grateful and that she loved him—inexpressibly. She couldn't possibly have done anything to cause him to act so . . . strangely, when he came home. But then she grew fearful at the thought of what might have prompted such conduct.

Yet how foolish that was. For he had not behaved in that manner out of anger; his actions were meant to be loving caresses, in a way. Merely lustful. And he had danced with her quite roughly, wild with an unrestrained merriment that had frightened her, for she wasn't used to Olav behaving in such a manner. But that didn't necessarily mean that anything had happened to him. Perhaps all men acted like that once in a while. Teit certainly had.

Teit. She felt a jolt pass through her. It had reminded her of Teit. The memory of him had become as distant and unreal as everything else that had vanished beyond the horizon as she traveled farther and farther away with Olav. Yet now it had again become terribly close and alive, the memory that Teit had once possessed her.

She gave a shriek and flinched, trembling all over as Olav suddenly came up behind her. She hadn't noticed that he'd come in.

He'd been standing in the doorway, looking at her, the tall and slender young woman bending over the table, narrow-shouldered and delicate, working slowly and clumsily as she kneaded the cheese with her long, thin fingers. He couldn't see her face beneath the wimple, but he sensed that she was feeling downhearted.

He was ashamed of acting toward her as he had when he came home a while ago. It wasn't seemly for a man to behave toward his wife in that way. He feared that she would feel mistreated.

"Did I startle you?" Olav spoke in his customary manner, calmly and with a hint of tenderness in his demeanor. He stepped forward to stand beside her, a bit embarrassed. Then he picked up a clump of the cheese that she was shaping into balls and ate it.

"I never did this sort of work before I came here," she told him apologetically. "Dalla would never let me. I don't think I've gotten enough of the whey out of the curd."

"I'm sure you'll learn," her husband consoled her. "We have plenty of time, Ingunn.

"I regret buying that horse, but Stein goaded me into it," he added as he looked down. He blushed and laughed uneasily. "You know it's not like me to act like such a fool. I was just so happy when you came out to greet me . . ." He glanced at her as if asking forgiveness.

Ingunn bent lower over her work, her cheeks bright red.

She's just not capable of doing much, thought Olav. All this unfamiliar toil is wearing her out. If only the old man in the alcove would remain calm tonight. Rheumatism tugged and yanked so badly at his poor body that he often lay awake for hours at night, whimpering loudly. And that meant there was little peace for the young folks in the main hall.

Olav Ingolfssøn had collapsed completely the moment his young kinsman released him from the burdens of running the estate. He had labored hard at Hestviken, even though so few traces remained of his efforts. Now he surrendered entirely to the afflictions of old age. The two young people treated him kindly. Olav found it heartening— although he couldn't actually say why—that he was at long last living under the same roof as a man who belonged to his father's lineage. And it made him happy to see Ingunn showing such kindness and concern for the frail old man. He had been a bit disappointed to see that she cared little for the daughters of Arne or their father, whom they had now met. Olav, on the other hand, took a strong liking to his father's cousin. Arne of Hestbæk was a man of fifty, white-haired but handsome and stately. The family resemblance between him and Olav was striking. Arne Torgilssøn had greeted Olav with great pleasure and invited him to be their guest at Christmastime. Olav wanted very much to do so, but Ingunn wasn't eager to go.

For that reason he was glad that she at least seemed to be fond of Olav Half-Priest, despite the fact that the old man caused them a considerable amount of trouble. He was often restless at night, and he made quite a mess whenever he concocted various remedies and salves for himself. An old dog slept in his bed at night, the warmth of the animal's body meant to soothe the rheumatism in his bad leg, but the dog was filthy, mean-tempered, and thievish. Yet Ingunn patiently helped the old man, speaking to him with the gentleness of a daughter, and she was also kind to his dog.

Both of the young people found it amusing to sit with Old Olav and listen to him talk in the evening. There was no end to everything he knew about men and families and estates in all the districts surrounding Folden. Based on what he'd heard from his father, he was able to tell them about the great strife that followed Sverre Priest's arrival in Norway. But Olav Half-Priest had personally fought for King Skule. Olav Audunssøn's great-grandfather, Olav Olavssøn of Hestviken, had been loyal to Sigurd Ribbung to the very end, and so he had fought *against* Skule. But when the duke was proclaimed king at the *Øreting*,[10] Olav Ribbung gathered supporters and headed north with his three sons to offer the new king his support. And his brother, Ingolf the priest, granted his son permission to accompany his kinsmen.

"We were then fifteen years old, both Torgils and I," said Olav Half-Priest, "but we certainly showed our mettle. I got this scar on my backside at Laaka. The Spring Pelts[11] kept mocking me for getting wounded in such a spot, but we had come to a deep valley with a stream running between clay hills, and the Birch Legs had us trapped both in front and behind—Torgils and me and three other lads. There were so many young boys fighting with us Spring Pelts. We called one of them Surt, and he had the angriest red hair I've ever seen on a man. When we followed Gudine Geig into the eastern valleys, we happened to take shelter at a small farm for the night, and when we awoke, the place was on fire. 'You've been sleeping with your hair pressed against the timbers, you devil,' said Gudine. 'Right, and then you blew on it,' replied Surt. Ha, ha, ha! Though what he really said was much less polite than I'd dare to repeat before Ingunn here. We were scattered about, lying on the floor, with Surt right behind Gudine. The gallery was ablaze, but we managed to get out and beat our way through the flames. Those Birch Legs were very careless about lighting fires on their farms. We jested that there were too many bathhouse fellows and baker lasses among them. But let me tell you now what happened to me and Torgils at Laaka. No, wait, first I'd better tell you a little about that man Gudine Geig . . ."

◆ ◆ ◆

Olav Audunssøn's Happiness   47

Olav could see that it distressed Ingunn whenever the old man badgered her and grew impatient, wanting to know whether she might soon have some news to reveal. She and Olav had been married now for five months, after all.

"We're doing what we can, kinsman," Olav would tell him with a laugh.

But the old man would then grow angry and say he shouldn't speak so lightheartedly about such matters. It would be better to make promises to God, so the Lord might bless them soon with an heir. Olav laughed and replied that there was no haste. What he didn't say was that he thought even though Ingunn had fully regained her health, she was having a difficult enough time managing the household and keeping her three maidservants working steadily.

But Olav Ingolfssøn grumbled that he didn't think he had long to live. He had known four generations of the paternal side of the family—great-grandfather, grandfather, father, and son. "I would very much like to welcome a son of yours, Olav, before I leave this earth."

"Oh, I'm sure you'll live long enough to greet both my son and my grandson," Olav consoled him.

But the old man was pessimistic. "Olav Torgilssøn, who was the first man of our lineage here at Hestviken, was married to Tora Ingolfsdatter for ten years before they had any children. And he fell before his twin sons even saw the light of day. I think that was his punishment for marrying Tora against his father's wishes. Ingolf of Hestviken and Torgils of Dyfrin had become foes, but Olav Torgilssøn said he refused to pass up such a good marriage simply because the two old men had once come to blows while drinking. Tora inherited the estate, for Ingolf was the last man of the old Hestviken family, who had lived here since Norway was formed. And Torgils Fivil was the last of the landowner lineage at Dyfrin. King Sverre gave the Dyfrin estate and Torgils's young widow to one of his men. Torgils Fivil had been married three times. In his youth he'd been named for the pale yellow flowers called 'fivil' because of the flaxen color of his hair and his fair, pale complexion, which have been passed down through the family ever since.

"So as you can see, our ancestor had plenty of reason to seek revenge against Sverre, in the name of the allodial estate and a father and three brothers. And that winter, when his wife noticed signs that their lineage would continue on the estate after they were gone, that was the same winter when folks living here around Folden rose up to avenge King Magnus, the lawfully crowned ruler, and strike down that man Sverre, who had no right to the realm and who wanted to abolish all our old rights and introduce new customs that we did not favor. Those living on the fjord and in the county of Oppland, the inhabitants of Ranrike and the river valleys, in fact nearly everyone in Norway was in agreement. Olav Torgilssøn was among the chieftains who had led the councils and he'd been the most zealous from the start.

"But you know what happened to those of us living around Oslo back then. The Devil always helps his own, and he carried Sverre Priest in his arms until he managed to bring the man safely inside the gates of Hell. That's what I think. Olav Torgilssøn was struck down out there on the ice, but several men from the district rescued his body and brought him home. So many men had fallen on top of Olav around his banner, that the Birch Legs hadn't stolen his corpse, and he was brought home clutching his axe. They couldn't loosen the dead man's grip on the axe handle, but when his wife went over and seized hold of the axe, he let it go. His arm dropped, but Tora stood there with the axe, and at that moment the child quickened inside her. It was as if the unborn boy had thrust out his fist. That's what she told her sons, who were born later in the spring. As soon as they were old enough to understand, she told them over and over that they had promised to avenge their father even as they lay in her womb. The axe was the one you now own, called Ættarfylgja, or Guardian of Kin. Tora was the one who named it. Before that it was called Jarnglumra, or the Weapon of Glumra.[12] The axe was given to Olav, for he was the older of the twins, when Tora sent the boys to a man named Benedikt, who was supposedly the son of King Magnus Erlingssøn. That was the first regiment the brothers joined.

"I remember well my paternal grandmother, Tora Ingolfsdatter. She was a generous woman and very wise, both God-fearing and kind to poor folks. A great deal of fishing was done from Hestviken during the time she was mistress here—and that was for as long as she lived. Your great-grandfather and my father obeyed her until her dying day. Grandmother sent her ships along the whole coastline, all the way down to the Gaut River and to Denmark. She wanted to find out if anything was in the works against the Sverre lineage, you see. Tora always knew about any such plans and ploys that were being hatched, and anyone who had a mind to fight against the Birch Legs received good support from the widow of Olav Torgilssøn. Tora had loved her husband beyond all measure. Olav Torgilssøn was short and fair-complexioned, but he was possessed of great strength, and he was a handsome man. He was somewhat coarse in manner, but that's how all men were in the time of King Magnus.

"Apparently Grandmother had never been fair of face. As I remember her, she was tall and so fat that she had to turn sideways and fold in half just to get through the door here in the new hall. She was half a head taller than her sons, and they were big men. But she was not attractive in appearance. Her nose was so big and so crooked that I don't know what to compare it to, and her eyes were like gull eggs. Her chins drooped down her neck, and her breasts sagged down to her stomach.

"At first she sent her sons to Filippus, the Bagler king,[13] but she soon grew discontented with him, for she deemed him to be an unenterprising, indolent, and placid man. So when Benedikt emerged as a leader at Marker, she told the boys to join him. His troops were mostly motley groups of roving fellows and all types of lowlifes, and my father always said of Benedikt that he was worthless as a chieftain. He was reckless and lewd and rather stupid, and his courage could not be counted on. Sometimes he was fearless, at other times fearful. But Olav was forever loyal to him, for he truly believed that Benedikt was the son of King Magnus, though perhaps not properly raised. This is what happened with Benedikt: at first his only followers were these bunches of riffraff who were called the ragtag youths, but then more and more respectable landowners decided to back him, since there was no better man of chieftain ability to be found. But they wanted to control Benedikt and not be controlled by their choice of king. After a while, when Sigurd Ribbung emerged with the support of the noblemen who were old Bagler chieftains, the chieftains of the ragtag youths took Benedikt with them as they switched their allegiance to Sigurd. And then Benedikt had to make do with being one of Sigurd Ribbung's lesser chieftains. But Olav Olavssøn always remembered that Benedikt was the first lord to whom he'd sworn fealty, and he continued to serve and honor him after this happened. Olav was a loyal man.

"Tora arranged good marriages for all her sons. For Olav she decided on Astrid Helgesdatter of Mork. They were very young, both of them only sixteen, but they lived well together and loved each other deeply. Their sons were Ingolf, your paternal grandfather, who was the eldest; then came Helge, who fell at Nidaros with King Skule; and finally Torgils. He was the youngest of the sons. He and I were the same age. The daughters of Olav and Astrid were Halldis, who married Ivar Staal of Aas in Hudrheim; and Borgny, the nun, who was a beloved holy woman. She died the year after you were born.

"Father was older when he married, for he wanted to be a priest. It was Nikulaus Arnessøn, the bishop himself, who ordained him. The bishop had the greatest affection for my father, for Father was exceptionally pious and learned and was able to copy books more beautifully than all the other priests in the bishopric. My mother, Bergljot of Tveit, was a merry woman who delighted in lavish things and entertaining guests. She and Father were unlike in temperament, and they never got on well, even though they had so many children. Five of us lived to adulthood. My mother was rather greedy when it came to money. Father was so generous that behind my mother's back he would steal from his own supplies to give away as alms. It got so bad that the townsmen caught wind of this and laughed. It doesn't look good, you know, for a priest not to be master of his own household. I remember once that Mother was angry about something. She picked up two pages of a book that Father had just finished copying and tossed them into the hearth fire. That time he beat her. Father was big and strong, and a daring soldier who had fought bravely against the Birch Legs. Yet toward those who were his Christian equals he behaved in a mostly gentle and placid manner. But Mother caused a good deal of discord. Between our estate in Oslo and the shoreline there was a patch of . . . it can't be rightly called ground. It was nothing more than a stretch of foreshore with scattered glasswort plants and bare rock. The townfolk were in the habit of taking a path across this area. Mother wanted to close off the path, but Father thought it would be unseemly for a priest to quarrel over such a petty matter. Yet there was endless strife because of that right-of-way, both between my parents and between us and our neighbors.

"When word arrived that priests here in Norway were to refrain from marrying, as was the custom in other Christian lands, Father ordered my mother to leave for Tveit, where she might make use of the estate and a large part of his property. But she and her kinsmen and my siblings were very angry, for they thought that Father, in his heart, was more glad than sorrowful at being forced to end their life together. I happen to know that my father had always thought it improper that priests should marry, and Bishop Nikulaus shared this view. But such was the custom when my father was young, and he had to do as his mother wished. My mother and siblings then left, and since then I have seen very little of them. My brother Kaare inherited Tveit, and Erlend was given Aasheim. Both estates have now been divided among many children. I stayed with Father. It had always been intended that I should become a priest. Father and I were happy living together, and we considered Halvard Church to be our rightful home. I was ordained as a subdeacon three years after King Skule fell. Grandmother Tora died soon after.

"But I was meaning to tell you about your paternal grandfather's father, Olav Ribbung, and his lineage. As you know, Ingolf was married to Ragna Hallkelsdatter of Kaaretorp. Tora was the one who had arranged for this good marriage for her grandson as soon as he came of age. Audun, your father, was only a couple of years old when our kinsmen and I left to support the Spring Pelts and King Skule. When Torgils lost his wits, Ingolf and Ragna were no longer happy living at Hestviken, and so they lived mostly at Kaaretorp. But one Christmas when they were here visiting, Ingolf decided to accompany his sister, Halldis, and her husband across the fjord to Aas and stay with them for a while. They set out in a heavy snowstorm, and everyone in the boat drowned.

"Olav Ribbung bore this misfortune so well that my father always said he'd never seen any man bear adversity in a more seemly manner. He always mentioned his brother as an exemplar of steadfastness and strength. Those twin brothers loved each other dearly. And so it was that he lost his son, daughter, and son-in-law. Olav merely said that he thanked God that his mother and his wife, Astrid, had both died before these ill winds had begun to ravage his children. He was left with a madman son, and he had no other remaining kin except his daughter Borgny, the nun, and the little lad Audun. Ingolf's widow later married a man south in Elvesyssel, and Olav agreed that Audun should be raised by his mother and stepfather. Olav Ribbung then took as his lawful son the boy that Torgils had sired with a maidservant here at Hestviken, but the boy didn't live long.

"It was three years after I became lame from the break in my leg that Ingolf and the others died. And I was not taking my misfortune well. It seemed to me unbearably distressing that I, young as I was, should become crippled and never become a priest. Back then my father always held up Olav Ribbung as an example for me. But I know that Olav took it hard when Audun refused to remarry after your mother died and decided not to stay here at Hestviken. And the lineage seemed destined to die out.

"But now there is every expectation that the family will blossom again, so young and fresh and fair as both you and your wife are. You must realize how I long to hold your son in my arms. Four generations have I known—five, if I count the matriarch of our lineage. And I would like to see the first man of the sixth generation before I die. Not many men are granted the privilege of knowing their kinsmen for six generations. But it would seem to me reasonable, Ingunn my dear, if your husband also longed fiercely to experience the same. His forebears have lived here at Hestviken since Norway was formed. Do you hear me, young wife?" he said, laughing slyly.

Olav saw Ingunn's face redden. But it was not the modest glow of longing and joy; it was the heated flush of shame that passed over her face. Her eyes turned dark and tormented. Out of compassion he looked away.

III

Ingunn went outside to the gallery of the loft room and stood there, watching the snow come pelting down. High above, against the pale clouds, the big, wet flakes looked gray as they whirled through the air, yet as they fell, they seemed a dazzling white, a flickering white mass against the obscured white heights close to Kverndalen.

After gazing up into that swirling snowstorm for a while, she felt as if she were being drawn up to hover there, just for a moment. Then she sank back down, and everything went black before her eyes. Again and again she sought to relive this sensation. The unbearable dizziness that suddenly overtook her now became, somehow, a sense of gentle well-being. But when she sank down, she couldn't see. Everything turned gray with black streaks and spun in circles.

It seemed strangely quiet, for the gulls were silent. In this sort of weather she'd seen how the birds would sit in the crevices on the slope below, and on the big rocks on the foreshore. Once in a while they would move slightly, though without making a sound. When she first came to Hestviken, she had thought that these big white birds with the great wingspans were more beautiful than anything she'd ever seen. Even their peculiar shrieks made her feel oddly happy. She had been brought to a strange land, far away from the places where she'd endured unbearable suffering. This summer, whenever she went out in the morning, she would hear the sea gently surging at the foot of the slope on which she stood, and she saw the fjord, stretching so wide and bright, and the distant desolate shore on the other side, and the circling white gulls shrieking hoarsely, as unreal as some sort of female guardian spirits—then she would feel quite lighthearted. The world extended so far and wide. Whatever had happened in some small spot, far far away, couldn't possibly carry much import. And surely it could all be forgotten.

But as autumn advanced out by the fjord, she began to feel unnerved by the fact that there was never any stillness. The eternal crash and thunder of the waves, the cries of the seabirds, the passage of storms over the forests close to the ridge—all of that made her feel dazed. If she merely crossed the courtyard on some errand, she would feel as if the storm were coursing through her ears and filling her whole head with noise. And rain and fog rushed in from the sea, robbing her of courage. She remembered what fall was like back home—the ground hard with frost, the sky clear and bright, the sound of axes hewing and dogs barking from one farm to the next; the sun filtering through the morning haze and the frost thawing to dew as the day progressed. And she longed for nothing but silence all around her.

It seemed as if she had slipped downward as the days and the year waned and darkened. Now she had reached bottom. They had passed the midwinter point and were heading back up. And she felt devoid of all strength when she thought about taking the upward path. The sun would soon rise higher and higher. It wouldn't be long before it steadily became clear that brighter and longer days were upon them. Spring was coming. Yet for her it was like staring at a towering mountain that she needed to climb over because of the burden she now knew for certain she carried. And she felt ill and dizzy whenever she thought about it.

How very still the air was now, in spite of the whirling snow. The flakes spun around, but eventually they fell straight down. The sea looked black as iron, what little she could see of it, and the drone from the shore sounded dull and sluggish in the mild snowy air.

Everything was now covered in snow. The path down to the wharf was completely blanketed. The footprints of the maidservants who had walked down to the foreshore, and her own footprints heading over here, had filled with snow. And all the whiteness was gradually fading to gray as the first shadows of dusk descended.

The door to the bathhouse down in the field burst open, and in the cloud of white steam that billowed out, she caught a glimpse of the men's bodies, dark against the snow. They ran up toward the barn where they'd left their clothes, pausing along the way to roll in the snowdrifts, shouting and laughing. She recognized Olav and Bjørn as the first ones out. They threw their arms around each other, wrestling and dousing each other with snow.

Ingunn picked up the basin of lightly salted and fermented fish called surfisk and wrapped her cloak around it. The basin was so heavy that she had to carry it in both arms, making it hard to see where she set her feet or how she might steady herself. She was afraid of slipping on the bare rock underneath the snow. Dusk had settled in more firmly, and the flickering light before her eyes made her feel even dizzier.

Olav came into the main hall and went over to sit down in the high seat in the middle of the gable wall. He was hungry and worn out. He sank down, content in the knowledge that it was Saturday and the sabbath eve. Three women began bustling around him, bringing food.

The hearth fire glowed red, with tiny low flames playing over the charred logs. Through the dim light in the hall, the man sitting in the master's seat was aware of the new sense of comfort that prevailed inside. Nowadays the table was always set up in front of the bench along the gable wall; cushions had been placed on the high seat, and a tapestry had been fastened to the timbers behind it. Next to the tapestry the axe Ætterfylgja hung in its old place along with Olav's big two-handed sword and the shield with the wolf's head and three blue lilies. Blue-patterned draperies had been hung around the bed at the south end of the hall, the bed where the master and mistress slept.

A faint light shone from the alcove. The old man was saying his evening prayers in a slightly lilting voice. Sira Benedikt might say what he liked, thought Olav, but his kinsman certainly possessed a good deal of learning; he could pray the canonical hours as well as any priest. When the old man was finished, Olav Audunssøn called to him, wanting to know whether he'd like to come out and eat.

The old man replied that he'd rather have a little ale and porridge brought to him in bed. Ingunn quickly filled an ale bowl and then took the food to him. At that moment the hired men came inside. Bjørn carried an armload of wood, which he tossed on the floor. He put more wood on the fire, then threw open the outer door and opened the hearth vent so the snow fell on the heat with a hissing sound. Ingunn stayed with the old man until the wood caught fire and the worst of the smoke had seeped out. Then Bjørn closed the door and the vent-hole.

Ingunn came in and stood in front of the table. With her knife she drew a cross in the air over the loaf of bread before cutting into it. The five men seated on the bench ate in silence, taking their time and eating their fill. Ingunn sat on the edge of the bed, nibbling at a little fish and bread, happy that the salmon was good, having fermented properly. The ale was their Christmas brew, and it could have been better, but the grain she'd had for the purpose was poor and mixed with all manner of unwanted seeds.

She glanced over at her husband. His damp hair was dark. His eyebrows and beard stubble gleamed golden on his face, which looked ruddy and weather-beaten tonight. He seemed pleased with the food.

The three maidservants had sat down on the bench next to the bed to eat their meal in front of the hearth. Herdis, the youngest of them, whispered and giggled every once in a while. That child was always so full of laughter and merriment. She showed the other girls a new spoon made of horn that she'd been given, and laughter spilled out of her. Then she gave her mistress a nervous look and did her best to stay quiet, but the girl just couldn't help tittering cheerfully.

The servants left soon after the meal was finished. The men had been out on the fjord since early in the morning, and considering how far it was from Hestviken to the church, they wouldn't be able to sleep long the next morning. Not when the snow lay as heavy as it now did on the road.

Olav went into the alcove to see to his kinsman. There was always something that the old man needed help with before he settled in for the night. Olav Ingolfssøn was especially talkative around bedtime and wanted to hear all about the fishing and the day's work on the estate. And for every bit of news he heard from the younger Olav, he would remember something or other that he insisted on recounting.

Ingunn was sitting on a low chair in front of the hearth, combing her hair, when Olav came back into the hall. She had partially undressed and wore only a short-sleeved white linen shift and a close-fitting, sleeveless undergarment of reddish-brown wadmal. Her luxuriant dark-golden hair hung like a cloak around her slender figure as she bent slightly forward, with the whiteness of her fragile arms shining through.

Olav went to stand behind her and took up handfuls of his wife's flowing hair, pressing his face into the tresses; they smelled so good.

"You have the most beautiful hair of any woman, Ingunn!"

He tilted her head back so he could look into her upturned face.

"But you've lost weight since Christmas, my sweet! I don't want you to do more than your strength will allow! And you must eat more. Or else you'll grow so thin that when it comes time for fasting there will be nothing left of you!"

He pulled off his tunic and shirt, then sat down on the edge of the hearth and let the fire warm his back. The sight of her husband's naked torso—the play of muscles under the milky-white skin when he leaned forward to take off his boots—aroused a tenderness in the young woman's soul. His robust health made her all the more aware of her own lack of strength.

Olav scratched his shoulder blades. Tiny drops of wine-red blood trickled down his smooth skin.

"He's such a rowdy bathhouse companion, that Bjørn," said Olav with a laugh. Then he bent down to the dog that lay with her pups on a sack next to the hearth. He picked up one of the pups. It whimpered as he held it up to the light; it had just started opening its eyes a bit. The mother gave a muted growl. Olav had bought the dog only recently, paying so much for the pregnant animal that folks again shook their heads at his grandiose conduct. But the dog was a rare, short-haired breed, with drooping, silky-soft ears—an excellent hunting dog. Olav examined the pups with satisfaction. It looked as if all five would turn out to be the same sort as their mother. Laughing, he placed one of the pups on his wife's lap, then stood up, amused to see how the mother dog issued an even more menacing growl yet didn't dare intervene.

The poor animal, her belly swollen and her legs still weak, struggled to creep closer to lick Ingunn's hands. There was such a soft and flimsy look about the animal that Ingunn suddenly felt unwell and a lump rose in her throat.

"Give the pup back to the mother," she said faintly.

Olav looked at her, stopped laughing, and returned the pup to its mother.

Mid-January gave way to mid-February, followed by *Gjømaaned*, the next almanac period that lasted until mid-March. The fjord froze over, and the ice stretched far south of Jølund. The days were growing longer and lighter. A frosty haze rose up from the fjord farther out, in open waters. Whenever clear days appeared, with a bright blue sky and sunshine, the whole world glittered white with rime. Olav and Bjørn went out hunting together.

Ingunn's one thought was how long she could continue to hide the news. Sobs surged inside her. With helpless despair she realized that she need not hide anything. She was Olav's wife, after all, the mistress of Hestviken, and she was to bring forth a child on the old estate where the same family had lived since bygone times. Yet she felt as if she should crawl under the earth to hide.

She knew that Olav was aware of what ailed her, but she still found herself unable to utter a single word about it. She observed the time of fasting along with everyone else, even though hunger clutched so painfully at her chest. She noticed that Olav would surreptitiously glance at her more and more often, as if with astonishment, a barely concealed concern in his eyes. Afterward he would fall silent for a long time. She was heartsick whenever she saw him behaving in that manner, worrying and wondering about her. But she couldn't bring herself to say anything.

One Sunday after they returned home from church, they were alone in the main hall for a short time. Olav was sitting on the bench. As she walked past him, he grabbed her wrist to stop her.

"My Ingunn, you must be kind to Olav Ingolfssøn and tell him your news. I don't think he will live past the spring, and you know how he has been waiting for this!"

Ingunn bowed her head, her face flushing bright red.

"All right," she whispered obediently.

Then her husband pulled her close, wanting her to sit on his lap.

"What is it?" he asked her in a low voice. "Are you so unhappy, Ingunn? Is he tormenting you terribly, this guest of yours? Or are you frightened?"

"Frightened!" For a moment anger seemed to flare in the young wife, and she looked like her old, impetuous self from the past. "You know full well what's wrong. You've never been anything but kind to me, yet now I have to go around here every day thinking about how I'm not worthy of your kindness!"

"Be still!" He crushed her hand in his. Ingunn saw how Olav's face seemed to close up. When he again spoke, he sounded disconsolate, even though he tried to speak calmly and gently.

"Ingunn, give no thought to what it would be better for us to forget. It's ill-advised for us to stir up memories that . . . that . . . And you know full well that I love you dearly, so I could never regard you with anything but kindness."

"Oh, I would be even less worthy if I could forget!"

She sank to her knees before him, hiding her face in her husband's lap and kissing his hand. Olav abruptly pulled his hand away, jumped up, and pulled his wife to her feet.

Ingunn leaned back in his embrace as she looked him in the eye and said somewhat defiantly, "Yes, you are fond of me. God knows I can see that. Yet I think, Olav, that if I offered to behave toward you as I used to do—capricious and haughty, always demanding that you should let me be the one to decide for the two of us—I hardly think you would tolerate that sort of behavior from me after what I did to you. Nor would you have much love for me."

"That's enough!" He let her go.

"I often wish that you would treat me harshly, the way you threatened to do back then."

"You wouldn't wish that," he said, with that cold little smile she knew so well from the past.

Then he fiercely drew her close and pressed her face against his chest.

"Don't cry," he pleaded.

"I'm not crying."

Olav lifted her face and looked down at her. He felt strangely troubled. He would have preferred to see her cry.

In the days that followed a sense of paralyzing anxiety would occasionally descend upon Olav. He felt as if everything had been done in vain. All it had cost him to buy peace for both of them had been in vain. The fact that he had buried his bitterness at the bottom of his soul and covered it over with all the old sources of his love—that too had been in vain. His life with her was an old, beloved habit from his childhood. When he took her in his arms, he was reminded of that first rush of passion in his life. Never had he allowed her to sense that he remembered her . . . weakness. That's what he chose to call it. And here he now stood, at a loss, realizing that he could do nothing about the feeling of shame that kept gnawing at Ingunn's heart.

Nor could he help himself from thinking about everything that had happened, now that he saw her in this condition. This would not be *her* first child.

When they first came to Hestviken to live, he had been very pleased with Ingunn's quiet manner, for he saw that it was happiness that made her such a gentle and compliant mistress. But now he found it vexing, because what she'd said was true: if she had behaved the same way she had in the past—always wanting to be the one in charge and always expecting him to yield to her wishes—he would not have tolerated such behavior from her anymore.

Then he pulled himself together, as if again taking up the burden he needed to carry. At home he always appeared serene and well satisfied, and he would respond cheerfully whenever folks spoke to him, seeming to be pleased that the old roots would now be putting out fresh shoots. He treated his wife kindly and tried to console himself by recalling that Ingunn had never been strong. The fact that she now felt unwell was no doubt causing a great strain on her fragile disposition. And her melancholy mood would probably improve after she regained her health.

Old Olav Ingolfssøn declined rapidly during the spring, and Olav Audunssøn tended to him as best he could. He often spent the night in the alcove with his kinsman. The old man was now in need of all sorts of help. A little oil lamp burned all night long, and the younger Olav would sleep in a sheepskin sack on the floor. When the elder Olav couldn't sleep, he would lie in bed and talk for hours, and by now the topic was always the family: how property and prosperity had come to the Hestviken men, and how it had later slipped out of their hands.

One night, when the two men were lying there talking, young Olav asked his namesake about Torgils Dirt Beard. He knew only bits and pieces about him, and he didn't think these haphazard details were any more pleasant than what he personally remembered about his mad great-uncle.

Old Olav said, "I haven't told you much about him before, but perhaps you ought to know more, now that you're going to be the head of our family. Is your wife asleep?" he then asked. "It would be better if she didn't hear this.

"It's true what people said about Torgils, that his conduct was cruel and faithless when it came to women—many women. And many folks spoke ill of me because I spent so much time with him—a man like me who was meant to be a priest. But I was more fond of Torgils than anyone else here on earth, and I could never understand all the gossip about the wicked life he led, for I never saw him seek out the company of women or flirt with young maidens when we attended a feast with dancing. And whenever the topic turned, as it often does among rowdy young fellows in the servants' quarters, to women and loose conduct, Torgils would sit in silence, most often displaying a scornful little smile. And I never heard him speak in a crude or discourteous manner. For the most part he was taciturn and calm in every way, a valiant, manly fellow who was skilled with weapons. I don't know whether he had any friends other than me; we had been foster brothers since childhood. His unruly behavior grieved me, yet I could never bring myself to say a word about it to my cousin. Father often chastised him with harsh words, for he too was very fond of Torgils. He would remind Torgils of the day that awaits us all, when we shall stand before Our Lord and answer for our every deed. My father would often say to Torgils, 'It would be better for you to be cast into the fjord tied to a millstone, as the brutes did to God's beloved Saint Halvard when he tried to protect an impoverished, innocent woman—but you choose to harm the poor and innocent.' Torgils never said a word in his defense. There was something secretive about Torgils. I never saw him go over to sit down next to a woman and speak to her, yet I noticed that women would grow uneasy if he merely looked at them; his eyes seemed to possess an evil power. He also had a certain power over men. For when the time of the Spring Pelts was over, Torgils lent the bishop his support—and later he was put in charge of the bishop's men. Yet it happened more than once that the bishop sought to dismiss Torgils because of the ugly rumors. When the story about Astrid Bessesdatter and Herdis of Stein came to light, the bishop threatened Torgils with excommunication and outlawry, and said he would expel him from town. Yet nothing ever came of that.

"It was at Christmastime, seven years after King Skule fell, that Torgils came home to Hestviken. During Lent, Besse and his sons, along with Olav, my paternal uncle, arrived in Oslo. It had been agreed that Torgils should marry Astrid as soon as it was possible after Lent. This was the only time that Torgils ever spoke to me of the matter. He told me that he wanted to stay here and not move to his wife's home, but Besse and his children were such good folks that he could not refuse; he would have to wed Astrid. Yet I could tell that he'd taken a dislike to her. I've never understood how a man could lead a young child into such misfortune when he didn't have a better liking for her. But Torgils replied that he couldn't help the way in which he always took against them.

"May God have mercy on his soul. He met Herdis Karlsdatter a short time later, and then he didn't come home for his own betrothal feast. My uncle Olav was beside himself with shame and anger at his son's behavior, but Torgils said that he'd rather flee the country than submit to taking a wife when he couldn't stand the sight of her. The situation got even worse when gossip spread about Torgils and Herdis. Uncle Olav and Father and the bishop all threatened and begged, but Torgils paid them no mind. Astrid Bessesdatter was not especially fair, but she was at least young, with a pink-and-white complexion. Herdis Karlsdatter was stout with sallow skin. She was thirteen years older than Torgils and she'd had eight children. Nobody could understand it. Folks said Torgils must have been bewitched. For my part, I thought it had to be the Devil's work. The Evil One must have taken full possession of my foster brother after Torgils behaved so heartlessly toward the young maiden Astrid. I said as much to him, but then he grew quite pale, with such a strange look on his face, and I was truly frightened.

"He said to me, 'I think you're right, my kinsman. But now it's too late.'

"And no matter how I beseeched and implored Torgils, it was like talking to a stone. Several days later we heard that Jon of Stein, who was Herdis's husband, had died."

Olav Audunssøn jolted to a seated position in the sheepskin sack where he lay on the floor. He stared in horror at the old man, but he didn't say a word.

Olav Ingolfssøn paused for a moment before he said, in a low, faltering voice, "Jon was on his way home from an assembly, where he'd spent the night, and two of his own loyal men were with him. He collapsed at the edge of the road and died at once. Jon was old and weak. God knows I don't believe that either Herdis or Torgils was to blame for his death. But as you can imagine, all sorts of things were said when it became known that Torgils wanted to marry the widow. Olav Ribbung said he wished the Bessessøns had struck down Torgils before this happened. He also said that as long as Astrid remained unmarried in the village with Torgils's son, he would refuse to allow Torgils to offend her kinsmen even more by marrying someone else. But if it was true that his son had taken up with a married woman, then he would ask God to bring down upon him the harshest of punishments if Torgils did not now give up his sinful ways, repent, and leave behind this whoring woman. His father also said he would rather tie Torgils up like a madman than allow him to marry Herdis.

"Not long afterward, Herdis suddenly died. I was with Torgils when he received the news, but I can't tell you what he felt. At first his eyes grew very big—I'd never seen the like—and then they narrowed and his whole body seemed to shrink and fade. But he didn't say a word, and in the following days he went about tending to his work as if nothing had happened. But I could tell that something was brewing, and whenever I wasn't in church, I stayed by his side, both day and night. I could also sense that he wanted me to be with him. But I have no idea when he slept. He would lie down fully dressed, he never bothered to wash or shave, and he started acting strange. He didn't look like himself.

"Herdis was buried in the cemetery of Aker Church. The next day the bishop sent Torgils up to Aker, and I went with him. It was the sabbath eve, and the nuns' leaseholder on the estate asked us to bathe. That's when I got Torgils to shave off his vile yellow beard stubble, and I also cut his hair. 'Well, now I'm ready,' said Torgils, and that made me uneasy, for he had such an odd smile. I saw how haggard and ravaged his face looked; both his hair and complexion were even more pale than before, and his eyes had grown so big, fading to the color of watery milk. And yet Torgils was handsome. But he hardly looked like he was alive as he sat there on the bench, motionless and staring.

"Finally I lay down on the bed to rest for a while and fell asleep. I awoke when someone knocked on the door three times. I jumped up.

"Torgils had stood up and walked forward as if asleep. 'They've sent for me,' he said.

"I ran over and grabbed hold of him. God only knows what I was thinking at the moment. But he shoved me aside, and then there was another knock on the door.

"'Let me go,' said Torgils. 'I have to go out.'

"I was a tall man, much taller than Torgils, and very strong in my youth, although never as strong as he was. He was as solidly built and sturdy of limb as you are, and possessed of great strength. I threw my arms around Torgils and tried to hold him back, but when he looked at me, I realized that in this instance no human being would be able to help him.

"'It's Herdis,' he said. And again there were three knocks on the door. 'Let me go, Olav. Never did I make any promises to the others, but to her I promised that I would follow, whether alive or dead.'

"Then he flung me aside so roughly that I fell to the floor, and he went out. Back on my feet, I grabbed my axe and ran after him. May God forgive me. If only I'd taken my book or my cross, things would have gone better, but I wasn't thinking. I was young, and at heart I was still more of a soldier than a priest. When it came right down to it, I trusted most to steel and blade.

"Out in the courtyard I saw them over by the passageway. The moon was shining through drifting clouds, the weather was mild, and the ground dark; that year we had no snow left down in the village. But it was light enough that when I went through the gate, I could see them ahead of me out in the field. The dead woman was leading the way; she looked like a wisp of fog and hardly touched the ground. Behind her raced Torgils, and I followed. At that moment the moon peeked out, and I saw Herdis stop. I knew what she wanted, so I shouted to her, 'If he promised to follow you, then he must, but he never promised to go *ahead* of you.'

"Yet it didn't occur to me to ask her to relent, in God's name, and to release him from his pledge. By now we were close to the church, where moonlight faintly lit the stone wall. The dead woman glided through the graveyard gate and Torgils ran after her. So did I. I made it through the gate in time to see Herdis standing by the church wall, stretching out her arm to Torgils. I swung my axe with all my might and hurled it so it flew over Torgils's head and clanged against the stone wall. Torgils dropped straight down, but the next second they fell on me from behind, throwing me to the ground so hard that my right leg broke in three places—at my thigh, my knee, and my foot.

"After that I knew no more until folks arrived for mass the next morning and found us there. By then Torgils had changed into the way you remember him. His wits had left him, and he was more helpless than a suckling infant, except that he was able to walk. Whenever he happened near an iron blade, he would howl like an animal and fall down as foam poured out his mouth. He was once the most skillful of any boy I'd ever met when it came to wielding a weapon. I heard that his hair turned completely white that first winter.

"I lay in bed year after year because of that broken leg. During the first years the bone splinters worked their way out of the wounds. Pus seeped out and stank so bad that even I couldn't stand the smell. There were many times when I sobbed my heart out and begged God to let me die, for the agony seemed to me beyond bearing. But Father was with me, and he helped me and implored me to endure the torment as befitted a man and a Christian. Finally my leg healed. But Torgils didn't recognize me when I came out here; that was five winters later. And Olav Ribbung asked me to stay away, for he couldn't bear to see his nephew dragging himself around like a wreck—I had to use crutches back then—because it was his own son who had caused my injury."

Olav Audunssøn lay awake for a long time after the old man fell asleep. His forebears had not been fortunate men. But they had endured through one hardship after another.

The lame old man now lying asleep in bed. His great-grandfather, who was his other namesake—he remembered him living here with that vile, mad son of his. Olav felt a surge of sympathy pass through him in acknowledgment of his connection to them. The old woman, Tora, and Ingolf the priest had remained loyal to a lost cause, to the dead and the forsaken who were their kinfolk.

He thought about the Steinfinnssøns, who might well be called fortunate men. Lively folks who had been free of sorrows. For them, misfortune was like a poison they had swallowed. They held on until they could vomit it up again, but then they died. And tonight Olav saw quite clearly that Ingunn was the same way. She too had suffered a misfortune that was like a mortal disease, and she would never be restored to full health. But Olav was fortunate enough to have been created in such a way that he could survive even without happiness. His forefathers had never given up on a lost cause; they had held aloft the old banner as long as there was a single scrap or thread remaining. In his heart he didn't know whether he regretted accepting Earl Alf's offer to release him from service. Yet he had accepted for the sake of the woman who had been entrusted to his care when they were both little children. And he would protect and love her, just as he had protected her when he was a boy and loved her from the first moment he knew he was a man. And if he never enjoyed any happiness with her, because she would always be an ill woman who was inept at managing a household, it made no difference. That's what he realized tonight. He would love and protect her until her last breath.

But in the bright light of day, Olav frowned when he recalled his nighttime thoughts. It was easy to imagine so many strange things when lying sleepless in bed. Ingunn had been healthy and happy during the summer, and more beautiful than ever before. Right now she was feeling utterly dejected, but the poor thing had never been good at enduring any sort of torment. After she had the child, she would no doubt be healthy and happy again.

For a moment it occurred to Olav that she must be thinking about the child she'd had the previous year. She had never mentioned him, nor had Olav had any wish to do so. He knew only that the boy was still alive when they'd left Oppland behind last summer.

IV

Ingunn was now thinking about Eirik day and night.

The memory of him had paled and seemed unreal during that first period of happiness. She recalled only hazily that she'd had a little son who had slept in her arms, suckled at her breast, and lain next to her, so tiny and warm and soft, and she had breathed in that sour-milk smell of him, while her tears had poured down on him in those dark, blind nights. And she had sent him away, as if she were tearing herself in half, before she moved toward that last terror and the uttermost darkness.

Yet all those fears lay like a sunken coast beyond the fevered nights she'd spent in a dark and clamorous sea, when she was flung high up on the waves and cast deep down in a state of dizzying helplessness. When she came back to the surface, Olav was there to take her in. And when happiness came to her, it felt as if the unhappy person she recalled could not have been her. Weeks passed when she didn't give even a single thought to her child. Or she would wonder, almost indifferently, whether he was still alive. And she thought it wouldn't have affected her much if she'd heard that he was dead. But then an unsettling thought might stir within her: How is he? Is Eirik being treated well? Or is he suffering terribly among those strangers? And suddenly one thing would vividly cut through all those distant and pale memories of the past year's misery: the little, persistent cries of the infant that only her breast could soothe for a while. The truth struck her with a raw and vile jolt. She was the mother of a whimpering infant who had been cast out among strangers far away in the world, and perhaps he was crying and crying for his mother, making himself hoarse and worn out at this very moment. But she would push these thoughts away with all her might. The foster mother had looked kind. Perhaps the woman was more merciful than the mother who had brought the child into the world. No. Ingunn pushed that thought away again and again. She would not think about it. And then the memory of Eirik would fade once more. She was here at Hestviken, and she was Olav's wife, and she felt inexpressibly happy. She could feel her youth and her beauty blossoming again. She would bow her head, radiantly modest and joyful, whenever her husband so much as looked at her.

But as the new child grew inside her . . . It started as a secret, corrosive ache that made her feel dizzy and nauseated, in fear of the shadows it might conjure up between her and Olav. Then it became a burden that weighed on her and hindered whatever she set out to do. And all the while, in everyone's eyes, it became the most import-ant thing about her, the fact that she was going to produce new life from the old lineage. Olav Ingolfssøn could talk of nothing else. If she had been the queen of Norway, and if the hope for the whole coun-try's peace and prosperity for generations to come were linked to the awaited child, the old man would not have viewed the approaching event as any greater than he already did. And when folks living in the area met the young mistress, they let her know they regarded this as welcome news. From the age of seven, Olav Audunssøn had been their only hope that he might continue the Hestviken lineage. Yet from that time on he had wandered far from those places where he belonged. After roaming for twenty years, he had finally come back to the allo-dial lands of his ancestors. Now that a flock of children promised to swell around him and his wife, something that had long been amiss would once again fall into place.

Even her own servants took a keen interest in what awaited their mistress. They had been fond of Ingunn from the start because she was so lovely in appearance and both kind and well meaning, and they'd felt a bit sorry for her because she was so utterly incapable of carrying out her household duties. Now they felt sorry for her when they saw how miserable she was. She would turn deathly pale if she merely set foot in the cookhouse when they were cooking seal or sea-birds. She would murmur that where she came from, she wasn't used to the oily smell issuing from the food. The maidservants laughed and urged her back outside, saying, "We'll manage without you, Mistress!" She couldn't serve the food without beads of sweat pouring down her face. The old cowshed maid would gently push her mistress down on the bench and stuff cushions behind her back. "Let me serve the food today, Ingunn. You can hardly stay on your feet tonight, you poor child!" she would say with a laugh, noticing how the young woman sat there trembling with fatigue. The maidservants were also worried how things would go for their mistress. She didn't look as if she could endure much more. And there were still three months before the birth, according to her own reckoning.

Olav was the only one who never expressed any joy about the child; in fact, he never mentioned it with a single word. And the house servants took note of that. But in her heart, Ingunn thought that once the boy came into the world, he would be no less remarkable in the eyes of his father than he would be to everyone else. Yet new little drops of the bitterness that frightened her began trickling forth.

She felt not even a spark of love for the child she now carried. Instead, she had such a longing for Eirik, and she harbored a grudge toward this new child to whom all the good things of the world would soon be offered, and whom everyone's arms would be ready to embrace when he arrived. For her, it seemed as if this child were to blame for Eirik having been abandoned and cast out into the darkness. Whenever she noticed folks looking at her with kindness, going out of their way to help her and spare her from all toil, the thought would race through her mind: when I was carrying Eirik I had to hide in a corner. Everyone's eyes stoned me with scorn and anger and sorrow and shame. Eirik was hated by everyone even before he was born. I hated him too.

As she now sat and sewed, she remembered how she had staggered around the room as the first pangs seized hold of her. Tora had unpacked the bundle she had brought of infant's clothing, the oldest and most worn of the garments she still had left from her own children. And Ingunn, the mother, had thought the clothing was good enough, more than worthy of this child of hers.

The maidservant who was sitting with her mistress looked on in surprise as Ingunn impatiently tore apart the delicate woolen swaddling she was hemming and cast it aside.

By now Eirik was just over a year old. Ingunn sat outside next to the house wall on the first summer evenings and watched the little child, who was Bjørn and Gudrun's youngest, totter and fall and pull herself up, and then stumble again on the soft green grass in the courtyard. Ingunn didn't hear a word of Gudrid's constant chatter. She was thinking: my Eirik, barefoot and poorly dressed like this child, is living with that impoverished foster family.

Old Olav died in July, a week before Saint Sunniva's Day,[14] and Olav Audunssøn held a splendid funeral feast in his honor. Among the women who came to Hestviken to help Ingunn with the preparations was Signe Arnesdatter, who had recently married the master of Skikkjustad. Her younger sister, Una, accompanied her, and when it was time for the funeral guests to go home, Olav persuaded Arne and the priest to let Una stay at Hestviken. Then Ingunn could be spared from any toil and concerns in the last months before giving birth.

Olav was a bit annoyed, for he couldn't help noticing that Ingunn did not like the girl. Yet Una was both clever and obliging, cheerful and appealing to the eye. She was small and fine-limbed, as light and quick as a wagtail bird, with fair hair and pale eyes. Olav had become quite fond of these cousins of his. Reserved and taciturn as he was, it wasn't always easy for Olav to feel comfortable with other people, but he seldom took a dislike to anyone. He accepted folks as they were, both their faults and their virtues, and he was pleased to regard them as acquaintances. Yet he was not averse to forming friendships with those he liked, as long as he was given time to warm up to them.

Olav Ingolfssøn had amassed a considerable pile of good timbers at the estate, and the previous autumn Olav Audunssøn had already done much to repair the worst damage to the buildings. Now that it was summer he had demolished the cowshed and proceeded to build a new one. The old structure had left the livestock standing in wet mire in the fall, while in the winter the snow would blow inside. The animals could hardly have suffered more cold than if they'd stayed outdoors.

One Saturday evening the servants gathered in the courtyard. The summer weather was beautiful and warm. The air was fragrant with the sweet smell of the first hay harvesting, and the scent of the linden blossoms gusted down from the steep cliff behind the outbuildings. The walls of the new cowshed had been raised, and the first beams had been placed. One end of the heavy central roof beam was leaning against the gable, with the other end resting on the ground. That's how the men had left it when they stopped their work midafternoon, as was the custom the day before the sabbath.

Now the young hired men got a running start so they could race up the slanted beam. They wanted to see how high they could go. After a while the other men joined in, along with their master. The game continued with shouts and laughter each time a man had to jump off. Ingunn and Una were sitting outside, next to the wall of the main hall.

Then Olav called to the young maiden, "Come over here, Una. Let's see how sure of foot you are!"

The girl laughingly refused, but all the men began urging her. She had laughed at them when they had to jump off halfway up the beam. Surely she could manage to run all the way to the top. Finally they went over and grabbed her hands to pull her off the bench.

Laughing, she pushed the men away and set off at a run. She made it a short distance up the beam but then had to jump down. Again she tried, and this time she managed to get higher up. For a moment she stood there swaying, looking so slender and lissome. She flailed her outspread arms a bit, while her little feet in their thin summer shoes that had neither sole nor heel clung to the beam like butterfly feet. But then she slipped off the side, the way a titmouse does when the bird fails to hold on to a timbered wall. Olav was standing below and caught her. Now the young maiden couldn't hide her eagerness. She ran up the beam again and again, with Olav running along underneath and laughing as he caught her in his arms every time she had to jump off. Neither of them was aware of anything else until Ingunn suddenly stood near them, groaning and winded, her face white as snow under the pale brown blemishes on her skin.

"Stop it right now!" she whispered, gasping for breath.

"Surely you know there's no danger," Olav assured her with a laugh. "Don't you see that I'm catching her?"

"Yes, I see that."

Olav gave his wife a surprised look. He could hear that she was on the verge of tears.

Then she tossed her head at the girl and exclaimed in a tone somewhere between a scornful laugh and a sob, "Look at her! She may be stupid but she should still have enough wits to be ashamed."

Olav turned toward Una. Her face was bright red, and she looked embarrassed. Slowly a flush rose to his face.

"It seems to me that you've lost all reason, Ingunn!"

"It seems to me," snarled his wife, her voice rising to a shriek, "that she's not a descendant of Dirt Beard for nothing. And there are more similarities between him and you than—"

"That's enough!" shouted Olav. "You're the one who should have the wits to be ashamed. How can you, of all people, speak to me like that?"

He stopped himself there, for he saw how Ingunn blinked her eyes as if he'd struck her in the face. Then she seemed to collapse with misery. Her husband reached out to grasp her upper arm.

"Come inside with me now," he said, not unkindly. Then he led her across the courtyard. She leaned against him with her eyes closed, moving slowly, with hardly the strength to set one foot in front of the other. He almost had to carry her. In his heart Olav was furious, thinking to himself: she's acting more feeble than she actually is.

But after he'd helped his wife to sit down on the bench and saw how wretched and unhappy she looked, he moved closer and caressed her cheek.

"Ingunn, have you completely lost your wits? How can you find fault with me for jesting with my own kinswoman?"

When she didn't reply, he went on.

"It's unseemly—worse than unseemly. Surely you must see that. Una has been staying with us for four weeks now, and she has tried to spare you from every task she possibly could. Yet this is how you reward her! How do you think she must feel?"

"It makes no difference to me," said his wife.

"But it does to me," replied Olav sharply. "Nor is it to our benefit that we behave in a way that will cause folks to speak ill of us," he added more gently. "You must realize that."

Olav went out to find Una. She was in the cookhouse, cleaning fish for the evening meal. He went over to stand beside her. He was so ill at ease that he didn't know what to say.

Then she smiled and said, "Think no more about it, my kinsman. The poor thing can't help it if she's unreasonable and bad-tempered right now. The worst of it is . . ." and here she let the cat hop up to get a piece of fish, "that I am of so little use, Olav. I've realized for some time now that she doesn't want me here. I think it would be best if I leave tomorrow and go to stay with Signe."

Olav replied with some vehemence, "It seems to me terribly shameful that she . . . that you should leave us in this manner. And how will you explain to Signe and Sira Benedikt why you did not stay?"

"You must know that they have sense enough not to take offense."

"Ingunn is the one who will be the most distressed," Olav exclaimed unhappily, "when she is herself again and realizes how badly she insulted our guest and kinswoman."

"No, not at all. By then she won't even remember this. Don't let it worry you, Olav." She wiped off her hands and then placed them on his upper arms, looking up at him with her clear, light gray eyes that were so like his own.

"How good you are," he said uncertainly. Then he leaned down and kissed her on the lips.

He had always greeted Una and her sisters with a kiss whenever they met or parted. But he knew, with a faint, sweet sense of alarm, that this was not the sort of kiss that belonged to the courtesies offered between close kinfolk who considered themselves of better standing than leaseholders. He let his lips linger on her fresh, cool maidenly lips. He had no wish to let her go, and he pulled her slender figure close, feeling a tantalizing and fleeting desire.

"How good you are," he whispered again, kissing her once more before he reluctantly released her. Then he left.

There was no sin in that, he thought, smiling derisively. Yet he couldn't forget the freshness of Una's kiss. It had been . . . Well, not what it should be. But there was no cause for worry. He had been annoyed with Ingunn. He'd never thought that she would behave in such an unreasonable and ill-mannered fashion. Yet it was most likely as Una had told him—no one should take to heart what Ingunn said or did during this time, the poor thing.

But the next day, after Olav had accompanied Una to Skikkjustad after mass—it was the feast day celebrating the discovery of Saint Olav's body[15]—and he was riding back home alone, anger again welled up inside him. Had Ingunn become the sort of woman who would suspect him of the very worst because she herself had sinned? Now he recalled that his wife had shown a dislike for his kinswomen before, during the previous autumn, when she was not yet ailing. Ingunn must be jealous after all. Even at Frettastein she had been quick to point out the faults and flaws of other women—the few that she encountered. And that was not appealing conduct.

Olav was angry with his wife. And then there was the fact that she'd dared to mention Torgils Dirt Beard. Everything Olav, as a child, had vaguely felt about his great-uncle had turned to open, hate-filled horror ever since he'd learned all about Torgils Olavssøn. The man had been an offender of women, and in the end, God had struck him down. The man was a disgrace to his lineage. Yet Torgils was the one everybody remembered, while the other Olavssøns who had lived and died with honor had been forgotten long ago. They could just as well be the ones he himself resembled most. Olav always felt ill at ease when he heard people say that he looked so much like Dirt Beard. But he also grew annoyed with himself for feeling a cold gust of mortal fear at the back of his neck whenever he heard such talk.

Even his worst enemy would not accuse Olav of chasing after women. During all those years he'd spent in exile, he could hardly remember even looking at a woman. When his maternal uncle Barnim urged him to take the beautiful miller's daughter as his paramour while he was staying at Høvdinggaard, Olav had curtly declined. She was certainly lovely, and he had no doubt noticed that she was willing, but he considered himself a married man, and he intended to remain faithful, even though his uncle teased him about this and laughingly reminded him of the girl called Ketilløg.

One evening Olav had sought out Ketilløg, an impoverished girl who sold her favors. He was in town with several other young lads, all of them dead drunk. In the morning, when he was once again sober, he happened to fall into conversation with the girl, and ever since he'd felt a certain affection for her. Ketilløg was not like other girls of that sort. She was intelligent and quiet in temperament, and she preferred a man who refrained from carousing or causing a ruckus or making trouble at the inn. Olav had continued to seek her out whenever his uncle had reason to send him to town. He would often go to see her and simply sit there, eating his provisions and asking her to bring him ale. He was very fond of watching the quiet way in which she walked among the tables to serve food and drink. But his friendship with her had not been any great sin. No sensible person would deem him unfaithful to Ingunn because of that girl. For several years after, Olav had often thought about Ketilløg. He hoped that she had not ended up in difficulty after helping him to flee when he chose to follow the earl. He wished he knew whether she'd been able to hide from the others at the inn the money he'd given her when they'd parted. And he wondered whether she had been able to carry out the plans she'd mentioned so often. She wanted to leave the inn and go to Saint Klara's convent, where she would seek employment with the sisters living there. She was much too good a person to stay where she was.

It was the secret guilt that Olav bore for murderously shedding blood that made him feel so uncertain. He felt defenseless against the Evil One. Olav was like a man who must continue fighting even though he's hiding a furtive, gnawing wound. His wife's lengthy illness and her unreasonable behavior, along with the fact that she herself was to blame for ensuring that he could never completely forget what must be forgotten—all this made him apprehensive and unsteady of spirit. And he felt a little shiver of desire whenever he recalled how good it had been to hold Una close.

It vexed him to think of Ingunn. It was her unwarranted behavior toward the kind and lovely young kinswoman that had brought this on.

But he would just have to endure things patiently. There was so little that could relieve Ingunn's misery right now.

That same evening Ingunn fell ill. It happened so suddenly that everything was over before the women who were summoned to help her had even arrived. Ingunn's own maidservants were the only ones with her when the child was born. And they had been terribly frightened and bewildered; that's what they said as they wept when they later spoke to Olav about it. They thought the boy was alive when they lifted him up from the floor,[16] but the next moment he was dead.

Never, thought Olav, had he seen anyone look as much like a piece of shattered and bleached wreckage that had washed up on the foreshore as Ingunn did, lying huddled next to the wall. Her thick, dark-golden hair lay in a tangled mass on the bed, and from her swollen, tear-stained face her eyes stared, blue-black and filled with unfathomable distress. Olav sat down on the edge of the bed and picked up her clammy hand to place it on his lap, setting his own hand on top of hers.

One of the weeping maids approached holding a cloth-wrapped bundle. She moved the cloth aside to show Olav the body of his son. Olav briefly studied the tiny, bluish, dead body, while the mother again burst into heartrending sobs. Quickly her husband leaned down to her.

"Ingunn, Ingunn, do not grieve so!"

Olav was unable to feel any lasting sorrow for his son. In a sense he was fully aware of how great the loss was, and he felt a crushing pang in his heart when he thought of the boy dying unbaptized. But he'd never had the peace to feel any joy of anticipation during the preceding months. Instead, he'd felt only a dim and hesitant jealousy for what they'd had, a fear for Ingunn, and a longing for the miserable time to pass. But it had never seemed real to him that the end result would be that he'd have a son on the estate, a little boy whom he would raise to be a man.

The neighbor women, who were now at Hestviken to tend to Ingunn, said that the mother was not particularly ill. Yet when it came time for them to help her sit up in the daylight hours, she had no strength. She would end up soaked with sweat if she so much as tried to bind up her hair in order to put on a wimple. And one mass after another was celebrated, but she never had enough strength to consider going to church to mark her recovery.[17]

All day long Ingunn lay on her bed, fully dressed, with her face turned toward the wall. She thought that she was the cause of the child's death. She'd felt no love for the infant when he lay inside her and fumbled for his mother's heartstrings. And now he was dead. The neighbor wives said that if skilled women had been with Ingunn when the child was born, he probably would have lived. But when they had come to Hestviken during the summer to see to Ingunn, she had insisted that the birth would not take place until Saint Bartholomew's Day. She was afraid those clever neighbor women would realize that Olav Audunssøn's wife had already had a child and spread the news throughout the district. On the morning when Ingunn awoke and became aware that the birth was about to take place, she got up and stayed on her feet for as long as she could. But this was something that Olav must never know.

Finally it could no longer be postponed. On the Sunday after Saint Mikael's Day, Ingunn Steinfinnsdatter would have to allow herself to be escorted to church. Olav had learned that four other women who had recently given birth would also be attending. One was the daughter-in-law on one of the largest estates in the northern part of the district. She had brought into the world a son who would inherit the allodial property; the church would no doubt be at least half filled with the family and friends accompanying her, wanting to make their devotions alongside her. Olav hardly dared think of Ingunn when she would have to kneel before the church door, miserable and empty-handed, while the others bowed low and received the lit candle, as the Psalm of David was sung for the women: "Who shall ascend into the hill of the Lord? or who shall stand in his holy place? He that hath clean hands, and a pure heart; who hath not lifted up his soul unto vanity, nor sworn deceitfully. He shall receive the blessing from the Lord, and righteousness from the God of his salvation." For Ingunn and for him, it would be the same as a judgment.

Olav had been reluctant to seek out Sira Benedikt ever since the day when Ingunn had driven Una Arnesdatter away from their estate in such a shameful manner. But one day he rode up to see the priest, asking him to be kind enough to come and console Ingunn.

Sira Benedikt had ordered that the bodies of all unbaptized children should be buried outside the churchyard fence. No one should cast out the bodies as they did with animals that had died without being bled properly. Nor should the bodies be buried in the wilderness as was done with criminals. The priest strongly admonished folks who believed in seeing the ghosts of little children who had been buried in unconsecrated ground. He said that dead children could not haunt the living, for they were in a place called limbus puerorum, a place they could never leave, yet they were happy there. Saint Augustine, who was the foremost of all Christian wise men, wrote that he would rather be one of those children than never to have been born at all. But when folks were so frightened that they lost both their wits and their health at those places where the bodies of dead children had been hidden, it was no doubt because they had such sins on their own conscience that the Devil had seized power over them and was able to lead them astray. For it was clear that any place where a mother had destroyed the child she carried would become most like an altar or a church for the Devil and all his demons, who would prefer to stay in that place forever after.

The priest was willing to accompany Olav home at once. Olav Ingolfssøn had strongly believed in the ghosts of little children, and he even thought that he'd once buried such a phantom. For this reason, Sira Benedikt was eager to dissuade Ingunn from such heathen beliefs and offer her comfort.

The mistress, pale and thin, sat with her hands clasped on her lap as she listened to their parish priest explain about limbus puerorum. It had been described in a book. A monk in Ireland had been seized with a spiritual rapture for seven days and seven nights. He had seen Hell and Purgatory and Heaven. He had also visited the place where unbaptized children dwelled. It was like a green valley, where Heaven was always behind clouds, to indicate that the children would never be blessed to see the visage of God. Yet light trickled down through the clouds as a sign that the goodness of God hovered over the children. And they seemed happy and content. They did not long for Heaven, because they didn't know it existed. Nor were they aware that they had been spared the torments of Hell and thus could be grateful for the reprieve, for they had never heard of Hell. There in the valley they played and splashed water at each other, for the land was awash with small lakes and creeks.

Olav interrupted the priest. "Then it seems to me, Sira Benedikt, that many a man would be tempted to wish he had died as an unbaptized infant."

The priest replied, "It's true, Olav, that at the baptismal font we are called to a great birthright. And it costs a good deal to become a man."

"Are the parents ever allowed to go there?" asked Ingunn quietly. "To see to their children and watch them play?"

The priest shook his head.

"The parents must take their own path, either up or down, but it never leads through that valley."

"Then it seems to me God is very cruel!" said Ingunn fiercely.

"That's what we humans are so quick to say," replied the priest, "whenever He does not do as we wish. I know it was of great importance to you and your husband that this child should have lived. He was meant to assume a large inheritance and continue the ancestral lineage. But if a woman carries a child who is meant only to bear witness to her shame and will have no inheritance other than his mother's milk—then, in many cases, the mother's heart cannot be trusted. She may choose to hide to give birth in shadow and shade, mistreating the child in both body and soul, or she might give the infant to strangers and then rejoice that she need never hear nor see that child again—"

Olav jumped up to catch his wife as she fainted and slumped

forward. On one knee, he laid her across his lap to hold her in his arms. The priest leaned over and quickly loosened the wimple that was tightly wrapped around Ingunn's neck. With her white face tilted back against her husband's arm and the arc of her throat bared, she looked dead.

"Lay her down," said the priest. "No, no, not on the bed. On the bench so she can lie stretched out and flat." Then he tended to the ill woman.

"She's not strong, your wife?" the priest asked somberly when he was about to ride home. Olav was holding the bridle of his horse.

"No," he said. "She has always been weak and frail. We were foster siblings, you see. I've known her since we were children."

V

In early spring of the following year, Norway's Duke Haakon made preparations for an incursion against Denmark. The Danish king would now be forced to reconcile with his outlawed chieftains under such terms as they and the Norwegians chose to dictate.

Olav Audunssøn set off for Tunsberg. He was one of the lesser chieftains under Baron Tore Haakonssøn. He was not entirely happy about being away from home that summer, for he was in the process of setting down roots at Hestviken. It was his ancestral estate and home district, after all, and for so many years he'd been an outlawed man without a home. He had restored the property from its state of decline so that this resource, which had long waned, was once again rich in earnings. And because he took a personal interest in the farmwork and seafaring ventures, he had grown fond of managing and tending to his own estate. He would have preferred to have Bjørn stay at Hestviken as overseer, but that was not to Bjørn's liking. In the end, Bjørn accompanied Olav as his armed squire, while an older man named Leif was to manage Hestviken along with the mistress.

Olav was also quite worried about Ingunn, who was to give birth again around midsummer. It was true that this time she was feeling much healthier than before. The whole time she'd been able to take care of her household duties and her role in running the farm. And she had learned a great deal and was not nearly as inept as she had been when they were newly married. But Olav was concerned, for he saw that Ingunn was awaiting this child with impatient eagerness. If misfortune were to strike the infant, the sorrow might well destroy her. And he felt as if he had a premonition of how things would go. He found it impossible to imagine that he'd find a child at home when he returned in the fall.

◆ ◆ ◆

No sooner had he arrived in Tunsberg than Olav Audunssøn met at every turn acquaintances from his outlaw years. Groups of Earl Alf's former retainers had sought out the late chieftain's kinsman and demanded that Baron Tore should accept their support. Among the Danish outlaws and their men who swarmed the city, Olav met many he had known when he was serving the earl. And one day a light sailing ship entered the harbor carrying letters from the Danish noblemen in Konungahella. The ship's captain, Asger Magnussøn, was from Vikingevaag, and he and Olav had been friends while Olav was staying at Høvdinggaard. They were also kinsmen, though very distantly related. In the evening Olav went into town with his Danish kinsman and got good and drunk; and afterward he felt much the better for it.

Baron Tore put Olav in charge of a small sixteen-oar vessel. During the incursion, his ship and three small warships from the ship works in the farthest southeastern section of Viken would sail under the command of Asger Magnussøn, captain of the Danish ship *Lindorm*, which the Norwegians called the *Yrmling*. The friendship between the Danes and their allies was often somewhat shaky, because this time the majority of the incursionary force was Norwegian. And the Norwegians were not hesitant to tout what they considered the goal of these raids. They said that Norway's King Eirik and Duke Haakon would lay claim to all of Denmark, as their rightful inheritance through their maternal grandfather, the holy King Eirik Valdemarssøn. They would also make the country taxable under the Norwegian crown. The Danes were not pleased to hear this. They ridiculed such talk, saying that their leaders, Marshal Stig Anderssøn and Count Jacob, would never allow themselves to be bound by promises to any king. They added that the Norwegians received reward enough for their help, whenever they used both hands to pillage the towns and fortresses of the Danish king. To this the Norwegians replied that when it came to dividing up the spoils of war, the Danes were sly devils who always managed to claim the best for themselves. The Norwegians outnumbered their ally in terms of manpower, but they were mostly farmers and seagoing folk and not as skilled in warfare as the Danes. Nearly all the Danes had spent years living in exile along with their outlawed chieftains. They had become hardened and fierce and didn't give a damn about any laws other than those honored among soldiers. On that score, Earl Alf's former retainers were an equal match with the Danes, and then some. Olav and Asger had their hands full keeping the peace among their men.

The incursionary fleet was under the command of Hunehals, the Danish fortress. Asger's and Olav's small ships were part of the force sent to attack the northern coasts of the Danish islands. They did not go near Vikingavaag. Olav had learned from Asger that the Danish king's men had stormed Høvdinggaard, burned the estate to the ground, and destroyed the stone hall. Sir Barnim Erikssøn had died with sword in hand. So there was no use thinking more about him, even though Olav had wanted to see his maternal uncle again. He would have a mass said for the man, and that would have to suffice. And besides, Olav now found himself less attached to his mother's family and country.

There was something foolhardy and careless about those low and defenseless Danish coastlines that sloshed right down to the glittering surface of the sea. Above the wide white foreshores towered the yellow of sand dunes, and tall trees grew all the way to the very end of the promontories. The trunks of full-grown beech trees and rugged oaks rose straight up above the storming sea. Grassy turf and tree roots dangled over the cliff edges like threads of a torn weaving. It looked as if the sea had grabbed and bitten off large pieces from the land's naked torso. Olav thought all of it hideous. No doubt there were lovely areas farther inland, with large estates worthy of chieftains, rich soil, wild boar in the forests, fat cattle in the meadows, and splendid horses in the paddocks. Yet he had never felt at ease here. His homeland was the Norwegian coast, with its ring within ring of protective rocks—skerries, reefs, and islets, the inner sailing lane, and finally the pale rock expanse of the mainland before the first streak of green hills crept down to the head of a bay, as if reconnoitering. The large estates were located inland, preferably on sites that could provide a wide view of whatever might approach.

Olav thought about his own home—the bay flanked by bare rocks, the estate atop the brow of the slope with the cliff called the Horse rising behind. Ingunn must have recovered from the birth by now. Perhaps she was standing out in the courtyard, looking again beautiful and young and slender as she and the child basked in the sunlight. For the first time he felt a great wish to see children back home at the estate. But that bright vision seemed remote and implausible.

He was now immersed in the same life he'd experienced when he was outlawed from Norway. Even the feeling of wearing a coat of mail was strangely pleasant; under its weight, all his physical strength seemed to have gathered. It was good to feel how the coat of mail cooled when he was at rest, and how it then closed in and stored the heat of his body during battle. It was like an admonition to conserve his energy and not waste it unless there was a definite intention and purpose. Tests of strength—on board ship during hard sailing, during raids on land—all demanded that a man be alert and vigilant, yet at the same time, deep inside, he must show bold determination, even if he was defeated by the very danger that he was doing his utmost to conquer. This was what dawned on Olav, though it was something he sensed rather than consciously thought. And occasionally he would feel a certain distaste when he recalled the two years he'd spent managing an estate and living as a married man. There was a vague ache in his heart, like a faint throbbing beneath the closed edges of a wound. Was he wasting his manly strength on such toil, clad in loose and shaggy work clothes, and with little idea what he might gain through all his efforts? He also felt a certain aversion to his memories of the intimate life he'd shared with the ailing woman. It seemed as if he were giving up his robust youth and unbroken health so that she might draw vigor from his vigor. And deep in his soul he didn't think it would do any good. It felt like he was swimming with a drowning companion clinging to his neck, and to be deemed worthy of calling himself a man, he would either have to save the other person or drown as well. Yet it was possible to feel a certain failure of courage at the thought that the end was inevitable; he would be dragged under, no matter how hard he strove to do his utmost, because a man could do no less.

If Ingunn had been healthy, and if it had seemed to him reasonable and a matter of course that they would produce children from his seed, and those children would in turn inherit everything he might have gained, then he would have felt differently when he thought about his role as husband. Occasionally, when he tried to convince himself that Ingunn might yet regain her health—and for all he knew, he now had a wholesome, bawling young son or daughter in the cradle back home—then he would long for his estate. But most often he felt no such longing. His solitariness gave him a deep sense of well-being; he had no other concerns than his duties as one of the many lesser chieftains in the incursionary force.

This life in the exclusive company of men suited Olav. The women he saw on shore—old and aging women who provided their food, loose girls selling themselves wherever men frequented—they were of no importance to him. There were wet days and nights on board ship and armed battles whenever they made landfall. So far it had not been Olav's lot to experience such confrontations very often, and he was not entirely displeased about that. Even the years he'd spent accompanying Earl Alf had not been enough to quell his loathing for unnecessary cruelty—and the Danes were certainly cruel as they set about ravaging their own country. Yet they probably would not have acted any differently if they were laying waste to some other country. They were used to such strife down there in the south; those coastlines had been ravaged and decimated and burned ever since Denmark was founded. Olav felt himself a stranger among his mother's people. In his youth he'd had a mind for war and battles, but only if there was a definite ending to the strife: either victory or defeat. Sometimes images would appear in his mind of an enemy assault on Hestviken, with him defending himself at the estate up on the mountain, with its back pressed against the cliff wall; he would drive the enemy down the slope all the way to the sea. Or else he would be struck down on his own lands.

The Danes were different, both more malleable and tougher. They allowed themselves to be chased—the farmers into dense forests, the chieftains across the sea—but then they returned the way sea swells recede and return. They lost and they won, yet neither outcome had any great impact on their hunger or their zest for life. And they seemed to have a strangely resilient tolerance for the idea that things would never be any different. They expected to be fighting for all eternity, losing and winning along those low, wet shores, and no victory or defeat would ever be the last.

Then Olav and the troops spent some time ashore. In town the men took shelter in overcrowded houses and estates. The air was hot and thick with the stench of sweat, boisterous talk, ale and wine, and belches and quarrels and disputes. Every night there were brawls in the streets and townyards. The military chieftains had a hard time keeping any sort of order and peace among the troops.

Rumors raced and flew. A ship's crew had supposedly gone ashore somewhere and seized an excessive amount of plunder. At Maastrand a group of Earl Alf's former soldiers had battled with some German merchants and then killed all the prisoners they'd taken. That was said to be their way of repaying an old debt on behalf of their deceased lord. The Danish king's fleet was reported to have taken the marshal's fortress on the island of Samsø, and folks said that Sir Stig Anderssøn himself had fallen. Among the Norwegians it was believed that Duke Haakon intended to take Denmark for himself. This was what had caused a disagreement with his brother the king, prompting King Eirik to sail home to Bjørgvin early in the summer. That was why the chieftains in the king's fleet, the noblemen from Vestlandet, along with some from Iceland, were pushing forward so fiercely. But the duke maintained a strict discipline among his troops; he didn't want to see them utterly destroy the land that he had decided to make his own.

Olav thought that while the chieftains might know which of these rumors were true or untrue, most of the rank and file in the incursionary forces had no idea. And the lesser chieftains, such as him, were considered to belong to the rank and file, not to the noblemen, whom the soldiers usually knew only by name or might occasionally glimpse. Yet the less the men knew about the chieftains, the more they talked about them. Olav was too proud to mention that he was related to many of the outlawed Danish noblemen, unless they happened to remind him of the fact. His own chieftain, Baron Tore, considered

Olav nothing more than a troop commander, on an equal footing with those men in charge of the ships crewed by farmers. He found Olav of Hestviken to be a decent man and a capable leader, though he'd done nothing to distinguish himself from anyone else. He'd had no opportunity to take any sort of action that might cause folks to pay particular attention to him.

This life Olav was now living did bring about one change. Whenever he thought about his secret fear that there was a connection between the guilt he carried and the fact that he'd had so little joy in his marriage to Ingunn, it would seem to him quite unreasonable. Such a notion had unwittingly grown in his mind over the past two years. But these men who were now his companions had stolen livestock from farmers, burned down houses and fortresses, and bloodied their swords not only in battle—many had killed and wounded innocent people for no apparent reason. Some carried precious items that they were exceedingly fearful of showing, since they had most likely stolen them from churches. And even though it was Duke Haakon's order that rape would be punishable by death, the women and girls who flocked among the soldiers whenever the men went ashore had probably not all entered into that sort of life willingly.

Olav's own confrontation with that Icelander Teit now seemed a matter of no importance whatsoever. Surely no one believed that all these fellows confessed every single sin to the priests who were on hand. The men couldn't possibly recall everything, nor could the priests manage to listen to such detailed confessions. No doubt many a man who confidently received Corpus Domini before setting off had great sins on his conscience that he'd forgotten to confess. That wretched Teit had his own actions to blame for his death. Now it seemed to Olav strangely foolhardy that he'd looked for portents in one thing or another—in words carelessly spoken by strangers, in dreams that he'd had, and in the hue and markings of his livestock. He'd ended up feeling that God's hand was hovering over him, wanting to force him to turn away from the path he was on. Here, among all these men, where he himself counted for so little, his own concerns also seemed to diminish. He'd seen and heard of the deaths of so many brave men. It was unreasonable to believe that the Lord would be overly zealous about whether Teit had been murdered. Or that God would bother to rebuke him, Olav Audunssøn, to seek atonement and salvation when there were plenty of prominent men who might be in even greater need—in particular the Danish nobles, judging by the way in which they attacked their own countrymen. Even Ingunn's misstep seemed to dwindle in importance. He had heard and seen so much out there.

One day in late autumn Olav headed into the fjord. The sun blazed in between the rain showers moving across the sea. There was a brisk wind, and the white foam splashing high up beneath the Ox greeted him from far away. Those living up at the estate had recognized his small sailing ship. Ingunn was standing on the wharf when he docked, her wimple and cloak flapping about her thin, stooped figure. As soon as Olav saw her, he knew that the same thing had happened again.

The child had been stillborn. Another boy.

Two months after New Year's Ingunn took to her bed once more. She had suffered a miscarriage, and this time her life was in danger. Olav had to send for the priest.

Sira Benedikt advised the couple to live apart for a year and to use the time to do penance and good deeds. As weak as Ingunn Steinfinnsdatter now was, the priest felt it was unthinkable that she would ever be able to give birth to a healthy child.

Olav was willing enough to follow this advice. But Ingunn was beside herself with despair when he spoke of it to her.

"When I'm dead," she said, "you must marry a young and healthy woman and have sons with her. I told you that I was broken, but you refused to let me go. I won't live long, Olav. Let me be with you during the little time I have left!"

Olav caressed her face and gave a weary laugh. She talked so much about him marrying again, yet she couldn't bear it if he looked at another woman or spoke two words to their neighbor women when he met them on the church hill.

During that spring Olav was plagued by sleeplessness, worse than the years before. His heart was heavy with compassion as he lay in bed and held the poor, ailing woman in his arms. But her clinging love made him ill at ease. Even when she slept, her thin arms were clasped around his neck, and her head rested halfway up his shoulder.

Olav was glad to escape from home when he set off for Tunsberg again in the spring. The summer proceeded the same as it had the year before. But every time he thought of home, he felt an ache in his heart. It didn't seem to matter that he'd had so little joy in his marriage with Ingunn. Losing Ingunn would be like losing half of his own life.

Yet she was happy and healthy when he returned home late in the fall. This time she was convinced everything would turn out well. But six weeks before Christmas she gave birth to a boy, more than two months early.

Shortly before this happened, it became known in the district that Lord Tore Haakonssøn had ordered the beheading of Bjørn Egilssøn in Tunsberg. After the first foray against Denmark, Bjørn had entered the baron's service, for he no longer wished to return to Hestviken. When the incursionary fleet headed back to Norway in the fall, Bjørn had been on board the ship on which Lord Tore himself was sailing home. Bjørn had ended up arguing with another man, fatally stabbing him. When the baron ordered his men to grab the assailant and tie him up, he had violently resisted, mortally wounding two men and inflicting lesser wounds on several others.

Gudrid, Bjørn's wife, had died in the summer. Now Olav Audunssøn thought he ought to help the children of this man for whom he'd held such affection. Torhild Bjørnsdatter had always kept apart from other people; she was taciturn and sullen. Olav had seen the girl only rarely, hardly exchanging more than ten words with her. For that reason, he didn't know how he was going to make his offer of help.

But now that Ingunn was confined to bed so close to Christmastime, there was no mistress at Hestviken to oversee everything that needed to be done, and there were more people staying at the estate because it was the season for hunting seal and auk. Olav pondered whether he should speak to Torhild Bjørnsdatter to see if she might move to Hestviken to manage the household. She was reported to be a skillful and hardworking woman, and the estate was in such terrible disarray that any housekeeper at all would be able to manage things better than the mistress. Even when she was well, Ingunn was not very capable, and she'd hardly had a single day of good health in three years. The food was so wretched that Olav had found it hard to hire men for the winter, and when strangers visited the estate, he dreaded seeing the shameful food that would be served at his table. That winter only the fresh fish and frozen meat didn't smell foul or taste surprisingly vile. And it was incomprehensible how little food there was in the storehouses—until Olav found out that many of the servants were stealing like foxes. He always had to serve ale bought in town, expensive though it was, because Ingunn's inferior brewing was notorious all along the fjord. Even the milk whey in the keg tasted putrid rather than merely sour. And Olav hadn't received any new garments that had been sewn for him on the estate since he'd married. His everyday clothes looked like the rags worn by a vagabond, and they were neither kept clean nor mended properly.

On several occasions he had suggested to Ingunn that they should hire a housekeeper for Hestviken, but each time she grew despondent, weeping and begging him not to inflict such shame upon her. It was useless for him to protest that illness was the master of any man and she should not regard this as shameful. He realized now that if he spoke to Torhild, he would have to do so without consulting his wife. Of greatest concern were the children in Torhild's care. She would have to bring the youngest ones with her, and that would no doubt cause some commotion, which Ingunn couldn't tolerate.

"Torhild's children." That's what everyone called the six offspring that Bjørn and Gudrid had left behind. The mother had been like a female rabbit, churning out one child after another. Her stepdaughter Torhild would pick up the newborn from the floor, place it on her lap, and let it suckle milk from a cow horn. Gudrid took no interest in anything but roaming around the countryside. In her early youth, Torhild had been betrothed to a prominent and respectable young boy, but he was a close kinsman of that man named Gunnar, whom Bjørn had had the misfortune to kill, and so the marriage never took place. Ever since then, Torhild had been cooped up in that impoverished home, doing the work of a man and a woman combined. Folks knew little about the maiden, yet they had only good things to say of her. She was not unattractive, but no one thought that Torhild Bjørnsdatter would ever be able to alter her fate. And by now she was no longer young; she had reached the age of twenty-eight or twenty-nine winters. The two eldest of her half-siblings were old enough to take jobs as servants, but whenever folks happened to mention this, Torhild would say that she needed them at home.

One Sunday, a short time after Ingunn had been confined to her bed, Olav saw Torhild Bjørnsdatter in church. She was standing farthest away on the women's side, and she was completely swathed in a long and full black cloak, which she held tightly closed. She had pulled forward the hood, but once in a while Olav caught a glimpse of her face, pale against the black woolen fabric. She resembled her father, with a high forehead and a long but finely curved nose. Her mouth was wide and colorless, her lips pressed together as if in silent restraint; her chin was strong and well-shaped. But her hair had a bleached look to it, with limp strands framing her forehead. The gray pallor of her complexion seemed streaked with smoke and soot embedded in her skin. She had big gray eyes, but they were red-rimmed and bloodshot, as if she'd had to stand too long over the cook pot in the cramped and smoke-filled hovel. Her hands, which kept holding the cloak closed even when she clasped them in prayer, were not big, though her fingers were long. But her skin was reddish-blue and cracked from frost, with black etched into all the folds and embedded under the worn-down fingernails. Even though the young woman was so well covered, it was evident she stood tall and straight-backed.

After mass Olav stood outside on the church hill to talk to some of the other landowners. For that reason he ended up riding home alone. His servants had gone on ahead.

Olav reached the place where the forest gave way to an open area with several big marshes and a small house at the edge of the largest of them. Beyond the outbuildings, the track diverged, with one section leading to Rynjul and south through the district. The smaller path headed down toward Hestviken. As Olav turned to take the road home, he caught sight of Torhild Bjørnsdatter standing outside the hovel. She had taken off her cloak and returned it to the woman who had lent it to her. When she became aware of the man on horseback, she turned on her heel and headed across the frozen marsh, moving as fast as if she were fleeing. But Olav had seen why she had kept the cloak wrapped so tightly around her. Underneath she wore only a shift made of coarse, undyed wadmal. An opening had been cut at the neckline and the sleeves reached to her elbows. Her arms were blue with cold. Also blue were her bare, thin legs, visible between the hem of the shift and the big, worn-out men's shoes on her feet. She had tied a strip of wadmal around her waist as a belt. Again Olav was impressed by how upright she held herself.

The clothing she wore was the sort that women workers wore on a summer day when they went out to cut grain. A memory passed through Olav's mind—of blue sky, sunshine, and warm air above the field where the women were walking, stooping to wrap their arms around the ripe, sweet-smelling grain. Now he watched the summer-clad maiden fleeing across the frozen marsh, heading for the forest where the branches were gray with rime. She must be terribly cold. She was bareheaded, her braid hanging thick and straight down her proud and erect back. Olav suddenly felt a great sympathy for her. He paused there on the path for a moment, watching her. Then he continued on for a short distance before turning his horse around to set off across the marsh.

The farm that Bjørn Egilssøn had owned was situated on the opposite slope. The alder thickets mostly hid it from the view of anyone traveling the path. Olav saw that quite a bit of work had been done since he'd last visited on some errand or other, two years earlier. Several small patches of ground seemed to have been cleared in the fall, although all the rocks and tree roots had not yet been completely removed. Farther up the hill the areas of grain stubble looked lighter than the rest of the marshy meadow, pale with frost. The little cowshed that Bjørn had built several years ago gleamed yellow with fresh timber, but he'd never managed to build the house. The family was still living in the round, earthen hut.

Torhild Bjørnsdatter appeared in the doorway when she heard the horseman. The children stood inside, peering from behind her. She stepped outside and stood up straight. Her face flushed slightly, and she gave the man an apprehensive look when he dismounted and she realized that he had some purpose in mind. Olav tied Apalhviten to a tree and then draped his gray fur cloak over the horse's back.

"You'll have to let me come in, Torhild. There's something I'd like to talk to you about." He didn't want her to stand out there freezing. She was now barefoot.

Torhild turned and went inside. She placed a threadbare fur coverlet on the earthen bench and invited her guest to sit down. Then she filled a ladle with goat's milk from a wooden cask that stood behind him on the bench. The milk tasted and smelled strongly of smoke, but Olav was fasting, so he thought it was good. The room was like a cave with a narrow aisle between the two earthen benches that took up the whole space. Torhild sat down across from her guest. She held a two-year-old child on her lap. A somewhat older girl stood behind, with one arm wrapped around Torhild's neck. The two oldest boys lay beside the hearth near the door, listening to the conversation between their sister and the visitor.

After they'd talked about other matters for a proper amount of time, Olav mentioned why he was there. No doubt she had heard how badly things stood at his estate. There was little hope that his wife would be able to handle even the smallest tasks this winter. If Torhild would be willing to help Ingunn and him during this difficulty, they could never thank her enough. Olav spoke of this request as if he were asking a favor. He'd taken a great liking to Torhild. She looked so strong, with those broad, straight shoulders, that high, firm bosom, and sturdy hips. She had certainly not allowed herself to be bowed by the fact that her life was confined to going between this hovel and the small cowshed.

Torhild offered some objections, but Olav replied that of course she could bring all six children to Hestviken. He hadn't actually planned to take in more than the two oldest, who might well be of some use, and the two youngest, who could not be separated from their foster mother. It had seemed to him likely that a place could be found out in the district for the middle children. Her livestock—a cow, four goats, and three sheep—could also be brought. And when the ground became passable for a sledge, they would come back to get the fodder she had stored. He would also make sure that the fields here at Rundmyr were fertilized and sowed in the spring.

In the end, Torhild agreed to Olav's invitation to move to Hestviken as soon as she could sew some clothing for herself and the children. Olav promised to provide the fabric, and he rode over with it the next day. There was no need for Torhild's fellow servants at Hestviken to know how poor she was.

Olav had intended to tell Ingunn of his agreement with Torhild that same evening. But when he went to see to his ill wife, she lay in bed looking so bloodless and weak that she seemed incapable of either listening or replying. For that reason Olav simply sat on the bed to keep her company. Her face was terribly ravaged. Her eyelids looked like thin, brown membranes over her sunken eyes. Her skin was gray with brown splotches across her cheekbones. The dark streaks that had appeared during her second pregnancy had never disappeared. Her white linen shift was held closed with a fine brooch; her neck was as sinewy as a scrawny bird's. Olav recalled that Torhild's gray woolen shift had been fastened with a sharpened piece of bone, but her neck was as round as a tree trunk and her bosom was full and high. She was healthy and strong, even though life had placed such heavy and wearisome burdens upon her. His poor Ingunn had an abundance of everything needed to ease the life of a young wife, yet here she lay for the fourth time in three years, without a child and without her health. Olav reached out to stroke her cheek.

"If only I knew how to help you, my Ingunn!"

He didn't manage to tell his wife that he'd hired a housekeeper until Torhild moved in with her entourage of children and animals.

Ingunn did not look pleased, though she merely said, "I suppose it's only right. You must have someone to manage things here. I was never any good, and now it seems as if I can neither live nor die."

Ingunn lay in bed well into the winter, and it looked as if what she'd said was true: she seemed unable to live or die. But then she began to get better, and by Lent she was able to sit up. Spring arrived early out by the fjord that year.

Everyone expected another military expedition, or *leiðangr*, to be levied that summer.[18] The farmers were desperately weary of this war with Denmark. No one believed that either the king or the duke would gain anything from it in the end. And they would lose the inheritance from their mother's side of the family that they had managed to squeeze out of their cousin, the previous Danish king, before he was murdered.

That spring Sira Benedikt let it be known that he would be going to Nidaros for the Olav Vigil in July.[19] Many folks in the district decided to join him, in order to have as large a group as possible on this pilgrimage, which every man and woman in Norway wished to undertake at least once in their life. Olav seized upon the idea that Ingunn should go along, thinking it might be restorative and offer some hope. It seemed a miracle that she had recently felt so well and was not suffering any ailments. She needed to take advantage of the situation.

At first Ingunn was greatly opposed to traveling unless Olav could go with her. But then it occurred to her that she would like to go home to visit her siblings, and she could accompany the pilgrims as far as Hamar. Olav wasn't happy with this; he wanted her to complete the pilgrimage so she might regain her health at Saint Olav's shrine. If she was well enough to travel as far as Heidmark, then she might as well continue the whole way. They would be traveling slowly, for there were many ill folks in the group. But when he realized how dearly she longed to see her siblings, he agreed to her plan.

Olav went with Ingunn as far as Oslo, where they stayed for a few days, buying and selling goods. One morning as Ingunn sat in the inn, Olav entered the room and began searching through their leather sacks for something. When he didn't find what he was looking for, he opened another sack and pulled out several small garments, suitable for a four-year-old child. He cast a swift glance at his wife. Ingunn was sitting with her head bowed, her face bright red. Olav didn't say a word as he stuffed the clothing back in the sack and then left.

VI

Haakon Gautssøn had purchased the Berg estate after Magnhild Toresdatter died. That was where Tora Steinfinnsdatter now lived, having been widowed more than a year earlier. From what Tora said, Ingunn realized that her sister had had a good life with Haakon, but she was also doing well without him. She was a very capable mistress. There was no end to Ingunn's admiration for her sister, who went about so briskly, displaying such keen competence on the estate, both outside and indoors, even though she was now so stout that it was quite astonishing. Tora still had that pure pink-and-white complexion, and the attractive, wholesome facial features, but her cheeks and the flesh of her chin had grown huge, and her body was so shapeless that she could hardly ride a horse anymore. Even her hands had become so fat that the joints were merely deep grooves, and yet Tora had full use of them. She was surrounded by a bustling prosperity, and her children were handsome and promising. She had given birth to six, who had all lived and flourished.

On the third evening the sisters were sitting together in the lofthouse before going to bed. Ingunn was seated on the doorstep, listening to the stillness. Deep in the forest a cuckoo called occasionally, and the grating cries of the corn crake came from the field. By now Ingunn had spent a long time in a place where even the air seemed to be constantly speaking, with the rushing and roaring of the wind, and the thundering of the sea as waves crashed below the slope. Here at Berg, beneath the quiet and clear vaulted sky, the little bird sounds merely seemed to make the silence even more audible. Ingunn felt as if she were partaking again and again of a refreshing drink. The bay was so endearing and small, its surface smooth with shadowy reflections from the dark forest of seaweed below. The last heaping of clouds hovered low over the distant heights. The weather had alternated between clear skies and rain showers during the day. Now, wafting up toward the sisters, came the sweet fragrance of hay spread out in the fields.

A sense of longing surged inside Ingunn, and without thinking, she suddenly spoke of the reason for her visit. For the past two days she had been struggling with whether to ask her question or hold it back.

"Do you ever see anything of my Eirik?"

"He is well," said Tora a bit reluctantly. "Hallveig says he is growing and thriving. She comes here every autumn, you know."

"Has it been a long time since you last saw him?" asked her sister.

"Haakon didn't approve of me going up there," replied Tora, again reluctantly. "And because I've put on so much weight, I'm not able to travel very far. But you must know that the boy is living with kind people, and Hallveig has only good things to say of him. I have a great deal to occupy me here at home, and little time to be wandering so far afield," she said, a bit annoyed.

"When did you last see him?" Ingunn asked again.

"I went there in the spring after you left for Hestviken, but after that Haakon didn't want me to go up there anymore. He said it would just keep the gossip alive," Tora replied impatiently. "Eirik was a handsome child," she added more gently.

"So that was three years ago?"

"Yes, that's right."

Both sisters fell silent for a while.

Then Tora said, "Arnvid went there to see him . . . several times during those first years."

"But not anymore? Arnvid doesn't go there anymore? Has he forgotten Eirik too?"

Tora unwillingly said, "You know how it is. Folks could never figure out who the father of your child was."

Taken aback, Ingunn hesitated before whispering at last, "And folks thought that it was Arnvid?"

"Yes. It was foolish to keep the father's name secret when the child couldn't be hidden away," said Tora curtly. "That made everyone think the worst . . . that a close kinsman or a monk was . . ."

For a moment neither sister spoke. Then Ingunn announced, "I'm thinking of riding up there tomorrow, if the weather holds."

"I think that would be ill-advised," replied Tora at once. "Ingunn, you must remember that all of us have had to suffer a great deal because of your misdeed."

"But you, who have six children . . . How do you think it feels to have had only one, and to be separated from him? I have been longing so terribly for Eirik during all these years."

"It's too late, my sister," said Tora. "You have to think of Olav."

"I *am* thinking of Olav. I have given him four dead sons. That's what he demanded, this child of mine whom I betrayed and abandoned. He demanded his mother. He has always, always been tugging at me. He sucked most of the soul out of my body, and he sucked the life out of those infants I carried inside me—this forsaken brother of theirs. They say that the first son I bore Olav still had a little life in him when he was born, but before I had a chance to see the child he died, unbaptized and without a name. You've seen all your children come into the light alive, and then grow and flourish. Three times have I felt the child quicken inside me, only to fall still and die. When the birth pangs started I knew that once again the only thing I could expect was to be parted from the corpse I'd been carrying inside me."

After a long pause Tora said, "You must do what you think best. If you think it will make things easier for you to see Eirik again, then . . ."

She patted her sister's cheek as they went inside to go to bed.

It was close to midday by the time Ingunn brought her horse to a halt at the opening in a fence in the forest. No matter how Tora had pleaded, she had refused to listen. And so she'd set off alone. The only bad thing that had happened to her was that she'd gone astray. At first she'd come to a small farm high on the ridge across from a little river. The people who lived there were the closest neighbors of the family at Siljuaasen, and two of the children had accompanied her down the slope to a spot where she could cross the river.

Now she paused for a moment, sitting in the saddle and looking out at the landscape. She saw endless waves of forest, one wooded crest after another, stretching all the way into the distance. To the north-west there were glints of snow beneath the bright, fair-weather clouds billowing in the sky. Far below and far away she caught a glimpse of Lake Mjøsa's waters, glittering at the foot of the wooded mountain. The land on the opposite shore looked blue in the warm sunlight, with green patches of farms and leaseholdings. From Hestviken no dwelling places were visible beyond the estate's own lands.

Homesickness and a longing for her child merged into a feeling of ravenous hunger inside Ingunn. She knew that she had this short interval to sate her hunger, but only once. Afterward she would have to turn back, bow her head, and once again submit to her unhappiness.

It seemed to her that down south near the fjord the sunshine was never this clear or reached as high in the blue sky. It felt blissful to be so far up on a mountain ridge again. Below and to her right was the steep, dark forested slope that she'd toiled to climb on foot as she led her horse. The roaring of the river at the bottom of the gorge ceased, grew stronger, then fainter. Right across from her, on the opposite side of the small, desolate valley, stood the little farm where she had first stopped, situated high up beneath a protruding cliff. Between her and the farm the air was a flickering and quivering blue above the slope.

Here, in front of her, she saw cleared ground. The farm buildings stood on a small hill by a meadow filled with tussocks and strewn with rocks. The buildings were low and gray, only a couple of timber-widths high. The small patches of cultivated land lay mostly at the foot of the hill, over toward the rail fence.

Ingunn got down from her horse and removed the guardrail. Up on the hill several gray-clad children came into view. Ingunn had to pause for a moment as her whole body began to shake. The children stood very still, peering at her. Then they turned on their heels and vanished. She hadn't heard a sound from them.

As she walked up the slope, a woman emerged, ducking her head as she stepped out of the doorway to one of the small houses. The woman seemed quite terrified as she watched the stranger approach.

Perhaps she thought what she saw wasn't human—this tall woman with the dazzling white linen wimple framing her flushed face, her sky-blue hooded cloak fastened with a silver brooch. She was leading a beautiful red horse with a light-colored mane. Ingunn hastened to call out, greeting the woman by name.

They sat inside for a while and talked. Then Hallveig went out to find Eirik. She didn't think the children were far away. They had been frightened by a lynx that had shown up to sit on the fence early in the morning. And they were shy about the visitor. The sight of a lynx was much more common here than visits from strangers.

Ingunn looked around her as she sat in the tiny room. The rafters were low, and everything was covered in layers of smoke. Wooden casks and tools lay scattered about, making it difficult to move around. A steady, wholesome snoring sound issued from an infant who was asleep in a cradle that had been hung from the ceiling. Then Ingunn heard a fly buzzing somewhere, a loud, sharp, insistent tone, unceasing, as if the fly were caught in a spider web.

Hallveig came back, bringing along a very small boy who wore nothing but a gray woolen shirt. Behind them swarmed all of the woman's own children, pausing in the doorway to peer inside.

Eirik resisted, but Hallveig pushed him forward so he stood right in front of this unknown woman. He raised his head for a moment and stared with astonishment at this splendidly clad person, before he slipped behind his foster mother to hide.

His eyes were a golden brown, the color of marsh water when the sun shines on it, and his long, black lashes curled at the ends. But he was fair-haired, with big, shiny curls around his face and at the nape of his neck.

His mother stretched out her arms and pulled the boy onto her lap. With a shiver of pleasure, Ingunn felt his head against her arm, his silky hair under her fingers. She pressed his face against hers. The child's cheek felt round and soft and cool; his little, slightly parted lips touched her skin. Eirik struggled with all his might, trying to escape this woman's fierce embrace, though he didn't utter a sound.

"I am your mother, Eirik. Do you hear me, Eirik? I am your rightful mother." She was laughing and weeping at the same time.

Eirik looked up but didn't seem to understand a thing. His foster mother sharply admonished him, telling him to behave properly and sit still with his mother. He sat there on Ingunn's lap, but neither of the women could make him say a word.

Ingunn kept her arm around the boy, with his head resting against her shoulder; she was aware of every inch of his body. She placed her other hand on his plump, brown knees, stroked his firm legs and his little, dirty feet. For a moment he reached down to brush his muddy fingers over his mother's hand, touching her rings.

Ingunn opened the sack she had brought and took out her gifts. The clothes were much too big for Eirik. His foster mother said he was quite small for his age. Eirik didn't seem to comprehend that the fine shirts and leather hose were for him. Even when his mother put on his head the red cap with the silver brooch, he didn't look happy. He remained puzzled and silent. Then Ingunn got out the loaves of bread that she'd brought and gave one to Eirik that he was not meant to share. It was a big round loaf made of wheat. Eirik eagerly grabbed it and hugged it to his chest with both hands. Then he ran outside, and his foster siblings followed.

Ingunn went over to the door. She saw the boy standing out there, with his arms wrapped tightly around the loaf, which rested on his round stomach. His bare, brown feet were planted far apart. The other children stood in a circle around him, staring.

Hallveig brought food for her guest: partially fermented trout, oat lefse, and a little cup of sour cream. The children were allowed to take out to the meadow the wooden container of milk from which the cream had been scraped. When Ingunn again looked outside a few minutes later, they were all sitting around the food. Eirik was on his knees, breaking off big pieces of the loaf to share with the others.

"He's a generous boy," said the foster mother. "Whenever I visit Berg, Tora gives me a loaf like that to bring to Eirik, and he always shares with the others, almost forgetting to eat any of it himself. That's one of the things that shows me he comes from high-standing folks."

Now that the children were all seated in a circle, Ingunn saw that Eirik's fair hair was very different from the wiry, white-gold tresses of the others. His hair, though disheveled, was curly and shiny. It wasn't golden but instead more like the palest brown of a newly ripened hazelnut.

Ingunn had to set off for home by midafternoon to ensure that she reached the village below before evening. She had not been able to overcome Eirik's shyness, and she'd hardly heard him say a word, except when he was talking to the other children outside in the meadow. His voice was so sweet, so sweet.

Eirik was to ride on her horse as far as the forest. Ingunn walked alongside, holding the halter in one hand and supporting the child with her arm as she kept on smiling at him, trying to coax a smile from his lovely little, round, sunburned face.

They were now beyond the fence, where no one could see them. She lifted the boy down and held him tightly in her arms as she kissed his face again and again, as well as his neck and shoulder. He stretched out his legs and made himself heavy in her embrace. When he began to kick at his mother with all his might, she grabbed hold of his smooth, naked legs, sensing with painful delight how firm and strong his little body was. Finally she sank down into a crouch, and while she wept and murmured fervent endearments to her child, she tried both to entice and to compel him to sit on her lap.

After a moment, when she had to shift her hold on him, Eirik managed to wriggle out of her grasp. He darted like a hare across the small clearing and disappeared into the bushes. Then came the banging of the gate.

Ingunn stood up, howling with grief. Then she staggered forward, bent over and sobbing, with her arms hanging limply at her sides. She came to a fence made of spruce saplings and saw Eirik racing up the meadow slope, moving so fast that his heels almost seemed to strike the back of his neck.

His mother stood where she was, weeping and weeping as she leaned against the fence. The withered, rust-red saplings had been felled to make an enclosure around a small field where the grain had just begun to grow, with the bristles still soft and closed, like some sort of newborn life. This was what always appeared in Ingunn's mind's eye later on, when she thought about her sorrow, although right now she was not aware of what she was seeing, for her eyes were blinded with tears.

Finally she had to go back to her horse.

VII

Late in the autumn Sira Benedikt Bessessøn fell ill and took to his bed. One day word came to Hestviken that the priest wished to say goodbye to Olav.

Sira Benedikt did not look like a dying man as he lay there, propped up with pillows. But the creases that had seemed merely shallow and sparse on his fleshy, weather-beaten face had now become deeper and more numerous. Yet he predicted with certitude his imminent death. When Olav sat down on the bedstead as requested, the priest absentmindedly took the riding gloves from the master of Hestviken's hands, stroked the leather, and then inspected the gloves, holding them up to his nose and eyes. Olav couldn't keep back a little smile.

They spoke for a while about all manner of topics, including Arne Torgilssøn and his daughters. Two of them were now married and lived in the area. But lately Olav had seen little of them or their husbands.

"Folks see less and less of you, Olav," said the priest. "And many are wondering why you always keep so much to yourself."

Olav reminded the priest that he'd been away on military campaigns the past few summers, and every winter his wife had been ill.

Again the priest spoke of his approaching demise, asking Olav to remember him with frequent prayers of intercession. Olav promised that he would. "But surely you have no need to fear what awaits you, Sira Benedikt. Not you," he added.

"I think it's something we all need to fear," replied the priest. "And I have always lived recklessly, for I paid little heed to small, daily sins. I said and did what suited me and consoled myself by thinking they were not great sins or mortal sins. It seemed to me that what I did out of weakness and an inherently imperfect nature could not carry much weight. Yet I was aware that in God's eyes all sins are more vile than sores. And neither you nor I would wish to live with a man and embrace him if he was covered with sores and scabs. I have benefited each day from the healing that cures with certainty the leprosy of sin. But you must know that even the most effective of healing remedies and the most costly of salves will only slowly cure the sore-disease if one day a man again begins to scratch and opens new lesions in his skin. The same is true of us. Our Lord cleansed us of sin with His blood and anointed us with His mercy, yet we carelessly commit again those deeds that had been mercifully subjected to remedy. And then we begin scratching as soon as he heals us, and we must stay in purgatory, bound hand and foot, until we are cleansed of scabs and contagion."

Olav sat in silence, fidgeting with his gloves.

"I'm afraid that I've harbored too great a love for my own kin. I thank God that I've never provoked them to sin or offered them support in an unjust cause; that's not something I've ever been tempted to do, for they are good folks. But on occasion I've been overly eager for their success and wealth—it is written in my testament that it shall all be restored. And I've been obstinate toward my foes and the foes of my kinsmen, short-tempered and quick to think badly of any man I did not like."

"And yet the rest of us will need to be rescued from the worst of the worst," said Olav, trying to smile, "if you consider this to be true of you."

The priest turned his head on the pillow and looked the young man in the eye. Olav felt his face turn pale under Sira Benedikt's gaze, and he suddenly felt strangely weak. He wanted to say something but could barely manage to speak.

"Why are you looking at me like that?" he whispered at last. After a pause he repeated, "Why are you looking at me like that?" It sounded as if he were pleading for himself.

The priest turned away and once again fixed his gaze straight ahead.

"Do you remember how I was always scowling at Olav Half-Priest because he talked so much about the sort of things he'd seen, things that I knew so little about? Now I think it may be that God deliberately opens one man's eyes to what He keeps hidden from another man. In my case, He never allowed me to see anything of what moves among us in this world. Yet here and there I too have caught a glimpse."

Olav kept looking at the priest as he listened.

"There is one thing that I've always been able to foresee," said Sira Benedikt. "I've always known—I suppose I should say almost always—when folks have been on their way to summon me to tend to a dying man. Especially to those who needed help the most, those who carried an unconfessed sin."

Olav Audunssøn gave a start. Without being aware of it, he lifted his hand slightly.

"Such a thing leaves its mark on a man. Few are so hardened that it leaves no traces that an old priest might notice.

"It so happened that one evening I was here at home, getting undressed. I was just about to climb into bed when it became clear to me that someone was headed this way, someone who was struggling with great difficulties and in desperate need of prayers of intercession. I knelt down and prayed that this person who was on his way might arrive safely. Then I lay down to rest for a while before I had to go out. But when I was lying in bed, I became more and more certain that someone was in grave danger. Finally I was aware of a presence here in the room with me, stirring fear in my heart, but I knew that it was a holy reverence I felt. 'Speak, Lord,' I prayed aloud. 'Your servant is listening.' And it felt at once as if a voice commanded me. I stood up, put on my clothes, and woke one of my servants, an old and trustworthy man. I told him to come with me up to the church. There he should go over to the bell tower and ring the middle bell. In the meantime, I went into the church and knelt on the altar step. But first I took a taper from the Virgin Mary's altar, lit it, and carried it to the church door, which I left wide open. The candle flame burned clear and unwavering, even though the night was wet and raw, with fog and a wind blowing in from the fjord.

"It didn't take long before a man arrived. He asked me to bring the final anointing and the viaticum to a person who was ailing. This messenger had been traveling for so long that he didn't think he'd ever reach me in time. He had been walking in circles, treading in his own footsteps for a long while, and he'd lost his way, ending up out in the marsh and rough terrain. But we made it in time to offer help to someone who needed it more than most.

"This is what I've been thinking about now. That the man acting as messenger was also someone who had conducted himself in such a way that evil spirits were more likely to guide his feet than his guardian angel, whom he'd grown accustomed to ignoring. So it might well be that his angel, or the angel of the dying person, then turned to me, causing me to go over to the church and order the bell to be rung.

"But when I returned home early in the morning and walked past the church, I saw that I'd forgotten to close the door. The candle was still there, burning in the candlestick, and it had not burned down, nor had the wind and rain, which had come in through the open door, put out the flame. I grew fearful when I saw this sign, but I gathered my courage and went inside to take the Virgin Mary's candle back to her, closing the door behind me. That's when I became aware of someone leaning over the candle to protect the flame, for around it I saw what looked like a reflection of the light falling on something white—either an arm or a scrap of clothing or a wing; I'm not sure what it was. I crawled up the steps on my knees, and when I reached out my hand to lift the candlestick, the flame went out. And I fell on my face, for I felt someone rush past me, either an angel or a blessed soul—but I knew that it had been face-to-face with its Lord and mine."

Olav sat motionless, his eyes lowered. At last there was nothing else to do, and he had to look up. Again he met Sira Benedikt's gaze.

He didn't know how long they remained like that, looking each other in the eye. But he felt time racing over them like a rushing and roaring stream, and he and the other man were standing on the bottom beneath the stream; that's where eternity dwelled, unchanging and unmoving. He knew that the other man saw the secret wound that was gnawing at his soul, gnawing its way outward—yet he was too cowardly to allow the healing hand to touch the malevolent, cancerous lesion. Feeling the utmost horror that the ailing spot might be touched, Olav gathered all his will and all his forces. He closed his eyes. He sank into blackness and silence; time stopped rushing and singing, but he felt the room spinning around him. When he again opened his eyes, the room was the same as usual, and Sira Benedikt lay with his head turned away on the pillow covered with green stars. He looked tired and sorrowful and old.

Olav stood up to take his leave. He knelt down and kissed Sira Benedikt's hand in farewell. The old man gripped his hand while he whispered several Latin words that Olav didn't recognize.

Then he left, and the priest did not try to hold him back.

The following week news came that Sira Benedikt had died. Folks in the district considered his death a loss, for they had appreciated him as a capable priest and a just and forthright man. But the villagers had never considered him to be possessed of particularly spiritual gifts. He was like one of their own in terms of both temperament and habits, and the learning he'd acquired was no more than was deemed necessary.

Only Olav Audunssøn felt strangely paralyzed when he heard of the priest's death. It seemed to him that a door had stood open, and he had vaguely trusted that one day he would have the courage to go through it. Yet he hadn't. And now the door had closed forever.

He hadn't spoken to Ingunn much about her visit back home to Oppland, and neither of them had mentioned the child.

But at Christmastime, Olav feared that the worst had happened once again. That was how he silently thought of the fact that Ingunn was clearly no longer walking alone.

Ever since Torhild Bjørnsdatter had come to Hestviken, Ingunn had shown more energy than in all the previous years of her marriage. This was not because she needed to do any of the work herself, for Torhild was so capable that she could manage all the mistress's duties on her own, and she had put things right at Hestviken. But it was as if Torhild's arrival had roused some sort of determination in Ingunn. Olav realized that his wife was offended that he had brought a house-keeper to the estate, and that he'd done so without consulting her. Yet Torhild was exceedingly amenable and helpful to her mistress, inquiring about her wants and wishes in everything, keeping to the background as much as possible, and living with her children in the small old house east of the courtyard. That's where Olav's mother had once lived. But he could tell that Ingunn was not fond of Torhild.

Fine handiwork was the only thing that Ingunn had excelled at during her youth, and she now took it up again. She sewed an ankle-length cotehardie for Olav. It was made of a foreign woolen fabric, woven in a black-and-green floral pattern, and she had adorned it with a wide border. Her husband had little use for such a garment, but Ingunn left the sewing of his work clothes to Torhild. When it came to the chores that needed to be done on the estate, Ingunn continued to be inept, yet she wanted to take part in every task. At Christmas she toiled to assist with the butchering, the ale brewing, and the cleaning of the houses and the clothing. She ran between the loft rooms and storehouses and wharf in heavy snowstorms that blew in from the fjord and covered the entire courtyard and the path down to the sea in a slippery, bright green slush.

On the evening before Christmas Eve, Olav came in and saw Ingunn standing on the bench, struggling with the old strip of tapestry that was to be hung on wooden pegs inserted in the chinks of the uppermost wall timbers. It was woven all in one piece and quite heavy. Olav went over to help Ingunn by lifting up the tapestry as she moved along.

"It doesn't seem wise for you to be working so hard," he said, "even though you're feeling well this time. That's all the more reason for you to be cautious, so that things will go the way we both wish."

Ingunn replied, "Things will go as fate has decided. And whatever anguish I'm meant to suffer, I'd rather it happened now so I won't have to wait and endure months of torment. Don't you think I know that I will never see the day when anyone calls me 'Mother'?"

Olav glanced at her. They were standing side by side on the bench. He jumped down, then lifted her down and stood there with his hands resting on her hips for a moment.

"You must not talk like that," he said faintly. "You can't be certain what will happen, my Ingunn!"

He turned away and began gathering up the wooden hooks and pegs that lay scattered on the bench.

"I thought you had intended to see the boy," he said in a low voice, "when you were at Berg in the summer."

Ingunn didn't reply.

"Sometimes I've wondered whether you might be longing for him," he said very quietly. "Do you ever long for him?"

Ingunn still didn't speak.

"Is he dead, perhaps? That child?" he asked gently.

"No. I did go and see him. He was so afraid of me that he scratched and kicked and behaved like a lynx kitten when I tried to hold him."

Olav felt old far beyond his years, worn out and sick at heart. This was the fifth winter that he and Ingunn were living together, yet it could just as well have been a hundred years. He reminded himself that the time must have felt even longer to her, poor thing.

Occasionally he tried to pull himself together enough to hope. If only it would go well this time. That was probably the one thing that might restore her happiness. And she had been feeling healthy for far longer than ever before, so perhaps the child would live.

For his part, any desire to have children had been wrung out of him long ago. He did think about the estate and his ancestral lineage, but they mattered so little to him. He also had a vague notion of something shadowlike, something in the distant future—when he had grown old, when the pain and worry and this strangely unhealthy and restless love of his were no more. For it was unlikely that she would grow old. And then his life might be like that of other men. Then he could seek reconciliation and peace for his tormented conscience. And then there might still be time to think about the estate and his lineage.

Yet whenever hazy notions about the future brought him to this point, a sharp pang would pierce his heart, the way a wound reopens and the edges gape apart. He was dimly aware that even though he had no peace and no joy, even though his very being was mortally wounded, he still possessed some measure of happiness, his own happiness, though it was unlike that of other men. Ill and nearly bled lifeless, his happiness still lived inside him, and what mattered was for him to find the courage and wisdom to rescue it, before it was too late.

Ingunn continued to feel more or less healthy as the new year arrived. But Olav gradually grew uneasy about seeing her behave in a manner that was so unlike her—bustling about in a constant, futile frenzy. He couldn't fathom how Torhild could stand having such a mistress. But calmly and patiently the young woman would follow Ingunn, completing all the work left behind in the wake of Ingunn's restless flurry.

That was how matters stood when, at the beginning of Lent, word came to Hestviken that Jon Steinfinnssøn, Ingunn's younger brother, who had never married, had died just before Christmas. It was then deemed necessary for Olav to travel north, even though it was winter, to see to his wife's share of the inheritance. For Olav Audunssøn, this seemed a portent.

For four nights he lay in bed with a candle burning, hardly sleeping at all. He lay there bargaining with his God and judge. He must find some way to save himself and this unhappy wretch whom he loved so dearly that he could see neither a beginning nor an end between them. For the boy to be given all of Hestviken as his allodial inheritance, and the right to be called the master's own son—that must be the full penance Olav would have to pay to the boy for murdering his father, the Icelandic vagabond.

One evening, after Olav had been at Berg for twelve days, he spoke of his intention as he sat in the main hall, drinking with his brother-in-law Hallvard Steinfinnssøn, while Tora kept them company nearby. He told them that the most important task of all still remained. He needed to bring home his son.

Hallvard Steinfinnssøn could only gawk, dumbfounded. Then he leaped to his feet.

"Yours! Are you saying that *you're* the father of that boy? And Ingunn had to crawl into the corner to give birth like a whore?" He pounded the table, his face blood-red with fury.

"You know full well what my situation was back then, Hallvard," replied Olav evenly. "If my enemies had found out that I was hiding here, without dispensation from the king, they certainly wouldn't have taken it well. And it could have proved a costly matter for their paternal grandmother and Fru Magnhild, if it came to light that they had harbored an outlaw such as myself."

But Hallvard cursed so fiercely that sparks flew off him. "Don't you think, Olav Audunssøn, that my grandmother and Magnhild would have gladly paid all they owned in fines because you, an outlawed man, had turned up here, rather than hear it said that one of our women had brought such shame upon herself that she didn't dare name the father of her child?" Hallvard then rattled off all the possible culprits that folks had guessed, each one more repugnant than the last.

Olav shrugged.

"I don't understand why you want to repeat those rumors. Now the truth will come out, after all. And if you'd told me a little earlier that such things were being said, I would not have waited so long. We thought we needed to keep silent for Magnhild's sake. But you must know that I've never contemplated doing anything other than acknowledging him as my son."

"You never . . . ? God knows what you were . . ." Hallvard stammered with a grimace. Suddenly he sat bolt upright, his eyes wide. "Is that true? I wonder whether Ingunn was equally certain about that. Or whether she believed that you would stand by what you had boasted, that it was a valid marriage, your bedding of her before you even had hair on your chin. If so, why did she go into the fjord?"

"Ask Tora," said Olav curtly. "She says the milk in Ingunn's breasts caused her to lose her wits."

"I also don't believe," said Hallvard slowly, "that Haftor would have brought a case against Magnhild for that reason. He had reconciled with you, after all."

"Believe whatever you like," said Olav. "It's true that Haftor and I had reconciled. It was because of the earl that I was outlawed at the time. You have been foolish all your days, Hallvard, but you can't be so stupid that you don't realize it would be more beneficial for your kinsmen to believe what I've said, even though you will lose the inheritance you would have received if your sister died childless."

Hallvard leaped to his feet and dashed out the door.

Yet when Olav was alone with Tora, he suddenly seemed to understand that what he'd now taken on was unbearably difficult. When she remained silent, he said with a mocking grin, "What about you, Tora? Do you believe me?"

Tora looked at him, though her eyes revealed nothing.

"I suppose I must believe you, since that's what you say."

And her words seemed to Olav like a physical weight at the back of his neck. Tired as he was, he had now assumed a new burden on top of the old. It was impossible for him to let any of it go, and there was nowhere for him to turn for help. He would have to endure it. Alone.

On the evening of the next day Olav returned to Berg with the child. Tora did her best to welcome her sister's son. Yet the boy seemed to notice that he wasn't truly wanted here at the estate. For that reason he stayed close to his newly found father, following close on his heels everywhere and leaning against Olav's knees whenever the man sat down. If the boy was allowed to hold his father's hand, or Olav picked him up and set him on his lap, Eirik's small, handsome face would beam with joy. And he couldn't help turning his head to look up at his father in delighted wonder.

After that, Olav didn't extend his stay at Berg any longer than necessary. On the morning of the third day he was already set to leave.

Eirik, who had been warmly tucked into the sledge, turned this way and that, peering about and laughing with glee. Once again he was going to travel by sledge. When his father came to get him at Siljuaasen, he had been allowed to travel in this same manner. The sledge had been waiting for them at the farm highest up in the district. The servant Arnketil, who was called Anki, laughed and chatted as he securely fastened the goods they were taking along. He was the kind man who had carried Eirik down on his back when the boy's father had come to get him. As for his father, he was a shapeless, looming figure, clad in a fur surcoat. Rime had settled in the fur of the men's hoods, just as the fur trim on Eirik's own ample cloak was white with frost.

Tora looked at the boy's happy, rosy face. His brown eyes were as shiny and bright as a baby bird's. Some of the tenderness she'd felt for Eirik as an infant now stirred in her heart. She kissed him on both cheeks in farewell and told him to give her greetings to his mother.

Olav returned home to Hestviken at an early hour, when the sun shone pale red through the frosty haze. They had left Oslo in the pitch-dark before dawn. When they reached the bay, he handed the reins to Anki, then lifted the slumbering boy out of the sledge and carried him up the slope to the estate.

Ingunn was sitting at the hearth, combing her hair, when Olav came in. He set the child down on the floor and pushed him forward.

"Go on, Eirik. Bid your mother good morning." With that Olav turned and headed back to the antechamber. From the doorway he saw out of the corner of his eye that Ingunn had knelt down and was moving close to the boy as she held out her thin, bare arms. Her hair dragged along the floor behind her.

Olav was standing outside in the courtyard near the sledges when Ingunn called to him from the doorway. In the darkness of the antechamber she threw her arms around his neck. She was weeping so hard that she shook all over as she pressed close to him. He placed his hand on her back. Under her hair and shift he felt her shoulder blades jutting out like sticks. With her long hair billowing over her weak and drooping shoulders, Ingunn reminded Olav, strangely enough, of what she'd been like when she was young. In her present bewildered state, and moving heavily as she now did, it wasn't easy to see traces of any wholesome beauty in her haggard face, swollen from crying. Yet it wasn't many years ago that she had been the fairest of women. For the first time Olav felt the full horror of her unfulfilled fertility.

He put his arms around her again. "I thought you would be happy," he said, for she kept on weeping.

"Happy?" she quavered, and now he saw that she was laughing in the midst of her sobs. "I think I'm happier than the angels. But surely you know, Olav, that I'm more fond of you than I would be of ten children."

"Go inside now and get dressed," he told her. "You're standing here freezing."

By the time he went back in, she had put on her clothes and wimple. She was going back and forth to the alcove, bringing out food from where it was stored in the winter. Eirik was still standing where Olav had set him down, although his mother had managed to take off his fur garment. When the boy saw his father approach, he quickly turned toward Olav and took his hand and smiled rather anxiously.

"No, go to your mother, Eirik," said Olav. "Do as I say," he added a bit sharply when the boy, out of shyness, drew closer.

VIII

When Eirik was living with his foster family at Siljuaasen and
was almost five years old, he realized that it was considered a great
shortcoming that he had no father. A year ago in the spring, when
they went down to the village for the Feast of the Annunciation, he'd
heard some folks say that he had been unlawfully born. It was the
same phrase that the men had used when they came to Siljuaasen to
hunt wood grouse, and they were no doubt referring to him. But when
Eirik asked his foster mother what it meant, she gave him a box on the
ear. After that she went about angrily muttering that they deserved a
good clout, all those people who would say such a thing of the poor
little creature, and of his mother as well. It was not the boy's fault that
he'd been born a wayside bastard. But Eirik could tell that it would be
better if he didn't ask any more questions about these strange words.
Clearly it was not a good thing to be, and that was why Torgal didn't
like him. Eirik wasn't sure how he knew this, but from what he could
gather, it seemed certain that Torgal, the father in the household, was
not his father.

Torgal, the farmer at Siljuaasen, was a kind and home-loving man
who was intent on teaching his sons. The oldest ones went hunting
with him in the forest, while the younger ones had to stay behind and
tend to chores on the farm. Their father instructed them and also
punished them if need be. But Torgal regarded Eirik as neither good
nor bad. He showed respect for his wife by never intervening in whatever she took on, and he considered it his wife's concern that she had
accepted this illegitimate offspring of a nobleman's daughter. It had
nothing to do with him. He let her take charge of both the child and
the money they received for his foster care.

Eirik knew that Hallveig was not his mother, but he didn't give it much thought, for she never treated him any differently than her own children. She was just as quick to mete out slaps and rebukes, no matter which child happened to get in her way when she was working. And she bathed all the children, in order of age, in the big wooden tub on the eve before the sabbath. Eirik was given a fur tunic to wear on winter's eve in mid-October. Then, as soon as the cuckoo was heard singing, he had to make do with nothing but a wadmal shirt, just like the other children, no matter what the weather. On those occasions during the year when the Siljuaasen folks went down to the village to attend mass, and Hallveig traveled on horseback, Eirik was allowed to ride behind her for the same length of time as the other children. And she would give each of them a loving kiss after she had received Corpus Domini.

They always had enough food. Salted fish or meat from game they'd hunted, along with a bit of bread and a ladleful of porridge. The children were given watery ale once in a while, and they drank water whenever the milk ran out in the wintertime. Eirik was treated exceedingly well, and he was happy living on that lonely farmstead deep in the forest.

Something was always happening, every hour of the day, for there were so many people and animals living on that small farm. Dense forest surrounded the fences in all directions. Behind the wall of rustling spruces and shiny-leaved bushes teemed a hidden and secretive life. Inside the woods there was a great bustling and coming and going; creatures kept an eye on everyone from the line of trees, enticing and drawing the boy all the way down to the fence. At the slightest movement or sound from within the forest, all the children would turn on their heel and race across the meadow, back up to the safety of the farm buildings. The children hadn't actually seen much of the otherworldly folk, but they'd heard the grown-ups speak of strange goings-on, so they knew about the troll on the heights of Uvaasen, and about the *hulder* who mostly kept to the marshy hills near Vaage-Stein, and about the bear. On a black-frost night during the previous year, the bear had been seen over by the cowshed, trying to break through the roof. That happened before Eirik could remember. Tiny blue-clad fellows and their wives lived under a rock firmly set in the ground up in the meadow, but those creatures were friends of theirs. Every once in a while Hallveig would take food out to them, and they, in turn, would perform many services for her. Eirik had often seen their footprints in the snow. Those who lived beyond the farm's fences were no doubt more mean-spirited. The boy didn't make much distinction between the forest animals and those other creatures who lived in the woods.

The sound of something moving through the thickets on a summer day, animal cries and other noises from the forest in the night, tracks in the snow on winter mornings, the dog named Beisk leaping up to howl on dark evenings without Eirik ever finding out what had roused the animal's attention—all these things belonged to the strange world beyond the farm, calling to the child. It was a hazy and dreamlike world, but real enough, except that Eirik was so young that he had to stay inside the fence. Farmer Torgal and the bigger boys went in and out, and spoke of peculiar things happening out there.

Eirik was allowed into the forest only on those occasions during the year when Hallveig took him with her to church. Then they would travel through the woods, heading down the long, long, ever-so-long path. And they would enter a new world that was even farther away and more dreamlike. The clamor of the bell echoing and resounding above the big, wide-open fields with large houses; the church hill crowded with horses and horses and more horses—small ragtag ones like their own horse at the bottom of the meadow, while up along the churchyard fence could be heard the whinnying of large, shiny foals with bristly manes and red and green and purple bridles adorned with glittery gold and silver. Inside the church stood the priests draped in gilt cloaks, singing between lit tapers on the altar. Some of the younger ones who wore white, ankle-length cotehardies swung golden incense burners, and the church was filled with the sweetest scent. Eirik's foster mother would push the children onto their knees and boost them up again, following the actions of those visible in the bright glow of the choir. Last came God. Eirik knew that. That's when the priest raised the small round loaf of bread, and the bell up in the tower began to ring, a pure and joyful chiming.

At the very front of the church stood an entire crowd of men and women wearing colorful clothing with gleaming belts and big brooches. Eirik knew that they were the ones who owned all the horses with the splendid saddles and the shiny swords left in the room under the tower. Eirik thought they were some sort of forest creatures, except that they went about their lives even farther away from his own life than those in the woods back home. Hallveig once pointed to one of them, the largest of the women, who wore bright red garments with three silver belts wrapped around her enormous stomach and a brooch like an ale bowl in the middle of her massive bosom. Hallveig said the woman was his maternal aunt. Eirik was none the wiser, for he had no idea what a maternal aunt might be. He'd heard of guardian spirits and angels, and sometimes a woman came to Siljuaasen and the children called her "aunt." Her name was Ingrid and she had a big hump on her back. But this woman in the church looked nothing like her.

Eirik had suffered a terrible fright when the imposing, blue-clad woman had come to visit. And he was the one she wanted to see; they told him that she was his mother. This made him very ill at ease, for it seemed both exceedingly dangerous and shameful. She was clearly one of the women who stood at the front of the church—the most distant sort of those creatures. By now Eirik had made his eldest sister explain what a wayside bastard was. She said that when women lay with men out in the forest, they got a wayside bastard. The blue-clad woman had birthed him, just as his foster mother Hallveig had birthed little Inga in the spring. And she had birthed all the other children in their home as well, except for him. With a shiver, the boy sensed that he'd been born somewhere outside and then brought in from the forest. He was terrified that he would be taken back out; that's not something he wanted. For a long time he went about in a state of great anxiety, fearing that the blue-clad woman would return to take him out to the place where she lay with a man he imagined looking like a blown-down tree with its roots up in the air. They passed just such a tree on their way to church. It lay on a flat, dry patch beneath a crag, and Eirik had always been afraid of that toppled, dead spruce, which seemed to have a hideous man's face among the tangled mass of roots. The boy thought the blue-clad woman must live in that sort of flat clearing in the forest, and he was meant to stay there alone with her and her wind-toppled man and the big red horse with the gleaming bridle. No one else would ever come there, neither people nor animals. But he refused. He wanted to stay here at home in the safe, open meadow and sleep indoors, and he never wanted to be separated from his foster mother and Gudda, his milk-sister, and Kaare and the other children and the dog Beisk and the horse and the cows and the goats and Torgal. And he didn't want to be hugged and kissed the way the strange woman had hugged and kissed him. For a long time afterward, he hardly dared venture three steps beyond the doorway, so frightened was he that she might come back, that mother of his. If only he'd had a father, then she couldn't have caused him any harm, for his sister had said that only children who had no father could be wayside bastards.

Eventually Eirik gave less and less thought to the visit. But one day during the winter, several men happened to stop at Siljuaasen as they headed for Østerdalen along a ski track through the forest. Again the boy heard strangers talking about him, but this time they mentioned his mother by name. They said she was called Paramour. Eirik had never heard that word before, but it sounded peculiar and threatening. As if she weren't human but instead some sort of bird. He vaguely pictured how Paramour might arrive, flapping that big blue cloak of hers like huge wings as she swooped down to get him. He became more and more aware of how precarious his position was, lacking a father he could turn to so that no one would ever dare seize him.

Then one day a father came for him. Eirik was not especially surprised by this. When he was led forward to stand in front of the man, he studied him carefully. Perhaps it was because Olav was so fair in complexion that the boy was drawn to him at once. This father with the straight, broad shoulders and erect posture. Eirik knew instantly that this was another person who belonged with those who stood at the front of the church, yet he was not afraid of him. The man wore colorful clothing: a leaf-green cotehardie, a silver brooch fastened at the chest, a gleaming belt, and a shiny dagger sheath. Eirik took a great liking to the big, strange axe that his father held between his knees as he sat there, with numerous rings on the hand resting on the butt of the axe. The more Eirik looked at Olav, the more pleased he was with his father. The boy calmly stood there, meeting the man's searching gaze. At the first hint of a smile on the man's face, Eirik's face lit up and he moved closer to Olav's knee.

"He's quite small, this son of mine, isn't he?" said the father to Hallveig as he reached out to lift the boy's chin for a moment. He said nothing directly to Eirik during his stay at Siljuaasen, but that was enough for the boy.

Hallveig wept a little, and Torgal lifted Eirik up when he said goodbye to his foster son. His siblings stood and stared at this boy who was about to leave with the two strangers. Eirik felt a pang in his heart when he heard his foster mother crying. He wrapped his arms around Hallveig's neck, and his lips began to quiver. But then his father called to him. Eirik turned around at once and trudged to the door, weighed down by the ankle-length fur tunic he wore.

Eirik and Olav became good friends as they traveled. His father said very little to him, letting his manservant, Arnketil, take charge of the boy. But Eirik knew that all the strange new things—the sledge and the horses, the different house they slept in each night, all the good food, and the countless folks they saw everywhere, many of whom spoke to him—were under his father's command. And his father wore a shirt and hose made of linen next to his body, garments he didn't take off at night.

The new mother Eirik found when he came to the journey's end made less of an impression on him. He didn't recognize her. When she asked whether he recalled that she'd visited Siljuaasen, he said yes because he could tell that was the expected answer. But he had no sense that this was the same woman. This mother wore brown clothing and was thick-waisted. She breathed heavily, taking long, slow breaths, as she constantly moved about, bustling in and out of the houses. He pictured the tall, blue-clad mother named Paramour with the brisk birdlike movements standing in the small clearing in the forest, where she lived with her tree-root man and the big red horse. Only when the new brown-clad mother pulled him close and repeatedly kissed him as she showered him with wild endearments did he have some notion that she and Paramour were one and the same—although they called this one Ingunn. Eirik didn't like being kissed and hugged in such a manner. The only kinds of kisses he'd ever received in his life were those belonging to Sunday mass, with fresh food and swigs from the ale bowls when they came home. Infrequent and festive.

Yet here he was given ale every day, and folks ate fresh food, both fish and meat, many days in a row, so perhaps it was the custom for the women to offer kisses every day as well.

Eirik would often go over to Olav, place his hands on his father's knees, and ask about all manner of things. Did the seal actually live in the forest that he could see across the fjord? And why were his two horses white? And why wasn't he the father of Torhild's children? And what were they going to do with the tallow they were cooking? And where was the moon headed when it flew so fast across the sky? Ingunn would watch the two of them with a strangely anxious air. For one thing, she feared that Olav would become impatient with the boy. She felt so inexpressibly humbled and grateful to her husband because of what he'd done for her when he brought home this child, for whom she'd been longing so desperately. Now she was afraid that the boy might pester Olav, or that her husband might grow angry with her child if Eirik demanded too much of his attention, though she hadn't noticed that Olav harbored any ill will toward Eirik. He paid little mind to the boy unless Eirik sought him out, but then he was always kind and answered as best he could all the endless questions. Yet it wasn't easy to make Eirik understand anything. The boy seemed to have very little sense in his head. He made no distinction between what was alive and what was not. He would ask whether the big stone on the foreshore favored seagulls most, and why the snow wanted to lie down on the ground. He couldn't grasp that the sun shimmering through the fog was the same one that shone on a clear-weather day. And once he'd seen a moon that was unlike all the other moons. The priest came to visit them one day, but Eirik didn't understand how he could be the same man that he'd seen in church, or that the priest could take off the garments he wore to celebrate mass and then ride about like other men. Occasionally Eirik would take it upon himself to explain things on his own, but everything he said was so odd and nonsensical— impossible to comprehend. Ingunn feared that the boy was quite slow and backward for his age when it came to intelligence. And she feared that Olav might find even more disfavor with the boy because of his lack of wits. Eirik was so handsome and so sweet that she couldn't seem to get enough of looking at him—but clever he was not.

And she felt a secret pang of disappointment because the boy so openly showed that he was more fond of his father than of her. That was also one reason why Ingunn strove to keep her husband and son apart as much as she could.

From the very beginning, Olav harbored no ill will toward Eirik. The violent emotions that had shaken him when he learned of Ingunn's faithlessness and that arose again and again whenever he recalled that another man had possessed her—all those feelings had faded into the distant past during these years of joyless marriage. His love for Ingunn was a certainty and a habit; it was woven into his very being the way the soil in a meadow is interwoven with tangled roots. But now his love seemed to him nothing more than an endless compassion for this poor, ill person whose life was his own life. A tenderness and concern for her—that was the heat still alive in his love for Ingunn, that was what pulsed and surged, flaring up and sinking down. His ardor was torpid, stirring only sluggishly, as if half-asleep. But with that his jealousy had also grown feeble and weak. On rare occasions, when he chanced to think of what had happened to Ingunn in the past, it all seemed so far away. And Olav couldn't see a connection between the shame and anguish of that time and this small boy who had now come to live with them on the estate. Eirik was here, and that was as it should be. God had made it known that Olav should take Eirik in, and after that there was nothing more to ponder or do about the matter. And Olav was almost inclined to feel affection for Eirik. The boy was a handsome child, and he so clearly courted his father's love. Olav, who had a hard time getting close to others, was always happy and astonished when anyone sought his friendship.

Olav often understood the thoughts behind the boy's strange and bewildering words better than Ingunn did. When she interrupted Eirik's stammered explanations with harsh rebukes and refused to leave the boy in peace so that he and his father might continue talking until they understood each other—then Olav, more than once, would feel a nagging impatience. He remembered, not in the sense that he could summon forth the memory in clearly formulated thoughts, let alone speak of it, but instead as brusque and fleeting visions, so much about the way in which the world had appeared to him, when *he* was a child.

IX

The ice on the fjord broke up, and spring arrived. The reddish gray rocks that reached down to the water were baked by the sun, and the sea spray beneath the Ox whitened as if newly born in the glinting sunlight. The ground turned green and released its sweet fragrance of grass and earth. Then came the time for sprouting leaves, filling the evening with the bitter, chill scent of new foliage all over Kverndalen.

One morning in May, Olav came upon a viper's nest on a hillside. He managed to kill three of the snakes. He put them in a wooden cup with a lid and took it along when he crept over to the cookhouse during the midday rest. The fat from a viper's entrails, as well as the snake's ashes, were good for many things, but they were more potent if prepared in secret.

Olav was about to slip inside the cookhouse when he heard voices. Ingunn was inside with Eirik.

The childish voice said, "Because Father gave me his breast, don't you see?"

"Gave you his breast?" Ingunn repeated in surprise. "What sort of nonsense are you talking about now?"

"But I'm not. Father said that I could eat the wings too, if I was still hungry, and by then there wasn't anything else left of the rooster, just the wings."

Olav chuckled as he stood there. Now he remembered. It was at the inn in Oslo. The woman had served him a roasted rooster, and the boy had shown a great fondness for the meat. Then Olav heard Ingunn speaking again.

"I'll roast a whole rooster for you, Eirik. Would that make you see that I'm just as kind as your father? I'll give it to you the next time he's away from home."

Olav walked back across the courtyard and headed east to the smithy. He felt strangely ashamed on Ingunn's behalf. Why would she say something like that? There was no need for her to wait until he wasn't at home to roast one of her own roosters for the boy.

Whether it was because the unfamiliar food lay too heavily in Eirik's stomach or there was some other cause, almost every night during that spring the child would awake screaming. Olav would hear Eirik give a shriek and jolt awake. The boy would crawl around and fumble aimlessly in the big bed at the north end of the room where he slept alone. Then the child would scream again, even louder, as if in the utmost terror.

Ingunn would tumble out of bed and go over to him. "Eirik, Eirik, my Eirik, hush, hush, hush, you'll wake your father. Oh, shush now. There's nothing here that you need to be frightened of, my little son!"

"You'd better bring him over here to us," Olav's voice, sounding wide awake, issued from the dark.

"Oh, has he woken you again?" lamented Ingunn. She came back with the boy and lay down. The two of them moved about, getting settled under the coverlet until they were comfortable.

"I wasn't asleep yet. What were you dreaming about again, Eirik?"

But at night only his mother would do for Eirik. He merely nestled closer to Ingunn and didn't reply to his father. They could make no sense of his dreams. The boy would rub something off his hands and fling it away, two or three times. Then he would sigh with relief and grow calm. A moment later both mother and son would be sound asleep.

Olav always had the hardest time sleeping in the spring. He seldom fell asleep before midnight, and he'd awake at dawn. On those early spring mornings the fjord was often as smooth as a mirror, pale blue and sparkling silver. The opposite desolate shore seemed as bright and delicate as a mirage. Olav would feel absurdly happy and lighthearted whenever he stepped outside on such a morning. He could hear Torhild Bjørnsdatter singing somewhere in one of the outbuildings. By then she'd already been at work for a long while. Olav and the young woman would meet out in the courtyard and stop to talk in the morning sunlight.

Several hours later, when he went back inside the main hall, Olav would sometimes pause to look for a moment at the mother and child, who were still asleep. Eirik lay with his face resting against his mother's neck, breathing with his lips slightly parted. Ingunn held on to the boy's shoulder with her thin hand, heavy with rings.

Two weeks before Saint Jon's Day, Ingunn gave birth to a little boy. Olav had the infant baptized at once. Audun.

The child was tiny, bluish-red, and terribly skinny. Once when the infant lay unswaddled on Signe Arnesdatter's lap as she tended to him, Olav wrapped two fingers around his son's hand. That tiny hand was so scrawny that it most resembled a chicken's foot. And it was just as cold.

Olav did not feel any strong love for the infant, nor any joy that at long last he had a son. The same circumstances had been repeated too often, and the mere suspicion that Ingunn might be once again carrying a child provoked in him a deep despondency. He had grown so used to giving up any hope that the misery might finally end in joy and happiness that he now needed time to take it all in.

But he saw that Ingunn was not of the same mind. Even though each time she had awaited nothing but bitter pain, against her own will her heart had trembled with hopeless and despairing love for the tiny unborn creatures. Audun was now the heir to all his brothers who had left behind not even a name or a memory.

Eirik was wildly happy to have a brother. From his life at Siljuaasen he knew that the birth of a child was the greatest of events. Then two or three strange women would come to the house, bringing with them good food, and candles would burn in the room every night. The infant was treated as the most precious thing. Those living outside the fence lurked about, ready to steal it, and the child's health and well-being were constantly discussed. In fact, the greatest danger at home occurred when the next infant was born and needed the cradle. The child from the previous year was left in the neglectful care of young siblings, always in the way and always susceptible to dangers.

But this was not something that Eirik had noticed. Here at Hestviken things were practically festive, with so many women present, each of them having brought a maidservant, and with a great abundance of food. But he and his father didn't get to see the candles burning in the room, for Ingunn and the new brother kept to a different house.

"He's my silken brother, but he's only your woolen brother," Eirik said to Torhild's two youngest children. They were all standing together, watching while Audun was tended.

Olav happened to be sitting with his wife at that moment and heard what Eirik said. He glanced over at Ingunn, who lay in bed, radiantly happy as she looked at her two sons.

His own son was the tiny creature the maidservant was swaddling. The other boy had bowed his healthy, beaming face toward the infant and was cooing over the little brother from whom he had unknowingly stolen his birthright.

It had caused a quiet commotion in the district when the Hestviken folks had so unexpectedly produced a five-year-old son who had been hidden away all this time.

Olav was not particularly well-liked in the area. He had been welcomed with open arms and warm goodwill when he returned to his own home, but little by little the villagers began to feel that he had refused their friendship and neighborly intentions. Olav kept to himself more than they liked, and he was quite reserved when he did venture out among other people, though he was never impolite. But this did nothing to improve their opinion of him, for it was thought that he wanted to appear more important than the other landowners, although he was taciturn, quiet, and unapproachable. Privately, it was hinted, with a little sneer, that Olav no doubt thought of himself as a royal retainer because he'd been one of Earl Alf's men, and on his mother's side he was related to those Danish chieftains who spent half of each year in Norway and feasted on the duke's food. Be that as it may, Olav still owned his allodial estate, whole and undivided, though he'd have to wait and see how long that would last, considering how times had changed. Even though he never shirked from his obligations, or ever refused to offer help when it was needed, no one had any real desire to ask Olav Audunssøn for a favor. When folks who were in some sort of difficulty sought out the rich landowner at Hestviken, he hardly seemed to bother listening to them. After they had explained, in great detail, the nature of their situation, he might ask at last, as if he'd been preoccupied with other matters, "Ah. And what is it you want?" No one could deny that Olav was generous with both charitable donations and loans, but if anyone wanted to ease their heart by discussing their concerns, it was ill-advised to seek such comfort at that particular estate. Olav would utter replies that made a person wonder whether the man was either stupid or indifferent. Unless folks were in the most dire need of a helping hand, they preferred to turn to someone else who would listen to them when they spoke and then offered an opinion as well as advice and solace—even if that person might not tender assistance without first complaining that he himself was not having an easy time of it, yet in God's name . . .

There was another matter that the villagers had noticed. No man had ever seen Olav get genuinely drunk or become loose-lipped while intoxicated. He drank no less than other good men at a feast, but it was as if God's gifts had no effect on him.

And slowly but surely a certain feeling grew in the district—a notion that was hazy and unformed, for no one actually knew on what it was based, but in all its vagueness it gained the strength of a certainty—that Olav was hiding something, a secret misfortune or a sin. The straight-backed and handsome young master with the wide, fair-complexioned face beneath the flaxen, curly hair . . . He was a marked man.

And it was a strange thing about the man's wife, the way she couldn't produce any children who lived. Little was seen of Ingunn Steinfinnsdatter, nor was the poor woman much to look at. But folks still remembered how lovely she had once been, and that was not so many years ago.

Then it became known that they did have a child, after all. During all these years they'd had a son who'd been hidden away, in some godforsaken place far north in her home district.

Conceived while the father was an outlaw? Was that right? Olav had explained how it had happened, keeping his account short and vague. Folks knew that the enmity with his wife's kinsmen had developed at that time and that the dying Steinfinn had placed in Olav's hands the daughter to whom the boy had been betrothed since childhood. Olav had accepted Ingunn as his wife, and it was impossible to interpret Steinfinn's words in any other way; that had been his wish. But the men newly put in charge of the girl's marriage had thought they could make other plans for the beautiful and wealthy maiden. Now Olav mentioned that during the summer before he finally became reconciled with his wife's kinsmen, he had secretly stayed for a time at the estate where Ingunn was living. But it had been necessary to keep his visit secret.

That's what Olav Audunssøn said. Yet folks started to wonder. Perhaps it wasn't certain that Olav had willingly accepted the wife that Steinfinn had pledged him to marry while he was a mere boy and under Steinfinn Toressøn's guardianship. Perhaps he had tried to wriggle out of a marriage that he'd been forced into as a child. People who had seen a bit of Olav and Ingunn's married life together—their servants and the women who had attended Ingunn when she was ill—recounted what they knew. Olav was undoubtedly kind toward his wife, after a fashion, but he was also sullen and said little at home. Days might pass when he didn't utter a single word to his wife. Ingunn never looked happy, and that was not so strange—living there as she did with that silent and surly husband, constantly ill, and giving birth to one dead child after another.

One day the new priest, Sira Hallbjørn, came to Hestviken.

He was quite a young man, tall and slender with a very handsome face, but his hair was a fiery red and folks thought that he seemed arrogant. In a short time he had attracted much disfavor. Hardly had he arrived in the district before he'd begun to quarrel with folks in every direction—about property belonging to the church, about the income due the priest, and about previous arrangements that Sira Benedikt had made with the landowners, agreements that this new priest had determined to be unlawful. Both the monastery on Hovedø[20] and its sister convent at Nonneseter owned estates and leaseholdings in the parish, as did several of the churches and charitable groups in Oslo. Their representatives were largely intelligent and well-meaning men who were on good terms with the local populace. Many of them had purchased gravesites at the cloisters, and when any of the Hovedø monks happened to visit church properties, landowners from far away would flock to the chapel to attend mass with them.

Sira Hallbjørn quickly ended up in disputes with the cloisters as well. On the other hand, the parish priest directed all his love toward monks of a new order that had recently come to Norway. They went about barefoot, wearing cowls of sackcloth and ashes, and the virtues that they were supposedly known for practicing included humility, modesty, and poverty. It was even said that these brothers begged for their daily bread as they wandered around, teaching both the lowly and the rich a true fear of God. If they had anything left in their sacks after vespers, they were to distribute it among the poor and then set off each morning as destitute and empty-handed as before. Sira Hallbjørn himself was neither humble nor modest. He was proud of his ancestry, having come from a noble family far away in Valdres, and he was ill-suited to teaching farmers a fear of God, for he was highly educated and spoke in a manner that few could understand. For that reason folks gained little from listening to him. Yet he couldn't stop praising these mendicant monks who called themselves Minorites.[21] He acted for them as a sort of protector, presenting them with large donations for the house they were building in town and trying to persuade his parishioners to do the same. But folks discovered this was likely because the duke greatly favored these new monks, while the bishop and most of the priests and learned men in town were against them, saying that the strictures of this order were dangerous and unwise. And people knew that Sira Hallbjørn had been sent to the area because, though his ancestry and remarkable learning meant he should have been destined for the highest positions of the church, he had drawn the ire of the bishop and the entire cathedral chapter in Oslo. He was haughty and quarrelsome, and he was convinced that he knew and understood and could learn everything better than anyone else. Yet the worst they could do to Sira Hallbjørn was to banish him to this good parish. His conduct was irreproachable in every other way, he had studied abroad for many years, and he knew everything there was to know about Norway's laws and rights, from the oldest times to the present day.

The purpose of Sira Hallbjørn's visit to Hestviken was to find out what Olav knew about the salmon fishing rights to a small river on the Hudrheim shore. Olav could tell him little. His paternal grandfather had sold to his brother-in-law the estate that owned the fishing rights, and since then the property had been divided up and passed to several different owners. Olav could tell that Sira Hallbjørn was annoyed that the master of Hestviken knew so little about the matter. Nevertheless, while the priest was eating, Olav asked him whether he could clarify something that was weighing heavily on his mind. "It has to do with my sons," said Olav.

He had heard that a child fathered by a man who at the time was considered an outlaw would consequently be without rights under the law, even if the mother was the banished man's lawful wife.

"No, that's not right," said Sira Hallbjørn, gesturing dismissively. "You've heard of wolf children? That's what they called the children of a banished man in the old days. Back then an outlaw was the same as a dead man. His estate was given to his heirs, and his wife was deemed a widow. If the man later won grid, or dispensation to return, he would have to ask her kinsmen again for permission to marry her and hold another wedding. But as you know full well, such a law cannot be recognized among Christian men. Neither a sin nor a judgment can sever the marital bond between a man and his wife."

"Ingunn's kinsmen refused to accept that what passed between us when we were young constituted a lawful marriage," Olav went on. "Her kinsmen did not give her to me with their consent until after Eirik was born."

"You need not worry about that. Whether the boy was lawfully born or not, he will have the same rights because the two of you were married with her kinsmen's consent. No one would argue that your marriage is not lawful."

"So that means that Audun could never step forward and dislodge Eirik from his rightful place as our oldest son?" asked Olav.

"Certainly not," said the priest firmly.

"Ah. I just wanted to ask you to clarify this matter for me."

"As is only reasonable," replied Sira Hallbjørn.

Olav thanked the priest for his kind explanation.

While Ingunn was convalescing, Eirik began talking about someone called Tøtrabassa. At first the grown-ups thought this was some beggar woman, one of several who appeared more often during that time when there was an abundance of food and drink in the house.

Oh yes, said Eirik, Tøtrabassa was a woman who carried a sack. But on another day he claimed that Tøtrabassa had come to visit and had played with him down in the field behind the barn. There was a little hollow in the meadow where he kept his playthings. Tøtrabassa was a tiny maiden. No one paid much attention to this, for they were all used to Eirik constantly spouting such strange foolishness.

But after a while he started talking about more playmates, and they all had such peculiar names: Tauragaura, Silvarp, Skolorm, Dølvandogg, and Kolmurna the Blue. It was impossible to know whether they were male or female, adults or children.

The servants on the estate began to worry. It still happened now and then that an entire household, both young and old, might leave everything behind and take up residence in the forest, either because some sort of legal case had been raised against them or because they were destitute. Then they preferred to seek refuge in the woods, at least during the summertime, rather than accept the charity of the parish. At that same time a fat sheep that had been kept on the estate disappeared, and the hired men thought that these friends of Eirik must be forest vagabonds of the type that lived mostly by pilfering and stealing. The servants kept an eye on Eirik when he went to play in the hollow, wanting to see whether any strangers, either children or grown-ups, came to him there. But no one saw anything. And one day the carcass of the sheep floated up in the bay. The animal had apparently fallen off the slope.

Then the folks at Hestviken grew truly alarmed. They thought it must be a matter of otherworldly creatures. They asked Eirik whether he knew where they came from.

"Oh, from over there under the cliff." But when he saw how frightened everyone looked, he too grew scared. "No, they come from town," he said. "They ride here in a sledge. Or maybe they sail in a boat," he corrected himself when Olav told him that no one could travel in a sledge from Oslo on a summer day, and he shouldn't be uttering such nonsense. "Well, actually, they come from the forest," Eirik then said. "Yes, that's right. Tauragaura said they live in the forest." Tauragaura was the one Eirik now talked about most.

Ingunn was beside herself with despair. It must be the evil spirits that had stripped all happiness from this estate, one generation after another. Now they were no doubt after her children. Eirik was kept inside the women's house to be safeguarded there. He talked on and on about these friends of his until Ingunn grew so despondent that it seemed she would lose her mind. She wanted Olav to summon the priest.

"You're not lying about all this, are you, Eirik?" Olav asked sternly one day after he'd listened to the boy replying to his mother's anxious questions.

Eirik's brown eyes took on a frightened look as he stared at his father and vigorously shook his head.

"Because if I find out one day that you've been telling lies, things will not go well for you, my boy."

Eirik looked at his father in surprise, seeming not to understand.

But Olav had begun to suspect that the whole thing was something the boy had made up, unreasonable as this seemed, for he couldn't fathom what purpose the child might have for spreading such useless and pointless lies. The next day, when Olav and a hired man set out to mow the meadow just below the hollow, Eirik was allowed to go along. Olav promised Ingunn that they would keep a sharp eye on the boy the whole time.

And that's what Olav did. He watched Eirik carefully. The boy puttered quietly and cheerfully about in the hollow, playing with some snail shells and pieces of stone that the fishermen had given him. He was utterly alone the whole time.

When the hired man and the maidservants went back to the estate for the midmorning meal, Olav went over to Eirik. "So they didn't come today, did they? Tøtrabassa and Skolorm and the others?"

"Yes, they did," said Eirik, beaming. And he began telling his father about all the games he'd been playing with them.

"Now you're lying, boy," said Olav harshly. "I've had my eye on you the whole time, and nobody was here."

"They took off running when you came over. They were frightened by your scythe."

"So what happened to them? Where did they go?"

"Home, I suppose."

"Home? And where might that be?"

Eirik pondered as he looked at his father with some nervousness. Then his face lit up, and he said eagerly, "Shall we go there, Father?" He held out his hand.

Olav hung his scythe from a tree branch. "Yes, let's do that."

Eirik led his father up to the estate, then out of the courtyard and over to the expanse of rock west of the farm buildings, where there was a view of the fjord.

"I think they're down there," he said, pointing to the little strip of foreshore far below.

"I don't see anyone," said Olav brusquely.

"No, that's not where they are. Now I know where." At first Eirik turned back toward the estate, but then he set off along a path down to the wharf. "Now I know, now I know," he called excitedly, hopping up and down and stomping in place as he waited for his father. Again he ran on ahead, then paused to wait and took his father by the hand, pulling him down the slope.

There he led the way to the farthermost warehouse, one that Olav almost never used, for these days not much went on in the bay. Only in the spring, before Olav traveled to the Korsmesse assembly in Oslo, did he keep any of his wintertime goods here. Right now the warehouse was empty and unlocked. Eirik pulled his father inside with him.

The water lapped and splashed against the posts under the warehouse floor. The building was drafty, the walls leaky, and the reflection of the sun on the water swayed in gleaming stripes across the walls and ceiling. Eirik breathed in the smell of the warehouse, his face glowing with excitement. He looked up at his father with an expectant smile, then led him, tiptoeing, to an overturned old cask in which Olav often stored pelts.

"Here," the boy whispered, squatting down. "In here. That's where they live. Can you see them? The cracks have gotten so big, otherwise we'd be able to see them better, but they're sitting inside eating. Do you see them?"

Olav toppled the cask over and gave it a kick so that it rolled away. There was nothing underneath except some debris.

Eirik looked up with a smile and was just about to say something, when he noticed the expression on his father's face. That stopped him short, and he gaped in fear. With a piercing shriek he raised his arms to fend off the blow and then surrendered to heartrending sobs.

Olav let his hand drop, realizing that he couldn't bring himself to strike the boy. So small and wretched did Eirik look as he stood there crying that his father felt mostly ashamed. Then he lowered Eirik's arms and led him over to a pile of rubbish. There Olav sat down, with his son standing in front of him.

"I see now that you've been lying. Every word was a lie, wasn't it? Everything you've said about those visitors of yours. Answer me."

But Eirik didn't reply. He stood there, staring in sheer bewilderment at Olav's face. He seemed not to comprehend a thing.

Finally Olav had to set Eirik on his lap in order to stop his bitter weeping. He admonished the boy again and again, telling him that he mustn't say things that were untrue or he would be punished. But Olav now spoke in a much gentler tone, occasionally stroking the boy's head. Eirik snuggled close to his father's chest and wrapped his arms around Olav's neck.

But Eirik still didn't understand. And when Olav saw this, he was filled with an anxious sense of alarm. This boy whom he held in his arms seemed to him so perplexing and odd. What in God's name had

possessed him to make up all those lies? It seemed to Olav so mean-
ingless that he began to wonder: did Eirik have his full wits about him?

Ingunn stayed indoors for nearly nine weeks after giving birth. She
wasn't especially ill or weak. Rather, she was feeling exceedingly comfortable in the cramped house where everything that was done was
for her sake and the child's, and she was shielded from anything that
might distress her. She lay in bed, taking the utmost pleasure in this
new happiness, with the infant at her breast and Eirik running in and
out of the room all day long. At last Olav began to grow impatient.
They had spent so many anguished years living together, and in all
that time Ingunn had always clung to him. Now she was happy and
healthy, and she had even regained some of the beauty of her youth.
Yet she had shut herself away from him with the children. But Olav
never showed any sign of his displeasure.

Finally, on the Sunday following Saint Lavrans's Feast Day, Ingunn attended church for the first time. Eirik was asleep when the
churchgoers set off at dawn, but he was outside in the courtyard when
they returned.

A new custom had taken hold, although many people did not favor it, and some claimed it was an arrogant insult to God. A young
wife attending church for the first time after childbirth, especially if
the infant was a son, would wear all day long the golden wreath, which
was the time-honored adornment of a high-born maiden, as a crown
on top of her married woman's wimple.

Ingunn had fastened over her white silk wimple the golden gar-
land. She wore a red gown and her blue cloak with the big gold brooch.

Olav lifted his wife down from her horse. Eirik stood there staring, awed by his mother's loveliness. She seemed to him much taller,
dressed as she was in such gleaming splendor, with the silver belt
around her slender waist. Slim and lissome, she now moved as nimbly
as a bird.

"Mother!" cried Eirik, beaming. "It's you, after all! You're Paramour!"

The next instant his father grabbed the boy by the shoulder and struck him on the jaw so hard that everything went black before Eirik's eyes. Blows rained down on the child, and he couldn't catch his breath to cry out. Only a wheezing squeak issued from his throat. Then Una Arnesdatter came running and seized Olav's arm.

"Olav, Olav, restrain yourself. The boy is so little. Have you lost your wits? Don't hit him so hard!"

Olav let the boy go. Eirik fell to the ground, collapsing onto his back. There he lay, gasping and panting, his face a pale blue. He had not been knocked senseless—it was partially deliberate that the boy acted as if he were dying. Una knelt down beside him and lifted him onto her lap. Then he began to cry.

Olav turned to face his wife. He was still shaking. Ingunn stood slumped forward; her eyes, nostrils, and open mouth looked like the empty holes in a skull. Olav laughed, harshly and angrily. Then he took her by the arm and led her inside the main hall where the maidservants were setting food on the table for the celebratory feast.

None of the churchgoers had heard what Eirik said. Yet they were all thinking the same thing: no matter what the child had done, it was an ugly sight, the way the father beat the little boy so fiercely. The guests seated themselves on various benches, waiting to be invited to sit at the table. Everyone was ill at ease.

At long last Una Arnesdatter came in, carrying Eirik in her arms. She set him down next to his father's knee.

"I doubt that Eirik will cause you any further trouble, Olav. You must tell your son that you're no longer angry."

"Did he tell you why I punished him?" asked Olav, refusing to look up.

Una shook her head. "The poor thing. He's been crying so hard that he has no strength to speak."

"You must never again say that word, Eirik," Olav then said, his voice muted but vehement. "Never again. Do you understand?"

Eirik was still fitfully sobbing. He didn't reply, just stared at his father, uncomprehending and frightened.

"You will never again say that word," his father repeated, placing a heavy hand on the boy's shoulder until, at last, the child nodded.

Eirik's gaze shifted longingly to the table that was now heaped with all manner of delicious food.

And then everyone sat down at the table.

Eirik was to sleep in Torhild's house that night, for there were so many guests staying at the estate. In the evening, when he left the main hall, Olav followed him out to the courtyard. Eirik abruptly halted and began shaking all over. With great dread he looked up at his father.

"Who taught you to say that ugly word? The name you called your mother?"

Eirik merely stared in fright as sobs rose inside him. Olav couldn't get him to answer his question.

"Don't ever say it again! Do you understand? Never again!" Olav stroked the boy's head, noticing somewhat shamefully that one side of Eirik's face was swollen and red.

The boy was just about to fall asleep when he noticed someone bending over him. His mother. Her face was burning hot and wet.

"Eirik, my son. Who told you that word? Who said that your mother was a paramour?"

The boy was wide awake at once.

"So you're not Paramour?"

"Yes, I am," whispered his mother.

Eirik threw his arms around her neck, pressed close, and kissed her.

X

Autumn came early that year. Around Michaelmas, bad weather set in. Rain fell as the wind howled day in and day out, except at those times when the storm was so strong that the clouds couldn't release any showers. This weather lasted for seven weeks.

At Hestviken the water rose over the wharves. One night the sea ripped away the posts under the farthermost warehouse. When the men went down there at daybreak, they found the old structure's back wall, which faced the mountain slope, leaning forward while the gable wall facing the fjord had sunk until the water reached halfway up. The whole thing was pitching on the rough sea like a moored boat. Each time the wrecked building was lifted up by a wave, it would sink down again, with water gushing between the timbers and even more pouring from a small slot under the gable eaves. Anki thought it looked like a drunken man hunched over the gunnel of a boat, vomiting.

Using broad axes, boat hooks, and ropes, the men had to free the wreckage and tow it away. Otherwise it would most likely end up slamming against the wharf and the warehouse where Olav had stored all the salt they had gathered during the summer, as well as the fish, what little there was of it. The fishing had been poor that autumn. While they were laboring at this task, Olav badly injured his right arm.

He paid little mind to it while he was toiling in the sea spray and stormy weather, which was so fierce that occasionally the men had to lie flat and crawl across the ground. But at dusk, as they walked back up the slope to the estate, Olav noticed that his arm hurt when he moved it. As he was opening the door to the main house, a burst of wind blew the whole door inward, pulling Olav along with it. His injured arm was yanked straight as he tumbled across the threshold and fell full-length onto the antechamber floor. Once inside, he had to be helped out of his soaked clothing, and Torhild put his arm in a sling.

The main hall was a loathsome place that evening. The entire room was filled with smoke, for it would have been unwise to prop open the door or the hearth vent in such weather. The smoke stung everyone's eyes and tore at their throats. When the men's wet garments also began to steam from where they had been draped over the rafters, the air soon grew so thick that they could have cut it with a knife.

Ingunn had retreated to the alcove with both children. There was less smoke, but it was so cold that they had to burrow under the covers. The men left the hall as soon as they finished eating. Olav tossed a few furs and cushions onto the floor next to the hearth and lay down so as to be lower than the smoke.

His arm was now swollen. His face was wind-burned, and both his head and his body felt hot, yet he would occasionally shiver with chills. In this mildly feverish state the storm sounded to him like all manner of voices as it howled around the corners of the house and banged against a loose shutter somewhere. Every once in a while he could make out the sound of the wind rushing through the forest up on the cliff above the estate. The deepest tone came from the turbulent fjord. From where he lay, Olav thought he could hear the thundering of the waves breaking against the slope on which the houses stood, as if the roar were coming from underneath and rising up through the bedrock.

Half-asleep, he lay there and pictured the enormous, white-crested waves arriving, the water brown with mud and sediment. Then he was again crawling on his hands and knees up the wet expanse of rock, with the boat hook clamped under him along with the rope that he needed to fasten to a crevice. The sea spray, as heavy as rain, kept on lashing him all the way up. At that moment small, brass-colored fissures appeared in the heaps of black clouds, and far below him, where the black and foaming-white fjord seemed as hollow as a cup, a single beam of sunlight glinted on the churning swells.

Then another vision appeared beneath his closed eyelids: a big marsh, pale with frost, the grass and heather furry-white with rime. But a trace of light was seeping into the morning haze, and he could tell that later in the day the sun would break through. There would never be a better time to set off riding with hawk and hound. The marshy hollows and small ponds scattered across the terrain were covered with shiny dark ice with tiny white air bubbles crackling underfoot. The deciduous-wooded slopes were bright and airy, for the trees and thickets were bare, and the fallen leaves gleamed on the ground. The spruce forest stood dark and fresh now that the frost had thawed. And then he felt the sense of anticipation, wondering whether to set off across rugged ground, or whether the hawk would head across the marshes and frozen lakes.

The only hawk Olav owned sat now on its peg in the hired men's quarters. The bird was ill, its feet reddish, and it didn't breathe as it should. It might be just as well to put an end to its misery; the hawk would never be able to hunt anymore. And Olav had lost his falcon last autumn.

Audun began whimpering again in the alcove. Ingunn hushed and soothed him for a while.

Torhild Bjørnsdatter brought several coverlets to spread over her master. Olav opened his eyes. From where he lay, he watched the girl's sturdy figure moving in the red glow from the hearth embers. Torhild quietly set about shifting the clothing that hung on the rafters.

"You're not asleep, Olav? Are you thirsty for ale?"

"No. I'd rather have water."

Olav propped himself up on one elbow. His bandaged arm hurt when he tried to reach for the water ladle. Torhild crouched down and held it to his lips. When he lay back down, she pulled the coverlet over his shoulder. Then he heard her over at the alcove, asking the mistress whether she wanted anything.

"Hush, hush," whispered Ingunn in reply. "You'll wake Audun, and he was just about to fall asleep."

Torhild banked the fire and left. Olav spent all night sleeping right there on the floor.

The harsh fall weather was not good for Audun. His eyes were inflamed by the incessant smoke, and he coughed a great deal.

Around Christmas the weather grew calm, and every morning the sun shone bright-red through the frosty haze. Early in the new year the fjord froze over, and the cold grew worse. At some of the surrounding farms, everyone had to move into one house and keep the fire burning in the hearth night and day.

The previous spring had been so good that the landowners had acquired as much livestock as they could possibly find room for. Yet even though the stables and cowsheds were now filled to overflowing, the animals froze so badly that folks had to wrap sacks and pieces of fabric around those it was deemed best to save. And spruce branches were spread over the floors so the animals wouldn't end up getting stuck to the icy clay. The dung was frozen solid every morning, so it was nearly impossible to muck out underneath them.

By Saint Agata's Day in early February, folks in the area said that men would be able to travel across the ice all the way to Denmark, although no one had any reason to go to that country. The kings of Norway and Denmark had reconciled during the previous year.

It was at this time that a case was brought against Olav because he had stayed home in the summer when the duke had gone to Denmark to negotiate a reconciliation at Hegnsgavl. Olav had joined the *leiðangr*, or expeditionary fleet, for three summers in a row as a lesser chieftain. During the fourth summer, Lord Tore Haakonssøn had half-promised Olav a reprieve. Lord Tore wanted him instead to provide to the baron's troops two fully armed men and also pay for their provisions. Olav had not done so, nor had he joined the military expedition in the spring. This time the call to arms had required far fewer conscripted men because the duke was heading south merely to negotiate terms. Yet Olav landed in trouble, and in the severe cold around mid-Lent, he was forced to ride once to Tunsberg and then several times to Oslo, first to explain his absence from the *leiðangr*, and then to raise the funds to pay the fine. He lost a fair number of livestock that winter, and the white horse he had purchased from Stein died.

◆ ◆ ◆

The two young children filled the cramped house with commotion.

Eirik had developed a nasty habit. Olav gradually learned that the boy was quick to lie. If Olav asked him whether he'd seen a particular house servant, Eirik would always eagerly say yes, he'd just talked to that person indoors, or out in the courtyard, and then he'd recount what the servant had said or done. Usually there wasn't a word of truth in what he reported. Some of the servants, as well as Ingunn, hinted that the child might have second sight, since he was unlike other boys. Olav had little to say to that, though he kept an eye on Eirik. He could see no indication that the boy's behavior was anything other than sheer deceit.

Eirik's other bad habit was that he would annoyingly recite and sing several verses that he'd made up, keeping at it until Olav's head began to ache and he had a great desire to clout the child. But he hesitated to lay a hand on the boy ever since he'd beaten him so mercilessly on that day when Ingunn returned from her first church service after giving birth.

In the evening Eirik would kneel in front of the bench and line up his snail shells and animal teeth in rows. Then he would chant:

Four and five of the fifth dozen
four and five of the fifth dozen
fifteen mares and four foals
I received in the day and in the night
four and five of the fifth dozen
horses I owned the next day.

He would then repeat the same verse about cows and calves, sheep and lambs, sows and piglets.

"Hush now," his father told him sharply. "Didn't you hear me say that I want some peace and quiet from all that droning and chanting of yours!"

"I forgot, Father," said Eirik with alarm.

Then Olav asked, "How many horses would you like to have, Eirik? Four and five of the fifth dozen or a hundred horses?"

"Oh, I want many more than that," replied Eirik. "I want . . . twenty-seven!"

That's how little grasp he had of what he was actually singing.

Audun was constantly whining and fussing. Ingunn boasted of her son, claiming he was the loveliest child, and that he'd also been growing stronger of late. But Olav saw the fear festering in her eyes whenever she said such things. Eirik would repeat what he heard his mother say and lean over the cradle, murmuring endearments and reciting his rules for his silken brother, as he continued to call Audun.

Olav felt oddly pained whenever he saw this. Audun seemed to him the most pitiful of creatures. His scalp was always covered in scabs, he had sores in his mouth, and his body was scrawny and tender and failed to thrive. This son of his had never prompted in Olav any sort of paternal joy. The fact that he was the father of this poor, ill, whimpering child seemed to him grievous and bitter when he saw Eirik leaning over the infant in the cradle. The older boy looked so lively and healthy, so handsome with those gleaming nut-brown curls falling toward Audun's wrinkled face as he patted his brother.

One day Olav asked Torhild what she thought of Audun.

"No doubt he'll get better when spring arrives," said Torhild. Yet Olav sensed that she didn't believe her own words.

At Hestviken they had let the livestock out, and in the daytime the animals were sent up to the old moss-covered meadows in Kverndalen. That's when Audun fell gravely ill. He'd had a cough all winter, and he'd suffered frequent bouts of diarrhea, but this turn in his health was worse than any other.

Olav could tell that Ingunn was about to collapse from fatigue and worry, yet she continued to seem oddly calm and composed. She insisted on keeping watch over the child night and day, while every remedy was tried that might help Audun—first those treatments that the servants knew, and then everything suggested by the neighbor women whom Ingunn had summoned.

Finally, on the sixth day, the boy seemed much better. By the time of the evening meal, he was sleeping soundly and securely, and his skin was not as cold to the touch. Torhild placed warm stones next to him in the cradle under the covers. Then she took Eirik by the hand and they left. She had kept watch almost as long as Ingunn, and she also had all the housework to tend to during the day. Right now her energy was spent.

Ingunn was so tired that she could hardly hear or speak. At last Olav persuaded her to rest. He removed her outer garments and made her get into bed. He promised that he would keep vigil along with the maidservant, and he would wake Ingunn if the child grew restless.

Olav got out three tallow candles. He stuck one on a candleholder and lit it. Although he usually had such a hard time falling asleep, tonight he felt sluggish and drowsy. When he stared at the candle flame, his eyes stung and watered. Then he shifted his gaze to the maidservant, who was spinning wool with her drop spindle, but he grew sleepy from watching and listening to the whorl. Occasionally he tended to the fire and the candle, then glanced first at the sleeping child and then at his wife. He drank some cold water or stepped outside for a moment, taking a look at the weather and reviving himself by breathing in the still, cold, spring night. Then he brought in a piece of wood and began whittling. That was how he kept himself awake until he'd set the third candle on the holder.

He jolted up at the sound of the cradle rockers thudding strangely against the dirt floor. The child was making an odd noise. The room was almost pitch-dark. The candle, nearly burned down to a stump, had fallen off the spike holding it in place. The wick flickered and smoldered in the melted wax on the little iron plate. The fire in the hearth were still crackling and smoking faintly from the embers underneath the wood. In two strides, without making a sound, Olav was over at the cradle. He picked up the child and wrapped him tighter in the garments he wore.

The tiny body strained, as if Audun wanted to free himself from the confining clothes. In the dim light Olav thought the boy was looking at him with a peculiar, plaintive expression. The child stretched out full length, then relaxed and went limp. He died in his father's arms.

Olav felt numb, both physically and in his soul, as he set the child's body down and covered it. He knew it was futile to think about when Ingunn awakened and . . .

The maidservant was asleep at the table, her head resting on her arms. Olav woke her and quietly but firmly shushed her when she was about to cry out. He told her to go and tell the house servants what had happened, but no one should come near the house. Ingunn must be allowed to sleep while she could.

He opened the smoke vent. It was daylight outside. But Ingunn slept on and on, and Olav sat with her and their dead son. Later, when he went over to look at his wife, he happened to dislodge her belt, and it fell to the floor with a clatter. Ingunn jolted awake and looked into her husband's face.

She sprang out of bed and shoved Olav aside when he tried to hold her back. She threw herself over the cradle with such force that it looked as if the dead child leaped into her arms.

As she crouched there, rocking the infant's body and sobbing with odd gulping sounds, she suddenly gave a start and looked up at her husband.

"Were you asleep when he died? Were both of you asleep when Audun drew his last breath?"

"No, no, he died in my arms."

"You . . . and you didn't wake me? Dear Lord, how could you not wake me? I'm the one who should have been holding him when he died. I'm the one he knew. Not you. You felt no love for your own child. No, you didn't. And this is how you keep your promise!"

"Ingunn—"

But she jumped up, holding in both hands the dead body high overhead as she screamed. Then she tore open her bodice and pressed the tiny dead boy to her bare skin and threw herself onto the bed so that she was lying on top of him.

A moment later, when Olav went over and tried to talk to Ingunn, she placed her hand on his face and pushed him away.

"Never will I be parted from my Audun ever again!"

Olav didn't know what to do. He sat down on the bench with his head in his hands and waited for her to calm down. Then the door flew open and Eirik rushed over to his mother, sobbing loudly. He'd been told what happened when he awoke.

Ingunn sat up, leaving Audun's body lying on the pillow. She pulled Eirik close, then let him go. She placed her hands on either side of his small, tear-stained face and leaned her own face against his as she wept, though much more quietly now.

On the day when Audun was buried, the weather was so beautiful.

Later in the afternoon Olav slipped away from the guests attending the funeral feast and went down to the rail fence surrounding the farthermost field. The sea gleamed and glittered, until the very air seemed to tremble with it. The low sea swells beneath the Ox shimmered white and fresh. Today a good, full smell emanated from the wharf, a smell that merged with the fine scent of warm earth and soil and new growth. The small waves rolling over the foreshore quietly trickled back out, carrying pebbles with them. Creeks raced and surged in many places, and up from Kverndalen came the rushing sound of the small river. Up there the alder trees were brown with blossoms, and the groves of hazelnut trees on the ridge dripped yellow catkins. It would soon be summer.

Olav could hear Ingunn approaching him from behind. Side by side they stood there, leaning on the fence and staring at the reddish-gray slope lit by the sun and glinting from the blue water.

All of a sudden Olav felt strangely ill and gripped by longing. To be on board a ship, sailing the seas with the horizon line in view in every direction. Or to be back home up north in the country, where the smell of soil and grass and forest billowed from the wide hillsides and mountain ridges, reaching as far inland as anyone knew. Here everything felt so small and cramped, this place on an insignificant inlet of the fjord and on these patches of land lined up along the desolate bay.

Olav said quietly, "Ingunn, do not grieve so for Audun. It was best for God to take home His poor innocent lamb. The child's only inheritance would have been to bear the burden of all our misdeeds."

Ingunn didn't reply. She turned away from him and walked back up to the estate in silence, her head bowed. As she neared the houses, Eirik came rushing to meet her. Olav saw that Ingunn shushed the boy as she took his hand and they continued on together.

XI

During the summer in the year after they'd lost Audun, Olav and Ingunn arrived in time for the midmorning meal at a farmstead in the village where they had offered to lend a hand. They had brought Eirik with them. The boy was now seven winters old, and he could easily become unruly whenever he was playing.

In the evening, after their work was done, everyone sat in the meadow near the house they had just finished thatching. Some of the young people began to dance, and Eirik and the other small boys ran about, shouting boisterously. They were giddy from drinking ale. Then they ran straight for the line of dancers, wanting to break up the chain as they hooted and laughed. They dashed among the older folks, jostling them aside and interrupting the conversations of the men. Olav had admonished Eirik several times, quite sharply at last, but that served to restrain the boy only for a moment.

Ingunn hadn't noticed any of this. She was sitting against the wall a short distance away with some of the other women. Suddenly Olav came over and stood right in front of her. He had Eirik with him. He lifted the boy up by the back of his shirt collar so he dangled from Olav's hand, the way someone might grab a pup by the scruff of the neck. Olav was red-faced and slightly drunk. The ale always seemed to have a greater effect on him than usual when the spells of sleeplessness had gone on for a long time.

"You need to control this boy of yours, Ingunn," Olav said angrily as he gave Eirik a shake. "I can't get him to obey me unless I clout him. Take charge of him now, seeing as he's yours." He tossed the boy so that Eirik practically fell into his mother's lap. And with that Olav left.

◆ ◆ ◆

Later that evening, when everyone had eaten and they were sitting over the ale bowls, someone began recounting stories. Then Sira Hall-bjørn told this tale:

"A rich merchant left home and was gone for three winters. You'll have to judge for yourself whether the man was more surprised than glad when, upon arriving home, he found his wife in bed with a month-old son lying beside her. But this man's wife was a sly and resourceful woman.

"She said, 'A great miracle has happened to me. I was pining terribly for you, my husband, while you were traveling far away. One day this winter I was standing in the doorway, and there were icicles hanging from the eaves. I broke off one of them and sucked on it as I longed for you with great anguish and the most ardent yearning. And then I found myself with child. Judge for yourself whether you and no one else must be his father. I have named him Jøkel, as that's what we call icicles!'

"The merchant had to make do with this explanation. He spoke gently to his wife and seemed exceedingly happy with his son, Jøkel. Whenever he was home, he always kept the boy near. And when Jøkel was twelve years old, his father took him along on one of his expeditions. But one day, when they were in the middle of the sea and Jøkel stood at the rail, the merchant went over to stand behind the boy. And when no one was looking, he pushed him overboard.

"When the man came home to his wife, he told her with a sorrowful expression and tremulous voice, 'A great misfortune has befallen us, and a heavy loss we must bear, my sweet. The boy Jøkul is no more. You see, the boat was becalmed at sea, the day was hot, and the sun was blazing right overhead. Jøkel was bareheaded and standing on deck. We told him most politely to cover his head with something, but he refused. Then he melted in the roasting sun, and there was nothing left of Jøkul, our son, except for a wet spot on the decking!'

"And with that explanation the woman had to be content."

Everyone laughed a great deal at this story. No one noticed that Olav Audunssøn was sitting with his gaze lowered as crimson shadows passed over his face. Even if it were a matter of saving his own life, he didn't think he would have dared to glance at Ingunn, who was sitting on the benches with the other women. A commotion suddenly erupted over there. Olav jumped over the table and pushed his way through the crowd of women. He lifted up his wife, who had fallen senseless off the bench, and carried her out into the fresh air.

What Eirik liked best was being allowed to accompany his father—either in the boat, when Olav set off by himself to fish with handlines, which he did occasionally, though mostly for the sake of amusement, or when Olav headed across the fields. Afterward Eirik would always go to his mother to recount what they'd done, his eyes shining. He was so eager to speak that he would stumble over his words as he reported everything that had happened and everything that his father had taught him. Eirik could now row and fish, tie big knots, and splice lines the way seafaring men did. Soon he'd be allowed to go out on real fishing expeditions with his father and the other men. He'd become quite good at shooting and throwing; his father said that he'd never seen the like.

Ingunn felt both despairing and tormented as she listened to the boy's chatter. This poor, trusting little boy of hers loved Olav more than anyone else on earth. It was as if the man's lack of friendliness made no impression on Eirik, who received only curt replies to his questions and would eventually be told to stop talking. Olav coldly rebuked him whenever the boy grew too lively and wild, and he would harshly demand that Eirik tell the truth, whereas his mother realized that the child had simply wrongly remembered something. But Ingunn didn't dare say as much to her husband, nor did she defend Eirik by reminding Olav that the child was so young. And she couldn't tell Olav, whom Eirik called Father, how dearly the boy loved him. She had to bow her head and keep silent. Only when she was alone with her son did she venture to show her own love for him.

Ingunn didn't know that Eirik's accounts of what his father taught him were true. That was why Olav's bad moods never frightened the boy for any length of time nor lessened his love for his father. Eirik and Olav got along much better when the two of them were on their own. That's when Eirik was more obedient and less restless, and even though he was constantly pestering Olav with strange questions, there was actually some sense to his queries. He devoured every word his father spoke, paying close attention with both his eyes and ears so that he forgot to spout his own songs and tall tales. Without giving it any thought, Olav felt warmed by the love that the child showed toward him. He would forget his displeasure from previous occasions and bathe in the warmth, just as he had always felt warmed whenever anyone treated him with kindness—a kindness that he found it so difficult to seek directly. He met Eirik halfway with calm goodwill. He instructed the boy in the use of weapons and tools that were still mostly playthings, and he managed to smile a little at Eirik's eager questions and talk to him the way a good father speaks to his young son.

They fished for ballan wrasse beneath the cliff north of the Ox, and Olav showed the boy the cleft in the mountain where an old otter had her den. Every year Olav would take away the pups—one year there were two litters—as well as the male. Olav said that as soon as the male was removed, the otter would find a new mate, and then he mimicked the otter's cry. Yes, when Eirik was a little older he would be allowed to go with him one night to get the otters. But when that would be, his father couldn't say.

Once when they went up to the forest to check on some traps where Olav hunted, he began talking about his childhood at Frettastein, back when he and Eirik's mother were young. "Your maternal grandfather," said Olav, and then he had to smile at a few things he recounted about Steinfinn, and Eirik laughed loudly. "One time I tricked Hallvard, your mother's brother, into going with me. He was very little at the time, you see, but I still took the boy along up to the lake where we had a boat we'd made from a log." But then Eirik happened to mention Tora of Berg. He remembered her. Olav fell silent and replied absentmindedly to the rest of the boy's questions. Finally he told Eirik to be still. It seemed as if dark clouds had suddenly descended upon everything.

But when Olav was with his hired men at the wharf or up at the estate, he would quickly grow much more impatient with Eirik if the boy started dashing about. The more people Eirik saw around him, the more boisterous and silly and disobedient he became. The men found the boy entertaining, but they noticed that the master disliked seeing them laugh at Eirik's chatter. They thought Olav was exceedingly short-tempered and stern with his only son.

But it was in Ingunn's presence that Olav felt the most goaded toward an impatient dislike of the boy. Many times Olav had a great urge to thrash Eirik and roughly squelch all his bad habits.

One reason was that Ingunn provoked in Olav a vague bitterness whenever she nagged the child. She would harshly tell Eirik to be quiet and behave in a seemly manner. Yet Olav knew full well that no sooner would he turn his back on the two of them than Ingunn would be on her knees, trying to win over the boy. He noticed how deeply she mistrusted his attitude toward her son. She would surreptitiously watch him whenever he was with Eirik. Olav knew in his heart that he had never caused the boy any real harm. Surely he could be trusted to discipline Eirik if punishment was warranted. Ingunn was the one who spurred Olav's indignation, but it was a lifelong habit of his to restrain himself whenever she was concerned. And over the past few years she had become an ill and joyless soul, and he had to be doubly cautious so as not to make things worse for her. Now, whenever Ingunn tested Olav's patience too severely, Eirik was usually the one to suffer.

The boy had come between husband and wife. He was the first one to seriously divide their hearts. In their youth, Olav had been forced to leave his foster sister behind when he fled the country. And he did have a sense that Ingunn had strayed onto a wrong path because he had left her on her own. Far too many burdens had been heaped on her shoulders when she had to seek refuge with her angry kinsmen, who considered her nothing more than a disobedient woman without honor. She was young and fragile and pampered, yet Olav knew that her nature was not the sort that would allow her to betray a husband with whom she had shared bed and board. He'd had a feeling that Teit was merely an unfortunate chance encounter. Olav's decision to get rid of that trusting fool was more because he thought it would be insurmountably difficult to repair the damage as long as Teit was alive and able to jabber about the truth—not because he had felt cuckolded by the fellow. Yet the murder, once committed, had done little to assuage the pain inside Olav. His desire to seek revenge because of the destroyed happiness had not been satisfied by the poor corpse up in the mountain pasture.

Now Olav saw that Ingunn loved someone else, and he wondered how often she wished her husband out of the way so that she might freely shower all her love on Eirik—the way a person smuggles out provisions to an outlawed friend behind the back of the master on the estate.

Along with this feeling of bitterness and disquiet, something like a phantom of the desires from Olav's youth stirred in his heart and senses. He longed to possess Ingunn the way he'd possessed her in the past, back when they were young and healthy. Back then, in spite of apprehension and worry, they had found joy in each other's arms. Olav had never entirely forgotten that time. The memory of her sweet beauty had caused his pity to burn with a painful tenderness. This poor, faded ruin of a woman to whom he was bound was the wreckage of the lovely, useless Ingunn he had once loved. And his will to protect her became now as fierce and stubborn as his will had once been to defend his right to take her as his wife.

A desire flared inside him to know that she too remembered the passion of their youth. Year after year a concealed loathing had protested in his heart whenever she clung to him, unwell and unreasonable and demanding the caresses that he knew his ill wife ought to be spared. Now, when she avoided him and hid herself away with what was hers, asserting that he could have no part of it, Olav was the one who would have gladly held her tight in his arms if only she would answer his questions: Have you forgotten that I was once your most beloved friend in the world? Why are you frightened of me? Have I ever willingly caused you sorrow in all these years? Surely it's not my fault that we've had so little happiness in our life together.

And then the dread would awaken, whenever he approached that tainted place inside him. Then the dull ache would become a torment that sparked and radiated through his whole being. What if it was true that all along he actually could have fended off the misfortunes that befell her? What if he had dared to surrender, both to the laws of men and to the mercy of God?

Olav noticed that his unaccustomed ardor now made Ingunn frightened and anxious. So he retreated and withdrew into himself, while his secret wound hammered and pounded. Why is she afraid of me? Does she know?

There were times when he almost believed that she did. And that everyone else knew as well. For he had not a single friend in his home district. So be it, he thought. But that was not the only thing. Olav realized that no one even liked him. Coldness and suspicion were directed at him from all sides. He thought he often glimpsed traces of malicious glee whenever misfortune struck him. Yet he couldn't rouse himself to feel indignant; he accepted the judgment without complaint. No doubt folks could see the secret mark on his forehead.

But when he thought of Ingunn, foreboding would tremble inside him. Did she see it too? Was that why she felt so cold in his arms? And was that why she looked frightened whenever he came near her son?

Olav always held an ale feast in the summer on Saint Olav's Day. He never prayed to his guardian saint. The lord of law would certainly not help him with an intercessionary word, except under one condition. Nevertheless, he wanted to honor Saint Olav in a seemly manner.

The floor was strewn with fresh greenery, and the main hall was adorned with tapestries, including the old weaving that was otherwise taken out only at Christmastime.

On the eve of Saint Olav's Day, Olav set about hanging up the lengthy weaving himself. He moved along the benches, fastening the woven tapestry to wooden hooks that he stuck between the uppermost timber and the roof. Eirik followed along on the floor, looking at the embroidered images. There were horsemen and longboats with men on board. He knew that soon the best picture would appear: a house with pillars and a shingled roof like a church, and guests inside with drinking horns and tankards on the table. When Eirik leaned down to take a closer look at the bundle of fabric still lying on the bench, he happened to tear down a long strip of the weaving that his father had just hung up.

Olav jumped down, yanked the boy away from the folds of the tapestry, and flung him across the room.

"Out! You're always getting in my way and making a mess of things, you little wayside bastard!"

At that moment Ingunn appeared in the doorway to the ante-chamber holding flowers that she'd gathered in the raised skirts of her cloak. All the flowers fell to the floor. Olav saw that she'd heard what he said.

He couldn't think of anything to say. Shame, anger, and confusion surged inside him. He stepped up onto the bench and resumed hanging the part of the tapestry that had come down. Eirik had dashed out the door. Ingunn picked up the flowers from the floor and began scattering them about. Olav didn't dare turn around to look at her. Nor could he bring himself to speak.

One morning several days later, Ingunn was sitting with Eirik on the crest of the cliff behind the Hestviken estate. She had been down at Saltviken, taking a path across the heights. It could be traveled on horseback, if need be, though the path was seldom used. Most people traveled by boat between Hestviken and Saltviken.

The sunlight was dazzling and there was a fresh breeze. From where Ingunn sat, she could see the dark blue of the fjord, dotted with white foam. The spray of the waves glittered white along the expanse of red-gray rock that jutted its feet out into the water along the shore-line. The morning sun still hovered over Hudrheim. From up here on the crest where she sat, she could see a little of the village on the slope. That was why she liked this spot. Up here the impatient roar of the sea was fainter and more distant. Back home on the estate the sound tormented her so much that it seemed to be coming from inside her own weary and dazed head. And there was always a taste of salt as well as a flickering of light from the sea in the restless air. It was not something that would ever cause her to flourish. It wore her out.

Eirik was reclining in his mother's arms, playing with a cluster of big bluebells. One by one he tore off the blossoms, twisted them around, and then blew inside them. Ingunn placed her thin hand on his cheek and looked down into his sunburned face. How handsome, how very handsome he was, this son of hers. His eyes looked a bit like marsh water when the sun shines on it, his hair was as fine as silk. It had darkened a good deal in the past year; his hair was now brown. Eirik scratched his head.

"Pick the lice off me, Mother. Ugh, they're biting so much in this heat!"

Ingunn laughed. She took her comb out of the pouch hanging from her belt and started cleaning the boy's head with slow, loving strokes. Eirik began to feel drowsy. Ingunn was lulled by the scent of the pine forest in the baking sun, the acrid smell of the haircap-moss on which she rested, and the ringing of bells from the cattle wandering farther along the slope above Kverndalen.

Then she jumped at a sudden sound. A dog came wading through the tall blueberry thicket. It sniffed at both of them, tumbled over their knees without making a sound, and then set off along the path again, heading down.

Ingunn's heart was still trembling from being awakened so abruptly. Now she heard horses' hooves clattering on the rock far below. Her head fell back against the trunk of the pine tree she was sitting under. Oh, why was he already on his way home? She had been so certain that he wouldn't be back until late in the evening, maybe not even until the next day.

She was instantly overwhelmed again by swarming terrors and anguish. What she had feared during the past month . . . She could feel that she had no more strength for it; this time it would be the death of her. And that was something she might almost welcome, if not for Eirik, because then he would be left alone with Olav. And in the midst of her agony a slight concern arose: Why was Olav already home? Hadn't he been able to complete his business in the neighboring village? Or had he quarreled with those folks? Maybe he was arriving home even more bad-tempered and taciturn than he was when he left.

Instinctively Ingunn had wrapped her arm around her child, as if she wanted to protect and hide him. Eirik resisted and broke free.

"Let me go. Father is coming." He stood up, and as he walked ahead of her along the path, his gait a bit uncertain and hesitant, Ingunn saw that his face had turned red. She followed.

She glimpsed the white horse between the trees. Olav was walking at the animal's side. When Ingunn caught up with the father and son, Olav was showing Eirik something that lay at his feet on the ground. A big lynx.

"I ran into this animal over on the mountain to the south," said Olav. "She was out early in the morning. She had kittens in the den; her teats are full of milk." With his spear Olav turned over the dead lynx. He shushed the barking dog that lay flat with its paws extended, as he held the bridle of the agitated horse. Eirik cheered with delight and squatted down to look at his father's bounty. Olav smiled at the boy. "We didn't find her den, even though it probably wasn't far away. But it was a scree slope covered by toppled trees. I suppose her foot-path must have been up in the trees."

"Will her young starve to death now?" asked Ingunn. Eirik pressed his hand against the light-colored fur under the lynx's belly, found the swollen teats, and squeezed them. The boy's hands were covered in blood. Olav was telling him that it had been easy enough to kill the lynx because she had wandered out into the light.

"Starve to death? Yes, or else they'll eat each other in the den. The strongest ones will survive. But they were born quite early in the summer. They must have been, since their mother had wandered away from them."

Ingunn looked down at the dead mother. Her kittens must have nestled together, soft and warm, snuffling for the milk sources in the light-colored pelt under her supple belly. The heavy thigh that the lynx had placed protectively over them was taut with muscles and sinews; her claws were like steel. When she licked her kittens, cruel white fangs must have been visible. The tufts of hair in her ears were there to make her even more vigilant and alert; the black pupils in her yellow eyes were like sharp slashes. She had been skilled at protecting and defending and disciplining her offspring.

And her own son? His mother was such a wretch that she couldn't protect her child. She was to blame for how things now stood, so that he had no one to protect him. And what he needed most was protection from the man he called Father.

"I can't believe that even Mary, the mother of God, would ask for mercy for a mother who forsakes her own son." That's what her sister Tora had said. Yet Ingunn had already forsaken her child when she allowed him to be conceived. She realized that now.

Olav and Eirik used clumps of moss to wipe off the blood that had dripped on the saddle and run down the side of the white horse. Olav then helped the boy into the saddle and placed the reins in his hand.

"Apalhviten is so steady that I'm sure Eirik can manage to ride him home, even though the slope is a bit steep from here." Olav followed a few paces behind, offering reassuring words to the boy and the horse. Then he turned back to the lynx and began binding the animal's limbs with several straps. Every so often he would glance up to check on the boy riding the big white horse, until they disappeared into the forest.

"No, we couldn't come to an agreement. It was futile to stay there and quarrel with those Kaaressøns," Olav was saying. "I think Eirik should have Apalhviten. The boy is seven winters old now, isn't he? He should soon have his own horse. And it would be unwise to let the child ride Sindre, as skittish as that horse is.

"Why are you crying?" he then said a bit sharply as he stood up from tending to the lynx.

"What would it matter, Olav, if you gave Eirik the fairest of foals ever bred, along with a silver saddle and a golden bridle, when you're unable to change how you feel? You can never look at the boy without resentment."

"That's not true," Olav angrily retorted.

"Heavy you are, you sow of the Devil," he muttered as he raised the lynx on his spear and lowered the weight onto his shoulders. "Be sensible, Ingunn," he then said, a bit more gently. "Will I ever have any joy of this son who will take my place on the estate when I'm gone if he is constantly made to hide under your skirts, especially now that he's old enough to need the guidance and discipline of his father? It's time for you to allow me to take charge of Eirik, or else we will never make a man of him."

Olav's big gray cloak flapped in the wind blowing on the crest, and the sides of his black woolen hat brim fluttered. He had aged a great deal over the past few years. Stout he was not, but his body had grown much huskier, both rounder and broader across the shoulders. And his light-colored eyes seemed smaller yet more piercing because his face was now brownish and weather-beaten. The whites of his eyes were bloodshot, no doubt because he slept too little.

Olav could feel that Ingunn was staring at him, and he finally had to turn his head. He met her aggrieved expression with an obstinate look in his eyes.

"I know what you're thinking, Ingunn. I uttered those words in anger. God knows I wish they were never said."

Ingunn ducked as if expecting to be struck. Olav went on, trying hard to remain calm.

"But you mustn't keep doing this, Ingunn. Stealing him away from me as if you fear that I would . . . Never have I punished Eirik with unreasonable harshness."

"I don't remember my father ever laying a hand on you, Olav."

"No, Steinfinn never bothered to take enough trouble for my sake that he would punish me. But I have never gone back on my word— not my word to you, Ingunn, no matter what happened. And now I've made it known to everyone that Eirik is our son, yours and mine."

Olav could see that Ingunn was nearly faint with fatigue. But it seemed to him that this time he could not give in. He was not about to find other words that would erase everything he'd said. And so he went on.

"You're doing all of us the greatest harm when you sneak off to the woods with your motherly love, never daring to take Eirik on your lap when I might see you. Keeping to the shadows and hiding away with the boy as if you were sneaking out to meet with a lover."

Olav took her hand and squeezed it tight without letting go.

"Keep that in mind, my dear. Treating Eirik in this manner is the worst thing you could do for the boy."

◆ ◆ ◆

Early in the day on the eve of the Feast of Saint Matthew, Eirik came rushing into the main hall where his parents were sitting. He was screaming at the top of his lungs. Right behind him came Kaare and Rannveig, Bjørn's two children who still lived with Torhild. Olav and Ingunn then heard what had happened.

The stoat that lived in the sod on the roof of the sheep shed had a new litter of kits. Eirik had tried to dig out the nest, even though Olav had told him they were to be left alone this summer. The stoat had bitten Eirik on the hand.

Olav grabbed the boy, picked him up, and set him on Ingunn's lap. Then he reached for Eirik's hand and hastily examined it. The bite was on his little finger.

"Can you hold him?" Olav asked Ingunn. "Or should I get Torhild? Quiet now, don't say a word to Eirik. We can save him if we act quickly."

The bite of a stoat was the most poisonous of any animal. If someone was bitten by an angered stoat, his skin would rot and fall off his bones until he died. Or else he would suffer convulsive seizures, for all stoats had the seizure disease. Only if the bite was on the very tip of a finger was it possible to save the person's life by cutting off the finger and cauterizing the wound.

Swift as lightning, Olav set about making everything ready. Among the small tools stored in a crack in the wall he found a suitable iron rod that he stuck in the fire while he told Kaare Bjørnssøn to blow on the flames. Then he took out his dagger and began sharpening it.

But the maidservant who had been summoned to hold Eirik started shrieking. Eirik was already frightened, and now he realized what his father was about to do to him. With a wail of the utmost terror, he pulled free from his mother and dashed about like a rat from one wall to the other, howling louder and louder, with Olav running after him.

The ladder to the loft above the alcove stood in place. Eirik raced up the ladder, and Olav followed. In the dark, among all the heaps of stored belongings, Olav finally caught the boy and carried him back down the ladder. Eirik kicked and flailed and bawled from under the skirt of his father's cotehardie, which Olav had been forced to throw over the child's head to prevent the terrified boy from biting him.

A quick glance at Ingunn told Olav that he couldn't expect any help from her. Torhild had now come in, so he handed Eirik to her, and the two older women servants stepped forward to assist. Eirik fought hard, screaming in mortal fear as they struggled to wrap a cloth around his head.

Then his father tore the cloth from his eyes.

"It's a matter of life or death, Eirik. Look at me, boy. You will die if you don't let me save you."

Olav's soul was in a desperate uproar. Eirik was Ingunn's last remaining child. She loved him in a way that she had never loved her husband, and if she lost him, that would no doubt be the end of everything. He had to save the boy; he had to do it, even at the cost of his own life! At the same time he felt a cruel desire and longing to finally strike a blow against this flesh that had come between him and her, to injure and burn. Yet something seemed to rise inside him from the very depths of his being, refusing to allow him to harm this defenseless child.

"Stop screaming like that," Olav snapped furiously. "You poor wretch, you pup, don't be so frightened, it's no worse than . . . Here, look at this!"

He slipped the tip of his dagger under the hem of his sleeve at his left wrist, then tore and ripped at the fabric until the sleeve of both his cotehardie and shirt hung in tatters all the way up to his shoulder. Quickly he rolled the shreds up so they wouldn't be in the way. Then he picked up the glowing iron rod with a tongs and pressed it against his upper arm.

Eirik had fallen silent out of both fear and surprise as he watched what his father was doing. He lay limply in the women's arms and stared. But now he again began howling with terror. Olav had vaguely hoped to instill courage in the boy, but all he'd managed to do was frighten the very wits out of Eirik. The smell of the scorched flesh, the sight of the spasm that passed over Olav's face when he pulled the iron away from the burning wound—all this drove the boy out of his mind. A streak of blood ran down the white flesh of Olav's arm when he lowered his hand. The dagger had cut his skin when he ripped up the sleeve.

All of a sudden Ingunn came forward. Her face was pale, but otherwise she was very calm. She took the child onto her lap and clamped his legs between her knees. Then she flung a corner of her wimple around his face and tucked his head under her arm. With her other hand she grabbed his wrist and held his little hand against the table. The maidservants helped hold the boy and stifled his awful cries of pain with more cloths as Olav cut off the injured finger at its base and then cauterized the wound before bandaging it. He did all of this more swiftly and expertly than he'd ever imagined was possible for him to practice doctoring.

While the women tended to the howling child, putting him to bed and offering him fortifying drink, Olav sat on the bench. Only now did he notice the pain in the burn on his arm. He was both ashamed and furious with himself for behaving so foolishly, mistreating himself so unnecessarily, like a madman.

Torhild came over to him, bringing a cup of egg whites and a container of puffball mushrooms. She was about to tend to his arm, when Ingunn took what Torhild was holding and pushed her aside.

"I can take care of my husband, Torhild. Go out and find some grass to wipe the blood off the table."

Olav stood up and shook himself as if wanting to be rid of both women.

"Leave me be. I can take care of the wound myself," he said with annoyance. "But find me some other clothes to replace these torn garments."

Eirik recovered rapidly. A week later he was sitting up and eating with good appetite the favorite foods that his mother brought to him. It looked as if the effects of the stoat bite would be no worse than the loss of his little finger on his right hand.

From the very start Olav refused to acknowledge that the burn on his arm bothered him; he tried to work and use his arm as if nothing had happened. But infection set in, and he had to bind up his arm.

Then he developed a fever, headache, and frequent vomiting. Finally he had to take to his bed and allow a man with doctoring skills to see to his arm. This went on well into Advent, and Olav was in the worst of moods. For the first time since their marriage, he was unkind toward Ingunn, often speaking to her in a harsh tone of voice. And he wouldn't stand for anyone even mentioning how the injury had occurred. The servants could also tell that Olav was not the least bit happy about the fact that Ingunn was once again with child.

When Eirik was well enough to be on his feet again, he doggedly and incessantly talked about his misfortune. He was inexpressibly proud of his maimed hand. On the first Sunday that the folks from Hestviken attended mass, he stood outside on the church hill and showed his hand to anyone willing to look at it. He was terribly boastful, both about his father's action, which he considered a great deed, and about his own stoic conduct. If Eirik was to be believed, he hadn't uttered a sound during this test of his manhood.

"I think that boy takes after the Devil himself, the way he lies," said Olav. "Things are bound to go badly for you, Eirik, if you don't rid yourself of such a vile habit."

XII

Around the time of Saint Blasius's Day in February, a guest
arrived at Hestviken who no one there had ever imagined they'd see.[22]
Arnvid Finnssøn came to the estate. Olav wasn't at home that day, and
the servants didn't expect him back until after the feast day.

Olav looked happy on the evening when he came into the main
hall in the company of his friend. Arnvid had gone out to meet him.
Olav accepted the ale bowl that Ingunn brought and raised a toast to
Arnvid, giving him a hearty welcome. But then he noticed that Ingunn
had been crying.

Arnvid said that he'd brought her some sorrowful news. Tora of
Berg had died in the autumn. When Olav heard that Arnvid had already been at Hestviken for several days, he was a little surprised. Had
Ingunn been weeping for her sister all this time? The two had never
been especially close, yet Tora was her only sister, after all. And right
now Ingunn had a tendency to weep easily.

Ingunn said good night as soon as they had finished the evening
meal. She took Eirik with her and left the hall. She said they would
sleep in the small women's house that night, "for the two of you will
no doubt want to share a bed. It seems to me you will have much to
talk about."

Again Olav was surprised. Was there something in particular that
his wife thought he and Arnvid would want to discuss, just the two of
them in private? Otherwise she could just as well have retired to the
bed in the alcove.

The conversation proceeded somewhat sluggishly as the two men
sat at the table drinking. Arnvid talked about Tora's children. It was a
shame that all of them were still underage. Olav asked his friend about
his own sons. Arnvid said they brought him much joy. Magnus now

had charge of Miklebø. He was married, and Steinar was betrothed. Finn was a monk at the Dominican monastery in Hamar. He was said to have good abilities, and next year the brothers wanted to send him to Paris, to the esteemed school there.

"You never chose to remarry?" asked Olav.

Arnvid shook his head. He fixed his strange, dark eyes on Olav and gave him a faint, shy smile the way a youth does when mentioning his dearest friend.

"I too plan to join the brothers as soon as we have celebrated Steinar's wedding."

"I see you haven't changed your mind either," said Olav with a little smile.

"Either?" Arnvid involuntarily repeated.

"And then both father and son will live at the monastery together?"

"Yes." Arnvid chuckled. "God willing, our roles may end up reversed so that I will have to obey my boy and call him Father."

They sat in silence for a while. Then Arnvid went on.

"It is on monastery business that Brother Vegard and I have come south. We wish to rebuild our church out of stone after the fire, but Bishop Torstein has need of his own workmen this year. So we thought we'd see if we could hire stone masons in Oslo. But Brother Vegard said it would be well if you could come into town, and preferably bring Ingunn along. Then he could see both of you."

"Ingunn hasn't the strength to travel anywhere. You can see that for yourself. And surely Brother Vegard must be exceedingly old by now?"

"I suppose so. Three score and ten, I think. He has become a sacristan. But I'm to tell you that you must come. There is something that he wishes most urgently to say to you." Arnvid lowered his eyes and added with some discomfort, "Something about your axe, the horned axe called Ættarfylgja. He has learned a great deal about it. That axe is supposedly the same one that was once at Dyfrin in Raumarike, during the time your ancestors lived there."

"Yes, I know that," said Olav.

"Well, Brother Vegard says that he heard an entire story about that axe of yours. In the past, it was said that the axe sang before a killing."

Olav nodded. "I heard it once myself," he said quietly. "On the day I stood in the cloister guesthouse, making ready to travel north. That was the last time I visited you at Miklebø, you know."

Arnvid paused for a moment before speaking. Then he said in a low voice, "You told me that you lost your axe during the journey."

"I'm not such a fool that I would set off through the forest with that mighty devil of an axe." Olav uttered a brief, cold laugh. "I took with me a small axe for chopping wood. That was good enough for me. But truth be told, I did hear *Ættarfylgja* ring. No doubt the axe would have liked to go with me."

Arnvid crossed his arms and propped them on the table in front of him. He didn't say a word.

Olav had stood up and was restlessly pacing around the room. Suddenly he stopped. In a loud voice and sounding defiant, he asked, "Did no one ever wonder . . . Was there no gossip after that man, Teit Hallssøn, disappeared from Hamar so abruptly?"

"Oh . . . Yes, there was some talk about the matter. But folks came to the conclusion that he must have feared the Steinfinnssøns."

"What about you? Did you never wonder what happened to him?"

Arnvid quietly replied, "It's not easy for me to answer that question, Olav."

"I'm not afraid to hear what you thought."

"Why do you wish me to speak of this matter?" Arnvid reluctantly whispered.

Olav was silent for a long while. When he spoke again, it was as if he were weighing every word. He didn't look at his friend as he said, "I'm sure Ingunn must have told you how things have gone for us. I've been thinking it was because God wanted me to pay the boy restitution for the killing of his father, that man I sent north and to Hell. That vagabond." Olav laughed. "Fool that he was, he had decided that he wanted to marry Ingunn, and 'provide for her and the child,' as he said. I *had* to get rid of him. You must realize that."

"I realize it's what you thought you had to do," replied Arnvid.

"Well, he struck first. It wasn't as if I tricked the fellow into an ambush. He came to me, forced his way into my presence, and wanted me to help him, the way a man would pay to marry off his paramour when he no longer wanted her."

Arnvid said not a word.

Olav went on, indignantly, "That's what he said, a man like him! He said that about Ingunn!"

Arnvid nodded. For a moment neither of them spoke. Then Arnvid said hesitantly, "They found the bones of a man among the charred timbers when they went up to the pastures in the spring—my leaseholders at Sandvold, in those mountain pastures on the slopes of Luraasen. I suppose that was him?"

"Satan! That was *your* hut? Maybe that's just as well—then I can pay you restitution."

"No, Olav! Stop!" Arnvid leaped to his feet, his face aghast. "What is your purpose in talking about all of this? What good will it do? It was so many years ago—"

"That it was, Arnvid. And I've thought about it every single day. But never have I said a word about what happened, not to a soul until tonight, to you. Was he given a Christian burial?"

"Yes."

"At least that's one thing that need not trouble me anymore. Thinking about . . . During all these years I've worried that he might still be lying up there. So that was one sin I didn't commit, allowing a Christian body to remain unburied. Did no one ever ask or try to find out who that person might be?"

"No."

"That seems to me quite strange."

"It's not so strange. The folks who live up there gladly do as I say, whenever I occasionally let them know of something I want."

"But you shouldn't have done that!" Olav clenched his fists. "It would have been better for me if the whole story had come out—if you hadn't helped me carry out my decision to hush up the matter. How could you lend your hand to do such a thing—you who are a God-fearing man!"

Arnvid suddenly began laughing so hard that he had to sit back down on the bench.

Olav flinched at his friend's abrupt outburst. Infuriated, he said, "There's that ugly habit of yours again. You start howling with laughter just when someone begins talking about . . . other things. You'll have to give that up when you become a monk!"

"I suppose you're right." Arnvid wiped his eyes on his sleeve.

Terribly agitated, Olav said, "You have never had to live in enmity with Christ, to stand before Him as a liar and a traitor every time you enter the Lord's house. But I have. Every day for . . . it will soon be eight years. Around here, folks think of me as a pious man, for I give as much as I can to the church and to the monastery in Oslo, as well as to the poor. I attend mass as often as possible, and two or three times a day whenever I'm in town. It's said that a person should put all his heart and soul into loving the Lord. And I do. It seems to me that God must know that. I didn't realize that it was within a man's power to feel such love until, through my own deeds, I broke with the Lord and lost Him!"

"Why are you telling me this?" asked Arnvid in anguish. "You'd do better to talk to your priest about such matters!"

"I can't do that. I've never confessed to killing Teit."

When Arnvid didn't speak, Olav said vehemently, "Say something! Can't you give me some advice?"

"It's a great burden that you're now placing on my shoulders. The only advice I can give you is what the priest would say. I can't tell you anything different than what you already know."

After a moment, when Olav remained standing there in silence, Arnvid added, "And that's not the sort of advice you want to hear."

"I can't." Olav's face turned stony and pale. "I have to think more of Ingunn than of myself. I can't condemn her to being left behind, all alone and poor, with neither good health nor joy, the widow of a murderer and a coward."

Arnvid replied somewhat tentatively, "I don't think it's certain that . . . It seems to me that the bishop might find a way out, seeing as it happened so many years ago . . . and since no blameless man was ever accused of the deed . . . and the dead man had sinned against you so grievously, and the two of you fought. Perhaps the bishop can find some way for you to reconcile with Christ, and give you absolution without demanding that you also admit to the murder in a court of law."

"Do you think that seems at all likely?"

"I don't know," replied Arnvid quietly.

"I can't risk it. There is too much at stake for those who have been placed in my care. Then I might as well not have done what I did to protect her honor. Don't you think I understood that if I'd made it known back then that the man had died at my hand, it would have been considered an act of little consequence? He was of no importance, whether alive or dead, and if you and the rest of my kinsmen had stood by me and testified that she was mine, the woman he had seduced . . . But Ingunn could not have endured it. She has always had so little strength. And if I made it known now, everyone around here would learn this about her, at a time when she is so worn out that . . ."

Arnvid waited a few moments before replying.

"I wonder," he said quietly, "whether she can better endure the alternative. If things go as they have all the other times, and she loses this child as well."

A tremor passed over Olav's face.

"No matter what," Arnvid continued, "she won't be able to endure this course many more times."

"Don't say that," whispered Olav.

"And then there's Eirik," Olav went on after a pause. "I promised God that I would treat Eirik as my own son."

"Do you think it does any good," said Arnvid, "to offer God this or that, promising Him all that He has never demanded of you, when you withhold from Him the one thing that you know He would entreat you to give?"

"The one thing? But that is *everything*, Arnvid. Honor. Life itself, perhaps. God knows that I'm not afraid of losing my life, but to lose it as a criminal—"

"Yet all that you possess was given to you by God. And He chose to share the death of criminals, in order to atone for all our sins."

Olav closed his eyes.

"I still can't," he said, his words nearly inaudible.

Arnvid spoke again. "You mentioned Eirik. Don't you realize, Olav, that you can't rightfully do that? You can't pledge to push aside an heir, for that would mean betraying your kinsmen."

Olav frowned angrily. "Those men of Tveit? Never have I seen them, nor did they deal with me as kinsmen should when I was young and had great need for them to step forward on my behalf."

"They did step forward after you fled to Sweden."

"But they might as well have stayed where they were, considering how little use they were to me. I would rather her son should have Hestviken."

"That will not make an injustice right, Olav. And neither you nor Ingunn can know whether it will bring good fortune to the boy if you pass on to him a gift that he is not entitled to receive."

"Ah, I see now. She must have spoken to you of what she has come to believe, that I hate her child and wish him ill. That's not true," Olav said forcefully. "As far as Eirik is concerned, I've never wanted anything but what is best for him. She's the one who has been corrupting him, teaching him to fear me, telling lies, and sneaking around me."

He noticed the expression on Arnvid's face and shook his head. "No, no, I'm not blaming her for that. Ingunn doesn't know any better, the poor thing. I haven't changed my mind, either, Arnvid. Do you remember that I once promised you that I would never betray your kinswoman? And I've never regretted making that pledge. Whatever the nature of my last hour may be, I will thank God for holding my hand when Ingunn was the one I was tempted to harm, and for revealing to me before it was too late that I was meant to protect and support her the best that I could. If I had returned to find her afflicted with leprosy, I still couldn't have helped remembering that she was my dearest friend, the only friend I had during all those years when I was a child and raised as a foster son among strangers."

Arnvid calmly said, "Olav, if you think it would be easier for you to judge what you should do to regain God's blessing if you did not have to worry about your family, then I promise to act as a brother for Ingunn, to care for both her and the boy. I will take them in, if need be."

"But you've given the Mikleb⊘ estate to Magnus. And now you've decided to enter the monastery." Olav spoke with a certain disdain.

"That doesn't mean I've sold off all my property. And I've managed to endure life in the world this long, so I suppose I can endure it to my dying day, if I have to. If my close kinsmen have need of me."

"Oh no," said Olav, again sounding scornful. "I refuse to allow you to think of such things for my sake, or for the sake of others, when I'm the one closest to them and charged with their care."

Arnvid sat there, staring at the dying embers in the hearth. He was aware of his friend standing in the semidarkness. I wonder whether he has any idea, thought Arnvid, that what he has placed on my shoulders tonight is no less of a burden.

With his foot, Olav pushed a stool over to the hearth and sat down. Then he turned to look at his friend.

"I've told you so many things now, but this is not what I'd intended to say. I told you that I yearn, day and night, to become reconciled with Christ, our God. I told you that Our Lord never seemed to me to be as loving—beyond all measure and in all ways—as when I felt that He had branded me with the mark of Cain. Yet it surprises me that I feel such a longing, for I have never seen Him treat other men as harshly as He has treated me. I have committed only one misdeed, and at the time I was so . . . incensed . . . that I can't even remember everything I was thinking. But it was because I judged that things would be worse for Ingunn if I didn't do it. By committing murder I would be protecting what remained of her virtue. And it ended up being so easy for me, as if it were fated to happen. Teit begged to travel with me, but no one saw us leave together. If God or my guardian spirit or the Virgin Mary had guided us to an inhabited farmstead that evening and not to those desolate mountain pastures below the slopes of Luraasen . . . Then you must know that things would have happened differently."

"Surely you didn't pray to God and the saints to advise you which road to take before you set off to . . . ?"

"I'm not entirely sure about that. But no, I can't say that I prayed at that moment. Yet during Easter I had done nothing but pray. And the whole time I felt such an aversion to killing him. But then it seemed as if everything arranged itself so that I was forced to commit the deed. And afterward I was persuaded to hide my action. And God, who knows all, must have known better than I where everything was headed. Why couldn't He have stopped me, even if I didn't pray for Him to do so?"

"That's what we all say, Olav, whenever we exert our will and then see afterward that it would have been better if we hadn't. But beforehand, I suppose that you, just like the rest of us, always think that you're the best judge of what would be of most benefit to you."

"I suppose so. Yet except for my actions following that misdeed, I have dealt with every man fairly and to the best of my ability. I do not have any goods in my possession that were obtained unlawfully, as far as I know. Nor have I passed on malicious rumors about man or woman; instead, I have allowed such gossip to cease when it came to my door, even if I knew the words to be true and not lies. I have been faithful to my wife. And there is no truth to what she believes, that I do not wish the boy well. I have treated Eirik as well as most men treat their own sons. So tell me, Arnvid, you who understand such matters better than I do . . . You have been a pious man all your days and displayed mercy toward all. Am I not right when I say that God has been harsher toward me than toward other men? And I've seen more of the world than you have."

Arnvid was sitting in a position so that Olav couldn't see him smile at these words.

"Especially in those years when I was an outlaw, living with my maternal uncle and later, when I was the earl's retainer. I've seen men who committed all of the seven deadly sins, carrying out cruel deeds that I myself would never do, even if I were certain that God had already cast me aside and condemned me to Hell. Those men were not afraid of God, nor did I ever notice that they thought about Him with love or felt a longing to meet Him. Yet their lives were happy and content, and many of them died a good death. I've seen that for myself.

"Why then shouldn't we be given some peace and joy, Ingunn and I? It's as if God were always following me, wherever I am, wherever I go, granting me neither calm nor peace. Instead, He demands impossible things from me, things that I've never seen Him demand of other men."

"How could I, being a layman, possibly reply to such questions?" said Arnvid. "Olav, can't you go back into town with me and speak to Brother Vegard about these matters?"

"Perhaps I will," said Olav in a low voice. "But first you must tell me this: Do you understand why things should be so much harder for me than for other men?"

"I don't suppose even you can know everything about those other men you mention. But surely you must realize that when you feel that God is following you, it's because He doesn't want to lose you."

"But He has made matters such for me that I can't turn back."

"Do you really believe that God is the one who has made matters such for you?"

"Yes. And I'm not to blame. It seems to me that I had to do what I did. Ingunn's life and well-being had been placed in my hands. But the beginning of all this, Arnvid, was when the Steinfinnssøns wanted to rob me of the marriage that had been promised to my father. Should I have found this acceptable and yielded to such conduct? Never have I heard otherwise than that God demands every Christian man should fight against injustice and the breach of laws. I knew of no other way to defend my right than to take my bride before they could give her to someone else."

Arnvid said with some effort, "That was what you told me when I . . . spoke to you about your conduct toward my kinswoman. But do you remember, Olav, that back then you didn't tell me the truth?"

Overwhelmed, Olav raised his head abruptly. He paused for a moment before replying. "No, I didn't. But I think," he said calmly, "that most men would have done the same if they stood in my shoes."

"No doubt they would have."

"Are you saying that God's hand has grasped me so tightly," Olav now said scornfully, "and Ingunn as well, because back then I lied—to you?"

"That's not something I can know."

Olav involuntarily tossed his head.

"I can't believe that was so great a sin. I've heard many men tell much worse lies, and needlessly so. But I've never seen God lift a finger to punish them. So I don't understand how it can be called just, the way He has dealt with me so harshly."

Arnvid whispered, "You must have quite a paltry perception of God if you expect His justice to be the same as man's. Not a single one of us children of Eve did He ever create the same. Why then should He demand the same conduct from all of His creations, to whom He has distributed such unequal gifts? When I first met you, back in our youth, I judged you to be the most truthful, just, and noble person. Cruelty and deceit were not in your nature. To you, God had granted the gift of loyal and respected ancestors."

Olav stood up, greatly agitated.

"It seems to me, if that were so . . . If it's as you say—and it's true that I've often restrained myself from doing such things that other men do every day, without remorse, for the sake of matters of lesser importance . . . It seems to me, that what you call God's gifts might as well be called an intolerable burden that He placed on me when He created me!"

Now Arnvid sprang to his feet. He went over to stand in front of Olav and said, almost menacingly, "Many a man might say the same about the character and disposition he has been given. Unless his faith in his Savior is as solid as a mountain, he will claim he was born to be the most wretched of men."

Arnvid then set his foot on the edge of the hearth and rested one hand on his knee as he leaned forward and stared at the embers.

"You often wondered why I longed to turn my back on the world—someone like me who has an abundance of wealth and more power than I have ever wanted to use, along with some measure of esteem. You say that I have been pious and shown mercy toward all. God knows whether you judge this to be so because I *love* my fellow Christians!"

"I thought you helped every man who sought your aid because

you were . . . kindhearted . . . and felt compassion for anyone who was in . . . difficulty."

"Compassion . . . Ah yes. Many times I've been tempted to take my Creator to task because He made me such that I found it impossible to do anything else. I had to take pity on everyone, even though I might not be fond of some."

"I thought," said Olav very quietly, "that you . . . supported me and Ingunn in both word and deed because you were our friend. Was it just for the sake of God that you held your hand over us?"

Arnvid shook his head.

"No, it wasn't. I've been fond of you since we were youths, and my affection for Ingunn began when she was a child. Yet there have been many times when I was desperately tired of all this. And suddenly I would wish more than anything that I might be left out of these efforts of yours."

"You could have told me," said Olav stiffly. "Then I would not have bothered you so much."

Again Arnvid shook his head.

"No, no. You and Ingunn have been my best friends. But I am neither pious nor good. And I often tire of everything. I wished that I could change the way that I am and become a harsh man when I failed to be kind. I wanted to let God judge people instead of doing so myself. There was once a holy man in France, a hermit. On behalf of God, he had taken on the loving deed of offering shelter to folks who traveled through the forest where he lived. One evening a beggar appeared and asked to take lodging with the hermit. Julian was his name, I think. The stranger was covered with leprous sores; he was ravaged by the disease and had a vile and vulgar way of speaking. He did nothing but complain about the kindness the hermit showed toward him. Then Julian helped the beggar undress. He washed and tended to the man's sores and kissed each one of them before putting the man to bed. But the beggar claimed that he was freezing and ordered Julian to warm him by lying down at his side. Julian did as the man said. Then everything that was unclean and hideous and coarse-sounding slid right off the stranger as if fastened to an invisible cloak. And Julian saw that it was Christ himself he held in his arms.

"But with me, things have been such that whenever I thought I didn't have the strength for all those people who came to me—telling me their lies and dumping their worries on my shoulders, demanding my advice and then doing as they pleased but blaming me when things went wrong; greedy and hateful toward one another, and claiming that I had helped everyone else—then it seemed to me that they must be disguised, and under the disguise I too would someday find my Savior and Friend. And I suppose that's what did happen, in a way, for He said that everything you do toward one of my little ones . . . Yet never did He throw off the invisible cloak and appear before me in any of those people."

Olav had again sat down on the stool. He was hiding his face in his arms. Arnvid said even more quietly, "Do you remember, Olav, what Einar Kolbeinssøn said that evening—his remarks that offended me so badly that I set upon him with my spear?"

Olav nodded.

"You were so young back then," Arnvid went on. "I didn't know whether you understood."

"I understood later."

"And since then . . . Have you heard the rumors about me and Ingunn?"

"Hallvard said something about that . . . when I went north to bring back the boy."

Arnvid took several deep breaths.

"I'm not so saintly that I didn't feel a stab to the heart, from both the insult and the gossip. And I often thought that God might grant me the one thing I had asked for: permission to serve Him under such conditions and wearing such garments, that I dared to show compassion as best I could without having folks whispering behind my back and besmirching my honor or calling me foolishly compliant. Or believing the worst of me because I took neither a wife nor a paramour after Tordis died."

Arnvid gestured with his clenched fist, then slammed it into the palm of his other hand.

"I often had the greatest urge to take my axe and mow down the whole lot of them."

Arnvid remained at Hestviken for two more days, but he and Olav were both taciturn and withdrawn in each other's company. They were embarrassed at having said too much on that evening. Now they felt as if they couldn't speak freely about even the simplest and most minor of matters.

Olav rode with Arnvid for part of the way north along the fjord, but when they reached the halfway point to town, he said he needed to turn back. He took out something he had hidden in the folds of his cotehardie—a hard object wrapped in a linen cloth. Arnvid realized it must be the footed silver goblet that Olav had shown him the other day. Olav now said that he wanted to give it to the monastery in Hamar.

"But this is such a costly gift. You should put it into Brother Vegard's hands yourself," Arnvid told him.

Olav replied that he needed to return home that evening. "But I might well come to Oslo to see him later."

Arnvid said, "Surely you must know, Olav, that it's futile to use gifts to buy reconciliation for yourself as long as you continue to live as you now do."

"Yes, I know. That's not the reason. I felt a desire to give something to your church. I spent many a pleasant hour in the cloister's old Saint Olav Church."

Then they bid each other goodbye and went their separate ways.

Olav didn't go to Oslo. Arnvid spoke to Brother Vegard, saying that no doubt Olav was unwilling to make the journey when Ingunn wasn't well enough to come with him. But she was greatly distressed at not being able to see the spiritual father of her youth, now that he was staying so close by. Arnvid suggested that the monk might borrow a sledge and travel south to pay a visit to Hestviken. Brother Vegard was more than willing to make the trip, but he'd felt ill ever since arriving in Oslo, and he was now suffering from a terrible cold. On Saint Peter's Day, freezing weather set in. Several days later the old man suddenly developed a lung infection, and on the third night, he died. Then it was up to Arnvid to deal alone with the hiring of stone masons, and he had his hands full with this task until he needed to head back north.

Olav persuaded Ingunn to stay in bed during the daytime after the weather turned bitterly cold. She hardly had the strength to move about anymore, now that the time for the birth was fast approaching, and her feet had frozen so badly that her skin was covered with big, open sores. Olav tended to them himself, smearing the sores with fox fat and pig bile. Ever since Arnvid's departure, Olav had treated his wife with great gentleness and concern. He had abandoned completely the surly and unkind behavior that he'd shown toward her during the fall and winter.

Ingunn lay curled up under the coverlets and whispered a faint "thank you" whenever Olav did anything for her. Silently and meekly she had submitted to his hostility and harsh words. Now she accepted his loving care with almost the same mute timidity. Olav surreptitiously kept an eye on her as she lay in bed for hours, not moving and staring straight ahead, hardly blinking. And the old, wild anguish again surged in his heart, as ardently as ever. It didn't matter that she was of so little use and brought him no joy. He couldn't lose her.

Ingunn was glad that she could hide away in this manner. She found herself seized by an unbearable shame every time she was again with child. Even before she'd had the first two, she had been tormented and embarrassed by how hideous she must look. Dalla's scornful words had become so etched into her mind that she had never recovered. She winced whenever she had to allow Olav to see her. Yet when he was elsewhere, she felt as if she couldn't go on unless his robust presence was near enough so that she might draw strength from him.

After it turned out that she could not bring to life a single one of the creatures that had grown inside her, one after the other, she became filled with a loathing for her own body. She must have been marked in some secretive fashion with something that was as horrible as leprosy so that she infected her unborn infants with death. Her blood and marrow had been spent, and the last remnants of her youth and beauty had long since been ravaged by these alarming guests who lived their hidden lives under her heart for a time, only to be snuffed out. Then she would feel the first warning pangs clawing at her back, and she had to allow women who were strangers to lead her over to the small house on the eastern side of the courtyard. There she surrendered to their hands, not daring to utter even a whimper about the deathly fear that filled her heart. And when the struggle was over, she would lie back, emptied of blood, emptied of everything. And it was as if the child had been swallowed up by the night, taken back into the gloom where she could find neither a name nor a memory. The women who had helped with the birth of the last stillborn infants had refused to let her even see them.

Yet sometimes she thought that what had happened with Audun was worse, much worse. By the time she lost the one-year-old child, he had already shown in many ways that he knew she was his mother. He had refused to be with anyone else, and he had loved her so much. But he probably still did. When they sang in Latin about *Omnes sancti Innocentes, orate pro nobis*, she knew that Audun was one of the innocents. And when she landed in purgatory, she would know that Audun was one of the holy ones praying for her. When her hour of grace arrived, perhaps Our Lord Himself or His Blessed Mother would say to Audun, "Go now and greet your mother."

She tried her utmost not to think about how things might go this time.

Whenever the men would come in for meals, Olav and Eirik together, the ill woman's big dull eyes would come alive with a deep and restless anxiety. Olav noticed then how alertly Ingunn would lie there, aware of every change in his expression and every word he spoke when he was with the boy. And he in turn was always on guard, never letting it show whenever he felt angry or impatient with Eirik.

The boy was certainly annoying. Olav felt only a modicum of affection for Eirik, now that the boy was old enough for his innate character to be fully revealed. Loud, boastful, bursting with tall tales, and always prattling in a way that was unbefitting a male. Eirik couldn't stop talking even when the men, weary and worn out, sat at the table having their dinner.

At Hestviken there was a servant fellow called Anki. Olav had taken him in six years earlier, and the man was now in his twenties. He was a dim-witted sort who might well be called half-mad, even though he was skilled at many types of labor. He'd always been Eirik's best friend. They would quarrel, partly in jest, until they both began to shout. Then Eirik would fly at Anki as he sat on the bench, pushing and tugging at him until he got Anki to join in the game. They shoved each other this way and that, tumbling into the middle of the room as they laughed and yelled and carried on, without giving a thought to the other men seated at the table who were in need of peace and quiet. Eirik was also blatantly disobedient. No matter what instructions his father gave him or what the boy was told not to do, Eirik would instantly forget every word of it.

Olav was also vexed that Eirik showed so little love for his mother, though he realized full well that his reaction was somewhat unreasonable. In the past, Olav had harbored a stifled bitterness because he knew that mother and son would cling to each other behind his back. Yet now he grew angry whenever he saw Eirik spending all day running about among the men and never once going inside to sit with his ill mother. Several years ago, Olav had taken it upon himself to teach the boy his prayers when he noticed that Ingunn didn't seem to realize it was time for the boy to learn such things. Now he had Eirik say a *Pater noster* and three *Aves* for his mother every evening, after he'd said a prayer for himself. The boy would rattle off the prayers as his father stood over him and then stand up during the last *Ave*. By the time he said "*In nomine*," he was already in bed as he quickly made the sign of the cross and slid full-length under the coverlet in the bed on the north side of the hall, where he now slept with his father. He would fall asleep at once. When Olav finished tending to Ingunn's feet and got into bed, Eirik would be curled up in the middle. His father would have to straighten out the slumbering boy's body and push him over to the wall in order to have any room for himself.

Occasionally Olav would feel a sharp pang when Eirik sought him out and chattered foolishly, boasting of his clumsy little attempts to be of some use to the hired men. If only the boy were the sort of person I could feel some affection for, thought Olav. Ignorant and trusting as Eirik was, he never sensed that his father was not as pleased with his company as he was with his father's. But Olav had made up his mind—he had claimed this child as his own and put him in a position so that, after he himself was gone, the boy would sit in the high seat here at Hestviken, although God knew, Eirik was an unlikely candidate to be raised as a noble landowner and the head of a large estate. The boy seemed to be a loose-lipped prattler and a liar, boastful and skittish, possessed of scant stamina, and born with little sense for what sounds were deemed to be seemly, calm, and appealing. But Olav would have to do what he could to teach Eirik good habits and thrash his bad ways out of him, even though he needed to leave the thrashing until Ingunn was stronger. The boy had to learn to behave as was suitable for Eirik Olavssøn of Hestviken.

Several years earlier, herds of deer had made their way up through the country on the west side of Folden, and there was now a surfeit of deer on Olav's property. They mostly kept to Kverndalen, up on the backside of the Ox, as well as in Olav's oak groves that were set inland, toward the village with the church. During the previous summer the folks at Hestviken had grown so much fodder that they had left some haystacks and bundles of foliage out in the fields. Now, in late winter, the deer came to the estate in the early hours to take what they could of the fodder left outdoors. One morning, from a hiding place behind several timbers, Olav shot a handsome young stag with ten-point antlers. After that Eirik was wildly eager to go with his father. He too wanted to fell a deer.

Olav laughed softly at the boy's chatter. Over the next few days the wind blew in from the fjord. He had Anki spend time outside in the morning so that the deer would catch his scent and stay away from the hay. He let Eirik go along. The boy lay on the ground, freezing cold, with his bow and spear nearby. But when he went back inside, he claimed he had both seen and heard the deer.

One night Olav awoke and went over to the door to see what time it was. Two hours before daylight, crackling cold and utterly still, except for a light breeze passing through Kverndalen from the east. At dawn the deer would no doubt arrive and take their tithe of hay. Olav put on his clothes in the dark, but he had to light a splinter of wood in order to select the best arrows. That's when Eirik awoke. His father ended up letting him come along, but the boy was allowed no weapons.

After they'd crept into the hiding place behind the timbers, Olav had a hard time getting the child to stay quiet. Eirik kept forgetting and insisted on whispering. Then he fell asleep. He was wearing a heavy fur tunic that belonged to his father. Olav wrapped the fur more securely around the boy so he wouldn't suffer frostbite. Right now, just before dawn, it was bitterly cold. He thought with satisfaction that now Eirik would not be causing any trouble.

Olav had to wait a good long time. The sky was already taking on a yellow glow to the east above the forest when he caught a glimpse of the deer emerging from the thickets. Four dark shapes headed toward the gray-brown fields. The ground was partially bare on the downward slope. The deer paused occasionally to scout the area and sniff at the air. Olav could now see that there was one stag, two does, and a fawn.

The warmth of anticipation and joy rushed through his frozen body as he raised himself up on one knee, brought the bow into position, and set the arrow. He held his breath. The stag stepped forward, proud and stately. Olav could see the animal against the snowdrift. It stepped up onto a ridge of old chaff and stood there with its hooves together. The animal's neck and head with the antlers were clearly visible against the yellow-tinged air. Olav silently gasped with elation. He hadn't seen this old fellow before—a stout body, thick coat, with a full crown, probably fifteen or sixteen points. The stag was on the lookout, moving its head back and forth. The distance was a bit far, but the animal stood in such a good position with the best target straight ahead. Olav took aim, his heart laughing with joy. That's when he sensed that Eirik was stirring.

The boy jolted up with a shout. He too had seen the magnificent antlers against the sky. Olav shot the arrow after the fleeing stag, managing to graze its shoulder, which caused the animal to leap high in the air. Then, taking long strides, the stag raced into the thickets, along with the other deer.

Eirik received a couple of well-placed blows on each side of his head, which he endured with a few little gasps, though he didn't cry out. He had sense enough to be ashamed of his actions and didn't howl. Besides, the thick fur hood he wore had blunted the blows.

"Don't say a word about this to your mother," said Olav as they walked back to the houses. "She doesn't need to know that, as big as you are, you still can behave like an untrained pup at the teat."

Later in the day Olav took his dog and followed the bloody tracks of the stag. He felled the animal and dressed the carcass up on the topmost ridge above Kverndalen. When he brought the bounty home in the evening, Eirik boasted that he was the one who had pointed out the big stag to his father when it came within shooting distance.

Olav didn't dare rebuke the boy, for he feared he might become too irate.

Groups of seals now headed into the fjord as spring approached. The farmers up in the villages took their boats to the edge of the ice to begin seal hunting in the waters to the south. Olav allowed Eirik to come along, but that did not go well. The boy grew terribly agitated and excited at the sight of the mass killings and the abundance of wildlife out there among the hunters. It was unbelievable that the boy had so little notion of what was proper behavior in any given situation. But once they returned home, he had a great deal to recount. It wasn't easy for Olav to listen to the boy's chatter without losing all patience.

By the time Saint Gregory's Feast Day arrived, the weather had turned, bringing a southerly wind and rain. That was seen as a portent of a good year, both on land and at sea.

Early the next day, Ingunn was alone in the main hall, lying in bed. It was quite dark inside because the smoke vent was covered with the transparent membrane made from a cow's stomach, and the hatch had been partially closed. It was raining outside.

Olav came into the room. He sat down on the bench and pulled off his boots, then wrung out his work tunic and shirt before going to his clothing chest to find other garments.

"Are you asleep, Ingunn?" he asked with his back turned. "How are you feeling?" he added when she replied in a whisper that she wasn't asleep.

"All right. Are you going off on horseback?"

Olav said yes. The ting at Vidanes was taking place that day. He went over to the bed, his torso naked, and set one foot on the step. "Do you think I need to change my hose as well?"

Ingunn involuntarily moved her head away.

"I think you should. They smell so foul."

"I don't suppose the other men who'll be there will smell any sweeter. Lately we've all been out hunting seal day and night, every one of us."

"But if you're going to meet with folks from other villages . . ." said Ingunn.

"Yes, all right, if that's what you wish." He pulled off his breeches and hose. Then he stood there completely naked, stretching a bit and yawning.

Ingunn felt her heart ache at the sight of his unblemished and well-formed body. It seemed hopeless that she herself should be so ravaged and miserable. It was such a long time ago that she had been young and lovely, and the two of them were such a fitting match. But Olav was still a young man, vigorous and handsome. He had become more muscular, mostly along his shoulder blades and in his upper arms. Under his smooth flesh the muscles rippled, strong and supple, as he stretched, raising his arms halfway up and then letting them drop. His skin was still a milky-white.

He came back over to his wife after he'd put on the red woolen shirt, hose made of black-dyed leather, and linen breeches.

"I suppose you think I ought to wear the blue cotehardie as well? Since you want me to look so finely attired?" he asked her with a smile.

"Olav?" When he leaned over Ingunn, she suddenly threw her thin arms around his neck and pulled him close, pressing her face against his cheek. Olav noticed that she was trembling.

"What is it?" he whispered. But she merely clung to him without saying a word.

"Are you ill?" He freed her arms from around his neck. Standing in that bent-over position was uncomfortable. "Do you want me to stay home today? I could ride over to Rynjul and bring back Una for you, and at the same time ask Torgrim to act on my behalf at the Vidanes *ting*."

"No, no." She squeezed his hand tightly. "No. I doubt there will be any change for me until after the springtide. But stay here with me for a little while." Her words sounded quietly plaintive. "Sit here for a while if you have time for it."

"I suppose I can." He held her hand and stroked her arm. "What is it, Ingunn? Are you frightened?" he asked softly.

"No. Yes. No, I don't know whether I'm frightened exactly, but . . ." Olav pushed the step away and sat down on the edge of the bed, patting her haggard cheek over and over.

"I was dreaming," Ingunn now said. "Right before you came in."

"Was it a bad dream?"

Tears began pouring down her cheeks. She wept without making a sound, though her voice was somewhat husky and hoarse when she spoke.

"The dream didn't seem bad while I was in the midst of it. Not then. I saw you walking along a path in the forest. You looked happy, and you seemed younger than you are now. You were singing as you walked. I saw you here at Hestviken too, out in the courtyard, and again you looked happy and healthy. I could see everything, even though I wasn't here myself. I was dead. I knew that. But I saw no children here—none."

"Ingunn, Ingunn, you mustn't lie here thinking such things." Olav knelt down so he could slip his arm under her shoulders. "There wouldn't be much joy for me here on our estate, if I should lose you, dear Ingunn."

"I have never brought you any joy."

"You are the only friend I have." He kissed her, bending lower over his wife so her face was completely hidden against his chest.

"If it's true what Signe and Una say," he whispered hesitantly, "that you are carrying a daughter this time . . . They were sons, all the other times. But a tiny maiden . . . Perhaps God will allow us to keep her."

The ill woman sighed. "I'm so weary."

Olav whispered, "Ingunn, have you ever thought that perhaps . . . that what I've given Eirik is no more than . . . restitution for his father's death?"

When she didn't reply, he asked, unable to hide a slight tremor in his voice, "Have you never wondered what became of him—that man Teit?"

Ingunn drew him closer. "I never believed that you did it."

Olav felt strangely overwhelmed, as if he'd suddenly emerged into bright light and was trying to distinguish what he saw. All this time she had *known*. But what had that meant? Had she understood the burden he was carrying? Or had she been afraid of his bloodied hands?

Ingunn looked up at him, then put her hands behind his neck to pull his head down to her. She kissed his lips, desperately and ardently.

"I knew. I knew. Yet sometimes I was afraid . . . when the worst happened to me and I was in the greatest despair . . . I couldn't help thinking that he might still be alive and had come to seek revenge from me. But I thought you must have done it, and that meant I was safe!"

Olav felt so odd, both numb and freezing cold. Was *that* what she'd thought? Ah well. No doubt that was all she could understand, the poor thing. He kissed her, gently and lightly. Then he gave a small, embarrassed laugh.

"You must let me go now, Ingunn. You're about to crush my ribs against the bedstead."

He stood up, patted her cheek again, and then walked across the room to his clothes chest and rummaged among the garments. Then he asked her again, "Are you sure, Ingunn? Wouldn't you rather that I stayed home today?"

"No, no, Olav. I don't want to delay you."

Olav fastened his spurs to his boots, picked up his sword, and flung over his shoulders the rain cloak made of thick, felted wadmal. He was already at the door when he turned around and went back to stand beside his wife's bed.

Ingunn sensed that he had suddenly become more distant and seemed more changed than she'd seen him in an exceedingly long time. His face was as rigid as stone and pale around his lips, his eyes were veiled and unseeing. He spoke as if asleep.

"Will you promise me one thing? If things should go as you . . . as you said . . . and this time it will be the death of you—will you promise me this? That you will *come back* to me?"

Now he looked at her, leaning over her slightly.

"This you must promise me, Ingunn. If it's true that the dead return to the living, then you must come back to me!"

"Yes."

Olav quickly bent down to touch his forehead to her chest for a moment.

"You are the only friend I've ever had," he whispered, swiftly and shyly.

Olav came riding home late in the evening, so wet and frozen that he couldn't feel his feet in the stirrups. His horse plodded along wearily, sending sprays of snow up over the rider with every step.

Clouds billowed and fog surged; the earth smelled damp. The evening was strangely steamy and hazy blue. Everything seemed to have dissolved. The forest and fields had dark bare patches between stretches of slushy snow. The fjord spoke with long gaps between each muted swell, like a sluggish pulse, but the river in Kverndalen roared, bursting with water. A sigh passed through the forest, snow fell from the boughs, water trickled and gurgled and sounded from every direction in the dusk. And the cold smell from the fields and the sea gave the first hint of spring and the growing season.

Up on the slope near the barn a dark figure came toward him. A woman wearing a hooded cloak.

"Welcome home, Olav!" It was Signe Arnesdatter. She hurried toward him as he drew nearer.

"Ingunn has made it through this time, and she is doing much better than anyone could expect." Olav had reined in his horse, and Signe reached out to caress its muzzle. "The child is so big and lovely. None of us have ever seen such a big and beautiful newborn infant. You'll just have to accept the fact that it's not a son!"

Olav thanked her for the good news. He sensed that if he'd been the same person as in his younger years, he would have leaped off his horse to embrace his kinswoman and kiss her. He was certainly relieved and glad, yet he couldn't fully take it all in. He thanked Signe for once again offering Ingunn such kind assistance.

It had happened so fast, Signe told him, that they weren't able to take her over to the women's house. Olav would have to make do with sleeping in the alcove while they kept watch over the mother and the cradle in the main hall.

But the instant Olav caught sight of Ingunn . . . Her face was a dazzling snowy white, and she lay on her side with one yellow-brown braid tucked under her cheek. Una was kneeling behind Ingunn in the bed, plaiting the other thick rope of her hair. On the other occasions when Olav had seen his wife lying in bed in this manner, her face had been hideously swollen and flushed bright red. This time she looked so unlike herself—wondrously beautiful, as if an unearthly light had settled over her ravaged white face. Her big, blue-black eyes glittered the way starlight is reflected in a well. And the realization slowly sank through Olav that a miracle had occurred.

Signe brought to him a tiny bundle, with strips of white linen crisscrossed around the leaf-green woolen swaddling clothes. She placed the infant in Olav's arms, saying, "Have you ever seen so fair a maiden, my kinsman?"

And again he felt himself caught up in something beyond belief. The face of a girl, exceedingly tiny, but fully formed and the loveliest of all! A newborn life, and to think it could look like this! Her eyes were open, dark and unfathomable, and her skin was as white and red as a briar rose, and she had a human's nose and mouth, but so small that he could hardly comprehend it.

Signe pulled back the swaddling so the father could see that his daughter also had lovely hair. Olav cupped his hand behind the delicate curve of the child's head. Resting in his palm, her head was no bigger than an apple and so sweet and soft to the touch.

Olav kept holding his infant daughter. A gift, that's what she was, a gift. It made him feel quite weak. He had never in his life felt so grateful, grateful beyond all measure. He laid his face against the chest of the swaddled child. Her face was so pure and delicate that he didn't dare go near it.

Una jumped down to the floor and then helped the new mother turn onto her back, with her braids lying on her bodice. The women took the infant from Olav before he sat down on the edge of his wife's bed. He held her hand for a while, now and then lifting up one of her braids. Neither of them spoke.

Someone brought him food and drink, and afterward they told him that he should retire to the alcove and go to bed. Ingunn needed to sleep. Then she quietly called to him.

"Olav," Ingunn whispered. "There's something I want to ask of you, my husband." She otherwise never called him that. "Will you do what I ask?"

"I will do everything that you ask." He smiled as if in pain, so infused was he with joy.

"Promise me that she will not be named after my mother. I want her to be called Cecilia."

Olav nodded.

He lay awake in the dark. Next to the wall Eirik slept as soundly as a rock. Through the door opening Olav could see the light from the hearth fire flickering over the wall timbers, rising and falling. But there was a glow, faint and golden and gentle, coming from the holy candle they had lit near the mother and child.

The women keeping vigil whispered and puttered about, rattling the water kettle and the hooks of the hearth rack. The newborn infant began to cry, and the cries called to his heart. Listening to her made him feel tender and happy. The women got up to rock the cradle, and Signe sang quietly and gently.

Here he lay before her door; it seemed as natural as a dream to be lying there and listening to the women keeping vigil as she slept. Ingunn slept sweetly now. She had given birth to the child, and now she would rest and once again become healthy and young and happy. A child had been born here on his estate—the first one. Everything that had gone before had been like an endless and unnatural affliction, an uncanny bewitchment that had befallen the unfortunate woman. The small, lifeless monstrosities that the women had brought for him to see, even though he was so reluctant to look at them—the sight of them had filled him with an endless loathing . . . And that poor little, misshapen child that had lived such a short and tormented life, until God had shown mercy and taken him home . . . In his heart, Olav had never been able to think of any of them as his children, the fruit of his and Ingunn's life together.

Never had he known what it felt like to become a father, to be a father. Not until now. He had a daughter, and that was something precious. This tiny, little Cecilia.

XIII

Cecilia Olavsdatter grew and thrived so well that the neighbor women said they could see a change in her from one day to the next. No one could understand how she managed to grow so plump, for Ingunn insisted on nursing the child herself, and there couldn't have been many drops of sustenance there. But the girl grew more in a month than other infants did in three. That's what Signe and Una boasted. Occasionally they would feed her spoonfuls of soured cream, or they let her chew on some deer marrow wrapped in a cloth.

Visitors who came to Hestviken wanted to see the little maiden, about whom word had already spread, for she was incomparably lovely. Folks let it be known that they thought Olav and his wife deserved this happiness, though it didn't make anyone favor the Hestviken master and mistress more than they had before. Olav was oddly unsociable, which made it a torment for people who had to deal with the surly man. No doubt that was simply his nature, because it had to be said that in terms of his actions, Olav had always shown himself to be a just and pious person, and quite helpful as well. His wife was inept and weak-minded, the poor thing, but she didn't seem to wish anyone ill. And so it was joyous news that they had finally had a child who looked as if she might survive.

But Ingunn continued to be sickly for a long time afterward. She must have injured her back, and by the time she was finally able to leave her bed, she still hadn't regained strength in her legs.

One Sunday Olav was returning home from church. The weather was beautiful. On this day summer had arrived. Light from the foliage and green meadows flickered in the wind that was following the sun's position, and every gust of air felt like a warm and wholesome breath from the growing grass and the budding trees and from the earth, which still held the dampness of spring. When Olav went inside and saw that Ingunn lay stretched out on the bench, he felt a bit worried. He told her that after he'd had something to eat, she must go with him to take a look at their best field. The grain had again come up lush and fine this year.

It was the field farthest away, facing the fjord and below the expanse of rock. Olav felt a special affection for that area, and he always sowed there the hardiest and best seeds. He fertilized the field with fish heads and waste from the wharf, which meant that it suffered less from drought than might have been expected, for the topsoil was not very deep. Yet the grain ripened there before it did in any of the other fields at Hestviken.

Olav had to carry Ingunn across the threshold. After he set her down outside the door, he saw that she walked as if she couldn't lift her feet. She shuffled forward along the ground, moving at a slow and unsteady pace, and when she came to uneven spots, she seemed on the verge of falling over. He put his arm around her waist, and she leaned heavily on him, placing one hand on his shoulder. At every third or fourth step she had to pause for a moment, and he noticed that she was sweating a good deal and trembling with fatigue.

When they reached the lookout area, Olav took the fur-lined winter cloak that he'd brought along and spread it out in a cleft between some rocks. There Ingunn would be able to lie down and watch the caressing wind as it seemed to groom the tips of the young leaves of grain, making bright flames ripple along the green slope. The ground was strewn with stones.

The sea and the land glinted and gleamed. The summertime waves rolled toward the mountain, then splashed and trickled their way back, carrying away pebbles from the foreshore. A gentle rushing sound came from the surge. But beneath the Ox the sea spray rose higher and higher; the wind was now moving to the southwest. Olav sat there, his eyes following a heavily loaded, high-sided ship that was heading along the fjord at quite a swift speed. He sank into his own thoughts. Hovering before him were ancient memories from the time when he was free as a bird and outlawed—back when he knew nothing of carrying someone else's burdens. He'd been alone, one man among many others, none of whom ever drew so close that he knew them well. That was something distant and pleasant to remember now, after all these years when he'd had the whole of Hestviken resting on his shoulders, and with his ill wife as close to him as his own flesh. He had struggled to keep going as he took along Ingunn, who was always unwell and suffering. It was as if he were fighting with one arm shattered and hanging uselessly at his side. Yet he didn't feel unhappy as he sat there in the midday sun. He wasn't thinking about the past in the sense that he wished to escape the present or was discontented with the way things had turned out for him with Ingunn. He was sitting there feeling comfortable albeit slightly melancholy, but what weighed on him was his boundless love for her; it seemed somehow too vast for him to contend with alone.

He turned toward Ingunn, wanting to say something to her about the ship in the fjord, but he saw that she'd fallen asleep. She looked as if she were dead.

Olav was surprised to find that he now felt a greater affection for her than ever before, and it was precisely because he could see for himself that all trace of her beauty had utterly vanished. Anyone who hadn't seen her in her youth would not imagine that this faded and old-looking woman had once been beautiful. She had been lovely in the same way fragile, delicate, and bright flowers were. Now her skin was stretched taut and shiny; it was sallow and mottled, and brown spots marked her lean face with the hollow cheeks and long jaw. Her tall and slender figure had long since lost its supple softness. Her narrow chest was as flat as a plank, her midsection a shapeless bulk. She resembled an aged and destitute woman who'd had too many children.

Olav sat there looking at Ingunn, not daring to touch her. Surely she needed to sleep. He merely reached out to tuck the tips of her wimple underneath so the wind wouldn't blow them in her face. Then he wrapped the edges of the cloak more securely around her. She looked so bloodless, and she mustn't get cold.

◆ ◆ ◆

Both Olav and the servants noticed that for every passing day Ingunn found it more and more difficult to walk. By the time Saint Jon's Day arrived, she could no longer get up from a seated position without help, nor could she set one foot in front of the other unless someone held her up and supported her. But she was still given help to get dressed every morning. Torhild was the one who did this now, because Ingunn's maidservant, Liv, was of no use at this time.

Olav had never been able to understand Ingunn's stubborn aversion toward Torhild Bjørnsdatter, which had lasted all these years. Torhild was the sort of woman whose equal would not easily be found. She was loyal, efficient, and strong. And no matter how unreasonable Ingunn might behave toward the housekeeper, Torhild continued to display a patient concern for her ill mistress.

Olav found it just as incomprehensible that Ingunn had directed her affection toward the girl Liv, who had become her maidservant the previous year. For one thing, the girl was practically the ugliest person Olav had ever seen in his life. At first glance it was questionable whether she was even human. She was short and unusually wide and fat, with especially squat, bowed legs. She had thin, red, scraggly hair. Her skin was reddish-gray and freckled all the way down to her chest, with freckles on her arms and hands as well. And she had the strangest, ugliest face, with little squinty pig-eyes, a pointed nose, and no chin. The lower half of her face sloped inward and merged with the sagging flesh of her throat. Nor was she a nice person. She was lazy, she treated both Torhild and the woman who minded the cattle with insolence, and she was quite stupid. Yet Ingunn had poured all her love on this girl. When it turned out that Liv had gotten herself in trouble during the autumn when she'd been given permission to go home to visit her parents during Michaelmas, her mistress had pleaded with Olav not to dismiss Liv from the estate. Olav hadn't planned to do anything of the sort. He knew that Liv came from an exceedingly poor family with many children, so it would be better for her to stay at Hestviken. But since she worked on his estate and was very young—only fifteen—he thought he would try to win justice on her behalf. He asked her who the father was. She knew only that he was a man who had accompanied her part of the way through the forest when she headed home at Michaelmas.

"Did he . . . treat you badly?" asked Olav.

"Oh no." Liv's whole face lit up. He'd been so kind and playful. He said his name was Jon.

"Ah. That's the name of every man who has no other name."

At any rate, Liv would soon be ready to be Cecilia's wet nurse, for it was simply wrong for the ill mother to have to suckle that big, greedy infant. Yet so far Ingunn had refused to hear of allowing anyone to take Cecilia from her breast.

Olav had summoned to Hestviken all the men and women in the surrounding villages who had any knowledge of disease and healing. None of them could say what ailed his wife, and most thought that her illness must have been caused by either treachery or envy. Olav knew that Ingunn had suffered the same sort of symptoms sixteen or seventeen years earlier, when she was staying at Miklebø. Back then Fru Hillebjørg had claimed that Kolbein was the one who had conjured some type of sorcery or witchcraft and had directed it at Ingunn. Olav now wondered whether there might have been some truth to the notion, after all. Perhaps she'd never been fully released from that evil power.

Then Olav happened to meet in Oslo a German merchant named Claus Wiephart, who in his youth had been held captive by the Saracens and learned from their wisdom. Olav brought him home, and this man saw at once what was wrong with Ingunn.

He wasn't able to say what had originally prompted the illness; there could have been various causes, but it was most likely due to the stars. For instance, Olav might have bedded her for the first time at a moment when the position of the heavenly bodies was hostile toward them, in terms of the stars under which they'd been born. It could have been a matter of less than an hour—slightly before or slightly after that moment and the constellations might have been particularly auspicious for them. But as it was, the effect on Ingunn, since she was the weaker of the two of them, might have been a disturbance of the harmony in her body between the solid substances and the fluids, such that the solid substances had diminished and the fluids had gained supremacy. She might also have been disposed at birth to this type of disharmony, but disharmony was undoubtedly the most likely cause of her weakness. Evidence of this was the fact that she'd been unable to produce male offspring who survived, except for the first son. A man's body was by nature drier than a woman's and required from the very beginning more of the solid substances. Yet Ingunn had been able to bring a daughter into the light of day. But this child had extracted more solid substances from her mother's body than Ingunn could spare. Claus Wiephart said that she was now in a state of decay, her bones and skin flooded with fluids—like a tender young sapling that floated in the sea until it became saturated with water.

First and foremost, they needed to dry out her body, said the German. The infant should by no means be removed from the mother's breast. Ingunn was given medicaments that would drive sweat and moisture out of her body; she was allowed very little to drink; and she had to consume charred and crushed animal bones, terra sigillata,[23] and hard, dried foodstuffs with heat-inducing spices added.

The learned man's claims filled Olav with renewed hope. It all sounded so reasonable. And from his youth he recognized the Latin words that the German now used. *Prima causa, harmonia, materia,* and *umidus, disparo, dispono.* All these words Olav remembered hearing said by Fat Asbjørn, Arnvid, and the monks at the monastery. And as far as he understood, Claus used the words correctly. Olav had seen for himself, during the years when they were growing up, that Ingunn's body was strangely weak and lacked sturdiness—which made him think of unripe grain. She had always been lacking in solid substances. Terra sigillata must surely be good for her. He knew it was beneficial for so many things.

Olav had learned about the four elements that form the human body, and he'd heard that the position of the heavenly bodies could affect a man's destiny. Fat Asbjørn had said that learned men here in Norway didn't know much about such matters; Christian men didn't need to ask about what might be written in the stars. But the Saracens were said to possess greater wisdom about the stars than any other people.

Olav felt inexpressibly lighter in his heart. Perhaps he'd been on the wrong track all these years. He had believed that he was the one who had brought the misfortunes down upon both of them, because he hadn't dared to break free from the sin he'd been living. And he *was* living a sin—that would be true as long as he wasn't willing to atone for the unfortunate deed he'd committed. Yet God must know that he couldn't do that. He couldn't risk the well-being and honor of his wife and child. In every other way he had tried to conduct himself as a Christian man. And surely God must know even better than he did how deeply he longed to seek peace with Him, daring to love Him with his whole heart, so that he could bend his knee and pray without lamenting over his own disobedience.

But what if he could now believe that all the misfortunes had a natural origin? Cecilia was the proof that God had released him from his debt—or would at least postpone punishment until his dying hour. And the weakness in Ingunn's body and soul had been caused by the stars.

But *Prima causa.* That was one of God's names. Olav knew that.

Ingunn herself said that she felt better after taking the remedies Claus Wiephart had prescribed. She still hadn't regained enough strength for her to move her lower body, but she had less pain in her back.

One evening just before Saint Olav's Day, Olav went over to the cookhouse. There was something he wanted to tell Torhild Bjørnsdatter before he forgot.

She was baking bread for the feast day. When Olav opened the door, the flour dust hovering in the air was gilded by the evening sun, and light flowed into the small room that was dark with soot. A sweet, yeasty fragrance rose from the round loaves baking on slanted stones that had been arranged around the glowing embers piled up in the hearth. Olav's mouth watered as he breathed in the scent. But Torhild wasn't there.

Olav had just turned to leave when Torhild appeared in the doorway. She was carrying a wooden platter that was so heavy she had to balance it on her head with her arms raised to hold it steady. And she had to walk even more erect than usual. Now, in the warm summer evening, the thin work garments she wore made her appear so lovely and lithe. She had on a short-sleeved wadmal shift, and her feet were bare. Her movements were agile, confident, and strong.

Olav took the platter from her. It was made from oak and very heavy. He carried it inside and set it down on the trestles. Torhild followed. From a basket she grabbed two fistfuls of crushed juniper twigs and spread them over the platter. A lovely scent wafted from her as she nimbly moved about. She smelled of flour and fresh bread and the wholesome heat of work. Olav threw his arms around the maidservant from behind and roughly pulled her close. He leaned his chin on her shoulder and pressed his cheek against her skin for a moment. Her neck was damp, both cool and warm at the same time. Then he let her go and laughed to hide his own confusion and shame at the foolish desire that had overtaken him so abruptly.

Torhild had turned as red as blood. When Olav saw this, he felt even more embarrassed. But she didn't say a word and showed no sign of anger. Calmly she removed from the stones the loaves that had finished baking and carried them over to the platter.

"You have the strength of a man, Torhild," said her master. When she didn't reply and merely went about tending to her baking, he added somberly, "You keep the entire household going. And you do more work than all the rest of us put together."

"I do my best," murmured Torhild.

"I wonder whether you think . . . Perhaps you think we ought to show you more appreciation? If so, you must tell me. I'm sure we could agree on—"

"No, I'm content with things as they are. By now I've managed to raise all the children of my family except for the two youngest, and you've certainly helped me greatly."

"Oh, there's no need to speak of that." Olav told her what he'd come to the cookhouse to say, and then he left.

◆ ◆ ◆

Ingunn continued to make use of the remedies prescribed by the learned German, but after a while the effects were no longer solely beneficial. She developed stomach pains and a burning in her throat from all the pepper and ginger. Yet she persisted for the longest time, struggling to swallow the dry and fiery foodstuffs, although it seemed to her that merely looking at the food caused her pain. And thirst tormented her day and night. Yet she endured everything with patience and seldom complained.

Then Olav had to be away from home for several nights, and Signe Arnesdatter came to stay with the ill woman while he was gone. Afterward Signe told Olav that it was sheer madness for Ingunn to keep Cecilia with her at night. Ingunn had not a drop of milk in her breasts anymore, and it was from hunger and anger that the child cried so fiercely every night, keeping her mother and everyone else awake.

Olav had never known any infant other than Audun, who was almost always crying, so he'd thought that was how they all behaved. By now Liv had long been nursing Cecilia in the daytime. Her own child had recently died, and the young woman had the milk of an otherworldly cow. The only sensible thing was for Liv to become Cecilia's foster mother and take care of the child both day and night.

But when they said this to Ingunn, she was beside herself with sorrow. She begged and pleaded with Olav not to take Cecilia away from her. "She's all I have left of myself. The price I paid for this daughter of yours was to end up lying here, lacking all strength and paralyzed from the waist down. If you have any affection for her, Olav, then take pity on me. Do not take Cecilia from me during the time I have left to live. It won't be long before you're released from this wretched life with me."

Olav tried to talk some sense into Ingunn, but she screamed and propped her elbows on the cushion underneath her, then raised her shoulders and struggled, as if trying to threaten her paralyzed body to get up. Olav sat down on the edge of the bed and spoke as gently to her as he could, but it was no use. Finally, after weeping and raging so much that she was exhausted, Ingunn fell into a doze. But even in her sleep she continued to sob and shake.

In the end, Olav had to promise his wife that she could continue to have Cecilia in her bed at night, but Liv had to sleep on the bench in the main hall so that she could soothe the child when she cried.

When Olav went to say good night to Ingunn before going to bed, she placed her arms around his neck and drew his head down to her.

"Don't be angry, Olav. I can't sleep without having her with me. I've always been afraid to sleep alone," she whispered. "From the very first night you slept with me, I haven't felt safe unless I could feel your arm around me. And now that will never happen again."

Olav knelt down, slipped his arm under her neck, and brought her head to rest against his shoulder.

"Would you like me to hold you this way until you fall asleep?" he asked.

Ingunn fell asleep almost at once. Then Olav settled the pillows more comfortably under her shoulders before quietly walking across the room to the north wall to slide into bed next to Eirik.

Olav kept a little oil lamp burning on the hearth at night, for he often had to get up to help Ingunn and turn her over. Now he also had to get up when Cecilia cried and carry the child to Liv, who seldom awoke.

He must have fallen asleep at last, and slept heavily. The child had apparently been crying for a long while, and so fiercely that she'd even managed to rouse Liv. In the faint light from the little lamp wick he saw the maidservant pad over to Ingunn's bed, carrying Cecilia in her arms. In the dim light, Liv's figure looked so shapelessly wide and short that he was reminded of tales he'd heard about weird creatures and troll women. Even though he knew it was unreasonable, he felt ill at ease seeing Cecilia in the arms of that foster mother.

The next day Olav came in to see Ingunn around noon. He and one of the hired men had been busy cutting hay in some of the outlying fields up on the heights. Beads of mist had settled on the nap of his short cloak, and his boots were heavy with wet earth and withered leaves. The raw smell of autumn wafted off him when he leaned over Ingunn and asked her how she was feeling.

With a shy little smile, he showed her what he was hiding in his hand: several big, pulpy strawberries threaded onto a straw, just the way they used to do it when they were children. The berries were soft and had left red speckles on the palm of his hand.

"I found these up by the mill."

Ingunn took the berries, forgetting to thank him. It was those tiny red flecks on his rough, worn hand . . . She found herself recalling their life together, from childhood and all the way up to the present. Twice he had bloodied his hand for her sake, and it was that hard, resin-stained boyish fist that had helped her climb over fences and opened to reveal gifts for her. Their life unfolded before her like a length of tapestry, one long weaving with little images of brief, ardent, and tender moments of lovemaking. In between there had been long spaces of waiting and loathsome, barren dreams. Then came the period of shame and distraught despair like a big, dark blot, and afterward all these years at Hestviken. All of it suddenly appeared before her like embroidery on a cloth background. A single weaving, the entire tapestry made from one long piece of fabric, stretching from their childhood days until now, until the end.

No doubt she had always known that Olav looked on her with kindness. She also had a sense that few men would have shown such patience toward her for such a long time, or been willing to protect and support her during all these years. She had certainly thanked him in her heart, sometimes with a burning ardor. But only now did she have a full view of how strong Olav's love had been.

At the moment he was standing next to the cradle. The rockers were thudding and thudding against the floor, and the child was gurgling and shrieking with glee as she vigorously drummed her heels on the coverlet spread beneath her. Above the edge of the cradle Ingunn caught a glimpse of the infant's tiny, flailing pink hands.

"Stop now, Cecilia, or you'll soon choke on all these wrappings!" Olav chuckled and lifted the child into his arms. Cecilia had been wriggling about so eagerly that the swaddling clothes had come undone, and the linen ties had gotten twisted around her arms and legs and neck, as well as her plump, fair body, so that it was a wonder she hadn't strangled herself. "Could you straighten everything out?" Olav said to Ingunn as he placed the child on the woolen coverlet in front of her.

"Are you lying here weeping?" he then asked sorrowfully. The tears blinded Ingunn so that she could scarcely see what she was doing as she tried to free Cecilia from the tangled ties.

"She's going to be just as fair-haired as all the Hestviken men are destined to be," said Olav. "And you already have seven little curls," he said to the child, stroking the front of her head where long tiny curls of yellow-white hair, like slivers of wood, had sprouted. "Are you in great pain today, my Ingunn?"

"That's not why I'm crying. I've been lying here thinking that even though you've been both kind and faithful to me for as long as I've known you, never has it been possible for me to repay your love."

"Don't say that. You have been a . . . gentle . . ." He couldn't think of another word of praise, caught off guard as he was, even though he searched and would have liked to please her. "You've been a gentle— and quiet—wife. Surely you know how fond I am of you," he said fervently.

"But now it's been almost a year," she whispered, sounding both bitter and embarrassed. "It's as if you don't have a wife, but instead a crippled sister that you must care for."

"Ah well. But since I love you so dearly . . ." replied Olav. "A sister, you say? Do you remember, Ingunn, those first years when we lived together and we slept in the same bed and drank from the same bowl, and we were like brother and sister? We didn't know anything else. Yet even back then, we felt happiest when we were together."

"Yes. But we were children. And I was still beautiful," she whispered, her voice more vehement.

"Yes, you were. But I fear that I was too childish to notice. During those years I don't think I ever thought about whether you were beautiful or not."

"And I was not a burden to you. I was both healthy and strong."

"No, Ingunn." Olav smiled faintly and caressed her arm. "You have never been strong, my dear friend, no you haven't!"

◆ ◆ ◆

It was a long winter for those living at Hestviken.

Olav stayed home the whole time. He didn't feel he could leave Ingunn for even one night. She was now suffering terribly in her bed-ridden state. Her body was emaciated, and she had developed such pain in her back that after she'd been lying in one position for a while, the pain seemed to rise up along her ribcage to fill her entire chest. The only thing that offered her some relief was to have the servants move and turn her frequently. She was no longer able to eat. They kept her alive by feeding her porridge made from sour whey and rye flour, soup, and milk, but only a few sips at a time.

She had tried to do a little handiwork as she lay in bed, but as soon as she raised her hands for a few moments, they would go numb. She couldn't manage to either sew or plait. She simply lay there, motionless. Never did she utter a word of complaint, and she would quietly and gently thank whoever came over to shift her position and straighten her pillows. Sometimes she would sleep a great deal during the day, but she rarely slept much at night.

Olav kept the fire burning in the hearth all night long, and he'd set a door into the alcove opening so that the space could be closed off and the main hall would stay warmer. The winter was not especially cold, but the constant smoke, night and day, was bothersome.

And night after night Olav kept vigil with his ill wife. Eirik would lie in bed behind his back, sleeping soundly. Liv slept on the bench, and Cecilia slept next to the wall in her mother's bed. Olav would doze off, but his slumber was not so deep that he couldn't sense whenever a spark flew from the fire or whenever Ingunn moaned faintly. Then he would get up and go over to her. All winter long he got undressed only when he went to the bathhouse to wash.

He would kneel next to her bed and slide the palms of his hands under her shoulders, then under her backside, and then hold the heels of her feet in the hollow of his hands for a while. In his heart he was waiting with grim dread for her to get bedsores. Right now was like the last smoldering glow of everything he had once felt for her body.

He didn't think he could bear to see Ingunn's skin rupture with sores that spread and ate into her flesh even as she was still alive. He had always had such a hard time tolerating the sight and smell of unclean wounds, even though he was ashamed of this weakness of his. In despair he begged God not to let this happen, as much for his own sake as for hers.

Now Olav went over to tend to the fire.

"Are you thirsty, Ingunn? Shall I hold you on my lap, Ingunn?"

Olav wrapped the bedclothes around her, then lifted her into his arms. He sat down with her on the small bench that had room enough for two to sit near the fire. Cautiously he raised her lifeless legs and placed feather-filled cushions under her feet on the bench. Then he supported her, with her hips and the small of her back resting on his thighs, her head leaning against his shoulder.

"Are you comfortable like this?" he asked.

Occasionally she was able to fall asleep when she reclined in this manner on his lap. And Olav would sit there for hours until his back was freezing and all his limbs felt taut and stiff. If he made even the slightest movement, she would awake. Then she would free her hand from the coverlets and stroke his face.

"I'm feeling much better now. Carry me back to bed, Olav. Go and get some sleep. You must be tired."

One night she said to him, "I have been a heavy burden for you, Olav. But have forbearance. It won't last much longer than this winter."

He offered no words in protest. He'd been thinking the same thing. When spring arrived, it would no doubt take her. And now he was finally prepared to accept that.

Yet as winter came to an end, Ingunn seemed instead to get a little better. At any rate, she livened up enough to ask about how things were going on the estate and with the fishing. She listened for the cowbells in both the morning and evening, mentioning each cow by name. And once she even said that when spring was in full bloom, they would have to carry her outside so she could take a look at the livestock one more time.

Cecilia was now exceedingly lovely and also big for her age. Ingunn took much solace in having the child with her in the daytime, but Liv had to stay with her too. At night Cecilia slept in a bed with her foster mother in a different house. Ingunn could no longer stand to have the plump, strong child in her bed. In her sleep, Cecilia would tumble on top of her mother, and when she was awake, she would totter around in the bed and then land heavily on Ingunn's paralyzed body.

Olav felt such a dislike for Liv that he avoided the main hall whenever the maidservant was present. He was also aware that Liv had taken to stealing things here and there, and he had good reason to suspect that she'd become too well acquainted with Anki and had subsequently taught the man to pilfer and lie. Arnketil had always been unreliable when it came to the words he spoke, but that had mostly been because he didn't know any better. What the two servants stole was never important enough to warrant any action, but Olav detested having dishonest folks on his estate. Besides that, much had fallen into disarray at Hestviken. He was so tired each and every day that he never managed to tend to all the tasks he should have seen to. And it was all too easy to slide downhill, as the saying goes.

He no longer saw much of Cecilia in the daytime. Gradually his love for his daughter became mixed with a deep ache. He felt a burning pain inside him whenever he happened to recall that blue and humid spring night when he returned home to find the infant in her cradle. The first time they placed her in his arms he had believed so strongly that she was a portent of a turn in their fate. Cecilia had come into the world to bring them happiness.

Olav loved this little daughter of his, but his love seemed to sink through him and settle at the bottom of his heart like a shy and mute living creature. During those first months he would often pause next to her cradle and reach out his fingers to touch her gently and playfully. And he was filled with a quiet and wondrous joy whenever he could make her smile. He would lift her up and hold her close for a little while, his movements awkward and clumsy. Cecilia, Cecilia. Yet now he would mostly pause some distance away when he saw her being carried from one house to another. He would smile to his daughter and wave, though this never prompted the slightest reaction from her. Even the fact that she was so lovely and that he recognized the fair complexion of his own ancestors in the child seemed only to increase Olav's melancholy.

These days Eirik drew little attention to himself. The nine-year-old boy instinctively avoided the grown-ups, for he could see that they were always of a somber disposition. On the large estate there were plenty of things happening, and plenty for the boy to do, so he set foot in the main hall only to eat and sleep.

During market days, close to the springtime celebration of Inventio Crucis, the Finding of the True Cross, Olav had to go into town. There he received word summoning him to the Dominican monastery.

The prior wanted to tell Olav that his friend, Arnvid Finnssøn, had died in the winter. In the middle of the previous summer Arnvid had donned the robes of a monk at the cloister in Hamar. But during the second week of Lent he had suddenly passed away. No one knew the cause. When the brothers had convened for the terce mass, the monk walking beside Arnvid had noticed him turn pale and stumble. When he asked in a whisper whether he was ill, Arnvid shook his head. But when they knelt for *Verbum caro factum est*, the monk saw that Arnvid was unable to stand up again, and when the mass was over, he lay senseless. The monks carried Arnvid back to the dormitory and placed him on his bed. He whimpered a bit now and then, but could not be roused. Yet around midday he regained consciousness and asked in a low voice to be given the last rites. Immediately after receiving the sacraments, he fell asleep, and when the monks came back from vespers, Arnvid was dead. It had happened so quietly that the brother sitting with him could not say when Arnvid had breathed his last.

The prior also told Olav that before Arnvid joined the monastery he had distributed many of his costly possessions among kinsmen and friends, and he had asked his sons to send to Olav Audunssøn two drinking horns. Yet Arnvid's sons were not of a mind ever to venture beyond their own district. It wasn't until they came to Hamar for their father's funeral that Magnus brought the horns to the monastery. And

Father Bjarne hadn't wanted to send such rare and precious items south until he could put them in the hands of one of the order's own men.

Olav was quite familiar with these horns from Miklebø. They were small but very costly: two horns with ends shaped like bird claws, embellished with silver and gilding. Olav and his friend had drunk from them on celebratory evenings when they were served mead or wine. Each horn held only enough for one man.

Learning of Arnvid's death had shaken Olav to his very marrow. He had no desire to remain in town among other folks, and that same evening he sailed for Hestviken.

There had been times when he'd thought of his friend and recalled their last conversation, and then he would feel such anguish at the way in which he had bared so much of himself before the other man. He had regretted this weakness of his so fervently that occasionally he'd even imagined that he might feel easier if he heard that Arnvid was no more. Yet he realized that this was the last blow; he had no strength left to fight against his own heart, now that he knew there was not a single person who shared the knowledge of what he'd done. He no longer had the strength to bear his secret all alone.

For the first time he saw the true nature of their friendship. He was the one who had made use of the other, and Arnvid had allowed himself to be used. Olav had lied to his friend, who had seen right through his deceit. Not just once, but in every instance, Olav had told Arnvid only what suited him best—even at their last meeting—and Arnvid had accepted his words and kept silent. Olav was always the one who had sought support, and Arnvid had supported him, just as he'd given to everyone else all that they asked him to give. And the reward that Arnvid received had felt like a flogging; he'd experienced the same reward as the man who has the courage to follow Christ's example. Yet Arnvid had found fault with himself. He had castigated himself for being an unfaithful companion every time he hadn't been able to see a clear path ahead, as well as every time his soul became filled with bitterness and scorn for the wretchedness of people—just as might happen now and then for a sinful man when he dared to follow in the footsteps of God.

♦ ♦ ♦

Olav stayed home for the spring farming, and he was even more taciturn than usual.

But one morning after he'd gone out with his servants to get them started on their work in the fields, he walked back to the estate alone.

Sunshine was flooding through the open smoke vent, casting light over the empty hearth, across the dirt floor, and partway up the bed where Ingunn lay. Both children were with her. Eirik lay with his head of dark curls resting against his mother's arm as his long legs dangled over the side of the bed. Cecilia crawled around on the woolen coverlet, then stood up halfway and uttered a shrill little cry of glee as she plopped down with a thump on the lifeless body under the covers. The small maiden wore only a bright red woolen shift. Her skin was pink and white, and her hair had grown so long that it now billowed in gleaming, flaxen ringlets around her face and at the nape of her neck. Her irises were such a pale blue that even the whites of her eyes seemed blue-tinged, giving the lovely little face the oddly alert look of an animal.

"Your mother can't bear to have the weight of you two on top of her, Eirik." Olav picked up Cecilia and set her on his lap as he sat down on the bedstead. For a moment he hugged his daughter close, but the child tried to pull free; she wasn't used to being with her father. Olav felt how good the sturdy little body felt in his arms, and her silky soft hair smelled damp and fresh.

When Cecilia wasn't allowed to go to her mother, she twisted around on her father's lap to lean toward her brother. Eirik picked up his sister, holding her under the arms so she could try walking. Cecilia stuck out her plump little stomach and stretched out both arms and one leg as she tilted her head back to look up and laugh at her brother. Then she lunged forward, making a series of furious little kicks and shrieking "ga, ga, ga" and laughing. She curled all her toes against the rounded swell of her soles that still had barely even touched the ground.

Olav slid his hand over the woolen coverlet that was strewn with half-withered flowers, the sort that bloom between spring and summer: heath peas, catchflies, buttercups, and large violets. Ingunn gathered the flowers into a bunch.

"I see that summer must be fast approaching," she said.

Olav was looking at the children. They were unusually lovely, these two children who would survive her. Eirik was a big boy now, tall and slim with a knife attached to the belt he wore around his slender hips. Olav could see how handsome he was. His face had lost its childish roundness to become thin and sharp with a slightly beaked nose and an arc of fine teeth. He had a brown complexion and black hair, with golden yellow eyes. Could his mother avoid thinking of who the boy resembled?

"Take your sister, Eirik. Carry her over to Liv. Your mother and I need to talk about something."

With both hands Ingunn raised the bunch of flowers to her face, her nostrils drinking in the acrid scent of plant sap and springtime.

"Now, dear Ingunn," said Olav in a clear and gentle voice. "Soon you will no longer have to lie here in bed and suffer such torment. I have arranged for passage on a ship to take us to Nidaros this summer, to the shrine of Saint Olav, so that you can regain your strength from him, the martyr of righteousness."

"Olav, Olav, you must not even think of such a thing. Never would I be able to make the journey. I would not reach Nidaros alive."

"Yes, you will." Olav closed his eyes for a moment with a pained smile. His face had now turned deathly pale. "For I dare to do it now, Ingunn. When I get there, to the shrine, I will confess my sin. I will voluntarily place myself in God's hands and atone for the deed I committed against His commandments and against the laws and justice of my countrymen."

She stared at her husband in horror.

With the same little smile, he said, "What happened to you back at Miklebø, that time when you got out of bed and walked . . . surely that was a miracle! Don't you believe that God can perform a miracle again?"

"No, no!" she screamed. "Olav, what are you talking about? What sin are you talking about?"

"That I killed Teit. I set fire to the hut where his body lay, and then never confessed to the deed. I have gone to confession all these years and diligently confessed to everything else, both big and small. I have received Corpus Domini along with all Christian men, attended mass and prayed and pretended that . . . pretended that . . . But that's over now, Ingunn. I won't do it anymore. Now I will place this matter in the hands of my Creator and whatever He deems should happen to me, I will thank Him and bless Him. I will bless His Name."

Seeing the horrified look of anguish on Ingunn's face, Olav fell to his knees beside the bed and laid his head on her lap.

"Yes, Ingunn. You shall not suffer anymore for my sins. If only you will *believe*, then you must know that help will be offered to you."

She slipped her hand under his face, trying to lift it. The entire bed was now lit by the sun, as was his bowed head. She saw that Olav's hair was streaked with gray. It wasn't noticeable unless the sun shone on it directly because he was so fair.

"Olav, look at me. In Christ's name, you must not think this way. I have plenty of my own sins to atone for! Do you remember . . ." She forced him to raise his face. "'What a monster you are!' That's what you said to me back then. You know what I would have done to Eirik if you hadn't arrived in time. Should I be the one to reproach God because He judged me unsuitable to raise children? I spent that whole winter thinking only how I might strangle the innocent life I could feel moving inside me."

Olav looked at her in surprise. He'd never imagined that she remembered that, let alone thought of it as a sin.

"I must be grateful for God's mercy," Ingunn went on. "That alone is why I do not have the murder of a child on my conscience. And no sooner was I saved from committing such a sin than I tried to do something even worse. Again God reached out His hand to me when I was halfway through the gates of Hell. I have long been aware of all this. I was not allowed to kill myself in Hell. Each day that I've lived since then has been on loan, a reprieve that I've been granted so that I might realize and understand.

"I do not complain, though I'm lying here in this manner. Olav, have you ever heard me utter a single word of complaint? I know full well that God has punished me, but not for a lack of love. Twice He has yanked me away from the fire, though I was determined to run straight into it."

Olav stared at her. A light seemed to be suddenly lit behind his eyes. He'd felt such an inexpressible love for her during all these years, yet he'd never expected her to have thoughts that went much beyond those of an animal, a fragile young doe or a bird, able to love its mate and offspring and mourn for its dead young. Easily frightened out of its wits, helplessly surrendering to wounds and pain. Never had he imagined that he could speak to his wife as he would to another Christian about what had been growing within his soul for years.

"No, Olav!" Ingunn took his hand and pulled him down toward her, then hugged his head to her emaciated chest. He heard her heart pounding wildly. "Don't say such things, my friend! Your sin . . . Surely it must be white when compared to my sins! Many times I've felt that these past years have been long and heavy to bear, but now it seems to me that they were nevertheless good years because I was living here with you, and you were always so kind!"

He raised his head.

"It's true, Ingunn, that our life together at Hestviken has been good in the sense that we've always been friends. Whether you were ill or healthy, I've always had you with me, and I have loved you more dearly than anyone else on earth, for I grew up separated from all my kinsmen and friends, and you were the one I spent the most time with back then.

"And God showed me such kindness that, in spite of everything, He allowed me to have you. And I now see that it would have been difficult for me to thrive here if I'd had to live at Hestviken alone without a single person that I'd known in my youth. Don't you see? That's why I can no longer bear to be God's enemy. I cannot of my own free will continue to live apart from Him. Let it cost what it may.

"Nor am I a poor man. That was something else that God spared me. He allowed many of my undertakings to succeed, efforts that I made to improve our circumstances. I now own more than I did when we arrived here together. And, as you know, we agreed on joint ownership, so half of our property is yours, no matter what happens. You and your children will not lack for a means of support."

"Don't talk like that, Olav. The fact that you killed Teit cannot be such a great sin. I've never told you this before, nor have I mentioned it to a single person, but he took me by force! I couldn't bring myself to speak of it; such a thing was too unbearable." She groaned loudly. "Yet I was not blameless, for I had behaved in such a manner that he must have thought I wasn't too good for that sort of conduct. But I hadn't imagined that things would end as they did, and then he used force . . . It's true, Olav, I swear it's true."

"I know that." He reached out his hand as if to stop her. "He said as much to me. I know full well that in the beginning the killing was of little importance, if only I had announced at once that he'd died at my hand. But I made the wrong decision, and now the guilt has grown, and I can see that it will continue to multiply and produce more guilt. I have to turn around now, Ingunn—or else I will become the worst of monsters. Things are such that I hardly dare utter three words, for I know that two of them are bound to be false."

She covered her face with her arm as she quietly moaned.

"You know," said Olav in a subdued tone, "it's not certain that the archbishop will demand that I stand in judgment before the king's representative. Perhaps he will find that it's enough for me to confess my sin before God. I've heard of other instances when a man was granted absolution for the most grievous of sins without having to destroy the honor and well-being of all his kinsmen. He was instead charged with making a pilgrimage to Jerusalem."

"No, no!" she cried again. "Then you'd leave us behind! You'd be sent to the ends of the earth!"

"It's possible," he said, placing his hand on her chest to soothe her, "that I might return home to you. And you know that you would stay here at Hestviken and manage things."

"But surely it would then come out that Eirik is not your son!"

Olav said quietly, "I've thought of that too, Ingunn. And it held me back as long as you and I had no child of our own. I worried that my distant heirs would drive you from Hestviken along with your son. But now we have Cecilia. You can leave the boy the full inheritance from your share of the property, and he will have a wealthy sister besides."

"Olav, do you remember what you once said? That what you'd given Eirik was no more than restitution for his father's death?"

"Yes, I remember. But I now see that I was wrong, Ingunn. To give my daughter's ancestral inheritance to the child of a stranger . . ."

"Cecilia. Cecilia will still be a wealthy maiden, Olav. She is both wealthy and born into honor from a noble lineage. And she will be beautiful too. She will not be the worst off if she has to settle for a sister's inheritance when you are gone."[24]

Olav's expression turned stony and closed.

"A child who has come into the world as Eirik has, is not entitled to ancestral property."

"No. You've always hated . . . my wayside bastard." She burst into tears, sobbing uncontrollably. "I've heard you call him that."

"Ah. That's just a curse that an angry man might utter, even when talking to someone who was lawfully born." He struggled to speak calmly but couldn't help the trace of bitterness in his voice. "But I admit that I regret my words. It would have been better if I'd called the boy something else when he vexed me so."

"You hate him," said Ingunn.

"That's not true. I've never treated Eirik overly harshly. God knows he has received fewer punishments than he deserved. I can't bear it when you look at me as if I were stabbing you with a knife the moment I speak to him a bit sternly. And you, in turn, spoil him terribly."

"Me! Here I lie without even seeing the boy from morning to night." She had picked up the flowers and was shredding them to pieces. "Weeks pass and he never comes to see his mother. He rarely has time to talk to me—except on days like today. But then you came and chased him out."

Olav didn't say a word.

"But should Eirik suffer for my misdeed? Then it would have been better if he'd never come into the light of day, even if it meant that I would have suffered death and damnation because of it."

"Be reasonable, Ingunn," her husband quietly pleaded.

"Olav, listen to me. Olav, have mercy on me! You've paid far too high a price for my life and my health. Is there any reason why you should wander the world as a poor and homeless pilgrim in the lands of Abyssinia among evil nonbelievers? Or if things should take the worst turn and you are stripped bare and disparaged, perhaps in mortal danger, called criminal and murderer—for the sake of that fellow? You, who are the best sort of landowner, fair-minded and gentle and forthright toward everyone."

"Ingunn, Ingunn. That's precisely what I no longer am. I'm a traitor to both God and men."

"You're no traitor. It cannot be considered a great sin that you killed that man. And you have no idea how it feels to submit to shame and scorn. But I do know. You have never known what it is to live without honor.

"I can't . . . No, so help me Christ and the Virgin Mary, but I cannot suffer such shame again—not even if I were allowed to live and regain all my strength. I would know that every person who looked at me knew of my shame and what sort of wife you'd brought back to Hestviken. And then my Eirik would be deemed unlawfully born, without rights or family—a child that some stray, foreign servant had conceived with me, seducing me among the sacks of wool up in the storeroom loft, as if I were a loose thrall woman running after men."

Olav stood there looking at her, his face white and set.

"No, if I were granted life only to suffer in that way, able to get up and walk but then have to face such consequences . . . forced to take your little Cecilia and my unlawfully conceived son by the hand . . . and with you gone, having left all three of us behind and defenseless . . . then I would no doubt long for the time when I lay here and waited for my back to rot and break apart."

She reached out toward Olav. He looked away, his face rigid and stony. But he took her hand.

"It shall be as you wish."

XIV

The following year, at the beginning of Lent, Torhild Bjørnsdatter moved back home to Rundmyr. Word spread rapidly through the
whole countryside that she'd been forced to leave Hestviken quite
suddenly because she was carrying Olav Audunssøn's child.

If such a misfortune had befallen some other man who had lived
like a widower for years although his ill wife was still alive, no one would
have talked much about it. All the best men and women in the villages
would have told thoughtless youths and folks who didn't understand
proper manners and customs that the less said about the matter the
better. Olav knew this. But he also knew that this was about *him*—and
he was considered more or less an outsider. Yet in this case he had
done no one any harm, as far as he knew. And occasionally this did occur to folks if they gave it some thought. They knew of no specific blot
or stain on his name, and it could not be said that he'd committed any
dishonorable or despicable deed. Olav Audunssøn had simply become
known as an unlikable person, the least pleasant of fellows.

In the brief sunny period after Cecilia came into the world—
before it became clear that her birth had cost her mother any remaining vestiges of health—the villagers had treated Olav with goodwill.
Now that the curse had been lifted that had prevented the master and
mistress of Hestviken from producing offspring who survived, Olav's
peers had rejoiced on his behalf. And they thought that perhaps the
man would be more amiable and not such a curmudgeon as he had
been before. In any cheerful company he would extinguish all joy and
merriment around him merely by the way he sat, staring vacantly and
without uttering a word. But Olav couldn't seem to meet them even
halfway. He was and continued to be the surliest of men, and no one
felt at ease in his presence.

Then a rumor began circulating about him that was considered most vile. While his wife lay in bed, paralyzed and suffering great pain, her body broken after so many childbirths, each one more grueling than the last, Olav had been whoring with the housekeeper on his own estate. Folks now claimed that this had been going on for years, and one or another reported that Olav had often brought the maidservant gifts from town, gifts that were much too costly for someone of her standing. He'd also helped her raise the children left behind by Bjørn and Gudrid. And the whole time he had kept the farm going for her back in Rundmyr, which was where she had now gone. There wasn't much distance between Rundmyr and Hestviken, so they weren't exactly hiding their shame. Folks had seen Torhild lumbering about in the full light of day, her stomach now swelling under her belt. She went back and forth from hovel to cowshed, carrying buckets, and she often walked a long way at the edge of the forest, cutting bark and branches from the trees. Suddenly folks began to dig up all the old gossip about Bjørn Egilssøn and Gudrid.

Olav's closest kin in the area, Signe at Skikkjustad and Una at Rynjul, had stood by him for the longest time, striving to defend their kinsman. Yet even they now fell silent, and they looked as though they felt uncomfortable if anyone so much as mentioned Olav of Hestviken.

Olav was aware of most of the things people were saying about him and Torhild. After he had given his confession to Sira Hallbjørn, the priest asked him whether he had anything else to add. That's when Olav learned of the rumors flying about. Folks said that he and Torhild had been carrying on for years, and some hinted that he might well have been the father of the child that Liv Torbjørnsdatter had given birth to during the previous year, out there at Hestviken.

On one of the first Sundays when Olav hadn't dared ride to church with the others, the weather had turned mild. He was wandering about the courtyard when he came upon a large basin used for washing clothes. The ice had thawed so much that water covered the top. Olav leaned over to look at his reflection. The face that peered up at him from the dark depths of the basin, slightly smudged and blurry, looked like the visage of a leprous man, with a pallor resembling specks of rime on his weather-beaten skin, and eyes that were bloodshot. The sight terrified him.

Olav had almost expected to feel relieved at not being able to set foot inside a church this year. He'd finally come to the decision that he could no longer bear to attend mass with his sin unconfessed. Yet it felt worse to be locked out. He'd thought that this harsh penance for breaking his marriage vows would also offer some sort of antidote for the old wound. But all he could think was that this latest sin of his merely brought him right back to his previous sin.

It had been the last thing he'd dared trust about himself—that nothing on earth could ever cause him to be unfaithful to Ingunn.

Not a word about his betrayal had been mentioned between them. Yet he knew that she knew.

The reason for all of this was that he'd suddenly felt he could no longer bear Ingunn's suffering. This was after that day in the spring when he'd told her that he couldn't go on living with a mortal sin working on his conscience and spawning new sin from one day to the next. Nevertheless, she had demanded that endure it he must; he had to go on for both her sake and the boy's. As ill and racked with pain as she was, she'd had the upper hand. No man worthy of being called a man could have refused someone undergoing such torment.

Nor could he humiliate himself so much that he would bring up the matter again. He pretended that nothing had been said and continued to help Ingunn through the long nights as he had before. But now that his heart had finally been emptied of all love and patience, it began to take a greater toll on him. Now he noticed every single day how weary and worn out he felt after the incessant nights of keeping vigil in the sickroom air. And the great bitterness in his soul was constantly accruing more little traces of bitterness each time he noticed that he was forgetful or sluggish in his thinking as he went about his work, his body slow-moving whenever he had a task to perform.

One night before midsummer, he'd gone outside close to dawn.

Ingunn had finally fallen asleep, and he wanted to breathe in the chill of the night air before he went to bed. Olav paused on the threshold for a moment to look out. Everything was quiet, light, and gray. The men out in the boats weren't expected back for several more hours. Everyone on the estate was asleep. Then he noticed a little plume of smoke above the cookhouse roof. At that moment Torhild Bjørnsdatter appeared in the doorway and poured some liquid out of a pot. Her hair hung dark and wet around her.

Olav had always found it so touching to see the way in which Torhild strove to maintain an orderly appearance, in spite of everything she had to do. She was always the first up and the last to go to bed, yet she found time to comb and plait her hair even midweek, and to change her clothes. Ingunn had given up any such semblance of tidiness after they'd been married less than four years.

Olav went over to Torhild, and they spoke for a few moments, instinctively whispering because it was so quiet. There wasn't a sound except for the birds that were beginning to stir. In reply to her question, Olav told Torhild that he'd managed to doze for a while, but now he was about to go to bed.

"Why don't you go to our house and lie down in my bed?" the young woman said. "You'll have more peace over there." Now that summer had arrived she and the children slept instead in one of the storeroom lofts.

Torhild lived in the house that had belonged to Olav's parents when they were first married. It was a small, old house that stood a bit removed from the courtyard, for it was situated next to the cowsheds beneath the cliff called the Horse, to the east and up toward the valley. Olav had made repairs so that the house was now nice and sturdy, although the space was quite cramped.

Torhild accompanied him up to the house and removed the stick she'd used to latch the door. The air inside greeted him like a pleasant breath; the floor had been strewn with juniper. The room was so narrow that the bed set at the gable end filled the space from wall to wall. In the dim light the hide coverlets shone as white as snow. Around the bed hung wreaths of flowers that were meant to keep away vermin and flies. Torhild had left everything in good order before moving out for the summer.

She invited Olav to sit on the bedstead so she could take off his shoes. He felt as if slumber were billowing up from the clean and fresh bed, rising over him like sweet, lukewarm water. He was already half asleep when he toppled onto the bed, barely aware of Torhild tucking his legs up and then spreading the coverlet over him.

When Olav awoke, he saw that the evening sun was casting a yellow glow over the meadow outside the open door. Torhild was bending toward him, holding a bowl of freshly strained, warm milk. He drank and drank.

"Did you manage to sleep for a while?" Torhild asked him before she took the empty bowl and went out.

His shoes stood at the foot of the bed. They were soft and had been thoroughly rubbed with fish oil. A clean everyday shirt had been laid out for him. The front was still damp where she had washed off the spots, and the rip that had been there when he last wore the shirt had now been mended.

More and more often during the summer Olav would go over to Torhild's house to sleep through the early morning hours. But each time he'd managed to rest up in that way, it was even harder for him to resume his nighttime vigils. He was clearly hungering for sleep and more sleep. It seemed to him that countless years had passed since he'd been able to get enough sleep.

Torhild would bring him a bite to eat when she woke him in the morning. If his clothes were wet when he lay down, he'd find them dry when he awoke, with all the rips and tears mended. Olav asked her not to do this, for it was Liv's job to do such things, even though she seldom did. Torhild had enough to keep her busy. But the young woman merely smiled a bit and shook her head.

Then Olav felt a desire rise inside him to possess her. For once in his life, he wanted to know what it felt like to hold a healthy woman in his arms, someone he needn't be afraid to touch. Yet he didn't think he'd ever actually intended to do this. Even on the morning when he reached out and grabbed her, he'd expected her to push him away, perhaps with anger. But she sank toward him without so much as a sigh.

During the fall and winter Olav moved about as if at the bottom of a sea of heavy fog. He felt such a loathing for himself, and sometimes he felt a loathing for her too, but he didn't have the strength to climb out of the mire. He consoled himself with the thought that when Torhild moved back into her house with the children, things would naturally come to an end, but that wasn't what happened.

Olav stayed with Ingunn from early in the morning until late at night. He hadn't been away from home a single night, except during a week's time when he joined the hunt for seal pups. Now that he'd betrayed his wife, he recalled his bitterness toward her as no more than a temptation from the Devil to which he'd succumbed. Ingunn, my Ingunn, how could I do that to you while you lay here, so patient and good, as helpless as a broken-backed animal? This is how our friendship has come to an end, with me betraying you.

Night after night Olav wrapped Ingunn in coverlets and furs and carried her about, the way someone would carry a child, so that she might have some respite from feeling the pressure of the bed beneath her. The wearier and colder and more sleep deprived he felt, the more relieved he felt as well.

He and Torhild had barely exchanged a word since that unfortunate morning. In all these years at Hestviken, Torhild had been practically the only person Olav had spoken with at any length—conversing as he would with an adult of equal standing. This he now recalled. He remembered what he owed to Torhild, and how he had repaid her. He could offer no explanation for his misdeed. She had known no other man before him. She had known only toil for the well-being of others, and she had never complained when life fell heavily upon her shoulders. Now he went about not daring to speak to her, and he prevented her from saying a word. Deep inside he knew full well what she had concealed for a long time and why this virtuous and honorable woman, who was no longer so young, had allowed him to take her without resistance. He'd noticed it in her silent caresses. But if she'd forgotten herself that one time and afterward tried to put her feelings into words, the shame would suffocate him.

He also thought about Bjørn, her father. If he'd been alive, he would have struck Olav down at once.

Olav realized that what had happened was not going to remain hidden. It was during the darkest time of the Christmas season that his fear turned to certainty. And in his despair, he was seized by temptation. It was as if the Devil, who all these years had been leading him into worse and worse terrain—walking ahead of him in a partially veiled and shrouded guise—now spun around and threw off his enveloping cloak to reveal his bared and naked face.

Olav knew that Torhild would do whatever he asked of her. In the past the two of them had often gone out in the boat alone. She would willingly go with him now. Even if she understood what he had in mind, he was convinced that she would accompany him. Then something might easily happen . . .

And Ingunn would be spared from finding out. He himself would escape from being exposed before every person living around the fjord as the most wretched and vilest of men. Since he already belonged, lock, stock, and barrel, to the Devil . . . He no longer had a soul to lose.

Yet he said no. Satan was the one presenting him with this way out, and he said no. Such a misdeed I refuse to do. It doesn't matter whether you have my chair ready in Hell. I know full well that I have nothing to lose—honor and hope of salvation and the happiness that I'd salvaged with Ingunn up until now—all of this I deliberately gave up. But you still won't get me to do this. I refuse to cause Torhild more harm than I've already done. Not even for Ingunn's sake.

Lord, have mercy! Holy Mary, pray for us! Not for me. I will not plead for anything on my behalf. But Lord, have mercy on the others.

◆ ◆ ◆

Well, now it's too late, Olav scornfully told the Devil. They know now, all of my servants, so you can spare me any more of your mutterings. Be still. You'll have me when the time comes.

Such a hideous silence surrounded him. The servants fell silent whenever the master came near. Hardly even a whisper was uttered at mealtimes. Olav sat in the high seat, and the housekeeper brought in the food to serve everyone. No one noticed the slightest change in Torhild's demeanor. She moved about as efficiently and diligently as always, from dawn to late in the evening. She was just as straight-backed and agile on her feet, although it was clear that she was no longer walking alone.

Ingunn turned her face to the wall whenever Torhild came into the room.

So many days had passed in the new year that Lent was quickly approaching, and neither Olav nor Torhild had yet mentioned what lay ahead of them. But one day after the midmorning meal, he saw her go up to the loft where foodstuffs were stored. And he followed. She was taking pieces of pork out of the salt barrel and scraping off the black scum that had settled on the meat.

"I've been thinking, Torhild, that there's not much I can do for you," said Olav, getting right to the point. "I can't offer you much help. But I want to do whatever I can. And so I thought . . . The property that I bought over in Hudrheim five years ago . . . at Auken . . . I will deed the land to you and give you the document. And I can continue to manage Rundmyr for you and your siblings, just as we've done all these years."

Torhild paused and stared straight ahead for a moment.

"I suppose it might be better if I didn't stay up there in Rundmyr," she said.

"It will be better for you not to have to live here in the village. Considering the position I've put you in," Olav said quietly.

"Auken . . ." Torhild looked at him. "That's no small gift for a woman in my circumstances, Olav."

"It was meant to be a three-cow farm, and there are several good fields over on the south side of the knoll where the houses stand. But as you know, no one has lived there in a dozen years, and the folks who leased the land from me haven't kept it properly cultivated."

Torhild turned to face him and held out her hand.

"Then I thank you, Olav. I know that you wish to do the best that you can for me."

Olav grasped her hand.

"I've treated you worse than anyone else," he whispered. "You had every right to expect a different sort of payment from me."

Torhild looked him in the eye. "I am no doubt equally to blame, Master."

He shook his head. Then he said softly, "Isn't the work going to be too much for you now? Taking charge of all the heavy tasks here on the estate?"

"No, no." She smiled faintly. "Although it might be best if I don't stay much longer at Hestviken."

Olav nodded stiffly. "But the houses over at Auken are in miserable condition, falling apart and with holes in the roofs. I'll have them repaired and replace the roofs, but you won't be able to move there until summer."

"I can stay in Rundmyr until then," Torhild told him.

"I can't think of any other solution," said Olav.

The following week Olav was away from home for several days, and by the time he returned, Torhild had moved back to the hovel in Rundmyr. That's when Olav realized that he missed her—more than he could say.

It wasn't that his love for Ingunn had diminished or changed. This was something that had emerged quite separately. As if in some sort of delirium, he had peered into a life that was utterly different from his own. And he'd seen what it might be like for a man to walk alongside a healthy and sensible wife, someone who would carry her share of their common burdens and do so with as much good judgment and with as much energy as he himself possessed—or thereabouts. And he could picture children, both sons and daughters, following in his footsteps, one after the other, without their mother being broken and slowly killed as a result of bringing offspring into the world. It wasn't that he wanted to exchange his fate for the mirage hovering before his eyes. He thought that if he'd known from the very moment that he met the young and fragile Ingunn what sort of dowry she would bring to him, he would still have reached for her with both hands.

Yet inside he felt a plaintive longing for Torhild. She had done him more good than any other person. And he had repaid her in the very worst way.

Eirik had noticed how things stood with Torhild, just as everyone else on the estate had, though he hadn't given it much thought. But a great silence now enveloped Torhild, and that caused Eirik to realize that something repugnant must have happened. And it probably wasn't just the fact that she'd gone astray, as so many of the other maidservants had.

The silence had spread like soundless rings in water when a stone is tossed in. And little by little, without hearing a word spoken about the matter, Eirik sensed that this eerie silence was also encompassing his father. Vague and troubling fears stirred in the boy's soul, but he couldn't understand what his father had to do with the fact that Torhild was with child. His father was married to his mother, after all.

Sira Hallbjørn sent word to Hestviken that this year Eirik Olavssøn must go to confession during Lent and receive the Easter sacrament. The boy was now in his tenth winter, and he should have begun taking part in the service the previous year. Eirik forgot all gloominess and worry on the morning when his father sent him off. The priest wanted the children to stay with him for a week to receive instruction. It was the first time that Eirik was to ride alone all the way up to the village church. His father had loaned him a small, light sword, and behind the saddle the boy carried a sack with gifts for the priest and provisions for himself.

The day after Eirik returned home, he asked Olav, "Father, who is my godmother?"

"Tora Steinfinnsdatter, your mother's sister who died." Olav wasn't certain about this, but he seemed to have heard it mentioned at one time. Eirik asked no more questions.

Memories that he hadn't thought about in years started swarming into the boy's mind. Half-forgotten feelings of uncertainty and confusion surfaced. The other children had talked of godmothers and godfathers. On the first day Sira Hallbjørn wanted to know what they had learned at home about Christianity. Eirik's father had taught him the Credo, Pater noster, Ave Maria, and Gloria Patri, but that was long ago, and Olav had stopped sitting with the boy to make sure he said his prayers. For that reason Eirik didn't know the prayers well, and he'd mostly forgotten what the words meant in Norwegian. Nearly all the other children had been better taught, and most of them had learned some of what they knew from their godmother or godfather.

Eirik remembered that while he lived at Siljuaasen the mother he'd had there had once pointed to a fat and splendidly dressed woman when they were near the church. She said that woman was his aunt, his mother's sister. But the woman hadn't so much as glanced at him when she walked past. Eirik wasn't even sure whether she was the same aunt they had visited when his father brought him home from Siljuaasen. At any rate, the boy had never heard that she was his godmother. For the first time it occurred to him to wonder why he had lived at Siljuaasen when he was little. He knew of other children who had been raised apart from their parents, but they were always taken in by kinsmen—folks who lived alone or who were old. For instance, he thought about the little maiden named Ingegjerd, who was so lovely and wore a silver belt around her waist like a grown maiden, except that the silver emblems were very tiny, and who could recite all the penitential psalms almost word for word. She lived with her godmother, and she practically ruled the estate belonging to the childless couple, who gave her whatever she wanted. But everything at Siljuaasen had been poor and cramped, and Hallveig and Torgal had had plenty of other children. And Eirik had never heard his parents mention those people again, so they couldn't very well have been kinfolk.

He was now fully aware of what wayside bastards and unlawfully born children were. And paramours. The memory of his mother's visit that had frightened him so badly now came back to him, quite vividly, but still a mystery. Words that he'd heard his mother murmur, mostly to herself, when she hadn't been able to hide her weeping . . . They too came back to him, and he recalled that his mother used to wear the keys on her belt, but then they were moved to Torhild's even before the rightful mistress of the estate took to her bed. And now that his mother lay defeated, paralyzed, and unable to do anything at all, his father had taken up with Torhild instead. She would soon give birth to a child, and Eirik understood that the child was his father's. But if his father was married, then this would be so great a sin that almost no man would dare such a thing. That must mean that his mother was merely his father's paramour.

And then . . . and then! A wealthy landowner might send his paramour and children away, banishing them to some small farm far from his own, while he took in another woman or decided to marry. Eirik had heard of this happening several times in the area.

Fear gripped the boy's heart, and he could neither sit still nor find any measure of calm. His father could send them away if he wished to do so. And Olav no longer held any affection for any of them. It had been years since his father had taken Eirik along, and he never taught him anything anymore; he barely bothered to speak to him. Nor did Olav pay any mind to Cecilia. And his mother lay in bed, in need of constant care and unable to do the slightest bit of work. What if his father ordered them away from Hestviken, all three of them, so he could take in Torhild and her child instead?

Eirik had always noticed his mother's dislike of Torhild, but he hadn't given it any thought. Now he understood. And hatred, which the boy had never before known, took root in his heart. He hated Torhild Bjørnsdatter so much that the mere thought of her made his cheeks turn white and caused him to clench his fists. He imagined that one night he would sneak up to Rundmyr . . . and kill this person who wanted to force his poor, ill mother and all the rest of them out of their home. He would drive his knife right into her evil, false heart.

But his father, his father . . . Eirik felt as if he held two arrows and didn't know which to set to his bow. Should he hate his father as well? Or should he love him all the more, now that there was a danger of losing him? For Eirik, Olav had always been the most splendid of men. His impatience, his reticence, and his aloofness had had little effect on the child. Eirik had shaken all that off the way a seabird shakes off water. He focused only on those occasions when his father had been different. First and foremost when the two of them had gone out alone, to the forest or at sea, and his father was the all-knowing and helpful person who had warmed and protected the child with his quiet, good spirits. Yet even at other times, Eirik had often sensed that his father wished him well. And then there was that time when his father had had to cut off Eirik's poisoned finger, and he'd pressed the glowing hot rod to his own flesh to show his son there was nothing to fear. In the boy's eyes, that had seemed a deed so stunning that he could hardly remember it clearly—it dazzled his mind.

Lose his father? The very thought evoked in Eirik a fiery and icy pain. Then he dreamed that he ought to do something—some manly action that would become renowned. He came up with many ideas but didn't know which to choose. Yet he imagined that when his father realized what sort of son he had, he'd understand that he was raising a boy who was worthy of him. And when Eirik had won his father's heart, he would tell Olav that he demanded honorable circumstances for both his sister and himself; and their mother should not be sent away, no matter how ill and feeble and troublesome she might be. But Eirik would drive Torhild so far away that he need never fear she would come back with her child and demand to take their place.

Even though Eirik's love for his father was stronger than ever, all sense of certainty and trust had vanished. And now the boy noticed that Olav held little affection for him, despite the fact that his father no longer reproached him; in fact, he barely paid him any mind.

Olav hardly thought of Eirik at all anymore. He merely noted with a vague sense of relief that the boy had grown calmer and was less in the way.

Eirik didn't utter a word to anyone about the troublesome thoughts that now preoccupied him.

Finally, one day in late spring, Olav stayed behind in the main hall after the servants had finished their midmorning meal and gone out. That's when he said, "I suppose you may have heard the news. Torhild has given birth to a son." He spoke in a low, hoarse-sounding voice.

"I heard about it." With an effort Ingunn tilted her head back far enough that she could glimpse her husband, who was reclining in the high seat. His face was pale with red splotches, his eyes swollen and bloodshot. She saw that he'd been weeping.

She hadn't seen him weep in all these years—not when Audun died, not when she herself was given the last rites, because the women tending to her thought that she would bleed to death. Only once had she ever seen Olav cry.

"How is he?" she whispered. "Torhild's child?"

"They say he is lovely and well-formed."

"You haven't . . . seen . . . your son?"

Olav shook his head.

"I haven't seen Torhild since she left us."

"But surely you want to see him?"

"I can't do more for her than I've already done. There's nothing I can do to remedy the boy's situation. So I don't think . . ."

Olav got up and walked across the room, intending to leave the hall.

Ingunn called him back, "What name did she give him?"

"Bjørn." Ingunn saw that sobs were about to overtake him again.

"That's the name of your maternal grandfather."

"I don't suppose she thought of that. It was her father's name, you know."

Olav was about to lean over his wife but then turned on his heel and left.

Ingunn saw no more of him until the evening meal. From Liv she'd heard that he'd gone straight to the estate's smithy, and no one had seen the master all day. He looked as if he'd been weeping the whole time.

Then night arrived. Olav and Ingunn were again alone in the hall, though Eirik was sleeping next to the wall in his father's bed. Olav tended to the ill woman as he'd done every night. Several times Ingunn saw that he was again on the verge of bursting into tears. But she didn't dare say a word, not to this man who now had a son, though he could never lead his own child to sit next to him in the high seat on his ancestral estate. But what about Eirik? she wondered. When she was no longer here . . .

Hazily Ingunn understood that it was not just sorrow over his own son that was making Olav so distressed.

Olav was not, in fact, thinking so much about the child. He was mostly weeping for himself. It seemed to him that the last of his honor and pride now lay shattered at his feet.

It wasn't until after Saint Olav's Day that Olav Audunssøn had repaired the houses at Auken enough so that Torhild Bjørnsdatter could move her household there. His hired men were to take her and her belongings across the fjord. Olav headed south to Saltviken on the day she moved.

Ingunn lay in bed listening. She'd had the servants leave both doors open to the courtyard. She heard the packhorses arrive, their hooves thudding on the ground. Then she heard the cowbells, the tapping of the cows' small hooves; and the children, Rannveig and Kaare, running about as they kept the flock of sheep and goats together.

Liv stood in the outer doorway, watching all the commotion expectantly.

"Torhild's taking the path down along the bay," the maidservant reported with great excitement. "I suppose she doesn't dare carry that wayside bastard of hers up here among the houses, after all."

"Hush, Liv!" Short of breath, Ingunn whispered, "Run down there . . . and ask her . . . ask her if she would . . . tell her I'd dearly like to see her child."

A moment later Eirik came racing into the room. His narrow, dark face was blazing, and his yellow eyes flashed with bitterness.

"Mother! She's coming up here! Shall I chase her off? That filthy hellish sow isn't going to bring her bastard child to our estate!"

"Eirik, Eirik!" Ingunn cried plaintively, stretching out her thin, waxy-yellow hand. "May God have mercy. Don't say such ugly words. It's a sin to sneer at that poor woman and call her names."

The boy was now quite tall and as slim as a reed, with slender limbs. Indignantly he tossed his head with the fine black curls.

"I'm the one who sent word for her to come here," whispered Ingunn. Eirik frowned, then turned on his heel. He went over to the bed on the north wall and plunked himself down, staring with an angry, scornful smile at Torhild when she came in.

The woman walked forward with bowed head. She'd hidden her hair under a kerchief of rough linen, tightly bound, but she was as straight-backed as ever. In her arms she held a bundle wrapped in a red-and-white-trimmed coverlet. It was strange that even as she came before Olav's wife, humble and sorrowful, she still moved with her usual dignity and calm.

The two women greeted each other, and Ingunn remarked that Torhild had good weather for the fjord crossing. Torhild agreed.

"I had such an urge to see your boy," whispered Ingunn hesitantly. "I suppose you'll have to let me take a look at him. You can set him here in front of me. You know I can't sit up," she said when Torhild held out the bundle. Then she placed the infant on the bed before the mistress.

With trembling hands Ingunn lifted aside the coverlet wrapped around the child. The boy was awake. He lay there, his big blue eyes staring, though not at anything in particular. A little smile, like a reflection of a light that only he could see, hovered over his toothless, milky-sweet lips. Downy fair hair peeked out from under the cap he wore.

"He's big, isn't he?" said Ingunn. "For his age. Is he three months by now?"

"He'll be three months after Saint Lavrans's Day."

"And lovely. I think he looks like my Cecilia."

Torhild didn't reply as she looked down at her child. The housekeeper didn't seemed to have changed, yet she looked somehow younger and more beautiful. It wasn't merely that her figure seemed even more well-formed than before. Her shoulders were broad, and she'd always had full breasts; her torso was as deep and wide as a man's. But now it looked as if her firm, full breasts were about to burst the bodice of her gown, and that made her waist appear even more slender than before. Yet that was not the only thing. The strongly etched features of her pale grayish face seemed to have softened and grown more youthful.

"The boy doesn't look as if he's suffering from hunger," said Ingunn.

"No, and I thank God for that," replied Torhild quietly. "He doesn't know what hunger is, and with God's help he never will, as long as I'm alive."

"I'm sure Olav will make sure that the boy never lacks for anything, even if you should be taken from him," said Ingunn softly.

"I'm sure you're right."

Torhild wrapped up the child again and picked him up. Ingunn held out her hand to say goodbye. Torhild bent low over her hand and then kissed it.

Then the words burst from Ingunn's lips. She could hold them back no longer.

"You finally got what you've wanted all these years, didn't you, Torhild!"

Torhild replied quietly and sadly, "I want to tell you, Ingunn—as truly as I hope that Christ and the Virgin Mary will show mercy to me and this child of mine—that I don't think I ever intended to betray you, my mistress. And your husband . . . you must know that he would never . . . yet it still happened, all the same."

Ingunn said bitterly, "Yet I noticed for years, before I lost my health, how you felt about Olav. You were more fond of him than anyone else. And that has gone on for more than three or four years."

"Yes. I've liked him better than anyone from the first moment I saw him."

Then Torhild nodded a silent farewell and left.

Eirik leaped up, spat after the woman, and swore.

His mother called to him quietly, her voice fearful. "Eirik, my son," she pleaded. "That is sinful behavior. You must never utter such vile words about any mother's child." Then she burst into tears and tried to draw the boy close. But he pulled away and ran for the door.

XV

When the end finally came, it seemed completely unexpected to Olav.

The winter following the misfortune with Torhild Bjørnsdatter passed much the same as the previous two winters. Everyone was amazed that Ingunn Steinfinnsdatter continued to cling to life; it had been more than two years since she'd been able to eat solid food. By now she had bedsores, and in spite of all Olav's efforts, they kept getting bigger. She took little notice of the sores herself, except for the ones under her shoulders that sometimes burned like fire. Linen cloths had to be spread underneath her, and even though Olav smeared a thick layer of liniment on the places where her skin had broken, the cloth often got stuck in the sores. Then it was a pitiful sight to see her suffering such agony. But it was surprising how seldom she complained.

One morning Olav carried Ingunn over to his own bed, and while Liv put a clean coverlet and linens on her mistress's bed, he tended to her back. He had placed Ingunn on her side. He was dizzy from fatigue, and his chest ached from the vile smell that now lingered in the room. Suddenly he leaned over his wife and cautiously pressed his lips to the moist, open sore on her gaunt shoulder blade. He remembered something he'd once heard, about holy men who kissed the sores before they bandaged the wounds of the leprous people they tended. But this time it was the other way around; he was the one who was afflicted with leprosy, even though he outwardly appeared to be healthy and unblemished. And surely she must be washed clean by now, after quietly bearing such torments for so many years and without protest.

He no longer blamed her for anything.

Ingunn knew that Olav found it hard to be locked out of the

church. One night, after he'd fasted on bread and water all day so that he was utterly exhausted by the time he was to keep vigil with his wife, she whispered as she pulled him close, "I don't mean to complain, Olav, but why couldn't I have died after Cecilia was born? Then you wouldn't have ended up in the worst of all misfortunes with Torhild."

"Don't say such things," Olav replied. But he couldn't bring himself to tell her that was not the cause of the misfortune. He had grown bitter toward Ingunn, and then he'd become indifferent and dejected, yearning for some respite from everything weighing on him. He no longer faulted her for that; she simply didn't know any better. For close to thirty years he'd been aware that Ingunn didn't understand much, and God had made it his responsibility to understand and respond for both her sake and his. She was naive—and inexpressibly dear to him. He blamed only himself. *Mea culpa, mea culpa.* It was no one else's fault.

Everything at Hestviken now fell into decline, both the farmwork and the fishing. If the master couldn't be bothered to take part . . . But he had to stay with his wife. Olav kept consoling himself that it couldn't possibly last much longer. Yet he always thought: not today and not tomorrow and not the next day. The end would certainly come soon, but there was still a little time left.

Easter came early that year, which meant that the market and assembly days in Oslo took place already in the week after the feast day of Saint Blasius. Olav had to go to town because goods had been left for him with Claus Wiephart. He'd entered into a form of trade partnership with the German, but he didn't trust the man any farther than his fingertips. The last few times Olav had also refused to stay with Claus because it had proved too costly. Until now he'd been able to excuse himself by saying that he wanted to stay with the Dominican monks; he'd been a friend of the order since his youth. But this year Olav couldn't very well stay at the monastery because he'd been banned from attending mass. So this time he had taken lodging at the main inn.

Olav was sitting in the large room of the inn on the evening of the last assembly day, eating his food and drinking the barely tolerable ale on offer when Anki came in and asked for Olav, the master of Hestviken.

"I'm over here," called Olav. "Is there news from home, Arnketil? Or why have you come?"

"God help me, Master. Ingunn is nearing the end. She was receiving the viaticum when I left."

She'd had a spell of diarrhea, but no worse than she'd often had before, and she'd been coughing badly for several nights. But no one had realized, when Ingunn collapsed in the morning, that death was near. Not until old Tore came in for the midmorning meal. As soon as he saw how the mistress looked, he went out, saddled his horse, and rode off to summon the priest. Once again Sira Hallbjørn was not at home—his parishioners were determined to complain about this to the bishop the next time he came to visit—but one of the priest's friars happened to be staying at the parsonage and acting as his substitute. Even before the man rushed to administer extreme unction to the ill woman, he told the house servants to send urgent word to their master. As things stood, it wasn't certain that Olav would be able to make it home in time to bid his wife goodbye.

There had been no real frost weather that winter, and beyond the islands in the fjord there were open waters, so Olav had come to Oslo by boat. Then freezing temperatures had set in for several nights, followed by a strong southerly wind, and then more freezing cold. Anki had been able to row as far as Sigvaldasteinar, but then he'd been forced to go ashore and borrow a horse. By now it was likely that much of the fjord was filled with treacherous ice, and it was hard to know what would be the quickest way for Olav to reach home. No doubt he would have to travel inland on horseback. He could probably borrow a horse from Claus.

Folks had gathered around Olav Audunssøn and his manservant to listen and offer advice. Several finely clad young squires wearing colorful caps and ankle-length cotehardies also came over. They'd been sitting farther back in the large hall of the inn, making a great deal of noise as they drank German malt ale and played dice. Now one of them spoke to Olav. He was a tall lad with a fair complexion.

His long, silky golden hair reached to his shoulders, as was the latest custom from abroad. Olav recognized him by sight. The young man was one of the sons of the knight at Skog, and he was accompanied by his brother. The other fellows were evidently attendants from the king's palace.

"I understand that it's of the utmost importance for you to reach home swiftly," said the young man. "You can borrow a horse from me. I've left a good, fast horse with the monks out in their paddock. Shall I take you there?"

Olav protested that it was too great an offer, but the young man had already gone over to tally up with the other players and finish his ale before collecting his cloak and sword. So Olav entrusted his baggage to Arnketil and then threw on his own cloak.

The snow screeched underfoot as they stepped outside. The air was still a clear green on the slopes, but the first stars had appeared overhead. "It's going to be beastly cold tonight," Olav said to his companion. They headed east through the lanes toward Gjeitabru.

Olav asked the young man about the route he should take. He was not familiar with the countryside east of the town and down to Skeidissokn. He'd never traveled overland from Oslo. The young man said he could ride the full length of Botn Fjord. The ice was solid enough, though it might not be safe in a few places. "But I'll be happy to go with you," he added.

Olav said that was far too much to ask; he was sure to find his way. But his companion, who was named Lavrans Bjørgulfssøn, was already eager to set off. "I've left my horse at Steinbjørn's townyard. If you wait for me over by the church, I won't be long." Then he turned on his heel and dashed back toward town.

The Franciscan church had not yet been consecrated. Instead, the monks said mass in another building on the estate, but Olav had heard that the church did have a roof, and that's where the brothers held sermons in the evening during Lent. Olav's first year of penitence would not come to an end until Easter, but he could freely enter this building, since it was not yet God's house.

It still seemed strange to him to be headed toward the church. He crossed the bridge and walked up the well-trodden path across a field where the snow shone gray in the gathering darkness. The gable end of the church etched a black silhouette against the star-strewn blue twilight.

It was colder inside than out. From habit, Olav knelt down as he stepped inside, forgetting that the Holiest of Holies had not yet been brought to this house. At the far end of the dark nave he caught a glimpse of the glow from an entire cluster of lit tapers; they were burning at the foot of a large crucifix that leaned against the pale gray stone wall. Next to it yawned the chancel arch, leading to a space that was pitch-dark and empty.

A little closer in the nave a solitary candle burned next to a lectern. Reading aloud from a book was a monk wearing the ash-brown supplicant's robes of the order. He stood on an overturned tool chest, and around him a group of twenty or so men and women had gathered, all of them wearing heavy winter clothing. Some stood, while others had dragged over pieces of rafters and up-ended casks to sit on. Their breath swirled like white smoke in the candlelight.

For Olav, the desolation and unfinished state of the room seemed like a hand tightly gripped around his anguished heart. The window openings high on the wall were covered with planks. The scaffolding from the walls still stood at one end of the nave. As his eyes grew accustomed to the dark, he could make out chests and barrels of plaster, trestle tables and remnants of beams. Yet what seemed most desolate of all was the gaping entrance to the black chancel. And above this image of the world, unfinished and deserted, rose the large crucifix with the glittering candle flames grouped at its foot.

It was unlike any crucifix Olav had ever seen. With every step he took forward, the immeasurable anguish and pain inside him surged up at the sight of this image of Christ. It was not merely a likeness; it seemed alive. God Himself in a death struggle, so bloody from being flayed, as if every wound that any human had ever caused another had lashed His flesh. His body was bent at the middle, as if writhing in pain, His head was bowed, His eyes were closed and streaked with the blood pouring from the crown of thorns and down to His parted and sighing lips.

Beneath the crucifix stood Mary and John the Evangelist. The mother had clasped her gaunt hands, one holding the other, and pressed them to her chest as she looked up. Her gaze was so filled with sadness, as if she were lifting the sorrows of all families and all ages up toward the Son of God and begging for help. Saint John's eyes were lowered, his visage contorted from pondering the mystery.

The monk was now reading words that Olav had known since childhood:

O vos omnes, qui transitis per viam, attendite, et videte, si est dolor sicut dolor meus. Is it nothing to you, all ye that pass by? Behold, and see if there be any sorrow like unto my sorrow.

The monk set the book down and began speaking. Olav heard not a word. Instead he saw before him the image of the cross: *et videte, si est dolor sicut dolor meus.*

Back home Ingunn lay in the throes of death, or she might be already dead. It didn't seem real to him, yet he now knew that this sorrow of his was like a bleeding wound on the crucified body. His own hand had delivered lashes to his God with every sin he had committed and every wound he had caused both himself and others. Now that Olav stood here and felt as if his own heart's blood were running black through his veins, torpid with sorrow, he also knew that his life, filled with sin and sadness, had been another drop in the cup from which God drank in Gethsemane. Then more words that he'd learned as a child came to him. He had believed it was a commandment, but now it sounded like a prayer from the lips of a sorrowful friend: *Vade, et amplius jam noli peccare.* Go, and sin no more.

Then it was as if his eyes lost their power to see, and all his blood flowed home to his heart so that outwardly he turned as cold as a dead man. Everything seemed to be inside him—his own soul was like this house, intended to be a church but desolate, without God. Darkness and disorder reigned inside, and the only sparks of light that burned and emitted warmth had gathered like this image of the outcast Lord, the crucified Christ, bearing the weight and the torments of his sin and his despair. *Vade, et amplius jam noli peccare.*

My Lord and my God! Yes, Lord, I am coming . . . I am coming, for I love you. I love you, and I acknowledge that: *Tibi soli peccávi, et malum coram te feci.* Against thee, thee only, have I sinned, and done this evil in thy sight. Olav had uttered these words a thousand times, but only now did he know they were the truth that gathered all truths into one, as if into a cup.

My God and my all!

Then he gave a start as he felt someone touch his shoulder. It was Lavrans Bjørgulfssøn. The horses were out in the courtyard. The young man told him there was a quicker way out, and then he headed through the church to the chancel. Now that Olav's eyes had adjusted to the dark, he could make out the altar—the bare stone, not yet consecrated and blessed, a cold and dead heart. There was a small door in the chancel.

"Watch your step. They haven't yet built the stairs." Lavrans jumped down into the snow. Two monks were standing out in the courtyard. One held the horses, the other a lantern. Lavrans had no doubt told them what was happening, for one of the monks came over to Olav. He was a brother who had spent time with Sira Hallbjørn, and he'd also once visited Hestviken. Olav recognized the monk but didn't recall his name.

"Your wife bore everything with such patience and gentleness. Ah well. Brother Stefan is with her over there. We too will remember her in our prayers here at the cloister tonight."

The bitterly cold north wind was at their backs as they rode across the ice. For long stretches the ice was as hard as steel, swept clean of the small amount of snow that had recently fallen. The moon wouldn't rise until the early hours of the morning. The night was black and strewn with stars.

"We'll have to ride up to Skog," said Olav's guide. "We need to get some furs for us to wear."

Olav saw that it was a large estate with many big houses scattered about in the darkness. Young Lavrans leaped down from his saddle, unencumbered by the heavy, ankle-length garments he wore. He stretched, twisting and turning his tall, supple body a bit before he went over to one of the houses and opened the door. Then he went back to his horse, gently murmuring to the steed until a man came out with a lantern. The glow seemed to glide across the snow.

"You should dismount, Olav, and come inside." Lavrans took a small burning torch from the servant and showed the way along the courtyard. "We still live in the same place we moved into when we married. My stepmother and my brother Aasmund live in the big house from my father's time." He seemed to assume that everyone knew all there was to know about the noble family of Skog.

"Your father is dead?" asked Olav, just for something to say.

"Yes. He died a year and a half ago."

"You're young to be the master of such a large estate."

"Me? I'm not so young. I'm twenty-three winters." He opened a door. They didn't seem to lock the houses here at Skog. The two men passed through an antechamber to enter a small room that was lovely and warm. Lavrans lit a thick tallow candle that stood near a bed hidden by drapes. He tossed the torch into the hearth, then he spoke to someone inside the bed. He slipped some women's garments behind the draperies.

A moment later a young woman emerged. She was dressed lightly, with a red cloak over a blue, ankle-length shift. She tucked several strands of dark hair under the wimple that she had wrapped around her narrow face with the big eyes. As she bustled about, lithe and robust and young, her husband climbed onto the bed and was partially hidden. From behind the draperies came the sounds of a small child, and the young master laughed loudly.

"No, Haavard, are you trying to pull off your father's nose? Let go, now. Or perhaps you want to find out if my nose has frozen off?" The hidden child burbled with laughter.

The mistress of the estate brought food from the alcove and offered their guest an ale bowl with foam spilling over the side. Olav thanked her but shook his head. Right now he could no more eat or drink anything than if he'd been dead. Lavrans pulled away from the child he was playing with as he lay on the bed. He came over to stand beside Olav and ate something without sitting down.

"I suppose you'll have to bring me some water to drink, Ragnfrid." Turning to Olav, Lavrans said, "My wife and I have vowed not to drink anything but water during Lent, unless we're keeping company with guests or are traveling." He cast a longing look at the bowl of foaming ale. With a crooked little smile Olav then accepted the proffered drink and took a sip before handing the bowl to the master, who could now join his guest and take a long swallow. The young man was probably not ready to bid farewell to the somewhat inebriated condition he'd been in when they'd left Oslo. The drunkenness had abated as they rode, but now he generously added to it.

For Olav, the single sip that he'd allowed himself to swallow seemed to have roused him from his trancelike state. Gone was the strange feeling that everything he saw and sensed was nothing but shadows, and that tonight God had taken him away from the paths that folks traveled and placed him alone before His visage in some desolate place, for He wanted this creation of His to finally understand. And Olav had heard all the external sounds from the visible world the way he heard the fjord speaking below the mountains back home at Hestviken, sensing rather than actually hearing. Voices reached him as if talking outside a closed hall where he was alone with the Voice that rebuked and complained, filled with love and sorrow: *O vos omnes, qui transitis per fiam, attendite, et videte, si est dolor sicut dolor meus!*

Yet now the door to the closed room had been thrown open, and the Voice fell silent. He was sitting in the house of complete strangers in an unfamiliar place, late at night. He was going to have to find his way through districts where he was utterly unknown as he traveled home. And there death awaited him, as well as the choice that he'd made more difficult for himself with every day and every year that passed as he postponed deciding. That too he saw. But now he would have to choose. That's what he understood as he sat there, feeling frozen and unwell, awakened from the oddly visionary state that had come over him. After experiencing that vision, or whatever it was, he could no longer go on as he had, only half-awake and hoping that one day God would choose *for* him and force him to decide.

So many times Olav had allowed himself to be led astray, taking paths that he hadn't wanted to follow. Long ago he'd seen the truth of Bishop Torfinn's words when he said, "For the man who is determined to do what he himself wishes, the day will come when he sees that he has done what he never wished to do." But Olav realized that this sort of willfulness was like throwing a spear with only hope to guide it. Yet his own will, deep inside, was like a sword. When he was called to Christianity, he'd been given free will, just as a chieftain gives his man a sword when he makes him a knight. Although Olav might have squandered all his other weapons, broken and damaged them, the right to choose whether he would follow God or forsake Him was like a shield, and his Lord would never strike it from his hand. Even if his faith and honor as a Christian man were now tarnished like the knight's sword misused by a traitor, God would not take it away from him. He would have to carry it with him among the Lord's foes. Or else on bended knee he would return it to the Lord, who still stood ready to lift him to His breast and greet him with the kiss of peace, then return his sword, cleansed and blessed.

Olav felt a fierce desire to be left alone with these thoughts, although he no doubt knew that young Lavrans had the best of intentions. And he realized it might be difficult for him to reach home tonight without the man's aid. Yet the young couple's resolute willingness to help caused him great discomfort and uneasiness. The woman knelt before Olav in order to help him change his boots. She'd found for him foot wrappings of thick wadmal along with heavy, shaggy hide boots lined with straw. The scent of her skin and hair, so warm and wholesome, rose up to Olav. He shrank back, as if trying to defend himself. The young mother breathed and radiated everything in life from which, step by step, he'd been led away until he saw tonight that he'd been utterly removed from all of it, as if he'd bound himself with the pledge of a monk.

The young man came over with his arms full of fur garments, wanting to find some that would fit his guest. Olav felt oddly disheartened by the fact that his body took up so little space inside the man's clothing, which seemed to swallow him up completely when he put them on. Olav had broad shoulders, while Lavrans looked quite slim, but the young man was no doubt bulkier than he seemed, and he was also quite tall. Feeling the pain of pride, Olav was loath to seem a lesser man than Lavrans Bjørgulfssøn in every way, in terms of size and reputation and power. This tall, fair-complexioned boy went about with such ease in the hall's warm air filled with the breath of women and children, issuing orders and taking charge of the wealthy knight's estate. A man who was helpful, kind, and content. Lavrans had a long face with strong, handsome features, but his cheeks were smooth and still childishly round. Life had not caused a single rift in his young, fresh skin—and no doubt it never would. He looked as if he were meant to go his own way through the world without ever witnessing sorrow.

Olav protested that he was certain he could find his way through the forest out to Skeidissokn. Lavrans shouldn't think of riding back home late at night in such freezing cold weather for his sake. But his host replied earnestly that since there hadn't been a proper snowfall lately, there would be no clear track through the forest. Anyone heading that way would need to be familiar with the roads via Gerdarud. And traveling at night? That didn't bother him in the slightest.

Out in the courtyard a servant was holding two fresh horses, both of them lively, handsome animals. The young master was a splendid rider, and he had the finest horses. Olav secretly fumed at having to accept a helping hand to climb into the saddle. No doubt it was because the boots he wore were too big.

They traveled through the forest for most of the way. The thin layer of snow was frozen hard and crisscrossed by wide, old tracks left by skiers, horsemen, and sledges. The moon was still not due to appear for a while. Olav realized that he could have easily wandered about for a good long time before he managed to find his way out of the forest on his own.

Finally they came to several small groves and saw Skeidis Church ahead of them on a flat expanse of ground. The moon, a little less than full, had just risen and was hovering above the low ridges to the northeast. In the slanting, wavering moonlight, the land seemed rippled with shadows, for the snow had been blown into drifts with gleaming bare patches in between. All of a sudden Olav happened to think of the night when he fled to Sweden, more than twenty years earlier. It was probably the waning moon that prompted the memory. He recalled that back then he'd also been forced to wait for the moon to rise, and then he'd gone out at about this same time of night.

He told his guide that from here he was familiar with the roads heading south. He thanked Lavrans for his help and promised to send his horse back north as soon as he could.

"Ah well. May God be with you, Herr Olav. I hope that things turn out to be better at your home than you expect. Farewell!"

Olav stayed where he was until the sound of Lavrans's horse had died away in the night. Then he turned onto the road leading to the southwest. The terrain was quite flat in this area, and the road was good and well-trodden for long stretches of the way. He could ride swiftly. Now there was very little distance between farmsteads.

The moon rose higher, extinguishing the smaller stars. And the greenish-white glow began flooding the vaulted sky, reaching across the white fields and the rime-gray forest. The shadows shrank and diminished.

A rooster crowed once through the deluge of moonlight and received replies from farms farther away. Olav became aware of how soundless and still this night was. Not a dog barked from any of the farmsteads, not a sound from any other animal, not a sound except from his own steed as he rode, utterly alone.

And again it felt as if he were transported to another world. All life and all warmth had sunk down to lie in the grip of frost and slumber, like the swallows on the bottom of the lake in winter. All alone,

Olav rode through a realm of death over which the cold and the moon arched in an enormous, echoing bowl, but from the bottom sounded the Voice inside him without ceasing:

O vos omnes, qui transitis per viam, attendit, et videte, si est dolor sicut dolor meus!

Bow down, bow down, and surrender. Place his life in those pierced-through hands, the way a vanquished man gives up his sword to the hands of the victorious knight. During the past year, after he'd become an adulterer, Olav had never wanted to think of God's mercy. Now it would be unmanly and dishonorable to seek it out. He had feared and fled from justice among men for such a long time. His misdeed had been committed so long ago that he might now be spared from paying the full restitution demanded by his peers, but was this when he should ask for mercy? It occurred to him that he, who had evaded the judgment of mankind, must not be so ready to slink away from the judgment of God.

But tonight, as he traveled beneath the winter moon like someone who had been pulled out of time and life, just below the rim of eternity, he realized that what he'd heard as a child was true: the sin above all sins was to doubt God's mercy, to deny the capacity of that heart, pierced through by the lance, to forgive. In the cold and dazzling light, Olav saw that it was this agony he had been tempted to undergo himself, to the extent that a man's heart could mirror the heart of God—just as puddles of water in the dirt of the road could contain the image of a single star, broken and trembling, beneath the starry depths of the night sky. It was on that night in his youth, many, many years ago, when Olav arrived at Berg. That's when he heard from Arnvid's lips that she had tried to drown herself, seeking to flee from his forgiveness and his love and his burning desire to lift her up and carry her to a safe place.

Tonight Olav pictured Arnvid's face, and his friend admonished him: you accepted everything I could offer you, you did not break our friendship, and for that reason you were my best friend. Olav then thought of Torhild. He hadn't seen her since that day when he'd been forced to send her away from his estate because she was carrying a child under her heart—and the child was his, a married man's. He had never seen his son, nor could he ever right the wrong done to both the boy and his mother. But Torhild had left without a bitter word for him and without lamenting her fate. Olav sensed that Torhild held such affection for him that she realized the best thing she could do was to leave without complaint. And in the midst of misfortune, it was her greatest solace that she would be able to do a good deed for him.

Even for poor sinners, the worst thing of all was when a friend in need refused to accept help. In spite of the fact that Olav had sunk into sin and sorrow, God had allowed him to keep his happiness in peace. He'd been allowed to continue giving to Ingunn, and never was it said to him that the measure was full. Again it was the words from his childhood lessons that rose up, illuminated, so that he now fully understood their meaning. *Quia apud te propitiatio est: et propter legem tuam sustinui te, Domine.* But there is forgiveness with thee, that thou mayest be feared. I wait for the Lord, my soul doth wait, and in His word do I hope.

The borrowed horse Olav rode was beginning to tire. He stopped in a field to let the animal catch its breath. Steam rose from its flanks like silvery smoke beneath the moon that was now shining from the highest spot in the heavens. Both Olav and the horse were covered with rime. He roused himself and looked around. Behind him at the edge of the forest stood a farm that he didn't recognize; before him was a big white, flat space surrounded by tall reeds glinting with frost and rustling faintly in the cold wind. A lake. No, he didn't know where he was. He seemed to have gone too far east inland.

The moon had sunk low in the southwest and lost its sheen, the sky had begun to lighten to a pale blue with a wisp of reddish-yellow above the land when Olav finally emerged from the forest and recognized where he was. He was near several small farms in the very south of the parish. The quickest way home to Hestviken was across the cliff called the Horse. Stiff, frozen, and deathly tired, he paused to stretch and yawn. He had dismounted to lead the poor, worn-out horse up the slope. Silently he patted the stranger's animal for a moment, stroking its muzzle. Rime and frozen froth clung to its coat. By now morning had fully arrived.

After reaching the top of the ridge, Olav stopped for a moment to listen. An unusual stillness forced its way inside him through all his senses. The fjord had fallen silent during the most recent freeze. For as far as he could see, the length of the fjord was rippled with gray-white ice. The southerly wind at the beginning of the week had broken the first icy covering and driven the floes toward shore. Last night's cold had then bound all of them into one vast carpet. A thin icy haze hovered over the world, frosting everything with a shaggy grayness. And the air was turning a faint reddish color in the sun that was on the verge of rising through the fog.

The monk came out of the house when the servants heard the horse out in the courtyard. "Praise God that you've come in time!" he said.

Then Olav stood beside her bed. She lay there with her thin, yellowed hands crossed over her sunken chest. She looked like a corpse, except that her eyes still moved slightly under the fragile lids. With a sharp stab of pain, Olav sensed that soon she would lie here no longer. For more than three years he had gone in and out of the house while she lay stretched out on the bed, martyred, without the strength to move anything but her head and hands. Lord Jesus Christ, had it truly meant so much to him that she should stay among the living!

The monk talked on and on about how good it was that she would finally be released from her suffering, considering how things had been for her lately, with the flesh of her back raw and bloody. So patient and pious. Yes, he, Brother Stefan, had prayed when he hastened to offer her the last rites: "May God allow all of us to be so well prepared to meet death when our time comes, as Mistress Ingunn is." The next moment she had lost consciousness and had lain in this manner for the past twenty hours. It was unlikely she would ever revive. It looked as if she would be allowed to die without a struggle. Then the monk began to ask Olav about his journey home; he couldn't stop talking.

"But we must make sure the master is given some sustenance!"

The maidservant brought ale, bread, and a plate of newly cooked and steaming salted ling. Olav felt instantly ill from the smell of lye rising up from the platter of fish. He refused the offer of food. Then the monk kindly placed his filthy and frostbitten hand on Olav's shoulder and urged him to eat. Olav felt a great loathing for this Brother Stefan. His cowl smelled terrible, and his face resembled a demon with that long, pointed, and seemingly boneless nose of his.

At the first bite of food, Olav nearly vomited. His throat burned, and his mouth filled with saliva. But after a couple of mouthfuls, he noticed that he was ravenous. While he ate, he stared straight ahead without realizing that Eirik was sitting in his place on the bench and fidgeting with something. When the boy saw that his father was looking at him, he went over and held out what had captured his interest. He was so eager that he forgot the aloof manner he usually adopted toward his father. Eirik had saved two pairs of shells from the walnuts that his father had brought home from town the previous year and was now making good use of them. He had filled the shells with the wax dripping from the taper at his mother's deathbed. He would give one to Cecilia and keep the other for himself. Brother Stefan's attention was drawn at once to what the boy was doing. He plucked off a clump of wax that had dribbled down the candle and discussed with Eirik how they could eventually prevent the joined shells from splitting apart.

Exhaustion overpowered Olav as soon as he'd eaten his fill. He sat in the high seat with his head tilted back against the wall timbers. His blood was pounding in his neck and up to his ears, and he couldn't hold his eyes steady when he tried to focus on anything. The flame of the holy candle burning next to the deathbed appeared to have doubled. Occasionally his eyelids would close entirely, and images and thoughts swirled inside him the way fog drifts ashore and tumbles around. But when he made an effort to open his eyes again, all was forgotten. He felt sluggish and empty, and the memory of the past night and everything he'd experienced seemed as distant as an old dream.

The tireless Brother Stefan came over to pester him again, wanting Olav to rest for a while on the bed at the north end of the hall. He promised to wake him if there was any change in his wife. Olav shook his head in refusal and stayed where he was. That was how the hours passed until close to midday.

Olav had slept for a while and then dozed a bit, when he noticed that Brother Stefan was busy tending to the dying woman. Kneeling, the monk raised his hand holding the crucifix to Ingunn's face. With his other hand he motioned urgently to Olav.

Olav rushed over to the bed. Ingunn was lying with her eyes wide open, but he couldn't tell whether she was actually seeing anything— whether she was aware of the crucifix in the priest's hand or whether she saw her husband bending toward her. For a moment a certain alertness appeared in her dark blue eyes, as if she were searching for something. Olav leaned over his wife, and the monk held the crucifix closer, but her faint, wavering unease did not diminish.

Then Olav went over to take Eirik by the hand and bring him to his mother's bed. The monk had begun reciting the prayer for the dying.

"Are you looking for Eirik, Ingunn? Here he is!"

Olav had placed his arm around the boy's shoulder to pull him close as they stood there. Eirik was now so tall that he reached to his father's shoulder. Olav couldn't tell whether Ingunn recognized either of them.

Then he knelt down, keeping his arm around the child. Eirik began quietly sobbing as he knelt side by side with his father to murmur the expected responses.

"*Kyrie, eleison,*" said the monk.

"*Christe, eleison,*" whispered the man and the boy.

"*Kyrie, eleison. Sancta Maria.*"

"*Ora pro ea . . .*" The two of them stared at the dying woman. Olav sought some sign that she recognized him. The boy looked at his mother, in terror and in wonderment, as tears poured down his cheeks, causing him to sniffle between replies. "*Ora pro ea, orate pro ea . . .*"

"*Omnes sancti Discipuli Domini.*"

"*Orate pro ea.*"

Ingunn sighed quietly and whimpered. Olav leaned closer. Not a word issued from her white lips. The three of them continued the prayer for the dying.

"*Per nativitatem tuam.*"

"*Libera ei, Domine.*"

"*Per crusem et passionen tuam.*"

"*Libera ei, Domine.*"

She closed her eyes again. Her hands slipped from each other and fell to her sides. The monk moved them back to her chest, crossing her hands as before. And he prayed, "*Per adventum Spiritus sancti Paracliti.*"

"*Libera ei, Domine.*"

"Ingunn, Ingunn, wake up, just for a moment, so I can see that you recognize me."

"*Peccatores,*" prayed the monk.

And the father and son replied, "*Te rogamus, audi nos.*"

She was still breathing, and her eyelids trembled ever so faintly.

"*Kyrie, eleison.*"

Olav stayed on his knees next to the bed, holding Eirik close, even after the prayer had ended. Silently he implored: let her awake, just for a moment, so we can bid each other farewell. Even though every night of the past three years had seemed as if he were walking with her down the road to Hell, he didn't feel he could part with her yet. Not until they greeted each other one last time before she went out the door.

Eirik was now lying on the edge of the bed, bitterly crying his heart out.

Suddenly the dying woman's lips moved. Olav thought he heard her whisper his name. Quickly he leaned closer. She muttered something but he didn't understand. Then she said more clearly:

"Don't go out there . . . it's not safe . . . out there . . . Olav . . . don't . . ."

He didn't know what she meant, whether she was speaking from a dream or what it was. Hardly aware of what he was doing, Olav put his arms around Eirik and stood up, setting the boy on his feet.

"You mustn't cry so loudly," Olav whispered as he led his son over to his place on the bench.

Eirik looked up at him in confusion. The child's face was swollen from weeping.

"Father," he whispered. "Father, you won't send us away from Hestviken, will you? When our mother dies?"

"Send who away?" asked Olav, distractedly.

"Us. Me and Cecilia."

"No, of course not." Olav fell silent with an abrupt intake of breath. The children . . . He'd forgotten about them when he thought about all those other things last night. He suddenly felt overwhelmed. But he couldn't think about this now; he had to push it aside. As if asleep, he sat down on the bench a short distance away from Eirik.

He didn't have the strength to worry about this now. But the children . . . He hadn't thought about them.

It was approaching late afternoon. Gradually those in the hall had grown tired of keeping vigil and waiting for the last breath. Liv had brought Cecilia in a few times, but Ingunn lay unconscious and the child was restless and noisy, so the maidservant had to take the little maiden out. The last time, Eirik had gone with them. Olav heard their voices outside.

He had sat down on the step to the bed. Brother Stefan was dozing at the table with his open breviary in front of him. The servants quietly came in, knelt down to whisper a prayer, and stayed for a short time before leaving again. Olav sank into a torpor. He wasn't asleep, but it seemed as if his head were filled with gray wool instead of a brain, so worn out and spent did he feel.

Once, when he again looked at Ingunn, he saw that her eyelids had opened partway to reveal her eyes shining beneath, unseeing.

During the first weeks after Ingunn's death Olav couldn't say when he actually slept. But he must have slept now and then, for there was still life in him. Toward morning he always felt as if a gray fog were flooding his head, confusing his thoughts and tangling them up. Then the haze settled, thick and gray, but it was as if he could still feel the pressure of his burden as he lightly dozed in the morning hours, aware that his mind, deep inside, was still preoccupied with the same matters. And through the fog he was aware of every sound in the hall and out in the courtyard. He longed just once to fall into a deep slumber, to sink down into utter darkness and forgetting. But as far as he could tell, that never happened; he was never able to enjoy a sound sleep.

It was the thought of the children that kept him awake.

He knew that on the night when he rode home to Ingunn's deathbed, he'd reached a decision. He had said yes to God. I will come, because You are my God and my All. I will fall at Your feet, because I know that You long to lift me up to You.

But the children . . . It seemed to him as if both he and God had forgotten them. Until, that is, Eirik had asked whether Olav intended to send them away from Hestviken.

Olav couldn't understand how the boy had come up with such an idea. Surely it couldn't have occurred to him naturally.

And then Olav thought about Ingunn's last words, pondering what she'd said.

"Don't do it, Olav. Don't go out there, it's unsafe out there."

Perhaps she'd been merely speaking in her dreams—dreaming that he was about to venture out onto unsafe ice. But it was also possible that, lying there as she did, as if her soul were not in her body, she'd found out what had happened to him that night. Perhaps both Ingunn and Eirik had become aware of it, and so they had pleaded for themselves.

The children had no one but him. Hallvard Steinfinnssøn, who lived far north at Frettastein, was their closest kinsman. And Olav could just imagine how Hallvard would react if he now stepped forward to take the blame for a murder he'd committed twelve years earlier. His children would not be heartily welcomed by their uncle. And then Eirik's true identity would no doubt come to light.

Olav would also have to admit that he'd sought to push forward an illegitimate heir and steal the ancestral estate from his closest kin to give it to a stranger.

If Olav did what he'd decided on that night, he could see only one way out for the children. He would have to give Cecilia to the sisters of Nonneseter Abbey as an offering, along with what the maiden had inherited from her mother. And Eirik would have to join the church of the monks.

Olav felt deeply shaken. Was that the intention? Was his lineage supposed to die out with him because he'd knocked the crown from his own head when he committed a shameful deed? Was he meant to be a childless man because it wasn't right for such shame to increase the lineage? And the children he'd sired while he was defying God? Were they not meant to carry on the family after he'd brought misfortune to his kin? One son did he have, only one, but he couldn't allow him into the family. And his only daughter would be lost to the world behind the gates of a nunnery.

Eirik . . . Sometimes Olav found himself feeling sorry for the boy. It would be difficult for him to send the young lad back to those circumstances from which he'd once been willing to retrieve Ingunn's secretly born son. Occasionally Olav had also felt affection for the boy, in spite of everything.

It was mostly at night, when Eirik was asleep next to the wall in the bed they shared, that Olav thought he couldn't possibly consider sending the boy back to the fate determined by his birth.

At other times, when Olav heard the boy bothering the hired men or laughing as if he'd completely forgotten his sorrow at his mother's death, he felt that Eirik was now his main burden. The boy was the biggest obstacle, making it difficult for Olav to break through everything that separated him from finding peace and solace for what afflicted his soul.

Olav noticed that he was drifting further and further away from the decision he'd made on the night before Ingunn died. But he didn't know whether he was being drawn back into the old ways against his will, or whether he was voluntarily fleeing, because, when it came right down to it, he didn't dare step forward after all.

One night Olav got up and went over to the house where the maidservant Liv slept with his daughter. With great effort he managed to rouse the servant from sleep.

Liv huddled under the coverlet, blinking her little, half-closed pig-eyes, as she stared expectantly, both frightened and curious, at the master who stood next to her bed holding a candle. Under the locks of thick, gray-flecked hair, his face was furrowed and as pale as ashes, the firm line of his jaw obscured by a haze of stubble. He wore only linen garments under the black, ankle-length cloak, and his feet were bare in his shoes.

Olav looked down at the maidservant and realized that she probably thought he'd come to dole out the same fate he'd caused Torhild Bjørnsdatter. When Liv moved aside to make room for him in the bed, Olav gave a brief, harsh laugh.

"Cecilia," he said. "I was dreaming about her. There's nothing wrong with Cecilia, is there?"

Liv folded back the coverlet so he could look at the child. She lay asleep in the crook of her foster mother's arm, her little rose-red face burrowing into the warmth and partially hidden by her own gleaming, silky fair tresses.

Without another word, Olav set down the candle, leaned down, and lifted up his daughter. He tucked her inside the folds of his cloak, then blew out the candle and carried the child away.

Back in the main hall he let his cloak fall to the floor, kicked off his shoes, and crept into bed with his daughter, who was still sleeping soundly against his chest.

At first it seemed to him that he was just as unlikely to fall asleep as always. But it felt good to lie in bed, holding the tiny young life in his arms. Her hair was as soft as silk under his chin, and it smelled of sleep, both sweet and refreshingly sharp. Her little puffs of breath, warm and dewy, played over his chest at the base of his throat. Her skin was silky soft, her body firm and chubby and strong; her little knees, boring into her father's abdomen, were very plump. Olav allowed himself to love this child of his, the way a miser might allow himself to take out his treasure and wrap his hands around it.

But after a while the tiny maiden felt like a heated stone. The warmth of the sleeping child seeped inside the father, soothing the pounding and aching uneasiness in his heart. Warmth streamed through his whole body, and the strain he felt now dissolved into a sweet and gentle weariness. He felt sleep trickle inside him, a beneficence that he could now fully appreciate. With his chin buried in Cecilia's soft curly hair, Olav sank into a deep slumber.

He was awakened by the child's loud and furious wailing. The little maiden was sitting up, still partway on his chest, and howling as she rubbed her eyes with her small fists. Next to the wall Eirik had sat up in surprise. Then the boy leaned over his father to talk to his little sister in an attempt to calm her.

Olav didn't know what time it was. The hearth vent cover was closed. The small oil lamp placed at the edge of the hearth was still burning, so it must be quite early.

When Olav touched Cecilia, she grew even more furious and wild, flailing her plump little fists about as she screamed and screamed. Then she turned around and threw herself at her father, trying to bite him, but she couldn't get a good grip on his gaunt cheek. Eirik laughed merrily.

Then Cecilia began digging two fingernails into Olav's worn-thin eyelids, pulling them sideways, twisting and turning them. This amused her so much that she calmed down and stopped crying for a while as she did her best to annoy her father. Then she paused and looked around helplessly.

"Liv? Where Liv?" She began howling pitifully. "Num!" she shouted insistently. "Num!"

That was her word for food, Eirik explained. Olav got out of bed and went over to the alcove. He came back with a big piece of the best cheese, some flatbread, and a cup of partially frozen milk.

Holding the cup of milk that he wanted to warm, Olav worked to get the fire going in the hearth. Cecilia sat on the bed and stared furiously with her clear blue, kittenlike eyes at this man she didn't know, as she tossed bits of flatbread at him. She quickly devoured the piece of cheese until only the rind remained. "Num," she said and threw the last of the cheese on the floor.

Olav went to find more food for his daughter. She ate everything he gave her, and when there was no more, she began wailing again. She wanted to go to Liv.

When the milk was suitably warm, Olav carried the cup over to his daughter. She drank every last drop and then refused to let go of the cup, pounding it against the bedstead. It was a lovely wooden cup, delicately carved from a tree root, so Olav took it away from her. Cecilia grabbed his hair in both hands and tugged. Then she dug her claws into his face, making long scratches on her father's cheeks with her sharp little nails. She kept scratching him as hard as she could. Eirik tumbled around in the bed with laughter. He knew his sister better than his father did, and he reported that Cecilia had the temper of a troll. "She has scratched you bloody, Father!" he said.

Olav went to get more food, bringing all the delicacies he could find. But by now Cecilia had undoubtedly eaten her fill, and she knocked aside everything he offered her. This daughter of his did not seem at all suited to a nun's life.

Finally Olav had to let Eirik carry the furious child out and take her back to her foster mother.

One night Olav awoke to pitch darkness. The oil lamp had gone out while he was sleeping. For the first time since Ingunn died, he'd fallen into a deep, sound sleep. He felt strangely gentle and tender with gratitude, for he felt as if he'd been reborn and cured from a lengthy illness. That's how good it was to awake feeling rested.

He closed his eyes again, for the darkness was so intense that it seemed to be pressing against him. Then it occurred to him that he'd been dreaming while he slept. He tried to put together the fragments of his dream. He'd been dreaming about Ingunn the whole time, and about sunlight. A lingering brightness was still with him.

He'd dreamed that the two of them were standing together in the small hollow between the clay hills where the creek ran, north of the houses at Frettastein. The ground was still pale and bare, the grass withered and flattened from the previous year. But in between, along the bank of the creek and sticking out of the dead grass, grew several reddish-brown and dark green leafy shoots. He stood with Ingunn just below the big white boulder that filled the entire creek bed; the water sloshed over and alongside the rock in a small waterfall, trickling and gurgling into the pool below. They were watching several boats made of bark whirling around in the hole. Ingunn wore that old red gown of hers. Neither of them seemed to be fully grown.

During the entire dream, Olav seemed to be walking along the creek with Ingunn. He saw them standing together under a big spruce in the middle of a steep scree; this was farther down, where the creek passed along the bottom of a narrow hollow. Heavy, toppled rocks filled the small riverbed, and in the rough terrain on either side grew such an abundance of ferns, wolfsbane, fireweed, and raspberries that it was impossible to see where to set their feet among the stones that tipped and slid away. Ingunn was afraid of something and reached for both his hands as she moaned faintly. He too felt his chest tighten. Overhead he saw a thin strip of sky above the gorge. Clouds were gathering with the threat of thunder.

At one point they'd found themselves all the way down at the shore where the river spilled into Lake Mjøsa. He saw the bay's curving shoreline, strewn with dark gray and sharp-edged stones beneath the slope. Out in the fjord, the water was surly and dotted with gray foam. He and Ingunn walked along, evidently heading for a place where they could borrow a boat.

Olav realized it must have been that old expedition of theirs to Hamar that had come back to him, the memories confused and rearranged, as always happened in a dream. But the sweetness of the freshest time in their youth had been so vivid in his dream that the taste of it still lingered in his mind.

In a sense it felt as if, in his dream, he'd relived his entire life with Ingunn during all those years.

However that might be, he must have slept through a whole night in order to dream about all that. It must be close to dawn.

In the dark, Olav slipped out of bed and found some clothes to put on. He wanted to go outside to see how early in the morning it was.

As he stepped out of the antechamber door, he saw the spine of the Horse with its mane of forest at the very top, a black shape looming against the starry sky. Between the houses the courtyard was dark, but up on the ridge of the expanse of rock that rose up in the direction of the fjord, there was a slight brightening, like a glow from the moon on the ice. Yet toward the forest beyond Kverndalen the brightening was flickering and faint with low, slanting rays of moonlight.

Olav couldn't quite believe that he'd been so mistaken about the time. Hesitantly he crept along the row of houses and headed west through the courtyard toward the viewpoint on the slope. The path up was icy and slippery.

On the opposite side, the crescent moon touched the treetops, yellow as it sank. Beneath the matte, slanted rays lay the frozen fjord, its entire surface rippled with the faint light and pale shadows. On the slopes below him the icy ground still gleamed slightly. He realized that he hadn't slept more than three hours.

Again the light from the moon hovering above the mountain crest prompted Olav to think about that night when he fled, an outlawed man. Now the memory suddenly settled over him with an infinitely weary gloom.

He thought about his dream. It seemed an eternity since they'd walked along the creek, taking the path down the slope and out into the countryside. Now she was dead. She'd died only three weeks ago, yet it seemed such a long time since then.

He felt sobs tighten his throat. Tears filled his eyes beneath their burning lids as he stood there, staring at where the moon was now nothing more than a spark beyond the forest across from him. He wished he were able to weep right now. He hadn't wept when she died or at any time afterward. Yet on the two or three occasions when he'd wept since becoming full-grown, he hadn't been able to stop. As furiously as he'd struggled to keep from weeping, wave upon wave of sobs had overtaken him, and he'd been powerless to stop them. But now, tonight, when he was alone and wished that he might weep out here where no one could see him, he managed only a painful tightening in his throat and a few, solitary tears that spilled out at long intervals and turned ice-cold as they slowly ran down his face.

But when spring arrived . . . It suddenly occurred to him that he would travel somewhere in the spring. He couldn't abide staying here at Hestviken in the summer.

The moon had disappeared, and across from him the light had now faded from the forest. Olav turned on his heel and walked back to the house.

In the darkness, as he was about to lie down, he noticed that Eirik had moved so he was lying crosswise, filling up the whole space between the wall and the edge of the bed.

Olav was suddenly loath to touch the boy—whether it was because he didn't want to disturb him or because he had no desire to share the bed with him tonight.

The bed against the southern wall of the house stood empty. The bedclothes had been taken away, and the straw on which she'd died had been burned.

Olav went over to the alcove door and shoved it open. An icy cold issued from inside, along with what seemed to be the frozen and hazy odor of food—cheese and salted fish. Food was stored in the alcove in the wintertime, and the room was kept closed so all the warmth would stay in the main hall. But the bed was always made up, in case guests should arrive and need to stay the night.

Olav paused for a moment with his hand on the old plank of the doorframe. Under his fingertips he felt the carving that covered the surface: the snakes writhing around the figure of Gunnar.

Then he went inside, colliding with wooden buckets and barrels until he found his way over to the bed. He climbed up and lay down, closing his eyes against the darkness, as he surrendered to the night and no sleep.

Holy Days and Canonical Hours

Saint Blasius's Day . . . . February 3

Saint Agata's Day. . . . . February 5

Saint Gregory's Day. . . . . .March 12

Feast of the Annunciation. . . . . March 25

Inventio Crucis (Finding of the True Cross). . . . . May 3

Saint Jon's Day. . . . . June 23, Midsummer

Saint Peter's Day . . . . June 29

Saint Sunniva's Day. . . . . .July 8

Saint Olav's Day. . . . . .July 29

Saint Lavrans's Day . . . . August 10

Saint Bartholomew's Day . . . . .August 24

Saint Matthew's Day . . . . September 21

Saint Mikael's Day (Michaelmas) . . . . .September 29

All Saints' Day. . . . . November 1

Canonical Hours Celebrated in the Catholic Church

Matins . . . . 2 a.m.

Lauds. . . . . 5 a.m.

Prime. . . . . 6 a.m.

Terce . . . . 9 a.m.

Sext . . . . 12 noon

None . . . . 3 p.m.

Vespers . . . . 6 p.m.

Compline . . . . 7 p.m.

Times are approximate.

Notes

---

1   Birch Legs—A political group formed in 1174 in southeastern Norway around a pretender to the Norwegian throne when the rightful successor was disputed. The name derived from the practice of tying birch bark to their feet because they were too poor to have shoes. They continued to use the name after they came to power in 1184.

2   ting—A meeting of freeborn, adult men that took place at regular intervals to discuss matters of concern to the community on the local or regional level. The regional ting also served as a court of law presided over by chieftains, who settled disputes and ruled on cases of manslaughter and other crimes. By 1276 the four law provinces had agreed on a secular law code for the entire country ("Landslog"), instigated and formulated by King Magnus, who was subsequently nicknamed Law-Mender.

3   Gunnar Gjukessøn—According to the "Lay of Atli" in the Poetic Edda, Gunnar was king of the Niflungs. Along with his brother Hogni, he was invited to visit Atli, lord of the Huns. Gunnar accepted the invitation on their behalf in spite of warnings of treachery. Atli then offered to spare Gunnar's life in return for the Niflung treasure. But when Hogni was killed, Gunnar exclaimed that now he alone knew of the treasure's hiding place, which he would never reveal. He was thrown into a snake pit. He played the harp in an attempt to charm the snakes, but died when one of them bit him.

4   allodial property—Land that was originally defined as owned by a family from the times when there were burial mounds, meaning heathen times. According to Norwegian law, the family had to have possessed the land continuously for four or even six generations. The property right was passed to male kinsmen, but if there were no male offspring, a woman could be the heir.

5   *Miserere, mei Deus*—The first words of Psalm 51: "Have mercy upon me, O God, according to thy loving kindness: according unto the multitude of thy tender mercies blot out my transgressions."

6   Sira—The title for a priest in medieval Norway.

7   wealthy convent—Although education for girls in the Middle Ages was rare, some daughters of the nobility were sent to cloisters to receive instruction, both secular and religious.

8   nøkk—A menacing male creature believed to reside in Norwegian lakes, streams, and other inland waterways. The nøkk can assume various forms, usually with the intent of luring folks into the water to drown them.

9   hulder—An eerie supernatural figure, most often female, encountered in the forests and high mountain pastures. At first glance, she appears to be a young woman with lovely golden hair, but her cow tail reveals that she is not human. She is sometimes described as having a hollowed-out back.

10 The assembly known as the Øreting was held near Nidaros (today's Trondheim) and was a gathering of noblemen from the eight counties in Trøndelag. It became known as the only assembly that, through acclamation, could establish the rightful king of Norway.

11 Spring Pelts—The Norwegian word Vaarbelger literally means "springtime-shedder." The name was given to the rebels led by Skule Baardssøn in 1239–40 in his fight against Norway's King Haakon Haakonssøn. It was a derogatory term because pelts shed in the spring were of lesser value.

12 Glumra—Eystein Glumra (Eystein the Noisy) was a minor king on the west coast of Norway during the ninth century, mentioned in the Heimskringla.

13 Bagler—The Baglers (representing the more conservative nobility and favoring the church and its privileges) vied with the Birch Legs for control of all of Norway during the civil war, lasting from 1130 until 1217. When King Sverre died in 1202, the Baglers gained in power, and when Sverre's successor, King Haakon III, died after a reign of only two years, his infant son was left in Hamar, which was under Bagler control. The Birch Legs were credited with rescuing the young boy, who later became King Haakon IV. In 1209 the Baglers and Birch Legs agreed to recognize royal pretender Philip Simonssøn as ruler of Oppland and Viken in eastern Norway, while the Birch Legs backed Inge Baardssøn, who became King Inge II of Norway.

14 Saint Sunniva—According to legend, Sunniva, a tenth-century king's daughter from Ireland, was known for her beauty and wealth. A cruel heathen suitor threatened to wed her. To escape this fate, she and her people left Ireland in three ships without sails or oars. The ships drifted north and then east until they came to the coast of Norway. Sunniva and most of her companions went ashore on the island of Selja, but they were regarded with suspicion by the heathen folks who lived on the mainland. When Sunniva and her people were attacked, God saved them by burying them under large boulders. When Olav Tryggvason later came to Selja, he found that Sunniva still looked as if she were merely asleep. A church was built on the site, and Sunniva was canonized a saint. Her feast day is celebrated on July 8.

15 Feast day celebrated on August 3 to commemorate when the body of Olav was taken from the sandbank on the Nid River and moved to the high altar

in Klemens Church in Nidaros; his body had not deteriorated, and his hair and nails had continued to grow. This was one year and five days after he fell in the battle at Stiklestad. Bishop Grimkjell then declared that Olav was Norway's saint.

16 Women gave birth by kneeling on the floor, supported by women family members and skilled helpers summoned from the surrounding village.

17 The first time that a woman attended mass after giving birth was considered a religious celebration of her recovery. At times it also developed into a demonstration of her social status.

18 leiðangr—A military expedition, especially an official fleet levied by the king. Norway was divided into districts, and the farmers of each district were obligated to own the necessary arms and to build and equip a ship for the fleet. When warfare later centered on fewer, bigger ships, the farmers could still be conscripted into active service, although in smaller numbers than previously. Breach of duty to serve in a leiðangr was punishable by fines paid to the king.

19 The Olav Vigil was held at Nidaros Cathedral on the night of July 28, starting at 11 p.m. and continuing until prime at 6 a.m., leading up to the celebration of Saint Olav's Day on July 29.

20 Hovedø (Hovedøya)—A small island off the coast of Oslo, in the Oslo Fjord. The Cistercian monastery, Hovedøya Abbey, was built on this island in 1147.

21 Minorites—An order of Franciscan monks also known as Greyfriars, founded in 1209 by Francis of Assisi and devoted to a life of apostolic poverty. The Franciscans established themselves in Norwegian towns around 1240.

22 Saint Blasius's Day—A celebration in February honoring holy Bishop Blasius, who suffered a martyr's death in Armenia in 316. Norwegians also called the feast day Blåsmesse, associating it with the Norwegian word blåse, meaning "to blow." In some areas people considered it the first day of spring, while others said it was the time when the sea swells were highest. Wind on that day portended a year with many storms. No one was to use a spinning wheel, churn, or any other rotating tool, or else the livestock would develop a dizzying illness, causing them to spin until they dropped.

23 terra sigillata—A very fine clay slip that produces a soft sheen when applied to pottery and can be polished to a high gloss.

24 A sister's inheritance (søsterlut) was half of what a brother would inherit.

Sigrid Undset (1882–1949) was awarded the Nobel Prize in Literature in 1928, primarily for her epic novels set in Norway during the Middle Ages. The first of these classic works, the trilogy *Kristin Lavransdatter*, was published in Norway in 1920–22, and the tetralogy *Olav Audunssøn* followed in 1925–27. She was a prolific writer and published many novels, essays, newspaper articles, autobiographical works, and children's stories. During World War II she lived in Brooklyn, New York, and wrote passionately about Norway's plight and the grim situation in Europe. After the war she returned to her home, Bjerkebæk, in Lillehammer, Norway. In 1947 she received Norway's highest honor, the Grand Cross of the Order of Saint Olav, for her "distinguished literary work and for her service to her country." Her first novel, *Marta Oulie*, and *Inside the Gate: Sigrid Undset's Life at Bjerkebæk*, by Nan Bentzen Skille, are also published by the University of Minnesota Press.

Tiina Nunnally has translated many works of Scandinavian literature, including Sigrid Undset's *Kristin Lavransdatter*, which was awarded the PEN/Book-of-the-Month Club translation prize. Among her other works are translations of fairy tales by Hans Christian Andersen and *The Complete and Original Norwegian Folktales of Asbjørnsen and Moe* (Minnesota, 2019). She was appointed Knight of the Royal Norwegian Order of Merit in 2013 for her significant efforts on behalf of Norwegian literature abroad.